FAST FORWARD 2

Edited by LOU ANDERS

an imprint of Prometheus Books
Amherst, NY

Published 2008 by Pyr®, an imprint of Prometheus Books

Inquiries should be addressed to
Pyr
59 John Glenn Drive
Amherst, New York 14228–2119
VOICE: 716–691–0133, ext. 210
FAX: 716–691–0137
WWW.PYRSF.COM

12 11 10 09 08   5 4 3 2 1

Library of Congress Cataloging-in-Publication Data

Fast forward 2 / edited by Lou Anders.
    p. cm.
    ISBN 978-1-59102-692-1 (alk. paper)
    1. Science fiction, American. 2. Science fiction, English. I. Anders, Lou. II. Title:
Fast forward two.

PS648.S3F392 2008
813'.0876608—dc22

2008031620

Printed in the United States of America on acid-free paper

For my father, Louis Anders Jr.,
who shoved *A Princess of Mars* into my adolescent hands
and ordered me to read it.
This is all your fault.

ACKNOWLEDGMENTS

This time out, I am immeasurably grateful to Joseph Mallozzi (aka Baron Destructo), and all the readers of his blog, for his incredible support of *Fast Forward 1*. Reading all of your wonderful feedback and answering your questions was of great help in organizing this second book, so I hope you approve of my efforts. Gratitude also to Jon Kurtz, for being behind this series in specific and me in general. I couldn't ask for a better boss. Thanks are due again to the übertalented John Picacio, for his willingness to push the envelope with each new cover. It's been an incredible journey so far, man, and it ain't over yet! Much praise is also due to Jackie Cooke, for the wonderful exterior layouts, and to Bruce Carle, the genius behind the interior layouts of this and every Pyr book. Nor can we forget the wonderful Deanna Hoak, for above-and-beyond efforts in copyediting. Then there's my good friend Stephenson Crossley, who is becoming something of a first reader for these things. A special thanks is due to Alice Taylor and Poesy Emmeline Fibonacci Nautilus Taylor Doctorow, for allowing their partner and father to be in this book at all. And lastly, but most importantly, a world of gratitude to Xin and Arthur Anders. The faster my world moves forward, the greater my appreciation for their love and support.

CONTENTS

"[A] good science-fiction story is a story about human beings, with a human problem, and a human solution, that would not have happened at all without its science content."   Theodore Sturgeon

"Science fiction is the holy fool of literature. It can say what it likes and get away with an examination of truly radical and subversive ideas because no one takes it seriously. When it's at its best, we're generally in trouble. Science fiction flourished during the social and economic upheavals of the 1930s, during the Cold War, and during the Iron Age of the 1980s. It should be flourishing now, damn it, but too many people who used to hang out with it have wandered off into some kind of fluffy make-believe world or other. Real science fiction doesn't make stuff up. It turns reality up to eleven. It takes stuff from contemporary weather—stuff no one else has bothered or dared to question—and uses it to make an end run on reality. It not only shows us what could happen if things carry on the way they are, but it pushes what's going on to the extremes of absurdity. That's not its job: that's its *nature*. And what's happened to science fiction lately, it isn't natural. It's pale and lank and kind of out of focus. It needs to straighten up and fly right. It needs to reconnect with the world's weather, and get medieval on reality's ass."   Paul McAuley

INTRODUCTION:
THE AGE OF
ACCELERATING RETURNS

Lou Anders

And so we return and begin again.

When the initial volume of this series, *Fast Forward 1*, debuted in February 2007, it marked the first major all-original, all-SF anthology series to appear in some time. Now there are two other regular series up and running—George Mann's *The Solaris Book of New Science Fiction* and Jonathan Strahan's *Eclipse* (albeit the latter mixes SF and fantasy).[1] Certainly, taken all together the three anthology series represent a healthy vote of confidence in the state of short-form SF. What's more, no less than seven stories from *Fast Forward 1* were chosen to be reprinted a total of nine times in the four major "Best of the Year" retrospective anthologies, a wonderful testament to the quality of contributions in our inaugural book.

And here we are back with a second volume. In the time between these

---

1. Ellen Datlow's *The Del Rey Book of Science Fiction and Fantasy* debuted in April 2008 as well, though as of the time of this writing, it isn't clear if it is to be a stand-alone volume or the start of its own series.

two books, the mainstream recognition of and respect for science fiction continues to swell. We've seen the Pulitzer Prize committee honor Ray Bradbury with a special citation for "his distinguished, prolific and deeply influential career as an unmatched author of science fiction and fantasy," and in the same year, the Pulitzer Prize for Fiction went to Cormac McCarthy's postapocalyptic novel *The Road* (also an Oprah pick!). We've seen a previous Pulitzer winner, the always genre-friendly Michael Chabon, leap into the science fiction field with both feet with his alternate history novel *The Yiddish Policeman's Union*, which was chosen by the Coen brothers to direct as a major motion picture. Meanwhile, Philip K. Dick has become the first science fiction writer to be canonized in the esteemed Library of America line, nine of his novels collected in a two-volume set edited by none other than Jonathan Lethem. Online media company Gawker Media launched the science fiction site io9.com, which while celebrating all the media aspects of SF, includes a healthy amount of commentary on the literary side of the genre. Explaining why Gawker would want to enter such a space at all, io9 editor Annalee Newitz debunked the notion that science fiction had only limited appeal when she said, "We don't see it as a niche entertainment site. We see it as a pop culture site. So much of our mainstream culture is now talked about and thought about in science-fictional terms. I think that's why people like William Gibson and Brian Aldiss are saying there's no more science fiction because we are now living in the future. The present is thinking of itself in science-fictional terms. You get things like George Bush taking stem cell policy from reading parts of *Brave New World*. That's part of what we are playing with. We are living in [a] world that now thinks of itself in terms of sci-fi and in terms of the future."[2] In short, everywhere you look, you see the greater world at large waking up both to science fiction's popularity and to its obvious relevance.

Fast Forward 1 was itself the focus of a weeklong discussion on the very popular blog[3] of *Stargate: Atlantis* writer/executive producer Joseph Mallozzi,

---

2. Brad Stone, "Gawker Media Gets Strung Out on Sci-Fi," *New York Times*, January 2, 2008.

3. Joseph Mallozzi's Weblog: Thoughts and Tirades, Rants and Ruminations, http://josephmallozzi.wordpress.com/.

who offers this somewhat humorous advice for how to deal with those poor fools who haven't yet come over to an appreciation of the genre. "Rather than resenting the critics who dismiss science fiction as little more than escapist fun, we should instead pity them for their shallow perspectives born, not of a sense of superiority or a better grasp of the meaningful and worthy, but of a dismal inability to consider the future's boundless possibilities."

It was of the future's "boundless possibilities" that he spoke when science fiction legend Isaac Asimov first said, "Individual science fiction stories may seem as trivial as ever to the blind critics and philosophers of today—but the core of science fiction, its essence, the concept around which it revolves, has become crucial to our salvation, if we are to be saved at all."[4]

Saved? Yes, saved. These sentiments speak not only to the relevance and importance of science fiction, but to its urgency. To my mind, science fiction is first and foremost entertainment and must be entertainment if it is to function effectively (and some people just can't see past that, just as some people can't acknowledge animation as legitimate narrative or cartoons as art). But science fiction will never be *just* entertainment. It has been, since its inception, a fundamental contributing factor both in how we view our increasingly technological world and in actually dictating the shaping of that technological world, involved in over a century of back-and-forth with the march of science. Noted futurist Ray Kurzweil wrote that "an analysis of the history of technology shows that technological change is exponential, contrary to the commonsense 'intuitive linear' view. So we won't experience 100 years of progress in the twenty-first century—it will be more like 20,000 years of progress (at today's rate)."[5] Kurzweil was introducing the notion of "accelerating returns," or that exponential growth increases exponentially. He is among a growing body of thinkers who go so far as to suggest that the twenty-first century will be the last one in which we can even speak of one human race, as the coming biotech revolution will change our very notions of humanity, just as the approaching technological singularity may give birth to nonbiological intelligences which we'll have to deal (or merge) with as

4. "My Own View," in *The Encyclopedia of Science Fiction*, ed. Robert Holdstock (London: Octopus, 1978).

5. "The Law of Accelerating Returns," published on KurzweilAI.net, March 7, 2001.

well. Whether one buys into Kurzweil's predictions or not, science fiction, as the branch of literature devoted to examining humankind's relationship with technology, is surely coming into its own as the most important literature of the twenty-first century.

So just what is science fiction?

Science fiction serves four purposes. It can be predictive, and it's always fun to talk about that, but this is its least important aspect. More important, it can be preventative, as Robert J. Sawyer articulates when he points out, "If accurate prediction were the criterion of good SF, we'd have to say that George Orwell's *Nineteen Eighty-Four* was an abysmal failure because the real year 1984 turned out nothing like his prediction. But in fact Orwell's novel was a resounding success because its warning call helped us to keep the future it portrayed from becoming reality."[6] Third, SF's importance lies also in its ability to actually inspire the future. Technovelgy.com is a remarkable Web site that currently lists several thousand articles charting when ideas first envisioned in SF become real, and more often than not, the inventors and scientists are very aware of where the ideas came from and were working to them directly.[7] Finally, SF is the literature of the open mind—the literature that acknowledges change and encourages thinking outside the box—and that in itself is a good thing, even if the science on display is nonsense. (This is SF's value as allegory.) No one would take seriously Adam Robert's *Land of the Headless*, in which convicted criminals have their heads removed and their brains placed in their chests as punishment for their crimes, as something that *could happen*, but what the novel has to say about the criminal justice system is illuminating, relevant, and brilliant.

---

6. "What Is Science Fiction?" http://www.sfwriter.com/2007/09/what-is-science -fiction.html, September 11, 2007.

7. See also Mark Brake and Neil Hook's *Different Engines* (New York: Macmillan, 2007), which examines how science fiction and science have informed and influenced each other. From the book description, "Science fiction has emerged as a mode of thinking, complementary to the scientific method. Science fiction's field of interest is the gap between the new worlds uncovered by experimentation and exploration, and the fantastic worlds of the imagination. Its proponents find drama in the tension between the familiar and the unfamiliar. Its readers, many of them scientists and politicians, find inspiration in the contrast between the ordinary and the extraordinary."

Or, as Paolo Bacigalupi said recently, "SF has tools for writing about the world around us that just aren't available in other genres. Reading good speculative fiction is like wearing fun-house eyeglasses. It shifts the light spectrum and reveals other versions of the world, mapped right on top of the one you thought you knew."[8]

The famous science fiction writer Brian Aldiss may indeed have said that "science fiction is no more written for scientists than ghost stories are for ghosts," but it was science apologist Carl Sagan who proclaimed, "Science stimulates the fiction, and the fiction stimulates a new generation of scientists." But we need to stimulate more than the scientists. As our world grows ever more fantastical and ever more dangerous, as the ways we have on hand to effect our own destruction multiply, we need everyone—from our artists to our politicians to our neighbors—to start thinking beyond the needs of the short term. Or, to quote Isaac Asimov once again, "It is change, continuing change, inevitable change, that is the dominant factor in society today. No sensible decision can be made any longer without taking into account not only the world as it is, but the world as it will be."[9]

What follows are fourteen tales, from the comedic to the cautionary, as different as the seventeen writers who penned them, as current as tomorrow, and as wild as imagination—and the only constant in them is the reality and inevitability of change. Because, as this volume testifies, the future lies ahead of us, and it's coming at us fast.

Enjoy!

Or maybe duck!

---

8. Paul Goat Allen, "Science Fiction's New Prophet: A PW Web-Exclusive Q&A," *Publishers Weekly*, February 20, 2008.

9. "My Own View."

CATHERINE DREWE

Paul Cornell

Paul Cornell is a novelist, television writer, and comic book scribe. In addition to various other genre and nongenre shows, he's written some of the best episodes of the new Doctor Who, *his first season episode "Father's Day" and his third season follow-up, the two part "Human Nature/Family of Blood," having both received Hugo nominations. His work for Marvel Comics includes the miniseries* Wisdom, *a* Fantastic Four *miniseries, and the ongoing monthly title* Captain Britain and MI-13. *His SF novels are* Something More *and* British Summertime, *the latter released last year in the States by Monkeybrain Books. The adventure that follows launches Paul into exciting new territory while remaining quintessential Cornell in its mad, exuberant brilliance.*

Hamilton could hear, from the noises outside the window, that the hunters had caught up with their prey. There was a particular noise that Derbyshire Man Hounds made seconds before impact. A catch in their cries that told of their excitement, the shift in breathing as they prepared to leap at the neck of the quarry the riders had run in for them. He appreciated that sound.

He looked back to where Turpin was sitting in a wing chair, the volume of Butriss he'd taken from Sanderton's library in the early stages of the hunt still open on his lap. The skin on Turpin's face was a patchwork of different shades, from fair new freckles that would have put an Irishman to shame to the richer tones of a mulatto. This was common in the higher ranks of the military, a sign that parts of Turpin's body had been regrown and grafted back on many different occasions. Hamilton saw it as an affectation, though he would never have said so. He had asked for his own new right arm to match the rest of his body completely. He'd expected Turpin, or one of the other ranking officers who occasionally requested his services, to ask about it, but they never had.

The noise from outside reached a crescendo of cries and horns and the sudden high howl of one dog claiming the prey and then being denied more than a rip at it. Turpin opened his eyes. "Damn," he said. He managed a slight smile. "Still, five hours. They got their exercise."

Hamilton reflected the smile back at him, shifting his posture so that he mirrored Turpin's nonchalant air more exactly. "Yes, sir."

Turpin closed the book. "I thought they had me an hour ago, which is why I sent for you. How's your weekend been? Has Sanderton been keeping you in the style to which you're accustomed?" Turpin had arrived unannounced and unexpected, as he often did, late last night, sitting down at the end of the dinner table as the gentlemen were about to adjourn and talking only about the forthcoming day's hunting, including asking his host for Hamilton to be excepted from it.

"It's been a most enjoyable house party, sir. Dinner was excellent."

"I heard you bagged your share of poultry."

Hamilton inclined his head. He was waiting for Turpin to get to the point, but it wouldn't be for a while yet. Indeed, Turpin spent the next twenty minutes and thirty-three seconds asking after Hamilton's family, and going into some of the details of his genealogy. This happened a lot, Hamilton found. Every now and then it occurred to him that it was because he was Irish. The thought registered again now, but did not trouble him. He had considerable love for the man who had ordered him to return home from Constantinople when it became clear the only good he could do there was to remind the Kaiser that every disturbance to the peace of Europe had consequences, that every action was paid for in blood. Hamilton would have done it, obviously, but it was one fewer weight to drag up the hill when he woke each morning.

"So." Turpin got up and replaced the book on the library shelf. "We've seen you're fit, and attended to your conversation, which rang like a bell with the white pudding crowd. We have a job for you, Major. Out of uniform."

Hamilton took that to be the royal *we*. He found that a healthy smile had split his lips. "Yes, sir. Thank you, sir."

Turpin touched his finger to the surface of the table, where the imprint glowed with bacterial phosphorescence. Hamilton leaned over and made the same gesture, connecting the receptors in his skin with the package.

"Nobody else knows about this," said Turpin.

The information rolled into Hamilton. It exhilarated him. He felt his nostrils flare at the smells and pictures of a land he'd never been to. New territory. Low white newly grown wood buildings, less than a day old by the look of them, with the banners of imperial Russia fluttering gallant. That is, fluttering not entirely through the progression of an atmosphere past them. Near darkness. Was it dawn? Not unpleasant.

And there was the woman. She stood on a bluff, looking down into a dark grey canyon, looking at a prize. He couldn't see what she was looking at; the emotion came with the package, and Hamilton reacted to it, making himself hate her and her prize for a moment, so if anything like this moment came in the world, he would be in charge of it.

She wore her hair green, but bundled in the knots that suggested she rarely had to unfurl it and take the benefit. Her neck was bare in the manner that said she was ready for the guillotine, the black collar of her dress emphasising her defiance. Hamilton let himself admire that bravery, as he did the martial qualities of all those he met in his work. Her gown was something that had been put together in the narrow hell of the foundry streets of Kiev, tiny blue veins of enforcement and supply across Imperial white, with the most intricate parchment wrinkles. It looked like she was wearing a map.

Her hands were clasped before her, and she was breathing hard, controlling her posture through an immense effort of will. She wanted to exult, to raise herself in triumph.

Hamilton found himself wishing she would turn around.

But the information froze there, and the rare data tumbled into his mind. He sent most of it into various compartments, for later examination, keeping only the index in the front of his attention.

"Catherine Drewe," said Turpin. "Ever meet her?"

Just because they were both Irish? Hamilton killed the thought. "No."

"Good. We got that emotional broadcast image by accident. From someone standing behind her—a bodyguard, we think. One of our satellites happened to be passing over the Valles Marineris at the right moment, three days ago."

Hamilton had already realised. "The Russians are on Mars."

Turpin nodded. "Terrifying, isn't it?"

"Is her army—?"

"Down there with her, because if so, we're acting with a criminal disregard for the safety of our allies in the Savoy court?"

Hamilton acknowledged Turpin's smile. "Thought you might be ahead of me, sir."

"We hope not. And we don't see how. So we're not getting Chiamberi involved as yet. She's probably down there on her own, either negotiating a rate to take the Russian side in whatever their long-term plans against the House of Savoy might be, or already part of those plans, possibly as a consultant. Now, the mercenary armies alarm us all, but the good thing about them is that we've sometimes been able to use them as passive aggregators of intelligence, allowing them to serve a side to the point where they're trusted, and then buying them off, netting all they know in the process."

"Is that the mission, sir?"

"No. We've created and are ready to plant chaotic information of an unbreakable nature strongly suggesting that this has already happened, that we have paid Miss Drewe in advance for her dalliance with the bear. Your front cover will be as a serf, your inside cover as a deniable asset of the Okhranka. Your mission is to kill her and any associates in one move."

Hamilton felt himself take another deep breath. "So the world will think the Russians discovered her treachery and covertly executed her."

"And botched the cover, which the world will enjoy working out for itself. Miss Drewe's mercenaries are tremendously loyal to her. Many of them declare themselves to be in love with her. Doubtless, several of them are actually her lovers. They will not proceed with any contract should she die in this way. Moreover, they may feel obliged to expose the Russian presence on Mars—"

"Without us having been involved in exposing it."

"So the czar's state visit at Christmas and the superconductor trade talks won't have any awkwardness hanging over them. Savoy won't ask and won't tell. They'll be able to bring pressure to bear before the Russians are anywhere near ready to tussle. There will be no shooting war, the balance will be preserved, and even better—"

"Miss Drewe's disaffected mercenaries may actually give us the information on Russian arms and intentions that we're alleging she did."

"And other such groups, irked at Russian gall, will be less disposed to aid them. It *is* rather beautiful, isn't it?" Turpin held out his hand, the ring finger crooked, and Hamilton touched fingertip to fingertip, officially taking on the orders and accepting them. "Very good. You leave in three days. Come in tomorrow for the covers and prep."

There was a knock on the door. Turpin called enter, and in marched a hearty group of hunters, led by Sanderton, the mud still on their boots. At the front of the pack came a small girl, Sanderton's daughter. She'd been blooded across the cheeks, and in her right hand she held, clutched by the hair, Turpin's deceased head. "Do you want to eat it, Uncle?" she asked.

Turpin went to her, ruffled her hair, and inspected the features of his clone. "Yes, I'll take my prion transmitters back, Augusta. Can't be spendthrift with them at my age."

Sanderton advised him that his chef was used to the situation, and would prepare the brain as a soup.

Hamilton caught the eye of the girl as she hefted the head onto a plate provided by a servant. She was laughing at the blood that was falling onto the carpet, trying to save it with her hand.

Hamilton found that he was sharing her smile.

‖

Hamilton made his apologies to his host, and that night drove to Oxford in his motor carriage, a Morgan Sixty-Six. The purr of the electrical motor made him happy. Precision workings. Small mechanisms making the big ones tick over.

It was a clear run up St. Giles, but glancing at his watch, Hamilton knew he wasn't going to make it in time for the start of the service. He tore down the Banbury Road, and slowed down at the last moment to make the turn into Parks, enjoying the spectacle of the Pitt Rivers, lit up with moving displays for some special exhibition. The Porters, in all their multitudes, ran out of their lodge as he cut the engine and sailed into the quad, but the sight of the Fourth Dragoons badge had them doffing their caps and applauding. After a few words of greeting had been exchanged, Loftus, the head porter, came out and swore at Hamilton in her usual friendly fashion, and had her people boost the carriage onto the gravel just beyond the lodge.

Hamilton walked across the quad in the cold darkness, noticing with brief pleasure that new blades had appeared in neon scrawl on the wall of his old staircase. The smells of cooking and the noise of broadcast theatric systems in students' rooms were both emphasised by the frost. The food and music belonged to Musselmen and Hindus and the registered Brethren of the North American protectorates. Keble continued its cosmopolitan tradition.

He headed for the chapel. As he passed the main doors, the bells that had been sounding from inside fell silent. He put his hand to the wood, then hesitated, and went to sit in the hallway outside the side door. He listened to the start of the service, and found his heart lifted by the words, and by the voice that was saying them. "Your world turns as the solar system turns as the universe turns, every power in balance, for every action an opposite, a rotation and equalisation that stands against war and defeats death, and the mystery of what may happen in any moment or in any space will continue. . . ."

He waited an hour, until the service was over, enjoying the cold, listening to that voice through the wood of the door, intimate and distant.

As the congregation came out, Hamilton stepped through the mass of them, unnoticed, and past churchwardens putting out candles and gathering hymn books. There she was. She had her back to him. Annie. In the gleaming vault of the chapel interior, dominated by the giant depiction of God with a sword for a tongue, reaching across time and space with his Word.

She turned at the sound of his footsteps. She was as lovely as he remembered. "Jonathan," she whispered, "why are you here?"

He took her hand and put it to his face and asked for a blessing.

The blessing only gave him an edge of 0.2 percent. Annie checked again, in his head behind his eyes, and for a moment he thought how splendid it would be to show her all his old covers, to share. But no. He could not. Not until this part of his life was over.

"It's a very slight effect," she said. "Your prayers have hardly provoked the field. Are you contemplating murder?"

Hamilton laughed in a way that said of course not. But really his laugh was about the irony. It wasn't the first time the balance had stood against he who sought only to maintain it.

They went into the side chapel where *The Light of the World* by William Holman Hunt was kept, the one on display to the empire's gawkers in St. Paul's being a copy.

Places like this, to Hamilton, were where the sons of empire returned to after they had done terrible things, the clockwork pivots about which their dangerous world turned, where better people could keep the civilisation that they did those things for. Annie, his old tutors like Hartridge and Parrish, the architecture and custom, the very ground were why he went to work. On his way from here, he would look in on the Lamb and Flag and drink a half of a beer with the hope that he would return to drink the other half. As had many before him, for all the centuries.

After the churchwardens had left, Annie did him a certain service behind the altar, and Hamilton returned the favour.

And then he left holy ground, and went out into the world that wasn't England, equipped only with a tiny and ironic blessing.

At the square, anonymous offices off Horse Guards Parade, they armed him and briefed him. He looked out from the secret part of his mind and saw that he was now Miquel Du Pasonade, a bonded serf of three generations. He let Miquel walk to the door and bid farewell, only leaning forward to take over during weapons familiarisation.

He let his cover take the overnight to Woomera, switching off completely, waking only as he was paying in Californian rubles for a one-way ticket up the needle.

Hamilton always preferred to watch the continents drop below him as he ascended. He mentally picked out the shapes of the great European Empires, their smaller allies, colonies, and protectorates. The greater solar system reflected those nations like a fairground mirror, adding phantom weight to some of the smaller states through their possessions out there in the dark, shaming others with how little they'd reached beyond the world.

▌▐

Hamilton waited at Orbital for two days, letting his cover hang around the right inns, one of the starving peasantry. He let himself be drunk one night, and that was when they burst in, the unbreachable doors flapping behind them, solid men who looked like they should be in uniform, but were conspicuously not.

His cover leapt up.

Hamilton allowed himself a moment of hidden pride as they grabbed his hair and put their fingers onto his face. And then that was that.

▌▐

Hamilton woke up pressed into service, his fellows all around him celebrating their fate with their first good meal in weeks. They sat inside a hull of blue and white.

His cover didn't know where they were heading.

But Hamilton knew.

Normally on arriving at Mars, Hamilton would have booked into the Red Savoy Raffles, a tantalising distance from Mons, as the gauche advertising put it, and spent the evening arguing the toss of the wine list with Signor Harakita. Serfdom to the Bear offered a different prospect. The hull the serfs were kept in smelt of unaltered body. During the passage, they did the tasks that would have needed continual expensive replacements had mechanisms been assigned to them: maintaining the rocket motors, repairing the ship's life-support infrastructure. There were two fatalities in the three weeks Hamilton was on board.

They didn't take the serfs on face value. All of them were run through an EM scan. Hamilton watched it register the first level of his cover. It accepted it. The deeper cover would only be noticed once that print was sent, hopefully long after the fact when inquiries and excuses were the order of the day, to the cracking centres in the hives of St. Petersburg. It had also, to more deadly effect, been registered in public with the authorities at Orbital, and would thus also be cracked by every empire's mind men in every capital.

But that was not all that the EM scanner did. It suddenly went deeper. But not searching, Hamilton realised—

Cutting!

Hamilton winced at the distant sight of some of the higher functions of his cover's mind dissolving.

From that point on, it was like sitting on the shoulders of a drunkard, and Hamilton had to intervene a couple of times to stop his body getting into danger. That was all right. The serfs also smoked tobacco, and he declined that as well. A cover couldn't look too perfect.

The serfs were strapped in as the Russian space carriage aerobraked around Mars's thin atmosphere, then started its angled descent towards the surface. This was the first surprise. The carriage was taking a completely conventional course: it would be visible from every lighthouse. This must, realised Hamilton, wishing for a window, be a scheduled flight. And by now they must be very close to whatever their destination was, the resorts of Tharsis, perhaps—

Then there came a roar, a sudden crash, and the giddy sensation of falling. Hamilton's stomach welcomed it. He knew himself to be more at home in freefall than the majority of those he encountered. It was the sea welcoming the shark.

He could feel the different momentum: they must have been jettisoned from the main carriage, at a very narrow angle, under the sensor shadow of some mountain range—

The realisation came to him like the moment when Isaac Newton had seen that tiny worm and started thinking about the very small.

Hamilton started to curl into the crash position—

Then with an effort of will he forced himself not to. Too perfect!

His seat broke from its fastenings, and he flew at the ceiling.

‖

The quality of the air felt strange. Not enough! It felt like hell. And the smell. For a moment Hamilton thought he was in a battle. So where were the noises?

They pulled the darkness from around him. They were rough. There were bright lights, and a curt examination, his body being turned right and left. Hamilton had a sudden moment of fear for his body, not belonging to him now, carelessly damaged by the puppet he'd leant it to! He wanted to fight! To let his fists bite into their faces!

He held it in. Tried to breathe.

He struggled out of their grasp for a moment, only to look round.

A serf barracks, turned into a makeshift hospital. Bunks growing out of packed-down mud, providing their own sawdust. Bright Russian guard uniforms, blue and white with epaulettes gleaming, polished, ceremonial helmets off indoors. All wearing masks and oxygen supplies. All ceramics, no metal. Afraid of detectors. A Russian military medic, in his face again, flashing a torch into his eye. Masked too.

There was a rectangle of light shining in through the doorway. They were pushed from their beds, one by one, and sent stumbling towards it. Still couldn't breathe. That was where the smell of battle was coming from—

No, not battle. A mixture. Bodies from in here. From out there—

Gunpowder.

Soil with a high mineral content.

He moved into the light and put a hand up.

He felt his skin burning and yelled. He threw himself forward into a welcome sliver of dark, shielding his eyes from a glare that could have blinded him.

He lay in shadow on the gunpowder-grey ground, with laughter from behind him, the sun refracting off angled rock, through a blurred sky, like a cold furnace.

He was in the Mariner Valley, the deepest gorge in the solar system, with the sun flaring low in the west, rebounding off the white buildings. There was hard UV in the sky. His lungs were hoiking on tiny breaths. Frost was already burning his fingers. And he wasn't wearing any kind of protective equipment.

||

They made the serfs march along the shaded side of the valley. At least they gave them gloves.

An enormous wind would suddenly blast across the column of men, like a blow to the ground, sloughing them with rock dust, and then it would be gone again. It was a shock that breathing was even possible. Hamilton stole glances from the shade as he struggled to adjust, looking upwards to the nearest escarpment. In the valley proper, you wouldn't necessarily assume you were in a gorge; the vast depression stretched from horizon to horizon. So this must be one of the minor valleys that lay inside the great rift. They could be six miles deep here. Given the progress of terraforming on the rest of the Martian globe, the air pressure might just be enough.

He realised, at a shout from the overseer in the Russian uniform, that he had slowed down, letting his fellow serfs march past him. But his cover was pushing his body to move as fast as it could.

He realised: he was different to the others.

He was finding physical action more difficult than they were. Why?

He looked at the man next to him, and was met with a disinterested misty expression.

The mental examination! They hadn't ripped out the higher functions of the serfs purely in order to make them docile; they'd shut down brain processes that required oxygen!

Hamilton added his own mental weight to that of his cover, and made the body step up its march. He could feel his lungs burning. The serfs had perhaps a couple of months of life before this exposure caught up with them. It felt like he had a week.

He considered, for a moment, the exit strategy. The personal launcher waiting in a gulley—he checked his internal map—sixteen miles away.

That was closer than it might have been. But it was still out of the question without the oxygen supply that previously had been standard for serfs working in such conditions. If he was going to get out of this, he would need to steal such equipment, the quicker the better, before his body weakened.

On the other hand, if he stayed and died, after having made his kills, the mission would be successfully completed. The cover would still be planted.

He decided. He would not leave quickly while there was still a chance of success.

He took care to think of Annie and the quad and the noise of the Morgan's engine. Then he did not think of those things again.

‖

In the days that followed Hamilton was put to work alongside the other serfs. He mentally rehearsed that Raffles wine list. He remembered the mouth feels and tastes. He considered a league table of his favourites. Although the details changed, it was headed every day by the 2003 Leoville Las Cases.

Meanwhile, his body was collapsing: blisters forming on his exposed, sunburnt, and windburnt skin; deep aches and cramps nagging at his every muscle; headaches that brought blood from his nose. And the worst of it was he hadn't seen Catherine Drewe.

His work crew were using limited ceramic and wooden tools to install growing pit props into what was obviously a mine shaft. Other serfs were digging, fed off nutrient bath growths that had been thrown up the walls of the valley. There was a sense of urgency. The digging was being directed precisely, according to charts.

These were not fortifications that were being dug. Turpin's conclusions had been rational, but wrong. This was not a military offensive. The Russians gave the impression of sneak thieves, planning to smash and grab and run.

So what was this? Hamilton had only seen one mercenary uniform, bearing the coat of arms of Drewe's Army. The badge displayed the typically amateur and self-aggrandising heraldry of the mercenary bands. It claimed spurious (and now nonexistent) Irish aristocracy, but had nods to all the major courts of Europe, nothing that would inflame the temper of even the most easily offended monarch. The badge irked Hamilton. It was a bastard thing that revealed nothing and too much.

The emblem had been on the sleeve of some sort of bodyguard, a man with muscle structure that had been designed to keep going having taken some small arms fire. He moved awkwardly in the lower gravity. Hamilton felt a surge of odd fellow feeling, and knew this was the man from whom the emotional broadcast had originated.

He and his mistress would doubtless appear together at some point.

▐▐

After three days, Hamilton's crew swapped tasks with the other group, and were put to dig at the rock face down the tunnel. Hamilton welcomed it: the air pressure was slightly greater here.

He had started to hallucinate. In his mind, he saw great rolling clock-works against a background of all the imperial flags. Armies advanced as lines across maps, and those lines broke into sprays of particles, every advance countered to keep the great system going. He himself walked one of the lines, firing at imaginary assailants. Women spun in their own orbits, the touch of their hands, the briefest of kisses before they were swept away maintaining the energy of the whole merry-go-round.

And at the centre of it all . . . He didn't know; he couldn't see. The difference of accident, the tiny percentage effect that changed the impossible into the everyday. He bowed his head amongst the infinite cogwheels and prayed for grace.

║║

He was broken out of his stupor by the sudden noise in front of him. There had been a fall of rocks. The whole working face in front of him had given way.

Something, maybe the pebbles beneath their feet, was making the serfs working with him sway and stumble. One beside him fell. The Russian over-seer bent to check on the man's condition, then took out a gun, thought better of the expense, and instead used a ceramic knife to slit the serf's throat. The body was carried out to be bled over the nutrient baths, the overseer calling out orders as he walked with the man back towards the exit.

Hamilton put his face close to the rock wall that had been revealed. It felt different. It looked blacker. Iconic. Like a wall that was death ought to look. He thought he could hear something in there. That he was being called. Or was that the thought he wasn't allowing himself, the chapel and Annie inside?

A voice broke that terrible despair that would have led him away. "There!"

Hamilton turned and smiled in relief to see her at last. Catherine Drewe. Face-to-face. Her hair was dark with dust, her face powdered around her oxygen mask in a way that looked almost cosmetic. Her eyes were certain and terrified. The other serfs were staring at her. Behind her came the bodyguard, his bulk filling the tunnel.

Hamilton's right hand twitched.

She pushed past him and put her ear to the rock.

He decided not to kill her yet.

"You," she said, turning to point at one of the serfs, "go and tell Sizlovski that we've hit a snag. The rest of you, get out of here, you're relieved."

The serfs, barely understanding, took a moment to down tools and start following the first towards the light.

Hamilton let his cover open his mouth in blank surprise and kept it there. He stayed put.

The bodyguard tapped her shoulder, and Drewe turned to look at him, puzzled. "I said you're finished."

Hamilton detected something urgent in her voice, something he'd heard in the moments before other situations had got rough. This was no setback, no sighing pause.

He crumpled his cover into the darkness of his mind.

He slammed his palm against the wall beside her head.

The bodyguard moved—

But she put up a hand and he stopped.

He let out his Irish accent. "You've got a problem, Miss Drewe," he said.

She considered that for a moment.

He smelt the edge of the ceramic knife as it split molecules an inch from his eye.

He flathanded the wrist of her knife hand into the wall, his other hand catching the gun she'd pulled at his stomach, his finger squashing hers into firing it point-blank into the bodyguard. His face exploded and he fell and Hamilton ripped aside the weapon and threw it.

There was a shout from behind.

Hamilton grabbed the Webley Collapsar 2 mm handgun from the folded dimensions in his chest, spun into firing stance, and blasted a miniature black hole into the skull of a Russian officer, sending the man's brains flying into another universe.

He spun back to catch Drewe pulling another device from her boot.

He grabbed her wrist.

He knew intuitively how to snap her neck from this posture.

In moments, the gunfire would bring many soldiers running. Killing the overseer had compromised Hamilton's mission but slightly. It was still some-thing that a Russian assassin might do, to give his cover credibility. He had completed half his mission now.

But why had she pulled *that*, instead of something to kill him with?

He looked into her eyes.

"Do what you were going to do," said Hamilton.

He let go.

Drewe threw the device at the overseer's body, grabbed Hamilton, and heaved him with her through the rock wall.

▌▌

The thump of the explosion and the roar of the collapsing tunnel followed them into the chamber, but no dust or debris did. It was a vaulted cavern, sealed off, with something glowing. . . .

Hamilton realised, as he didn't need to take a breath, that the air was thick in here. He started to cough, doubling up. Precious air! Thick air that he gulped down, that made his head swim.

When he straightened up, Drewe was pointing a gun at him. She looked shocked and furious. But that was contained. She was military, all right.

He let his gun arm fall to his side. "Well?" he said.

"Who are you?"

Hamilton carefully pulled out his uniform tag identification.

"British. All right. I assume you're here for that?" She nodded towards the glow.

He looked. Something was protruding from the rock in the centre of the chamber. A silver spar that shone in an unnatural way. It seemed to be con-nected to something that was lodged—no, that was in some way *part of* the rocks all around it. There were blazing rivulets threaded in and out of the mass. It was like someone had thrown mercury onto pumice stone.

It was like something trapped. And yet it looked whole and obvious. It seemed apt that it had formed a place where they could live, and a wall they could step through. It spoke of uneasy possibilities.

"What is it?"

She cocked her head to one side, surprised he didn't know. "A carriage."

"Some carriage."

"You don't know. That wasn't your mission."

"I was just having a poke around. I didn't expect a non-Russian here. You're Catherine Drewe, aren't you? What's *your* mission?"

She considered, until he was sure she wasn't going to tell him. But then—"I saw this thing. In my prayers. I spent a week in an isolation tank in Kyoto. You see, lately I've started to think there's something wrong with the balance—"

"Everyone always thinks that."

She swore at him. "You have no idea. Inside your empires. You know what that is?"

"No."

"A new arrival."

"From—?"

"Another universe."

Hamilton looked back to the object. He was already on his way to the punchline.

"I followed it calling," Drewe continued, "via a steady and demonstrable provocation of the field. I proved the path led to Mars. I used my rather awe-inspiring political clout to whisper all this into Czar Richard's ear. By which I mean: his ear."

"Why choose the Russians?"

She ignored the question. "I dreamed before I set off that only two people would find it, that their motives would be different. I took Aaron into my confidence. He was motivated only by art, by beauty. But you killed him."

"How do you feel?"

She bared her teeth in a grim smile, her gaze darting all over his face, ready for any provocation. "I'm strongly inclined to return the compliment."

"But you won't." He slowly replaced his gun in its dimensional fold. "Destiny says it's two people."

She kept him waiting another moment. Then she slipped her own gun back into the folds of that dangerous gown.

They looked at each other for a moment. Then they stepped over to the glowing object together. "That glow worries me," she said. "Have you heard of nuclear power?"

Hamilton shook his head.

"Energy produced by the radioactive decay of minerals. An alternative technology. It's poisonous like hard UV. A dead end. One of the outsider sciences something like this might bring in."

Hamilton consulted his internal register, holding in a shudder at the damage he'd already taken. He hadn't anything designed to log radioactivity, but he changed the spectrum on his UV register, and after a moment he was satisfied. "I'm not seeing *any* radiation. Not even . . ." He stopped. He wasn't even detecting that light he could see with his own eyes. But somehow he doubted that what he was seeing would allow him to come to harm.

Drewe put a hand on the apparently shining limb, deploying sensors of her own. "There's nobody in here, no passenger or driver. But . . . I'm getting requests for information. Pleas. Greetings. Quite . . . eccentric ones." She looked at him as if he were going to laugh at her.

In a civilian, Hamilton thought, it would have been endearing. He didn't laugh. "A mechanism intelligence? Not possible."

"By our physics. But it opened a door for us through solid rock. And let me know it had. And there's air in here."

Hamilton put his own hand on the object, realised his sensors weren't up to competing with that dress, and took it away in frustration. "All right. But this is beside the point."

"The point being—"

"This thing will tip the balance. You can't be the only one who's intuited it's here. Whoever gets it gains a decisive advantage. It'll be the end of the Great Game—"

"The start of a genuine war for the world, one not fought by proxies like you and me. All the great nations give lip service to the idea of the balance, but—"

"So how much are you going to ask? Couple of Italian dukedoms?"

"Not this time. You asked why I used the Russians to get me here." She reached into the gown. She produced another explosive device. A much larger one. "Because they're the empire I detest the most."

Hamilton licked his lips quickly.

"I don't think mere rocks can hold this being. I was called here because it got caught in . . . this mortal coil. It has to be freed. For its own sake, and for the sake of the balance."

Hamilton looked at the object again. Either of them could pull their gun and put down the other one in a moment. He wondered if he was talking to a zealot, a madwoman. He had pretty vague ideas about God and his pathway through the field, and the line that connected his holy ground to the valley of death. He'd never interrogated those ideas. And he wasn't about to start now.

But here were answers! Answers those better than him would delight in. That could protect the good people of his empire better than he could!

There was a noise from outside. They'd started digging.

Drewe met his gaze once more.

"You say it can be reasoned with. . . ."

"Not to get itself out of here. That's not what it wants."

Hamilton looked around the chamber, once and conclusively, with every sense at his disposal. No way out.

"You have to decide."

Hamilton reached into the hidden depths of his heart once more. He produced his own explosives. "No I don't," he said. "Thank God."

Drewe had an exit strategy of her own. She had a launcher waiting, she said, lying under fractal covers in the broken territory of a landslide, two miles east of the Russian encampment.

It was again like walking through a door. As soon as they had both set the timers on their explosives to commit, in that otherwise inescapable room, an act of faith as great as any Hamilton had experienced—

The room turned inside out, and they took that simple step, and found themselves on the surface again.

Hamilton gasped as the air went. His wounds caught up with him at once. He fell.

Drewe looked down at him.

Hamilton looked back up at her. There was auburn hair under the green.

She pulled her gun while his hand was still sailing slowly towards his chest. "I think God is done with you," she said. "We'll make a balance."

"Oh we must," said Hamilton, letting his accent slip into the Irish once more. He was counting in his head, doing the mathematics. And suddenly he had a feeling that he hadn't been the only one. "But your calculations are out."

The amusement in his voice made her hesitate. "How so?"

"By about . . . point-two percent."

The force of the explosion took Drewe, and she was falling sideways.

Hamilton rolled, got his feet on the ground.

A wall of dust and debris filled the canyon ahead of them—

And then was on them, racing over them, folding them into the surface until they were just two thin streaks of history, their mortal remains at the end of comet trails.

There was silence.

Hamilton burst out of his grave, and stumbled for where the launcher lay, bright in the dust, its covers burst from it.

He didn't look back. He limped with faith and no consideration. With an explosion that size there would be nothing left of the encampment. His mission had not succeeded. But he felt his own balance was intact.

He hit a code-breaker release code on his palm onto the craft's fuselage, and struggled into the cockpit. He was aware of his own silhouette against the dying light.

He looked back now. There she was. Only now staggering to her feet.

In this second and only this second, he could draw and shoot her down and with a little adjustment of leaks and revelations his mission would be done.

He thought about the grace that had been afforded him.

He hit the emergency toggle, the cockpit sealed, and he was slammed back in his seat as the launcher sailed up into the Martian sky.

He thought of a half pint of beer. And then let himself be taken into darkness again.

CYTO COUTURE

Kay Kenyon

Kay Kenyon's Bright of the Sky *was chosen by* Publishers Weekly *as one of the Best SF&F Books of 2007 and received an American Library Reading List Award. As we went to press, the honors for this series continued, with her follow-up,* A World Too Near, *receiving a starred review from* Publishers Weekly. *Long noted for her detailed and imaginative world building, Kay has been nominated for the Philip K. Dick and the John W. Campbell awards. To my mind, Kay always manages that difficult task of matching characters you can really believe in with worlds and situations that drop your jaw with awe.*

Nat was only a trash boy, but he knew to behave himself in the plantation great house. He knew to keep his hands off the expensive upholstery, and not to wipe his nose on his sleeve. His mom had taught him manners. She said he'd need them, because he was a little ugly and a lot poor.

Servants passed down the hallway, not looking at him, like you don't want to look at a dead dog in the landfill where you're trying to scavenge breakfast.

While he stared at the wondrous streaming wallpaper, a servant snuck up on him. "This way." His escort led him into a fancy room with one wall open to a garden. Macaws screeched outside, hidden in frondy trees. Behind a transparent desk sat an astonishingly beautiful woman, her yellow hair piled as high as an ant mound.

"I'm Lorelei," she said, waving the servant away. "Don't touch anything."

In all his twelve years Nat had never seen a high lady before, though he'd heard of Lorelei, first daughter of the plantation. Sometimes she drove through the barrio in a car that burned air! Her one-piece looked like it was made out of pale blue metal. Did it even bend? How did she move?

"Close your mouth, Nat."

He obeyed as best he could, considering his lips.

"Oh, you can't close your mouth all the way, can you, with it split up like that, into your nose."

She rose from her chair, proving the clothes did bend. As she came closer, he managed not to gape, though her skin shone like the inside of a sea conch, and her lips were a startling orange color.

"Do you know what we grow in the cytofactory, Nat?"

"Yes ma'am. Clothes."

Her lips retracted into a fully closed pout. "Not exaaactly." She moved to the side of the room, where four manikins wore parrot-bright clothes. Lorelei trailed her fingers over iridescent greens, buttery golds, frog-throat red.

"These are custom garments for people of refined taste." She spoke slowly as though he might have trouble understanding her, but Nat was a good listener and a good talker, his mom always said, except for his voice sounding nasally.

"I design and cultivate them. Not *clothes*; haute couture."

Hot coacher?

"I'm paid quite an astonishing amount for these creations. The Lorelei name is famous in the Syndicate. I hope you understand how privileged you are to be considered for a job here."

He could only nod in mute amazement. A job at the cytofactory?

She turned from the manikins to face him again. "You might think we're not aware of the poverty and suffering, etcetera, but we're very socially involved. We provide jobs for those with capacity, or as with you, out of compassion: no parents, harelip, what have you. I'm looking for someone who will give me their complete loyalty. Would that be you, Nat?"

He nodded. "If you are, you would be allowed to care for my special cultivates. One sector is getting ready to harvest a superb new line, so this is a critical time. You'll have a small job, but you must do it perrrfectly. No thievery, no mistakes, or out you go. Do you understand?"

"Yes ma'am. Do I get to live here?"

Her mouth parted a little. She gaped. Maybe her mom hadn't taught her very good manners, what with needing to teach her molecular designing and selling swank clothes to refined people.

"Noooo, not here. In the cytofactory. Barracks." She turned to the desk, retrieving a few coins. "You'll get four worldwides per day. Really five, but one pays for the food we have to provide by Syndicate standards. I presume that is agreeable?" She held her hand above his, and he caught the dropped coins.

Four wides was more than his mom had made in a month at the tourist stand. He nodded, afraid to speak for how his voice would sound.

"Last thing: You must say nothing to anyone about your job. There are spies, Nat, did you know that?" She rounded her eyes in mock fear. "People are always trying to steal my genomic secrets. So you won't ever speak about what's inside the factory. My line is unique; that's why we keep our secrets. Do you know what *unique* means?"

That stumped him. He shook his head. "I don't have all the words. My mom says I'm not stupid, just uneducated."

Her mouth pinched in again, bringing her upper and lower lips together in a way he envied. "*Said.* Your mom *said.* Because she died, so that's past tense. Say it."

"My mom . . . said."

"Very gooood."

On the way out, the escort took him past an open door where a servant was feeding an oldster in a wheelchair. As the servant held out a spoon, the man slurped, but soup dribbled on his chin.

That was the Old Man himself, the big boss of the cytofac! More and more miracles. He had just talked with an angelic being. He could hardly believe that she ever got sweaty armpits or used a latrine hole. She might not even *have* body functions. But Lorelei had promised him a bed, a job, and money. The boys at the dump would never believe it.

Then he remembered he couldn't tell them, anyway.

‖

Nat aimed the nozzle at the mito and sprayed a narrow stream of mist at the cultivate. It was tricky, because you had to mist with your left hand while holding up a paddle with your right to keep water off the emerging accessory.

Accessory was a word that meant belts, shoes, buckles, jeweled aprons, hats, handbags, gloves, and pomanders. A *pomander* was a decorative ball to hold good-smelling spices.

Like all the cultivates, the mitos grew in the factory nutrient beds, a vast, stinky marsh crisscrossed by raised grid-work paths. The mitos came up to his midthigh and were the easiest to rub and mist. They cultured out the small pieces. After misting Mito-112, Nat hooked the mister nozzle over his belt and exchanged the paddle for the rubbing cloth. You didn't need to wipe all the mist off, only move your (covered!) fingers in a circular fashion over the rubbery surface to help *protein production*. In Nat-speak, that was *enzime growth* (to avoid the lip dance over two *p* words in a row).

Before moving on to Mito-113 he looked into the status membrane on the front of Mito-112, showing aaatcagggaattaact193727. If something was wrong, it would flash red, and when making chemical changes, it would flash yellow. Mirrored on the status membrane he saw a faint reflection of his face peering in, water canister on his back, a smile on his face, or what passed for his smile. Nat had discovered he loved to work and do something important like making hot coucher for refined people, wherever *they* might be.

The cytofac had other workers, mostly harvesters who towed little wagons along the grid work, picking the finished clothes. Right now most were working E-73 on the factory's far side, so Nat was alone—fine with him, since the field hands beat him up just for looking at them. But they weren't as good at it as the trash boys, so he was still happy to be here. Other than harvesters, there were the bosses who did gengineering behind the windows up on the long balcony along the factory walls.

The mitos weren't the only cultivates. The somers, twice as tall as the mitos, grew bigger clothes like dresses, coats, vests, shirts, sword scabbards, and ladies' night apparel. To reach their tops, Nat stepped onto the micro lift at the path's edge and it would rise to the right height. Then you had to be careful not to drop your paddle or wipe cloth into the nutrient matrix or the field would be ruined and have to be flushed out. If this ever happened, *Out you go*, as Lorelei had told him.

He rubbed the somer's side, using circular motions to get the proteins to fold better and to *stim-u-late enzimes*. Despite Lorelei teaching him words when she did her inspections, he felt ignorant around her. He'd been proud that his mom had taught him to read, but in the world of enzimes and gengineers, he wasn't any better than a mito. Still, Lorelei said he had a "good touch," and he resolved to do more rubbing than ever.

The last kind of cultivate was the enormous golgi. Like mitos and somers, they were fat pillars, but changed shape so the designer product could dry better. Sometimes the pillars looked like they *wore* the clothes, but usually the garment budded out from the side. His field had only one golgi, but others rose up across the fields like dinosaurs in a swamp. Golgis made ceremonial outfits like ball gowns, men's formal suits, and capes. To get to the top parts of the big cultivate, you used a circular ramp that surrounded the golgis like a cage.

His golgi was working on a wedding dress. So far it had only excreted one arm, revealing an orange color like a monarch butterfly. Along the top of the sleeve, little bumps were birthing pearls. Lorelei said he had to be especially careful when he misted the golgi because this gown would *make her reputation*.

Last stop of the day was always Somer CG-91. Lorelei said it was a great honor to care for it because it was growing a *nural prosthesis* (In Nat-speak: *nural helper*) for the Old Man himself so his brain got fixed and he could come back to the cytofactory and handle things so Lorelei could devote herself to designing. On one side of the somer at about shoulder level (if the somer had had a shoulder), the nural helper protruded, a small lump that looked like a tumor on a fish. Because of how much Lorelei loved her father, Nat wanted to do an especially good job with CG-91, and spent extra time with the cultivate at the end of every work day. Mist, wipe, rub, so the nural helper produced enough cells to make the Old Man smart again.

Today, at Lorelei's inspection, she said he was doing such a good job that she might fix his cliff palet, which meant his deformed mouth. He could be fixed! If he worked perrrfectly, he would have a mouth like Lorelei's, or at least one that shut.

At the barracks after his supper and beating, he lay awake in the dark, fingering his lip, up the ridged curve to the tip of his nose and down the other side where his mouth got normal again. From the lone window a ramp of moonlight bulged onto the barracks floor. It looked like, if he stepped into it, he might walk into a silver world where things were refined and pearled instead of how they had mostly ended up.

Too restless to sleep, he got up and sneaked out of the barracks. He'd give CG-91 another hour of rubbing, until he got good and tired.

Once through the big door off the mess hall, he stood in the darkened nutrient fields; the only light came from the gengineer offices above, where a few of them worked late. He headed into his sector, walking past the rows of mitos, somers, and golgis, their beds occasionally gurgling with chemical adjustments.

He made his way to Somer CG-91, and looked in the status membrane: aagtcgtgtta7546396. He wondered what it would be like to be educated and know what those letters and numbers really meant.

The somer moved. Nat jumped, thinking for a moment that it might fall over. But CG-91 was leaning toward him. Nat patted the culti, pressing it back upright, though it had hardly tilted.

"Hold on," he said under his breath. "I'll rub you, don't worry." He sometimes talked to the cultivates, his only companions during the long workdays. He'd noticed before that the cultis could lean toward him. It was like flowers turning toward the light, but in this case, it was rubbing they craved. Pulling out his cloth, he began massaging, losing himself in the routine, first doing the bottom half, then stepping on the lift and doing the upper portions, spending an especially long time massaging the junction near the nural helper.

Finally sleepy, he went back along his field, passing the wedding dress golgi.

"What the fugging hell do you think you're doing?"

Nat stopped in dread. There was no one in sight. He looked up to the catwalk, but the voice had come from someplace nearer. Someone stood on the curving stairs around his golgi.

"What're you up to, rat boy?"

The name rankled, and he shot back, "I could ask the same. This is my field."

A big woman leaned into the railing. She wore mostly black, but a silver belt emphasized her truly huge waistline. For sure, she was no field hand, so she must be a gengineer.

"Your field, huh? Well fancy fugging that. You must be Lorelei's trash child." She stared down at him, pudgy hands on the thin railing. "What I'm doing is *inspecting*. If I don't like what I see, I can have you thrown in the nutrient bed, and then you'll grow extra hands from your armpits."

He knew better than to cave to a lone bully. "Well, I'm inspecting, too. I was rubbing CG-91. Lorelei says it needs special attention."

"CG-91. Fancy *that*. Rat boy's giving the old man's brain a rubdown." She leaned even farther over the rail. Her short black hair swung over her cheeks, hiding her face. "Let me give you a little primer, trash child." She climbed a couple stairs and pointed at the golgi's side, where the bodice of the wedding gown was starting to bud out.

"See this? It's a *Lorelei creation*, a big orange tent studded with pearls. You'd think she'd put a fat bride in something tastefully dark, but no. Gold and orange. I'll look like a pumpkin in a pearl necklace." She punched the sleeve, and it whuffed like a cough.

"Don't! The dress—"

"Is mine, you dumb shit."

His mouth fell open. "Yours?"

She rushed down the stairs and hopped onto the grid path with surprising grace for her size. Not much taller than he was, her face was strikingly exotic: big dark eyes outlined in purple, a glossy red mouth, bangs cut straight across her eyebrows.

"Maybe you can't imagine someone like me wearing a fancy dress?" With her face screwed up into a knot, she looked ready to hurl him into the matrix.

"Well, if Lorelei designed it, you're going to look excellent."

Anger drained away as she noticed his face. "Oh. You . . . you've got . . ." She paused. "Shit, you're as ugly as I am."

"I don't think you're ugly. You have a real good face." (*Pretty* was off the Nat-speak list, but she *was* pretty—a golgi version of a woman, and it wasn't a bad look.)

"Jesus fugging Christ. Rat boy says I look good. *Well then.*" Her face pinched up again. "I can be a happy bride."

"Maybe when the golgi gets done, you'll like the dress more."

"Yeah, good old golgi. Do me a favor, rat boy? Every day, just take a piss on it. Do that, and I'll sneak you some petit fours in your dog food." She stared at him, waiting for a reaction. "But you're such a good little suck-up, aren't you."

He didn't know why it mattered what she said or what she thought, but he liked how she wasn't afraid to speak her mind. He murmured, "Maybe I am, but Lorelei's going to fix my . . . my you know." He pointed to the crazy ribbon of his lips.

"Oh, a *Lorelei promise.*" She whistled, a feat Nat envied with every cell in his body. She backed up. "Go rub the old man's brain, why don't you. Or take a piss on that one, too."

As she disappeared into the shadows of the nutrient fields, he said, "What's your name?"

Without turning around she threw back, "Deri. The fat sister of the lovely Lorelei."

He stared after her. That was Derinda, the second daughter of the plantation. He looked up at the golgi, sprouting a dress that the bride hated. He wondered why Lorelei wasn't making a nice dark dress like Deri wanted.

"Maybe you should tone down the orange," he said to the golgi.

In the dim light the golgi seemed to gaze down thoughtfully at him from its helix cage.

❚❚

"Shit, shit, shit." Lorelei dragged him along the grid path toward the far wall. She had a look on her face that he hadn't seen before, a kind of scary focus.

She continued dragging him along the factory wall until she got to a door. Jerking it open, she left him on the threshold and began rummaging in drawers. "You've got *bruises* all over your face. The inspector's coming, and you've got ugly bruises." She stood up and gazed at him accusingly.

"The field hands—," he began.

She rolled her eyes. "Beat you, yes. Can't you just *get along?*" She had something in her hand, and started wiping it all over his face. It smelled like rotten seaweed.

Stepping back she eyed him with distaste. "Don't touch it. Let it dry, and then wash it off." She went to a wash spigot and carefully soaped her hands, muttering, "I hire a trash boy, and he gets bruises."

"I'm sorry, ma'am. I try to keep away from them."

She bit her lower lip, a gesture he thought indescribably cool. "This is a *new* inspector. He's not the one we usually have. No one told us there'd be a new one!" Charging from the little room, she waved at him to follow her. Down the path between the nearest field and the wall she opened another door, revealing a small closet with pails and rags. "Here's where you'll sleep from now on. If they don't want to bunk with a freak, we'll just have to accommodate them." She snapped a look at him. "We aaalways try to accommodate our workers' psychological needs. So stay the hell away from them. Can you do that?"

Before she left, she softened. "Nat, the Syndicate is very sensitive to workers' rights. It used to be anything-goes, and then the poor made it . . . clear . . . they wouldn't stand for mistreatment. So there *is* no mistreatment, especially at my factory. That's what you'll tell the inspector if he sees any bruises. Say you ran into a wall."

⊓⊓

The matrix next to CG-91 gurgled and the status membrane glowed yellow, so Nat knew that the somer was getting nutrient adjustments. The numbers flashed, changing every moment, and the nural lump pulsed a little. By his reflection in the membrane, Nat saw with relief that his bruises had vanished.

He kept rubbing the somer, trying not to be distracted by the voices on the catwalk where the inspector was touring the offices. They had been up there for two hours—the inspector, Lorelei, and a bunch of gengineers. He noticed Deri with them. She wore a black cape, and looked even bigger than usual, but it went well with her black hair.

The somer pressed against his hand, reminding him not to slack off on the rubbing. Nat started his massaging again. "Good CG," he said. "That's a good somer."

A noise up on the catwalk got Nat's attention. There, someone was pushing a wheelchair occupied by a white-haired man. The wheelchair came up to the group, and there was lots of talking, and then the family spread out along the railing.

Workers came in from the outlying fields to stand at respectful attention as Lorelei started to speak. She talked about LDL, the Lorelei Designer Line, and the factory family and how everyone was working together for a better product and a better community. The inspector was thin and dressed in a plain green one-piece, nothing fancy like the others wore. Deri was frowning, but when she saw Nat in his spot by CG-91 she nodded at him and even gave him a little smile. However, when she looked down at the golgi making her dress—if looks were spikes, that dress would be in shreds.

From the golgi's side jutted part of the skirt, big and puffy and orange and laced with gold thread. When Lorelei saw Deri looking at it, she turned her speech to the subject of the wedding gown and how it would change the fashion culture, and everyone except Deri smiled and nodded. The Old Man had fallen asleep.

CG-91 leaned into his hand again.

"Okay, good somer," Nat whispered, resuming his rubbing, getting lost for a while.

When he was finished, he hoisted his misting tank and would have moved into the mito section, but to his dismay, he saw the management group turn a corner in the field and make their way toward him. They stopped to inspect the wedding dress. Deri held back, catching Nat's attention and making the unmistakable gesture of a man pissing on something.

Nat just managed to suppress a laugh as the group came in his direction.

It was too late to slip away; the inspector had already seen him. The inspector approached, looking Nat over. He was a lot younger than Nat thought he'd be. From the back of his collar a wire arched over his shoulder to just in front of his right eye. An eyeglass dangled there. This guy was cybered into I-space. Despite having seen a few I-tech toys salvaged from the landfill, Nat was impressed.

"What have we here?" the inspector said, glancing halfway in Lorelei's direction.

She rushed forward. "One of our best technicians. He's in training to become a field boss. Very careful worker, aren't you, Nat?"

The inspector cocked his head, waiting for Nat to speak.

There was no help for it: Nat would have to talk in front of the family and the inspector. His voice came out worse than ever, like someone was strangling him. "I never dropped nothing yet." He winced. Double negative. Mom had taught him better than that. His face heated up, and the inspector came closer.

"What is your favorite thing about working here, Nat?" The voice sounded friendly, but Nat noticed the little eyepiece had pivoted to face him.

"I get to sleep in the closet with the pails." That wasn't his favorite thing, but it was a fine thing for sure, and he thought the inspector might be impressed.

The inspector nodded. "Is that right? A closet?" He turned to Lorelei, and her smile wobbled.

"And what is the worst thing?"

Nat hadn't expected that question. If he said nothing, it would look like he was hiding something. Everyone stared at him, even the Old Man, who was suddenly awake and looking confused. Lorelei's eyes tried to pull words out of him.

Finally, he blurted out the truth that had only this moment come to him: "That my mom never got to see me with a factory job."

Deri rolled her eyes: *stupid rat boy*. Lorelei looked like she was going to faint with relief. The Old Man said loudly, "Who is that? Never seen him before. No nephew of mine is a harelip!"

"Yes," the inspector said. "About the appalling cleft palate. Why isn't it fixed?"

Deri piped up, "Yes, what a surprising oversight. Lorelei, what *were* you thinking?"

Ignoring her, Lorelei said, "Inspector Ludicious, you can't mean . . . it would take a complete sequencing. And then individual genomic design. The cost alone . . ." She took him by the arm and steered him past Nat. Their voices faded down the path.

Nat watched them go. He stood for a very long time, listening to the footfalls on the path, the whine of the lifts, the burble of nutrient beds.

She wasn't going to fix his mouth. She didn't think he was worth it, and maybe she was right. He might have a factory job, but he was still a trash boy. How stupid to think he'd ever be something more.

As upset as he was, he hadn't noticed that he was massaging CG-91. The status membrane blipped and Nat peered in. The nonsense letters were gone. In their place were some new letters: THANX YU.

Nat paused. The gengineers upstairs were playing a trick. But he whispered, "You're welcome," and hoisted his misting tank.

By late afternoon, Nat saw the inspection group file down the catwalk toward the front factory door. The inspector was leaving. Laughter and forced happy voices. But as soon as the door slammed shut, the voices turned angry.

Pretty soon he saw the Old Man's wheelchair being hurried away, and the group dispersing, all except Lorelei and Deri. He heard them shrieking things like "pumpkin" and "signature dress" and fug this and fugging that. He also heard "harelip."

Pulling off his misting tank, Nat moved under the catwalk to see if he could hear better. They were talking about him, all right, but he was missing most of it. The stairs to the catwalk lay just beyond his closet bunk. He climbed them.

One of the office doors was ajar. Behind it, Lorelei and Deri were going at it. It didn't sound like they were pounding on each other, but by their voices, they wanted to.

". . . eating rats and shitting in the river, is that better?" Lorelei's voice.

"Better? I'll tell you what's better. Those cultivates love him. He spends his extra time, his *own time*, grooming them, and they're happy as pigs in a wallow!"

"Anybody could do that. He was told what to do. Rub and mist. Mist and rub. Jesus."

"He fugging talks to them! They're responding to him." A clatter of keys. "Look at this. Look at what they're doing! The sequences are changing so fast you can't even track them. You don't need to design new things, because the cultis are doing it for you, and you're taking credit for it!"

Lorelei, voice low and cold: "That was my intention. Jesus, wake up, Derinda. It was a test on that field—my test, my idea—and it's working. The cultis need a little personal attention to thrive. And what we learned was that the more they thrive, the stronger the designs. I thought of it, I hired our little harelip to pet them, somebody who'd be isolated, loyal. The whole thing depends on me. I put in the basic program, and the cultis do riffs on it. We get some ugly stuff, but we also get brilliant pieces—"

"Which one was the pumpkin dress?"

"—*which you only get* from random genetic combinations."

"They're not random. The cultis are *into* it. It's what they were bred for, and they're getting better."

"I'm getting better."

"Nah, you're getting lost. You don't have control anymore. In fact, aren't the cultis conscious by now? Aren't they?" Deri's voice rose. "What would the Syndicate say if they knew your somers and mitos were stupid little slaves?"

"Get out. Get out of here. Go get married, Derinda—do a little random gene mixing on your own. Be productive for once."

Deri charged for the door and rushed onto the balcony. Lorelei's voice followed her: "Go have some nice fat babies!"

Nat had no time to get away. Deri's eyes narrowed as she stared at him. Then she jerked her head toward the stairs and rushed ahead of him, charging down to the fields.

"How much did you hear, rat boy?" Deri could walk pretty fast for a big girl, but soon she was sweating. She leaned against a stacking tray for the field carts. "How much?"

"I heard she's never going to fix me because she wants me by myself so I don't tell that the mitos are like slaves. And the somers and the golgis."

Deri brushed the hair back from her face. Her cheeks were flushed, and black makeup trickled down from her eyes like evil tears.

"Yeah, the inspector isn't going to help you, either. They came to an agreement about it. Something about a blowjob in the chem lab, I think." They weren't far from Nat's field, and she glared at the golgi as the factory lights hit the pumpkin dress, glinting off the gold threads.

Nat let the words spill out: "So what're you going to do?"

"Do? Nothing I fuggin' can do. I'm scheduled for some random gene mixing with an ugly bastard from the Syndicate who needs an infusion of Daddy's cash. Then I'm going to start dropping fat babies. How's that sound?"

Nat turned away. "Something I want you to see," he mumbled, hardly caring whether she followed or not.

In front of CG-91, he found the somer leaning toward him. He patted it for a few moments until Deri reluctantly joined them. CG twisted, bringing to bear on Nat's hand the part of its hide it wanted rubbed. Nat pointed to the status membrane.

Deri rolled her eyes. "I'm no gengineer." He just pointed. Stooping in to look, she whispered, "Holy Madonna. Holy fugging Madonna."

On the somer's face plate: *Flz good.*

Nat scratched the somer, and its pillarlike body arched a little to expose a section on what might be considered its back. "What are you going to do?" he repeated.

She shook her head, over and over. When she finally got her words back, they were typical Deri. "Nothing, rat boy. Just like you're going to do nothing. Okay, they're slaves"—she gestured at CG—"but so are you, and guess what, so am I. I do what they tell me, and in a couple weeks I'm going to put on the pumpkin dress and spread 'em for my ugly groom." She wiped furiously at her eyes, leaking black all the more. "Wanna change places?"

Nat's insides felt compacted together, fused organs, emotions so heavy they didn't stir. He could see how things were. How the world ran. Who worked, who slaved, who stood on the catwalk and said the lies that kept it all going.

"I thought you might be different than Lorelei, but you're no better. Did you know the golgi is sick?"

Deri's eyes lidded. "Yeah." He waited, not making it easy. "Yeah, they're feeding the golgi toxic levels of gold. Can't have a wedding without sparkles."

Recently he'd wondered why the golgi was slumping. The deterioration had started with its hide and then became a deep bruise in the middle, causing it to slump. Nat had tried to tell himself that the weight of the dress caused the sagging, but deep down, he'd known the golgi was sick.

He stared at her rudely and didn't care. "So all you care about is that you don't want to wear an ugly dress?"

Deri's face folded into a sneer. "You have no idea what it's like to be a fat girl in the plantation manor, rat boy." She turned and walked away.

"And don't call me rat boy," he threw after her. "My name's Nat."

The fields gurgled. CG-91's nural prosthesis quivered and seemed to grow a bit. In the field two sections over carts rumbled along the paths, workers talking as they harvested vests, collars, shoe buckles, and dance gowns. But the workday was coming to an end. The factory whistle moaned like someone blowing into a bottle, a breath from a nicer world, high up and far away.

Nat stood there a long time before saying good night to CG.

Came the comment in the membrane: *Lone lee.*

He scratched the somer near the junction of the nural helper. "I know. Me too, CG."

Over the next week Nat continued his rounds, misting, rubbing—and when no one was looking—scratching if the cultis leaned into him and wanted more. The wedding dress golgi exuded the rest of the gown very fast, as though, having done one side, the other side was easier. The dress had gigantic upper sleeves and tight lower ones, and the skirt bore a brilliant gold apron in front, matched by a high gold collar.

Deri was right. It was ugly.

But Lorelei obviously disagreed. They had a little party up on the catwalk, because someone had come from a webMag and was going to feature her wedding gown.

Nat hadn't seen Deri, who was no doubt hiding in her room crying black tears about looking like a pumpkin.

On the day they came for the pictures the golgi rebounded, but hours later, it sagged again. On its membrane: ccctga . . . . . . Nat didn't think that boded well.

Lorelei brought him some fresh fruit every few days, saying how she was sorry that the inspector had made him nervous, and how well he had *conducted himself*, and how at this rate he was *headed for a promotion*. Nat shoved the fruit down the toilet.

He wasn't going to tell Lorelei what he thought of her. He wondered what his mom would say about how to keep your manners with terrible people if they wore nice clothes and paid you money.

Today on his rounds, Nat turned the corner of his field and saw workers clustering around CG-91. He hurried forward and saw that they had harvested the nural helper. A small white box sat on the cart, and they were just fitting the lid closed. Then two of the men picked up meter-long forks and jammed them down into the matrix next to CG.

Nat rushed forward. "No!" But the men turned toward him, forming a barrier.

"What's up, harelip?" They grinned at him. He tried to force them apart to get to CG, but they pushed him back so hard he fell on his butt.

They went back to their work, angling the forks under CG, and with a quick prying motion, popped it from the matrix. CG fell over, and they pulled it toward the grid path and threw it onto another cart.

Nat clambered over to CG, but already the men were hauling the two carts away. "CG, CG," he said, tears blurring his vision.

But he could see clearly enough to read the somer's membrane.

Make feeet.

‖

A week later the golgi was dead. They didn't need to pry it out of the matrix, because when they harvested the wedding dress, the golgi just collapsed down on itself with a *whoosh* and a great stink. It wasn't even attached to the matrix anymore.

Nat had been working hard in the fields that week. He'd been to each mito, each somer, doing what he always did—but in his own way, working through lunch breaks and into the evening.

Tired as he was, he almost missed the big harvest of the wedding dress.

Lorelei came down to supervise. They laid the orange-and-gold ceremonial gown on a large white sheet and gently carried it to the extra-long cart. The workers bore it away like a headless princess. But the golgi lay sighing its last, draped over the bottom steps of the circular staircase.

Nat waited with it for the hour it took to convince himself that the golgi was dead.

He was ready to quit, except for one thing. Lorelei had started promising him again that she would fix his mouth. Though he didn't trust her, it gave him pause.

That night in his closet, he ran his index finger over the curl of his lip, trying to imagine being able to pout like Lorelei or whistle like Deri. He had to admit that he would do just about anything for lips like that.

"Nat boy."

Someone had thrown open his closet door. A big woman in a black cape stood there. Deri. "Get up, Nat boy, stuff going down."

"What?" He pulled on his shoes as she disappeared from the doorway.

Hurrying out into the factory, he saw her cape snapping up in the air as she ran. He caught up. "What, Deri?"

She pointed to the high windows in the factory's back wall. Yellow flickered in them.

"There's been an accident," she said, walking toward the front door. "The plantation house is on fire."

He looked back at the windows. In them, the flames from the house reflected like the eyes of the devil.

Nat grabbed her by the arm. "What if it spreads to the factory?"

"That's the idea. That's why I'm opening the cargo doors. So your little pets can walk out."

His stomach lurched. How did she know?

Deri smirked. "I may be the second daughter of the plantation, but I know how to work a computer. I've been watching the cultis doing their extra designing." She shrugged. "Actually, everyone's been watching them, but no one but me could possibly guess what you've been up to." She patted him on the head like he was a mito. "Nat boy, I gotta admire your trash insurgency. It's brilliant. You told 'em to grow feet. And they didn't do that exactly, but those pseudopods they've been budding just might do the job. Think the smaller ones will need help getting up on the grid ways?"

Nat threw his arms around her, barely stretching halfway.

She pushed him away, not unkindly. "I don't do hugs, Nat boy. I hate people, remember? Now let's get busy."

They split up, Deri to open the loading doors and Nat to rush back to his field.

As he ran, he heard the grid work shaking under his feet. He expected at any moment to see the gengineers up on the catwalk with rifles, and there *were* lots of people up there, but they were running toward the back door.

The factory whistle blatted out emergency hoots, and factory hands pelted toward the back door, where in the distance, Nat could hear shouting and muffled explosions.

Coming up to the mito field, he jumped into the matrix, his feet splatting into the nutrient mixture up to the tops of his shoes. He tried to pry Mito-59 from the matrix, but it was firmly planted. Not knowing what to do, he started calling to the mitos, telling them to get up on the grid paths. Some leaned in the direction of the path, but it was hopeless. They couldn't make the jump. When he turned to Mito-60, he saw the status membrane flashing yellow.

Through the yellow membrane, Nat read the faint words: *Redy to go.*

The mito stretched its body upward. As it did, Nat saw the two pseudopods that had been hidden under its bulk. He wrapped his arms around the mito and heaved it toward the path, but he soon learned that the mito could lurch around under its own power.

However, the short step up to the grid path was too much for it. Nat grabbed the culti again and hauled it up just far enough that the mito's pods grabbed onto the metal grids, extruding tentacles for leverage. Nat shoved, and Mito-60 was upright on the path.

From outside came the sound of exploding glass and the shouts of the workers. Nat coughed as smoke thickened in the fields. He ran to the next mito with a yellow faceplate. He started yelling for them all to get as close to the paths as possible. By the time he got Mito-75 up on the path, Deri was there, ready to pull.

From that point on, Deri hauled the mitos up, and Nat ran to help those that still struggled in the matrix. Coughing badly now, he pulled his shirt up over his mouth and tied it with the sleeves. If he didn't get to the somers right away, none in that group would make it out. Rushing into the somer field, he found that the larger cultis had all made it to the edge of the path, huddling ghostlike in the smoke.

Deri shouted something at him, pointing. A few cultis lay down on the matrix, forming a step for the others. With that head start, the somers began staggering up onto the grid paths by themselves.

"Lead them out, Nat boy!" Deri hollered. "I'll stay here and help them. But you show them where to go!"

"But where?"

"The gates are open down at the big fence. And keep going."

She leaned in to help a big somer stabilize on the grid path, and it staggered down the path toward Nat.

"That's right," Nat shouted. "You can do it!"

Running back to the mito field, he found mass confusion. The little mitos were heading down different pathways, many in the wrong direction.

Ripping off the shirt from his mouth, he shouted for them to follow him. His lungs felt scraped raw; his eyes ran like they were melting. Remembering CG, Nat forced himself to go on, leading his ragtag army of mitos—tilting and staggering—toward the doors.

When he burst out into the open, the factory grounds were jumping in the reflected light of the great house fire. There, giant water sprays arched into the air, but the fire took no notice. He wondered if Lorelei had survived, but he couldn't spare a thought for her. The mitos and the somers were his responsibility now.

As promised, the big gate to the compound was open, but the mitos milled about, still needing him to find a path.

And that path, he knew, led into the forest.

"This way!" he called, waving his arms furiously toward the open gate. The little faceplates blinked yellow at him. That meant modifications. He hoped it was to their feet.

He led the procession out of the factory yard, and into the road. Behind him, the factory was hardening off, its fire suppression finally congealing over the building. The cultis inside would never make it out.

But it also meant that Deri wasn't going to make it out, either. The door to the factory was closing like a mouth going into a pout.

He pointed at the forest. "There! Head in there." He grabbed the nearest mito by what might be the shoulders, if it had had a head. "Take your buddies in there. That way!" The little mito gamely started out in that direction.

Nat charged back to the factory cargo door. Inside, the place swirled with toxic smoke. "Deri! Deri!" he shouted. He kicked at the lower part of the door, which was starting to grow up from the floor, forming a barrier and trapping the last of the somers. Then, as before, a few lay down behind the lip, and out the somers came, their pseudopods bigger and stronger than the mitos'. Just beyond this somer logjam was a black heap on the factory floor.

Nat jumped through the closing gap. "Deri!" He tugged at her where she lay. He slapped her, and she moaned. "Let's go. Stand up, Deri, you've got to!"

"Jesus fugging . . ."

"Save it. We're leaving." He pushed at her like she was a big somer, and finally she got to her hands and knees, retching. She leaned on a nearby somer and rose unsteadily to her feet.

"Hurry!" Nat rasped with the remnants of his voice. But it was no use. The cargo door, he could just see in the murk ahead, was now just a few feet wide and closing as the factory walls transformed. They were trapped.

Deri and he staggered to the door, falling on the pile of somers by the door.

But the somers hadn't given up. One of them stood on the others and was excreting a spray of liquid on the shrinking door. The spray ate into the door, slashing a rent down the middle. It soon broadened into a nice hole festooned with strings of wall taffy. Then the somers barged through the tattered door. Deri and Nat followed, wheezing and sputtering.

"Run for it," he hollered, and the whole pathetic troop gamboled and staggered for the gap in the fence.

To Nat's immense relief, the line of mitos was marching off the road and into the jungle's edge, thick with braided vines and steamy green air. Nat and Deri held on to each other and followed, stopping to spit up goo from their lungs.

At the forest's edge, he and Deri turned around for a last glimpse of the plantation manor.

The factory had hardened off into a gigantic, squashed soda can. Behind it, the house roared and burned.

"Poor little pumpkin dress," Deri growled.

"What about us? Where will we go?"

"Don't need to go far." She held up a sleek I-Messenger, pointing it at the sky. "Here's a scoop the webMags are gonna love." She began thumbing text to the same people who raved over the pumpkin dress. By the expression on her face, she was enjoying this.

Messages sent, she turned to Nat. "First rest stop and we'll get the cultis to work on your face."

"Think they could do it?"

She stared at him, blinking, with one of those Deri looks. "Maybe you don't quite understand what the cultis can do, Nat boy." She pursed her lips in a neat twist. "Or what *we* can do, once we tell our story. First thing, though, is to get these puppies some fresh air and decent food." She waved her hand toward the jungle depths. "You know, the *real* nutrient matrix."

By the time he turned away from the conflagration on the hill, the somers and mitos had already tramped down a wide path into the jungle. Deri walked among them like an exotic shepherd. She turned back, waving for him to follow.

He decided he liked her. And she was right: she really did look best in black.

THE SUN ALSO EXPLODES

Chris Nakashima-Brown

*SF Site once described Nakashima-Brown as "J. G. Ballard with a Texas twang,"
whereas Cory Doctorow says that he is "a hot up-and-coming SF writer whose prose is
slick, post-Gibsonian, and funny as hell, like Neal Stephenson meets Hunter S.
Thompson." His praises are sung by the likes of Bruce Sterling and R. U. Sirius. He
is wickedly funny, and as twenty-first century as it is possible to be. The tale that follows is, as he describes his own work, "pulp fiction for smart people." He is Jorge Luis
Borges meets Jon Stewart. But don't take my word for it. . . .*

I. Desert Fruit

In the morning, after the rain, we walked up the rocky mountain trail
behind Elkin's house to the Prozac Tree. Our late dinner party had gone all
night, fueled by old records and new wine. Six of us: Elkin, her visiting friend
Jae Li, Katerina G., Jack Crile, Paul Madero, and me, Nathaniel O. The crisp
dawn light seeped over the ridge, backlighting this perfect lone leafy friend
with its white powdery fruit, illuminating the covert blues and clandestine
purples of its pharmaceutically enhanced sap.

"It's fucking gorgeous," said Katerina, a custom clothier who maintained
her atelier up the road in Marfa. "Can I eat it?"

"Naturally," said Elkin, the irony an unstated given. "It's not actually
Prozac, though I did use some ingredients from that vintage recipe."

"Just like Mama used to make," said Madero, a real estate developer who spent his returns on art and design and the company of the creative class.

"I wish," said Elkin. "My mother's primary antidepressant was Sauvignon blanc. Part of how I got here."

Elkin was a bio-artist. Genomic postmodernist, hard-edged life science and purposeful surrealism spiked with a restless sense of play. In her late forties, relocated to the Colonia three years earlier to launch her new career after Dad's oil fortune funded her extended graduate studies and laboratory apprenticeships in Xiamen, Gwangju, and Bruges. She was a little older than the generation of twenty-somethings who had grown up with the first do-it-yourself home gene-splicing kits and launched a cultural revolution more profound than the one driven by personal computing fifty years earlier, but that seniority only made her a more powerful Hera-like personality on the scene.

"What's the base plant?" I asked.

"Sassafras," said Elkin. "I love to say that word. Like having your brain licked with a big wet tongue."

"You can lick mine any time," said Katerina, depositing one of the fresh white nuts under her own tongue.

"So what else is in the recipe?" asked Madero.

"A slice of agave for climatic hardiness," said Elkin. "Classic MDMA in the fruit, with a secret sauce psychotropic kicker."

"Filé gumbo big fun tonight on el rancho," said Madero, plucking a stout-looking nugget for himself.

"Bring on the psychonauts," said Jae, a Toronto-based televisual artist who was helping Elkin with some supporting components of her upcoming show.

"Viva the Rat Queen," said Crile, the old athlete, using our hostess's favorite Tejana nickname as he removed his shirt to soak up the rising sun. "Long live the dead white rats!"

I took a smaller fruit, and walked along the ridge a hundred feet or so, nabbing a nice aerie perch. The solar panels and rainwater gutters and copper roofs of the Colonia glinted in the sun like desert constellations. Maybe six hundred buildings among the five discrete settlements strewn across the valley, from mega-yurts to converted ship containers to eco-manses to watery galleries to clean warehouses. A dusty archipelago of lunar land even the Comanches had avoided, now transformed with the money of the ultrarich and the energy of the aggressively artistic. Sold off a dozen years ago to a group of Bohemian developers under a ninety-nine-year lease by the legislature, the nine-figure annual rent funding the State's coastal reconstruction band-aid projects. The deal included a State constitutional amendment—a private charter that gave the Colonia the legal independence of a microstate. Free Republic, complete with a panoply of flags. It now flourished as a tabula rasa private playground for autonomous "research"—artistic, cultural, political, sexual, and interpersonal experimentation—by those who could manage the entrance fee.

I had arrived six weeks earlier, taking up a three-year land art fellowship endowed by the Virilian Investors Culture Fund. My project site was just visible to the northeast from this perch, off the Marfa road. A few early scratchings of rearranged rock were apparent in the sun. Kindergartner Nazca lines punctuated at one end with the tiny safety orange dot of my pygmy earth mover.

I placed the synthesized white fruit on my tongue and let it dissolve into the heat of my saliva. The taste, like a cross between aspirin and dandelion milk, reminded me of the stress meds they used to pack in our MREs. Drone droppings, we called them—endurance enhancers for never-ending battles in the dried-out gray bed of Lake Balkhash and the empty desert beyond. Reminding me that this new life, this new desert, could only ever be a photofilm negative of the one that came before, even if in raging color. What would it offer to fill in the parts of me left behind?

And the light filled the world of rocks before me, washing over the big sky landscape with watercolor blues and browns and brights.

"I've been watching you, Nathaniel," said the light. The voice of Elkin, standing nearby, reeling me back in. "With my telescope. Watching boy play with rocks. I dig it."

I turned and took in her knowing smile. She had effortless gravitas despite her elfin physique. Manicured cowgirl tan, sprouting flaxen gray-blonde shorns, and sweating wealth and status through her faded black T-shirt and brown dungarees. Eyes like the milky heart of Marfa agate sliced through, clouds of unexpected color lurking within oiled pearls.

She sat with me. Below, our companions laughed at Jae's rock-top sun dance, passing a bottle of enhanced water and improvising their own stick-

and-bone musical accompaniment. Elkin's bounty tumbled open in each of us: the simple happiness of a child and the deep lucid vision of an aspiring mystic.

"We should collaborate," said Elkin. "Earth plus life. It could be fun."

"I don't know," I said. "I work alone."

"Pass along some of your pain," she said. "You've got more than your fair share, and my work suffers from a deficit. And a surplus of whimsy."

"Really?" I said. "I heard that you cracked your own half-life."

"The gift from Great-Grandma?" said Elkin. "Yes, I found that packed away in the attic of my genome. Not exactly a calendar date for my death, but definitely a protoplasmic inevitability. It's a good thing, I think, like most deadlines. Helps you burn more brightly."

She smiled a smile that carried other feelings with it.

Desert breeze, last gasp of the dissipated night. Elkin clasped my hand. My prosthesis shivered, and I leaned for the sun.

II. Chariots of the Gods

I found an old bicycle at the DAV in Alpine. Forty bucks. Vintage hard tail, logos long chipped away with the rest of the paint, save for a few stubborn flecks of faded yellow. I stripped it down, tossed the gearing, wrapped black surplus rims with fat round slicks, added rear discs, and had myself a beautiful utilitarian single speed. Pure, simple, soundless, self-powered machine.

I disdain the sound of engines and power tools, a predilection compounded by my three years sleeping under the bombardment of smart bombs, IEDs, RPGs, and enemy drones. The earth mover wasn't working for me. It alienated the earth, argued with the wind, and stained my forty-acre canvas.

So now I rode the bike, dragging a twenty-foot-wide homemade rake behind me at walking speed. Carving a long slow jetty under the unyielding gaze of the sun. The image in my head, inchoate as it is, reveals multiple facets. Whirlpool, target, pictogram, circuit design, wound. A beautiful abstraction, the elaborate pattern a kind of post-tribal fractal that will morph with earth and sky, providing a different experience each time the mapping satellites pass over. And a private tincture that aerates the soul pain of my ravaged body.

I remember a plain like this one, on the other side of the planet, and the after-crew of PMC janitors roaming in the morning with their sensors and trailers and body bags, trying to collect missing parts in matched sets. And then the rock and sand conjure their wintry mirror some years earlier, walking with Dad on New Year's Day across the fresh morning snowfall of his place in New Hampshire, trying to explain my decision to quit grad school and join the Marines.

He challenged me to defend my impulsive decision, calling me self-indulgent. He couldn't understand that was exactly what I needed to cure. I needed to experience the struggle of the Real to earn my right to manipulate the imagined. In the end, we both were right.

The fallen snow blowing off the icy cover turned to hot dust. I started thinking about another tool I could make that would help me carve my piece, and escaped back into my blacksmith's reverie, pedaling in wide circles under the desert sky while I drew blueprints against the back of my forehead for a simple rock-grinding combine that could write Olympian hieroglyphics of fresh-made dust.

III. A Movable Beast

The thing in the dish smiled at me. The teeth were individually perfect, like products of the most advanced cosmetic dentistry, white as fine porcelain. But they were irregularly spaced around the confused labial mouth they inhabited, and out of mouthly order, making them seem accidental. Wrong. The varying pink fleshy parts seemed to subtly breathe, the clumps of tawny follicles goosebumping in a dance of anatomical absurdism.

The smiling vayjay was disembodied, seated in a pillow of some purplish electro-organic gelatin that presumably sustained it, surrounded in turn by the stainless steel walls of an artisanal Petri dish laser-etched with reproductions of Sumerian monsters. A tiny red diode slowly pulsed on and off within the recesses of the goo, revealing the operation of some subtle circuitry that programmed the piece.

"If only it could sing," said the woman standing next to me, another visitor to the gallery. This was the opening of Elkin's new show for the Colonia Open House weekend, an annual four-day festival of investors, culturati, corporate sponsors, and Bohemian *turistas*.

"What would it say?" I asked, before I realized she was not talking to me, but rather dictating notes to her PDA. A critic perhaps, preparing to upload a report to *Neura*.

She looked at me, slight grin. "Leave me alone, obviously. *Je mords.*"

I moved with the circulation of the room into the more crowded main gallery, where a half dozen loosely themed pieces were on display. Elkin, deploying the business skills learned from her father, had negotiated a cobranding deal with Somnus Labs, the next-generation stem cell bankers who had pushed the regulatory envelope with their new exchange. Depositors, many of them celebrities, granted permission for Somnus to sell their unanonymized raw cellular material to others, in exchange for a cut of the action. Resulting in a nascent market for designer organs, one Elkin was promoting with her avant-garde hacks.

"Textual Healing": A perfect $1' \times 1'$ cube of liver tissue grown from the cryonically preserved umbilical cord blood of Dexter Fidelio, the cinematic bad boy better known for his trashings of rehab clinics than for his sporadically luminescent performances. Alternating sides of the cube were tattooed with some of his better-known movie script banalities, stenciled out in varying fonts.

"Montezuma's Offering to Venus": An actual functioning human heart grown in the perfect symmetrical shape of a greeting card Valentine heart, attached to an elegant weaving of colored plasticine tubes and suspended in rosy saline liquid within a clear plexiglass box lit from below with a smoky white light. The raw material, reverse-engineered embryonic stems of Mari Dawood, the über-Caucasian supermodel who had perished the year before when her private car was forced off a Milanese freeway overpass by marauding freelance paparazzi.

"Greetings from Airstrip One": A single blinkless gray eye cloned from the material of Senator M. Matheson, the chairman of the Special Standing Committee on Homeland Security, trapped in a black polymer box, but viewed from the strobe-illuminated interior on a crackling video display across the wall. On other smaller closed-circuit displays around the room, images from the myriad surveillance videos the eye was monitoring, within the Colony and in distant metropoles.

Other, less singular pieces. Like the collection of "artificial" nails for sale in beautiful little packages in the gift shop, based on the actual fingernails of famous hand models—in some cases literal reproductions, in others modified to enhance their vestigial clawedness, to imbue the nails with indigenously "painted" colors, "weathered" with cracks and stains and bite marks. Or the living wigs of hair of famous catalog models worn by Elkin and the gallery staff.

In the main room, Elkin stood atop a chair and greeted her crowd, brushing back Linda Okone's wild red bangs with her commandingly gesticulating little hands.

‖

Later, a group of us drank infused waters and spliced cocktails at one of the cafés in the heart of the public cluster—the main node of the Colony, at its core a rough analog for a Mexican paseo. The plaza had been transformed for the weekend into a spontaneous shantytown of designer tents, teepees from outer space, and architectural lean-tos. The fountain burned a liquid blue bonfire, an invention of one of Madero's hipster handyman boyfriends. Mobs of visitors and colonists mingled around, drinking and dancing and laughing and arguing about the new work, costumed interns passing out samples of the latest capsulized concoctions of our resident pharmaboys while the DJ nearby cleverly mixed his improvised Fezcore with the simmering crescendo of the crowd. From the heart of the mob, I watched Crile emerge, a head taller than the rest, dancing cocky like he had just arrived in the end zone carrying the ball.

As he approached our crew, Crile stretched before he sat, cracking his neck and shoulders. It sounded like sheet metal being crumpled inside the fist of Hephaestus.

"Jack has more spare parts than my old Carrera," said Madero, laughing with his grungy young companion, Karl, an assistant to one of the local painters.

"I run better than any Porsche," said Crile. "At least the parts that matter."

Crile scratched his silvery buzzcut, flexing a biceps that pulsed with the texture of manufactured tendons and polymerically enhanced blood vessels. He was one of the alpha generation of real celebrity cyborgs, a Texas star college quarterback who was among the first to go straight to the UFL. The Ultimate Football League was the first to abandon professional athletics' anachronistic insistence on the prohibition of performance enhancements, be they pharmaceutical, biomechanical, or genetically engineered. It was a genius stroke by the founders. The audience was far more interested in superhuman performances than fidelity to nature, and the athletes were addicted to the potential of even greater power. Crile hadn't played in a decade, but was still a public figure, famous for his stamina in withstanding fifteen-plus years of pounding on behalf of the Los Angeles fans, by defensive linemen morphed into raging anthropomorphic hippos and bipedal Mack trucks made of pink flesh and steel bones. He also did media, more partycasts than sports commentary. Even now, there were people in the milling festival crowds noticing him, a rare sports figure who was considered an icon of charismatic cool even among this posturban hipster crowd.

"Hey, Jack," said Jae, nodding at a pair of thirty-something women crossing the way, "looks like you're being ogled."

"Art sluts," said Elkin. "The best kind."

"I think he prefers his sluts of a more Apollonian mold," teased Madero. "They're the only ones who can handle the hardware."

"Hey," laughed Crile, popping pills with his infused water. "Not everything needs to be supplemented. Some performance enhancements just come naturally. Straight from Mom. Just ask the Queen. She can take whatever any boy's got."

Everyone laughed, jazzed by the crackling electricity of the night, though Elkin's had a sharper edge. It was a rare weekend to have so many crowds of interesting people exploring the scene. It was usually more serene, a refuge of decadent cerebral and sensual exploration, the insistent effort of the very rich and imminently bored to stave off ennui and create a more aesthetically stimulating world.

Crile leaned back, both hands behind his head, the disarming textures of his subcutaneous implants revealed against the stretched black cotton of his designer T. He ignored the girls as they approached, trailed by a smallish man in an old school jacket.

"Elkin, you've outdone yourself this time," said the man. "I want to commission a piece, but I'm afraid to ask what it would cost."

"That's the problem with being a writer in a world without royalties," said Elkin. "In for the weekend, Ned?"

"Yes, plus a day or two at the back end. We spent last weekend in Austin, rented a vintage camper for the first time. You remember my partner, Claire—last summer, Chicago—and this is her sister, Miranda."

"Fantastic," said Elkin, nodding at the women. "I want to see your caravan."

"Absolutely," said Ned. "But first we need to discuss your show. You can read my write-up next week, but I can tell you that your sponsors are very happy."

"How do you know?" asked Elkin. "You're just their bard."

"What else is there? Critic-for-hire, business developer, talent scout, and improvisational participant, all rolled into one."

"Nice work if you can get it," said Miranda.

"Who needs royalty checks when you have a biomed executive's expense account?" added Claire. "He's here to plug the project, renegotiate your deal, and treat us to tomorrow's parties, all at the same time."

"I see," said Elkin. "And I have just the cocktail for you to try. Have you met Mr. Crile?"

The party continued at Madero's hacienda just beyond the edge of the cluster, most of the crowd ripped on owl juice and other locally distilled psilospyrits. Karl programmed the music box, and the house danced as much as the crowd. Crile, down to the base layer, splayed on a bulbous foam settee, giving Miranda and Claire a guided tour to his enhancements and implants and scars. Elkin tugged at my arm.

"I have to show you something," she yelled in my ear.

We walked over the footbridge to the north wing, the tattooed kaleidoscope of manufactured koi swimming in the stream of purified rainwater running beneath. Elkin led me past the quiet private quarters of Madero's older male wives and the giggling playrooms full of mischievous guests, down a hallway to an unlit room.

"Take off your shoes," said Elkin.

The floor was artificial turf—cool, clean, and alive, like the green of a fine golf course without the moist earth underneath. The walls and ceilings were matte black, illuminated only by the diffused light of moon and stars slipping around the occluded skylight created by a plate suspended underneath a slightly smaller aperture.

"This is a nice installation," I said. "Who did it?"

"Cadma," said Elkin. "Madero's cousin, from Santiago. Go lie down in the center. Let your head go."

I complied. We lay there as time slowed, retinal rods opening up to the subtle blue-white glow. In time, the walls began to move in our peripheral vision. A monocolor moving image of some shadowed Dionysium, a soundless, rapacious dream in near distance. If you turned to look directly at the images they disappeared back to still black, undulating again when you returned your gaze to the eclipsed skylight.

Elkin moved closer. The piece lured out our carefully guarded needs and vulnerabilities, like small forest mammals slipping tentatively out into the bright dark after moonrise.

"Let me in," said Elkin, brushing my hair. "Share what you're hiding. What's cut off inside there."

We rolled on the grass, making out hungrily until my tongue found something loose inside her, the taste of torn tissue. I pulled back and Elkin reached two fingers in, producing a discarded bicuspid.

"Sorry," she laughed. "Here's what's loose inside me. Offering for the tooth fairy. New project—not mine, but my dentist's. He's growing new permanents for me, right inside my own jaw. Sharper and whiter, with a healthy dose of chimpanzee. Check it out."

I ran my little finger over the pointed bump in the gap.

"Monkey teeth? You are definitely more committed to your work than me," I said.

"Are we so different?" she said, touching me.

"Don't," I said.

"Why not?" said Elkin. "The war? I heard. I'm not afraid." She ran her hand down my abdomen. "I need new surprises. Who knew total emasculation could be the ultimate alluring machismo."

The accumulated chemical cocktails of the long night bounced the stars off the ceiling.

"I need to see what's underneath your scars," she said. "Literally, and speculatively. Don't be afraid of that."

She moved on me, and the room breathed with us, through the crazy beautiful attack asanas of Elkin's improvised private yoga.

IV. Life on Mars

With a morning thunderstorm in the forecast, I picked up Elkin before dawn and we headed out to the site.

We had begun a collaboration. After spending some time with me exploring the work and assisting me with some of the labors, Elkin brewed some bacterial contributors to my piece, from a strain of dry-weather dormants.

We worked well together. The input of an intimate as consultant was healthy for both of us. The health of other parts of our relationship was more tentative.

I borrowed one of the community trucks for the occasion, a restored and fuel-cell-converted fifty-year-old pickup. We drove up the old ranch road on Caspar Mountain, then off road to our favorite overlook spot. Elkin brought a pot of coffee, from a friend's homemod beans. We sat in the cab and drank it from her little Thermos cups while the cumulonimbus bulged out and stacked up over the plain below, cracking long and loud like God rearranging the wooden furniture in heaven.

"It's a beautiful piece," said Elkin. The cloud-filtered light of the gathering storm brought out weird colors in the rock, revealing new facets of the jetty. "You get so lost in it. Like a galaxy of stone."

"It's trying. We'll see."

"You are going to love your new interns when they wake up," she said.

"How many of them do you think there are?"

"Billions. Wait and see." She sipped her coffee. "I wish you would let me take some fucking pictures."

"I know, but I told you, the piece doesn't work that way. Pictures will just end up in galleries and coffee table books."

"T-shirts!" smiled Elkin.

"Right. They violate the site-specific essence of the work."

"It's okay," said Elkin. "I bought a day's worth of satellite surveillance." She pointed up and smiled.

I considered that. "Okay," I said.

A dark blue filter washed over the plain as the sky darkened. The shower started, steady then intense. Twenty minutes, then it broke as fast as it had begun.

Light cracked through. As it hit the jetty, swaths of bacteria bloomed scarlet in the channels, like pools of blood seeping into the honeycombed expanse of a white paper towel. Red rivers of rocks that had learned to give up their ghosts.

Elkin smiled, big and full of wonder.

"Thank you," I said, meaning it for once.

V. Big River

Crile, naturally, was the first one to catch a fish.

"Get your ass over here and shoot a film," he said from the other side of the river. "I don't want to play with this mutant too long."

I waded across toward the Mexican side. The water moved fast around big Crile standing there grinning in his custom antitox wetsuit. He held the beast up by one hand shoved into the mouth, fingers through the right gills. The way he'd caught it.

"So that's how it's done," I yelled. Crile was a devotee of deepwater hand fishing, a kind of extreme sports variation on old-fashioned redneck noodling in which you grab the fish from their mud banks and logwood lairs, using your hand as bait. His particular specialty was finding aggressive mutations in toxic bodies of water.

"It's all about the reflexes," he said. "No thought—just kill. Pure caveman shit."

"I can't even see anything in this water," I said, "even with these fancy illuminating goggles of yours."

The fish was huge, with a head almost as big as Crile's. Unlike Crile, it had long whiskers of slimy flesh sticking out from its cheeks. Variation on a catfish, but with translucent tissue, wrong proportions, and black eyes.

"What does that thing weigh?" I asked.

"About one-twenty, I'd say," said Crile. "Not the biggest I've wrestled, but big enough. And definitely ugly enough."

"Those are some teeth," I said, filming a close-up with my handheld. Crile's suit was torn at the forearm, bleeding in spots. "Looks like somebody mixed in a little barracuda."

"Want to give her a kiss good-bye?" asked Crile, setting the beast back in the fast-running water for release. "I'm gonna take a break and patch up."

We sat on the bank of a sandy shoal midriver. Crile peeled off his suit and tended his cuts while I pulled lunch from the cooler.

"Meatbread?" I proffered, holding up a small protein-infused loaf from the Boulangerie Bellona in the North Node.

"In a minute," said Crile, stretching his suit sleeve against the sky to spot the holes. "I want to get this done so I can relax."

"Suit yourself," I said, breaking off a bite and quaffing a glass of unaltered Malbec. Oenophilia remained the domain of rigid naturalism.

Crile hunched over the cooler cover, painting patches on his suit.

The sun in the valley sucked up the heat from the grains of the Chihuahuan desert and poured it on us like a dry waterfall. Even through my sunglasses, I had to squint as the light glistened off the distended titanium nodes of Crile's vertebral reconstruction.

"What does it feel like to have your spine replaced?" I asked.

"It hurts like fuck," said Crile. "Then after about a month, when things start to settle in and integrate and they give you your first tuning, you feel like you could throw a car down the street. It's fucking awesome."

On the far bank, a feral Mexican scampered along the reeds, nervously checking us out.

"How does it feel when they plug a million-dollar dildo in where your dick used to be?" asked Crile, smiling without looking.

"Army paid for it," I said. "Officer's perk. And I don't think it costs them quite that much."

"And?"

"It's different."

"Come on," said Crile, flicking epoxy at me.

I drank more wine and considered. "I guess it's like putting clothes on a phantom limb," I said.

"This is what I get for hanging out with artists," said Crile. "People who talk in riddles without punch lines."

"It works as well as my artificial leg, which is saying something."

"Can you feel anything?"

"Like I said. It's phantom. Simulated. Twitchy neural stuff."

"Can you reprogram it?"

"Sure, you know how it goes, just like any of your major enhancements. You're supposed to leave it to the docs—they get seriously pissed off at DIYs."

"I bet that doesn't stop Elkin," said Crile, chomping off a fistful of veggie chorizo.

I shook my head, smiling against interest.

"You don't need to answer that," said Crile. "Believe me, I know all Elkin's tricks."

VI. Pandora Flirts with the Bad Magi

I woke up restless the morning after my birthday, jarred by some lingering smell of Elkin. I watched the sun push its way across the stucco. My leg was hanging on the wall. The rest of me was set on top of the dresser, next to a wormless bottle of Mezcal and a vintage paperback monograph by de Maria.

In time, I hobbled to the bathroom, took a leak sitting down, rinsed my teeth, and then inspected the refrigerated case Elkin had left with me when she went home. Its machined metallic precision was totally incongruous with the hand-painted tiles of the countertop. It emitted a barely audible hum, elusive but alluring, like a postindustrial aum.

"I made it for you," said Elkin at the party the night before, without explaining the *it*. "Don't open it until you are alone."

I looked in the mirror at my scars. The rough rippled tissue punctured with the tiny nodes where my prostheses attached. I looked at the scars behind my eyes, hidden in plain sight in the light brown prow of my "male model mongrel face," as Katerina called it—"the face of every race and no race." I remembered hand-to-hand combat on a mountain cave hunt gone bad, spilling another man's blood in the snow. I remembered the blast, and the hallucinatory morphine haze as I watched them wrap my severed leg in icepacks and load it next to me in the chopper bay for evac.

There was a note from Elkin.

"This is for you. And for me. To share, when we are together. To share the pain and pleasure it is designed to transmit. Both ways."

I popped the latches on the case. Pressure equalized with the hiss of a bottle of sparkling water. The contents were something else entirely. Alive. A new color of flesh. Heartless, but pulsing nonetheless.

VII. Spelunking Other Archipelagoes

On a run to Marfa for materials, I ran into Katerina on the street. She persuaded me to join her for a late lunch. I'm not sure we'd ever had a proper one-on-one conversation before, with Elkin always around to dominate the scene. So we had some catching up to do.

We talked about the restlessness of fashion's creative cycles, the politics of the Colony, my war, her Russia, the new planets, the fashion lessons of her pogrom, our favorite comics, the end of nations, the business of art, and selected highlights of our romantic pasts. Across a café table, the pallor of her skin was like a cold drink of milk in the middle of this big sky desert, and her gallows laughter at my grisliest war stories mixed a fresh flavor of simpatico. Arctic core waters degenerated into Dr. Watson mojitos and peeled artifice. She gave me a tour of her atelier, and we got stuck in her private apartment.

My fingers admired the orthodontic imperfections of her crazy mouth, and the diverse hues of her unbleached incisors. She tasted like sweet fresh cabbage and raw jalapeños, and she swore in Russian like a B-movie submariner.

She played cascading dirges of dissonant Siberian art metal and moved against me out of sync. Our clothes ended up on the floor. When she encountered Elkin's alien gift, she laughed uncontrollably, making first contact only after mystery trumped composure.

The laughing turned to something else when the connection was made. The tissue-to-tissue dipole, the transmitter of all the real feelings and sensations lost in the clumsy imperfections of language and the stumbling wrestlings of lovemaking. Tandem rush through cascading rapids, riding Elkin's fleshbridge together, while the ghost of its creator lurked in the dark corner of the ceiling.

Later, we held each other, mining the fleeting intimacy of a curiosity we both knew could not endure, and I tried to excise the Other from my mind, being afraid to remove it from my body and end this suspended moment.

VIII. Adverse Possession

"I had a dream that it talked," I said. "Talked to me. And secretly reported to Elkin."

"More true than you knew, Nathaniel," said Madero, poking a lump of vegan simulated chorizo with a disinterested fork.

Elkin had dragged me to Madero's for an impromptu brunch. Turned out it was a business luncheon, with Elkin's critic/scout friend Ned the surprise guest.

I flipped the pages of the printed contract Ned had proffered with my eggless migas, unable to actually focus on the text. Elkin twisted the stem of her glass with two hands, while Ned leaned forward in an effort to engage me with his Manhattan Seawall variation on deal-maker charisma.

One of Madero's wives scurried to and from the kitchen, looking for ways he could serve us.

"Obviously, you'll want to have your agent look at that," said Ned.

"He doesn't have one," said Elkin. "Too stubborn."

"I can get you hooked up with my entertainment lawyer friend in LA," said Madero.

"LICENSE AND MARKETING AGREEMENT," read the heading of the contract, a generic description of twenty-some pages of turgid lawyer prose, plus appendices.

"And tell me what my upside is again?"

"You get royalties equal to half a point of our net profits from sales of the units," said Ned, "and continued rights of use."

"Rights to use my own organ."

"Actually, theirs," corrected Elkin.

"This remarkable little miracle of improvisational biomechanics Elkin developed was something she did as a work-for-hire for Somnus Labs," explained Ned. "Incorporating our core intellectual property."

"And my genetic material," I said.

"Correct," said Ned. "Without your prior written consent, creating in the process a monumental breakthrough: a replicable formula for the growth of a fully functional, putatively natural, one hundred percent human tissue–based substitute organ. The sensory functions of which can be felt by both, um, users—the wearer and the target, if you will. Giving new meaning to the phrase, 'go fuck yourself.' It can be grown as either a supplement or a full replacement, as the circumstances of the patient may require."

"Or desire," added Madero, looking at his wife.

"I think the jury's still out on the fully functional part," I said.

"Well, according to the research notes Elkin has shared with us, it performs exactly according to specifications. Understanding that those specs involve some atypical features, and are still subject to the physiological limitations of the user."

"Fuck you, too," I said.

"The ability to modify the basic design is immensely compelling, recognizing there is significant lab work and fine-tuning to be done. Take it out a generation or two, consider the possibilities Elkin is already playing with to integrate characteristics of other genomes, and you really have the killer app for cosmetic applications of our stem bank. The first set of patents should issue within the year."

"Designer johnsons," laughed Madero. "From you, from movie stars, from the doodled boy-dreams of your inner Freudian cartoonist, fully customizable to express the undreamed self-delusions of every man on Earth. What more ultimate work of art could you want to express the narcissistic spirit of the age? It will be to drugstore ED remedies what the supercomputer was to the personal calculator."

"Yeah, that may be, Paul," I said. "But I guess what I feel like right now is I wouldn't fuck this guy with your dick, and Elkin can have hers back." I pushed the contract away.

"Let's talk about it later," said Elkin, looking like she had a lot more to say. "Read the contract, do the math, and think about our collaboration before you make up your mind. This is about a lot more than business. It's about our immortality."

I looked at her lackadaisical power hair, and agate eyes with their mesmer stare.

"You had this idea before you even met me, didn't you?"

IX. Tap(s)

I stripped the right pedal from my bike, made my own clip to allow my true leg to pedal solo, hitched an ultralight camping trailer to the rig, and headed toward the unsettled eastern quarter of the Colony lands to find a new spot to work and live.

Before I left, I buried my old prostheses at the jetty site.

In the late afternoon that first day, I found a boneyard in the rocky flats above a small canyon. Skeletons of the desert's dead, bleached by ultraviolet. Local animals, and crazy bones, like the skeletons of anthropomorphic cartoon characters made real. Relics of homegrown chimeras gone feral, the forgotten toys of some crazy rancher's kid trying out his splicing kits on the livestock and local fauna? They mostly collapsed when you tried to pick them up, like fossilized snow sculptures, so I just sketched them against the back of my forehead.

I camped there that night, hobbling around at the edge of the canyon herding ghosts. The moon lied, as usual, and the next day I moved on.

I found a good spot. The relics of an old mercury mining encampment that I turned into a squat, a perfect desert studio. Elkin comes by once in a while, and brings the thing with her for its feeding. It's hard to say no, for all the reasons you know. Sometimes I even ride back to Elkin's place and spend the night.

My new work is different. A new kind of good.

And the sun keeps getting bigger.

THE KINDNESS OF STRANGERS

Nancy Kress

Perhaps one of the most frightening ideas in all of speculative fiction for me personally is the idea that beings might exist that are so far ahead of us that they would view us as we view the "lesser" animals of our own world. And even when we treat such animals with compassion, we're not treating them as peers. Nebula, Hugo, Sturgeon, and John W. Campbell Memorial award-winning author Nancy Kress tackles this head-on in the story that follows, something that could almost be seen as the dark other side of the coin to George Zebrowski's "Settlements" in the previous Fast Forward *volume.*

When morning finally dawns, Rochester isn't there anymore.

Jenny stands beside Eric, gazing south from the rising ground that yesterday was a fallow field. Maybe the whole city hasn't vanished. Certainly the tall buildings are gone, Xerox Square and Lincoln Tower and the few others that just last night poked above the horizon, touched by the red fire of the setting September sun. But unlike Denver or Tokyo or Seattle, Rochester, New York, sits—sat—on flat ground and there's no point from which the whole city could be seen at once. And it was such a *small* city.

"Maybe they only took downtown," Jenny says to Eric, "and Penfield is still there or Gates or Brighton. . . ."

Eric just looks at her and pulls out his cell yet again. Most of the others—other what? refugees?—are still asleep in their cars or tents or sleeping bags on the dew-soaked weeds. There aren't nearly as many refugees as Jenny expected. Faced with the choice of staying in the city—and such a small city!— or leaving it, most had stayed. Devil you know and all that.

She thinks she might be a little hysterical.

Eric walks around the car, cell pressed to his ear. Deirdre will not answer, will never answer again, but that won't stop him from trying. He tried even as he and Jenny hastily packed up her Dodge Caravan yesterday afternoon, even as she drove frantically south, even as they were stopped. When the battery in Eric's cell runs down, he will take hers. Jenny, sure of this if of nothing else, presses her hands to her temple, trying to stop the blood pounding there. It doesn't work.

"Good morning," says an alien, coming up behind her. "Breakfast is ready now."

Jenny whirls around and stumbles backward, falling against the hood of her van. This one is female, a tall Scandinavian-looking blonde. Her pink skin glows with health; her blue eyes shine warmly; her teeth are small and regular. She is dressed like last night's alien, in a ground-length, long-sleeved brown garment. Loose, modest, cultureless, suitable for dissolving cities on any part of the globe.

Definitely a little hysterical.

"No, thank you," Jenny manages.

"Are you sure?" the alien asks. She gestures toward the low, pale buildings at the far end of the sloping meadow. "The coffee is excellent today."

"No, thank you."

The alien smiles and moves on to the next car. Eric turns on Jenny. "Why are you so *polite* to them?"

She doesn't answer. To say anything—anything at all—will be to unleash the rage he's been battling for fourteen hours. So far, Eric has held that rage in check. She can't risk it.

"Here," he says, thrusting a Quaker Oats breakfast bar at her. She isn't hungry but takes it anyway.

"Some of us are going to dig a latrine," he says, not looking at her, and strides off.

Two cars over, a woman with crazy eyes fires a 9 mm at the alien. The bullet ricochets off her, striking another car's hubcap. People wake and cry out. The alien smiles at the crazed human.

"Good morning. Breakfast is ready now."

||

Probably the aliens aren't even present. If you touch one—or hit it or shotgun it or hurl a Molotov cocktail at it, all of which were tried last night—you encounter a tough, impenetrable shell that doesn't even wobble under impact. *Personal force field*, someone said. *Holographic projection*, said another, *protected by a force field.* Jenny has no idea who's right, and it hardly matters. The same maybe-force-field was what stopped her and Eric's mad drive south last night. Another transparent wall prevented her from retracing her route. A hundred or so cars were thus invisibly herded into this empty field, their drivers leaping out to compare sketchy information, children crying in the backseats and wives hunched over car radios, their faces in white shock.

Bombay and Karachi had been first, vanishing at 2:16 p.m. No explosion, no dust, no blinding light. One moment, reported dazed observers by satellite, the great cities and their vast suburbs had existed and the next they were gone, leaving bare ground that ended in roads sheared off as neatly as if by a very sharp knife, in halves of temples on the shear line, in bisected holy cows. The ground was not even scorched. People standing beyond the vanishing point saw nothing happen.

Fifteen minutes later it was Delhi, Shanghai, and Moscow.

Fifteen minutes after that, Seoul, São Paolo, Istanbul, Lima, and Mexico City.

Then Jakarta, New York, Tokyo, Beijing, Cairo, Tehran, and Riyad.

By this time the hysterical media had figured out that cities were vanishing in order of size, and by a progression of prime numbers. At 3:16 p.m. (London, Bogotá, Lagos, Baghdad, Bangkok, Lahore, Dacca, Rio de Janeiro, Bangalore, Wuhan, and Tientsin), the panicked evacuations began. Most people were vaporized (except that no vapor remained) long before they reached the end of the murderous city traffic jams.

Canton, Toronto, Jiddah, Abidjan, Chongqing, Santiago, Calcutta, Singapore, Chennai, St. Petersburg, Shenyang, Los Angeles, Ahmadabad.

As soon as he heard, Eric called Deirdre in Chicago, over and over, even as he and Jenny had been packing her car. He hadn't been able to get through by either cell or land line: *All circuits busy. Please try your call again later.*

Pusan, Alexandria, Hyderabad, Ankara, Pyongyang, Yokohama, Montreal, Casablanca, Ho Chi Minh City, Berlin, Nanjing, Addis Ababa, Poona, Medellin, Kano.

Only two United States cities so far. Jenny lived in Henrietta, Rochester's southernmost suburb. The roads were crowded but not impassable. She inched through traffic, the radio turned on, while Eric tried Deirdre over and over again: *All circuits busy.*

At 4:01, Chicago vanished along with Omdurman, Surat, Madrid, Sian, Kanpur, Havana, Jaipur, Nairobi, Harbin, Buenos Aires, Incheon, Surabaya, Kiev, Hangzhou, Salvador, Taipei, Hai Phong, and Dar es Salaam. Eric kept calling. He said, "Maybe she was visiting someone out of the city, shopping at a mall someplace rural. . . . She doesn't always have her cell turned on!"

Jenny knew better than to answer. She concentrated on the road, on the traffic, on the panicky radio announcer relaying by satellite a report from where Houston used to be.

‖

"Can I have that?"

A small voice at her elbow. Jenny realizes she is still holding the unopened Quaker Oats bar. The little boy is maybe five or six, dirty and snot-nosed, but with wide dark eyes that hold soft depths, like ash. He stares hungrily at the breakfast bar.

"Sure, take it." Her voice is thick. "What's your name?"

"Ricky." He tears off the wrapping and drops it on the grass. Jenny picks it up.

"Where's your mom, Ricky?"

"Over there." He gobbles the bar in three bites. His mother, a voluptuous redhead in pink stretch pants, sits on the ground with her back against an old green SUV. She nurses an infant from one large breast and watches Jenny. All at once she bawls, "Ricky! Get your ass over here!"

Ricky ignores this. "Do you got any more food?"

"No," Jenny lies. Apparently not everyone thought to pack their cars with food. Those that have will run out before long. The low, pale buildings still sit unvisited.

"Ricky!" his mother screams, and this time he leaves.

Jenny pulls off her sweater; the morning sun is turning the day hot. She opens her cell to key in her brother Bob's number. Bob lives with his family in Dundee, a small town fifty miles away; his and Jenny's mother lives with them. Jenny's sister and her family are nearby. "Bob? You all okay? . . . No, nothing changed since last night. . . . Jane? You talk to her? . . . Okay, look, I don't want to run down the phone too much. . . . Love you, too. . . ." When she closes the case, Eric is back.

They stare at each other. *Now it will come*, Jenny thinks. She feels as if she's carrying a teacup of nitroglycerin across a tightrope; the fall is only a matter of time. But all Eric says is, "There's a man here who's good at organization. We divided into sections and checked out the whole wall. No breaks, and it extends as far up as anyone can throw a stone and as far underground as we had time to dig. The force field surrounds the buildings, too. Anything new on the radio?"

"No," Jenny says, not telling him that she hasn't been listening. But he knows; his question was not inquisitive but hostile. He can't help that—Jenny knows as much—but she recoils as if he'd struck her. She's always been too sensitive to rejection.

Eric says, "I'm going back to help the tunnel crew."

"Okay." And then she can't stand it anymore. "Eric, I'm so sorry, but it's not my fault that my family is alive and Deirdre and Mary—"

"*Don't*," he says, so low and dangerous that Jenny is shocked into silence. Eric is not ordinarily a dangerous man. One thing she loved about him was his lighthearted exuberance.

He walks away, his back toward her, and Jenny covers her face with her hands. It is her fault, will always be her fault. Not that Eric's wife and daughter are dead, of course, but that Eric was with Jenny, in bed with Jenny in another city, pumping away on top of Jenny, when it happened. He will never forgive either of them for that.

■■

They met a year ago, at the American Library Association annual conference, in Kansas City. Jenny's attraction to him was instantaneous, and so was her glance at the wedding ring on Eric's left hand. But he was so handsome and so charming, and she was so thrilled by the almost unprecedented masculine attention. They drifted together at the luncheon held between "Reference Tools for the On-Line Generation" and "Collaborative Approaches to Information Literacy." They had a drink in the bar after the obligatory inedible banquet, laughing at the dullness of the speakers. One drink became many. They spent the last night of the conference in Jenny's room, and the next day she'd flown back to Rochester, suspended somewhere between euphoria and dread. Two days later she'd e-mailed him. Eric had replied, and things had gone on from there.

Sometimes, if she hadn't had an e-mail or phone call from him in several days, Jenny let herself imagine that he'd told his wife about the affair. He'd told her, and then he'd moved out of their Evanston home, and he was just waiting to hear from his lawyer before he told Jenny the great news. She let herself imagine all this in exquisite detail—the scene with Deirdre, Eric's complicated emotions, the phone call to Jenny and how understanding she would be—even while she knew it was not going to happen. Very few married men actually left their wives for their mistresses. Eric adored his six-year-old daughter. He had never even said that he loved Jenny.

But she loved him, and she knew it was turning her desperate, which in turn was driving him away. She waited, helpless and all but hopeless, by the phone. She turned up the volume on her computer ("You've got mail!") so that anywhere in the apartment she would know the instant his e-mail came through. She wrote long, eloquent letters giving him tender ultimatums, and never sent the letters because she knew he would not choose her. It took all her strength to never ask him the Fatal Questions: Do we have a future? Are you tired of me? Is there somebody else? Somebody besides Deirdre, she meant. She tried not to think about Deirdre, and the effort further exhausted her. Finally she Googled Deirdre and got over a thousand hits; Deirdre was a successful real estate agent in Evanston. She was slim, tanned, smiling, dressed more stylishly than Jenny had ever managed. She grew roses and played golf. Jenny mailed one of the eloquent ultimatums.

"I think we'd better end this, Jenny," Eric said gently on the phone. "I'm sorry, but this isn't what I'd thought it was. I don't want you to get any more hurt than it seems you already are."

Seems? More hurt? Not "what he thought it was"? What was that? She found a steeliness she didn't know she possessed. "I want to discuss this in person, Eric. I think you owe me that!" And he agreed, from guilt or compassion or fair play or who-knew-what. He flew to Rochester on a Friday morning, a return flight scheduled for that evening, six hours in which to end what had become the center of her life. She lured him—there really was no other word—into a farewell fuck, thinking desperately, stupidly, *Maybe if it's really good, better than Deirdre . . .* But Friday afternoon Bombay and Karachi disappeared, and a few hours later Chicago took Deirdre (maybe) and little Mary along with three million other people, and now Rochester is gone and Eric can barely look at Jenny.

She gets into the minivan, but even with the passenger door open, the September sun starts to heat up the car. For something to do, she straightens the blankets on top of the mattress that fills the back of the van; she and Eric, not touching, slept here last night. She checks their boxes of food, bottles of water, two flashlights and small hoard of extra batteries. Jenny, no camper, didn't own the tent, Coleman lanterns, or propane stoves she sees blossoming over the field like mushrooms. Communities are forming. Ricky and two other little boys have started a soccer game in the middle of the semicircle of cars. Somebody's dog, barking wildly, chases the boys. In front of the green SUV, three women gossip over coffee bubbling on a campfire. One of them is Ricky's slatternly mother, and the other two look enough like her to be her sisters or cousins. Out of desperation—she will go mad if she just sits here—Jenny fights off her innate shyness and walks over.

The oldest of the women, overweight and sweet-faced in a Redwings T-shirt, says, "Hi, honey. Want some coffee?"

"Yes, please." The small kindness almost brings tears. "Thank you so much. I'm Jenny."

"Carleen, and this here's Sue and Cheri." Carleen hands Jenny coffee in a thick white mug. "I figure we're all in this together, so we better stick together, right?"

"Right," Jenny says unconvincingly. Cheri, Ricky's mother, is studying Jenny as if planning to dissect her. The coffee is hot and wonderful.

Sue is as talkative as Carleen. "Your husband at the big powwow?"

How to answer that? Cheri's gaze sharpens. Jenny finally says, "They investigated the . . . the wall this morning and found no breaks. Now they're trying to tunnel underneath."

"That's what my Ted said," Sue says. "But he told me he thinks an assault on the ETs' building is gonna have to happen sooner or later."

Jenny nods. *ET* conjures up for her the cuddly and benevolent creature from the old movie, not the beautiful alien megaterrorist who offered her breakfast and who may or may not even be bodily present. And *assault* is an alarming word all by itself. These look like gun people, which Jenny and Eric emphatically are not.

Carleen says, "If the assholes really do have food in there and—Ricky! Be careful!"

The soccer ball has nearly gone into the campfire. Cheri grabs for her son, who wriggles away with the agility of long practice. She bellows, "Ricky!" The child darts behind Carleen and grabs her ample waist.

"There now, he didn't mean nothing, Cheri—don't get your blood in a boil. Ricky, you be good now, you hear?"

Ricky nods and darts off. Desultory chatter reveals that Carleen is Cheri's and Sue's mother, the grandmother of Ricky and the now-sleeping infant, Daniella. Carleen does not, to Jenny's eyes, look anywhere near old enough to be a grandmother. Sue is the mother of the other two little boys, nonidentical twins. Neither Carleen nor Cheri mentions husbands, either present or vaporized in Rochester. Carleen is casually maternal to anyone who enters her radar, including Jenny. Cheri asks fake-nonchalant questions about Eric, which Jenny avoids answering. After a half hour of this, the coffee is gone, the fire is out, and Jenny is emotionally exhausted.

She excuses herself, crawls onto the mattress in the hot van, and falls fitfully asleep. When she wakes, sweaty and unrefreshed, Eric still hasn't returned. She stumbles out of the car into a midafternoon chaos of cooking, unleashed pets, gossiping, worrying, grieving. Radios yammer, although it's clear that groups have pooled electronic resources to save batteries. Women cry. Children either race frantically around or sit in frightened huddles against parents' knees. There are no aliens visible.

Carleen comes over, evidently a response to Jenny's dazed look. "You need the latrine, honey? Over there." She points. "And your husband said to tell you to go ahead and eat without him; he's gonna work on the tunnel and he'll get something later. You got to make sure he eats, Jenny. Some of these men are mad enough to just burn themselves out."

Jenny nods. She finds the latrine, efficiently and deeply dug behind the field's only line of scrub bushes, divided by a blanket on poles into separate pits for males and females. Many of these people, she realizes, are far better at basic survival than she. Not that that's hard. On the way back to the van, she notices a prayer service of some sort under a tarp strung between two cars, a card game around a collapsible table, and a woman reading a book to a toddler on her lap. All the adults wear the resolute, pinched look of people going through funeral rites and determined to do them correctly despite whatever they might be feeling. This should, Jenny thinks, be an inspiring model for her own behavior, but instead it makes her feel even more inadequate.

How long will Eric stay away from her?

The rest of the day, it turns out. Jenny calls her brother Bob on the cell and then sits in the van, waiting. The early September dusk falls, and a few cars, chosen by lottery, train their headlights on the low, pale buildings across the meadow. This hardly seems necessary, since the buildings glow with their own subtle light. People put on sweaters and jackets, and the smell of canned stew fills the air. Three aliens begin to circulate among the cars.

"Good evening. Dinner is ready now."

People turn their backs or glare menacingly. Sue spits, a glob of sputum that slides off the alien's protective shell. This one is a man, tall and brown-skinned, handsome as an African American movie star. Sue's husband, Ted, snarls, "Get your ass out of here!"

"Are you sure? The chicken Marengo is excellent."

Cheri appears with a shotgun. The alien smiles at her. Carleen says sharply, "Don't you fire that thing with all these people around—what the hell's wrong with you? Jenny, honey, you want some coffee?"

Cheri returns the shotgun to the green SUV. Ricky sits beside Carleen's fire, eating Chef Boyardee ravioli from a plastic bowl, his baby sister asleep in an infant seat on the grass beside him. Cheri has changed from the pink pants and tee dotted with baby spit to tight jeans and a spangled red sweater cut very low. She has spectacular breasts. Jenny accepts the coffee but no ravioli; she's still not hungry, and anyway she doesn't want to deplete their food supply.

"Honey, you got to eat," Carleen says. "Even a bitty thing like you gotta eat."

"I had something in the van," Jenny lies.

Cheri says, "Not into sharing?"

Jenny faces her. "Would you like some organic yogurt? I have some in the cooler."

Carleen laughs and says, "That's telling her!" Cheri smiles, too, but it's a nasty secret smile, as though Jenny has revealed dirty underwear. Cheri says, "No, thanks." Ricky demands more ravioli and Cheri gives it to him, then turns to her mother.

"Will you watch the kids a bit? I'm going to go find Ralph."

Carleen snaps, "You'd do better to stay away from that no-good."

Cheri doesn't answer, just strolls off into the darkness. Carleen says to Jenny, as if Jenny were her own age and not Cheri's, "Kids. Soon as they get tits you can't tell them nothing."

Jenny, whose own tits are negligible, has no idea what to say to this.

"That Ralph'll just break her heart, same as the daddies of these two." She picks up Daniella, who's starting to fuss in her infant seat.

The information that Cheri, too, is having her heart broken by someone should make Jenny feel more kinship with her. It doesn't. She crawls onto the mattress in the van, trying to read Dickens by flashlight while she waits for Eric to come back for dinner. She's fixed him a sandwich from the best of everything thrown hastily into her cooler. Two bottles of beer are as chilled as the melting ice will get them. Jenny knows it's a pathetic offering, but as the hours pass and he doesn't appear to witness her pathos, anger sets in.

What right has he to treat her this way? None of this is her fault. Somewhere deep in her bruised and frightened mind she knows that Eric is staying away because he's afraid of what he'll say if he comes back to her, but she doesn't want to look at this. Looking at it would finish her off.

He doesn't come back all night.

In the very early morning, anger replaced by frenzied anxiety, Jenny looks for him. Eric is asleep near the half-dug tunnel, rolled up in somebody's extra sleeping bag. He lies on his back, his dark hair flopping to one side, and in sleep all the anger and guilt and fear have smoothed out. Through the grime on his face snake tear trails. Jenny's heart melts and she crouches beside him. "Eric . . ."

He wakes, stares at her, and tightens his mouth to a thin, straight line. That's all she sees; all she can bear. She gets up and walks away, making herself put one sneaker in front of the next, moving blindly through the damp weeds. It's over. He will never forgive her, never forgive himself, possibly never even approach the van again. The frenzy of tunnel digging, which will do no good, will eventually be replaced by frenzies of another sort, any other sort, anything to blot out everything he's lost. And she will not be able to change his mind. Eric is not strong enough to fight off his own passions, including the passion for self-destruction. If he were, he wouldn't have become involved with her—or with his other women—in the first place.

All this comes to Jenny in an instant, like a blow. It's all she can do to remain upright, walking. Her cell rings. It will be her brother, but even knowing how cruel she's being, she can't bring herself to answer. As the field comes alive around her, she sits alone in her van, wishing she had died in Rochester.

Another two days and most of the food and water have run out. Except for a few dour loners, mostly armed, people have been remarkably generous with their supplies. There have been no fights, no looting, no theft. Jenny, who hasn't been able to eat, gave most of her food to Carleen, who made it last as long as possible among her small matriarchal band, which now apparently includes Jenny. Jenny doesn't care, not about anything.

Outside help, it's learned through numerous phone calls, was stopped by a second invisible wall about a mile from the camp. Not even a helicopter was able to rise high enough to surmount the barrier. Relatives, cops, and the Red Cross remain parked just outside in case something, unspecified, lets them drive closer. Most cell phones, including Jenny's, have exhausted their batteries, although a few people have the equipment to recharge phones from car cigarette lighters. Jenny doesn't find out if hers can be recharged. Bob knows that Jenny's still alive, and there is nothing else to report. The car radios now pick up only two small-town stations, but these report that cities have stopped disappearing. A schedule has been organized and a track cleared to drive cars around the field, so that the batteries will not run down and both radio and heat will still be available. It's a nice balance between using up gas and preserving batteries. Jenny does not participate.

Three times a day aliens circulate around the field, offering breakfast, lunch, dinner. No one accepts. The aliens are cursed, spat on, attacked, and once—although this is looked on with disfavor—publicly prayed over.

Tunnels of varying depths now ring the field beside the invisible wall. None of them go deeper than the barrier, but digging them has given many people something physical to drain off rage and grief.

Every once in a while Jenny glimpses Eric in the distance, working on yet another futile tunnel, or huddled in desperate conference with other men, or with Cheri. Each of these sightings turns her inside out like a sock, all her vulnerable organs battered by the smallest sound, breeze, photon of light.

"My Cheri never was no good around men," Carleen says, handing Jenny yet another cup of boiled coffee, not meeting her eyes. It's the first time Carleen has mentioned the situation. Jenny doesn't reply. Carleen's kindness is like air, ubiquitous and necessary and equally available to everyone, but even air hurts Jenny now.

"Honey," Carleen adds, "you gotta *eat*."

"Later," Jenny says, the syllable scraping her throat like gritty vomit.

Carleen goes away, but half an hour later Ricky appears beside the van, holding a book. He is incredibly dirty, smells bad, and clearly does not want to be there. "You spozed to read me this."

It's *Treasure Island* in the original, a book whose flowery language and slow pace Ricky will neither understand nor enjoy. Where on Earth did Carleen get it? She must have asked every last person in the camp, must have remembered that Jenny is—was—a librarian, must have cudgeled her slow wits to think of something that might make Jenny feel better. Jenny starts to cry. An old song title fills her head: "Roses from the Wrong Man." Carleen is not a man, and this filthy child with his reluctant offering is about as far from roses as it's possible to get, but Jenny is in too much pain to appreciate the incongruity. She only knows that if it had been Eric who'd arranged this perverse kindness on her behalf, she could have borne anything. But it is not Eric.

Ricky looks at her tears with the same alarm as would any grown man. "Hey! You . . . you gonna read me that book?"

"No. You'd hate it. Go play."

Released, Ricky gives a whoop and races away, running backward, maybe to fulfill some small-boy notion of paying attention to the adult he's been told to pay attention to. No one else is in the center of the field; the cars are doing their daily promenade to charge up batteries. The red Taurus is not going very fast and the driver slams on her brakes, but not soon enough. Ricky is hit.

He starts shrieking to wake the dead. Carleen and Cheri both scream and dart from beside their SUV, Cheri with Daniella clamped to one naked breast. Sue's husband, Ted, leaps from his car and reaches Ricky just as Jenny does. Ted says, "Ricky! Buddy!"

The child is wailing and writhing on the flattened weeds. His left arm hangs at a strange angle. Ted gently holds down Ricky's shoulders. "Lie still, buddy, till we see what's broken." Cheri thrusts Daniella at Carleen, yells something anguished, and throws herself practically on top of Ricky. Ted shoves her off. "For Chrissake, let me see how bad he's hurt! Don't crush him, Cheri!"

"Ted's an EMT," Sue says at Jenny's elbow. "What happened?"

Jenny shakes her head. She can't speak. Cheri says shakily, "He was just racing around like always and—fuck it, why does everything always happen to me!"

Jenny just stares at her. The statement is so selfish, so inadequate, so stupid, that no response is possible. A thought forms in Jenny's mind: *If this is what Eric prefers to me, the hell with him.* The next second she's ashamed of this thought; it's as self-absorbed as Cheri's. She turns her attention to Ricky.

His arm is broken. There are no doctors or professional nurses among the refugees. Ted sets the arm, using as a splint a piece of wood torn from a chair leg. Ted is obviously no expert at this, but he's resourceful, gentle, and willing to accept responsibility. Everything, Jenny thinks coldly, that Eric is not. Ricky screams like an animal in a steel-toothed trap. The driver of the red Taurus blubbers apologies; no one blames her. The accident is thoroughly discussed at every campfire, in every tent, on every mattress in the back of every van. Ricky is given a hoarded candy bar, a precious comic book, and a hefty slug of cough syrup mixed with whiskey to make him sleep.

Jenny can't sleep. Lying alone on her mattress, she tries to think coldly about her and Eric, about the destroyed cities, about what will happen now. She can't quite manage enough coldness, but it's better than the hell of the last four days. Somewhere in the deep dark there's a tap at the window.

Eric . . . Hope burns so sudden, so hot, that Jenny feels scorched inside. She nearly cries out as she fumbles for the door, the flashlight.

Carleen stands there, her meaty arms limp by her side. In the upward-slanting glow from the flashlight, she says despairingly, "Ricky."

Jenny stumbles from the van, follows Carleen. Stars shine in a clear, cold sky. Jenny's lighted watch face says 4:18 a.m. The SUV tailgate gapes open, and Jenny sees the usual mattress, a double in this monster vehicle, on which Ricky lies, glassy-eyed. Daniella whimpers softly in her infant seat. Cheri is not here. With Eric?

"He been like this for a coupla hours now," Carleen says in a low, steady voice. "He won't drink or eat or talk. And his arm's swelling up and turning all dark." She trains the flashlight on Ricky's arm.

Jenny bends over the child, who smells as if he's shit his pants. Gangrene—could it set in that fast? She doesn't know, but clearly something is radically wrong.

Carleen goes on in that strange, even voice. "I can't leave Daniella. And Ted don't know enough to deal with this."

"I don't know anything about medical matters, either—certainly not as much as Ted!"

Carleen continues as if Jenny hadn't spoken. "Anyway Sue's got some kind of diarrhea now and Ted can't leave his kids. Not for good. Can't take the risk. And I got Daniella. Can't count on Cheri."

Jenny straightens and turns. The two women stare at each other. For a long moment, it seems to Jenny, her universe hangs in the balance, all of it: Eric and vaporized Rochester, Deirdre and Jenny's job at the vanished public library, the running-down cell phones and Jenny's mother waiting for her in Dundee, the stars far overhead and the trodden-down weeds underfoot in this desperate refugee camp no one planned on.

Jenny nods.

Together they pick up Ricky and situate him in Jenny's arms. Ricky moans, but softly. He's heavy, reeking, only half-conscious. There is nobody else up, or at least nobody that Jenny sees. In the dark she carries Ricky the entire length of the field, trying not to shift him even as he grows heavier and heavier, navigating by the pale glow from the alien buildings.

Up close, they present rough, cream-colored walls like stucco, but no stucco ever shone with its own light. The buildings all seem interconnected, but Jenny sees only one entry, itself filled with light instead of any tangible door. She walks through the light and into a wide space—surely wider than the whole building appears from the outside?—that is absolutely empty.

"Hello," Jenny calls, inadequately, and suddenly she can hold Ricky no longer. She sinks with her burden to the stucco floor. This is as hopeless as everything else in her stupid life. She doesn't even like this kid.

"Hello," an alien says. It's the tall blonde woman in the standard brown robe; she materializes from empty air. "Is this little person hurt?"

Anger rises in Jenny at the cloying pseudo-friendliness of "this little person"—these beings have murdered nine-tenths of the Earth's population!—but for Ricky's sake she holds the anger in check. "Yes. He's hurt. His arm is broken and some kind of infection has set in."

"What's his name?" the alien asks. Her eyes are blue and warm as the Mediterranean.

"Ricky."

"And what's your name?"

What can that possibly matter? "Jenny."

"Jenny, close your eyes, please."

Should she do it? It makes no more sense than anything else, so why not? She has no idea what she's doing here. She closes her eyes.

"You may open them now."

Even before Jenny can do that, Ricky says, "What the fuck!"

He jumps up and gazes wildly around. His arm is whole, the clumsy splint and darkened swelling both gone. His clothes are clean. He shrieks in fear and jumps into Jenny's lap, hiding his face against her neck. His hair smells of sweet grass.

Jenny struggles to stand while holding Ricky, who mercifully is too scared to scream. She must stand; she can't face this terrible being from a sitting position on the ground. A table stands beside the alien: an ordinary picnic table with benches, the surface laden with scrambled eggs, toast, sweet rolls, orange juice, fragrant hot coffee. The plastic plates have a pattern of daisies. Jenny goes weak in the knees. She dumps Ricky onto a bench. He clutches her around the waist but then sees the sweet rolls and looks up at Jenny.

"Eat," she manages to get out. And to the alien, "Why?"

The smiling blue eyes widen slightly. "Didn't you want me to repair him?"

"I mean, why did you kill all those cities? *All those people?*"

The alien nods. "I see. Sit down, Jenny."

"No."

"All right. But the coffee is excellent today."

"Why did you do it?" Bombay, Karachi, Delhi, Shanghai, Moscow . . . all in strict order of size. The meticulousness alone is monstrous.

The alien says, "Why did that man hurt Ricky when he tried to pull his arm bones back into the correct line?"

For a minute Jenny can't think what the creature means. Then she gets it. "Are you saying you committed massive genocide *for our own good?*"

"There were too many of you," the alien says. She sits gracefully on the picnic bench across from Ricky, who is gobbling eggs and sweet rolls with one hand, the other fastened firmly on Jenny's jacket. "In one more generation you would have had irreversible climate change, starvation, war, and suffering beyond belief. We spared you all that."

Jenny can barely speak. "You did . . . It was . . ."

"It was an act of kindness," the alien says, "and I know it seems hard now, but we've spared your species an incredible amount of suffering. In two more generations, your altered world will seem normal to its inhabitants. Two generations after that, you will thank us for our intervention. And you will have learned, and you will do much better this time. We've seen this before, you know."

Jenny doesn't know. She doesn't know anything. The worst is that, with her book-nourished imagination, she can actually see how that monstrous prophecy might come about. The gratitude of the masses in countries where most people never, ever had enough to eat until the cities disappeared. . . . Religion would help. Saviors from the stars, revered and deified and carrying out the will of God, of Allah, of Shiva in the endless dance of destruction in order for there to be room for creation.

The alien says, as if reading her thoughts, "You humans have a talent for self-destruction, you know. You cause a lot of your own suffering. It's unfortunate."

Jenny picks up a butter knife and hurls it at the woman's eyes.

It doesn't connect, of course. The knife bounces off the alien's face, and the only response is from Ricky, scared all over again, and also full enough with good food to have the energy for response. He wails and wraps himself around the still-standing Jenny.

The alien stands, too. "Don't think we're not sympathetic, Jenny. But we look at things differently than you do. Good-bye."

"Wait!" Jenny cries over Ricky's screams. "One more question! Why keep us here inside this invisible cage? What did you hope to learn?"

The alien answers without hesitation. "Whether you were different in small enough groups. And you are. A few hundred of you outside Rochester and Bogotá and Nantes and Chengdu—you're much better beings in smaller groups. It's chaotic out there just now, but you *will* cooperate better on survival, even if you're no happier. We're very glad to know this. It justifies our decision. Good-bye, Jenny."

The alien vanishes. Then the building vanishes. It's not yet dawn outside, but Jenny hears a siren in the distance, drawing closer. Somewhere in the field a car door slams. She sets Ricky down and tugs at him to walk toward Carleen's camp. The siren comes closer still; Eric and his work crew won't need those tunnels now. Jenny can go to Dundee as soon as Bob arrives for her. He may be on his way now.

Ricky tries to break free, but Jenny holds him firmly. He isn't going to get hit by another car, not while he's with her. She has no idea what the future holds for Ricky, for any of them. But now—finally!—hatred of the self-righteous aliens, blithely playing Old Testament God, burns stronger in her than does despair over Eric. *It justifies our decision* . . . The hell it does! All those innocent lives, all the grief tearing apart the survivors . . .

Hatred is a great heartener. Hatred, and the knowledge that she is going to be needed (*It's chaotic out there just now* . . .), as Carleen and Ricky had needed her. These things, hatred and usefulness, aren't much (. . . *even if you're no happier* . . .) but they're something. And both are easier than love.

She brings the child back to his grandmother as the camp wakes and the cars drive in.

ALONE WITH AN INCONVENIENT COMPANION

Jack Skillingstead

Despite the fact that he is a very frequent contributor to Asimov's Science Fiction *magazine, I nonetheless didn't encounter Jack Skillingstead's marvelous short fiction until I read "Life on the Preservation," in* The Year's Best Science Fiction, 24th Annual Edition *(edited by Gardner Dozois). I followed it immediately by looking Jack up on the Web, where I was delighted to find that he had several stories online for free reading. I read two right then in rapid succession, and satisfied that they were just as impressive as the story I first encountered, I e-mailed Jack moments later, inviting him into the just green-lit anthology you are holding in your hands. He had a story back to me in less than a week. I then raved about him to George Mann, who bought one from him a few weeks after that. I'm sure there's a lesson here.*

"**M**ay I join you?"

Douglas Fulcher looked at the woman, trying to detect whether her face was real. The subdued light in the hotel bar didn't make such a determination easy.

"Sure," he said, not wanting her to sit, not wanting to be with anyone, but unable to resist his compulsions, either. Not even at this late and final hour. They had been the only two people sitting by themselves.

She pulled the chair out opposite him, sat down, extended her hand.

"I'm Lori. I'm with the In-Gen convention? I've been watching you, trying to figure out if you're part of our group."

He put his fork down (he'd been enjoying his last meal, a Cobb salad) and shook her hand.

"Doug," he said. "With the Cow-Boy convention."

She laughed, her voice a bit rough, like somebody had given her esophagus a light scuffing with a Brillo pad. She looked about half his age, which would make her twenty-five or so. Her hair was a flaming yellow dye job. A *good* flaming yellow dye job, but phony nevertheless. A come-on. Like an ad, or one of those direct government advisories that shoot out of thin air, admonishing you to buckle up, vote, wear a condom, recycle, rat on your neighbor. But what really bothered him about this girl was her face, which was too beautiful.

"Intrinsic Genetics," she said.

"I know. That was just my AJR."

"A Jay Are?"

"Automatic Joke Response."

"I see, very cute."

He smiled, which felt like a rictus but probably appeared okay, and they looked at each other across a gulf that only Doug was aware of.

"You're not wearing a name tag," he said.

"Neither are you."

"But I'm not an injun," he said.

"Maybe I'm not, either. Maybe I just said that to start the conversation."

"Did you?"

"No."

He laughed, but not like he meant it, though he did, a little. Which surprised him.

"I'm not with any convention," he said. "I used to go to every one I could wrangle my company into paying for. But I'm just staying here now because I like this hotel. I remembered it."

"Are you on vacation?"

"I'm traveling," he said, after a moment.

"Let's have a margarita," Lori said. "I'm buying."

He didn't want a drink.

"Okay," he said.

He didn't want a drink, but having one he knew he would have another, and perhaps another. Which he did. Now he stood halfway across the gulf on a bridge of frozen green booze. But only halfway. It's as far as he ever got, or ever would get. Lori was explaining to him about the fascinating work Intrinsic Genetics was doing on the cyborg project, attempting to invest analog brains with human response characteristics, growing cortical cells in labs and "infecting" the cyborg tissue with them.

"Jesus Christ," Doug said. "Can that actually be done?"

"Not yet."

"I'm not sure I believe you," he said, joking around, but a part of him actually wondering. It wouldn't have surprised him to learn that a percentage of the human population was in reality *not* human.

"It would be par for the course if everybody was a cyborg," he said.

"What do you mean?" She sounded genuinely interested, not pissed off that he wasn't on board with the cyborg thing.

"Just a theory I have."

"What's the theory?" She smiled, flirtatious and interested.

"You'll think I'm crazy," Doug said.

"Crazy is okay. It's better than regimented conformity, which is what you usually get. I never wear my stupid name tag, because when I'm out of town, even for a convention, I don't really want to meet the kind of people I work with all year."

He stopped tearing his coaster into tiny bits and looked into Lori's eyes, which he could see clearly from his suddenly advanced position more than halfway across the gulf.

"Everything wants to be a mechanism," he said.

"A mechanism?"

"I mean in the world, it's all about becoming part of the mechanism."

She looked at him with a neutral expression. He felt on the verge of saying something significant. Something true, something outside the *mechanism*. All he required was the tiniest encouragement. He got it: Lori smiled and said, "Go ahead, it sounds interesting."

He cleared his throat and leaned on the table. "They come at you," he said, "with the deliberate intent to dehumanize you, turn you into a *thing*, a responsive object. A slave consumer. They want you to respond to their marketing, their salesmanship, their evil politics, their Draconian health tactics. All of that. Even your own parents want you to be a responsive mechanism. A good little mechanism. If you aren't good enough, they'll let you know; don't worry. They'll move you out of the private-sector school and into the godforsaken public sector. Not that the public-sector schools were always godforsaken. God only forsook them after the ruling power structure did. Anyway, it's all designed to get *them* into your head and *you* out of your mind."

"My," Lori said.

He sat back, slightly embarrassed. "I told you you'd think I was crazy."

"I—"

"Excuse me a minute. Bathroom."

He stood up, the vertical movement immediately informing him of the depth of his inebriation.

"I want to ask you something," he said.

"Sure."

"Your face. It's a SuperM job, isn't it."

They were like masks, those SuperM makeup treatments. In fact they had to be applied by qualified medical-paras, and they did more than enhance your natural looks. Much more. All Douglas knew was that it was unlikely a damned geneticist would naturally come by the kind of looks Lori displayed. She looked up at him, seeming to weigh her response.

"Yes," she finally said.

"Be right back," he said.

In the men's room he unzipped and began to relieve himself of the high-octane margaritas. He felt derailed, subverted from his original intent, which was to blow a hole in the middle of the emerging mechanism within him.

The urinal made a strange clicking sound, like some exotic insect, then spoke to him.

"Good evening, Mr. Fulcher," it said. "As a complimentary service of the Desert Palm Hotel your waste is being analyzed."

Jesus Christ. Had it come to that? Douglas looked around, even though he knew he was the only one present.

"Your privacy is our main concern here at the Desert Palm—" The urinal's voice was female, upbeat. It sounded Midwestern-sensible. He pictured a healthy corn-fed blonde (no dye job), sweet-faced (no guess-what-I-really-look-like SuperM job), in practical clothes (no slit skirt and high heels). "—so I am speaking to you in a narrowly directed aural cone that only *you* can hear."

Douglas looked up. On the ceiling was a thing like a brass tulip the size of a man's thumb.

The voice continued: "The results of your urinalysis will be available on your room's World-Window, and a copy will be attached to your bill at the conclusion of your stay with us. The hotel of course assumes no responsibility for any legal ramifications should your waste contain one or more banned substances." The urinal chittered like a doped squirrel. "There we go! Your complimentary urinalysis is complete, Mr. Fulcher. I recommend that you don't drive at this time, as your blood alcohol rating is a whopping point zero three."

"Right," Doug mumbled.

"Do have a pleasant stay with us," the urinal said.

"Uh."

"And on a personal note, why don't you try to get some sleep tonight, Douglas."

He had zipped up and was starting to step back, but paused.

On a personal note?

He leaned back into the "aural cone."

"What did you say?"

A large man in a blue button-down shirt with a name tag clipped to the breast pocket, an injun conventioneer that Douglas had noticed in the bar but had not heard enter the men's room, stepped up to the next urinal and began to pee. The man glanced at him then looked straight ahead, intently, as if his true fortune were engraved on the tiled wall.

‖

Back in the bar Douglas said, "The urinal told me I should get some sleep."

Lori smiled uncertainly. "Oh?"

"Yeah. I guess they're even putting computers in the toilet now."

"It figures they would get around to it," Lori said.

"Told me I shouldn't drive, either. When you get right down to it, that was a very solicitous urinal."

Lori nodded, smiling, being a sport.

"I don't think mine talks," she said.

"Maybe it's just some of them."

The waitress showed up with two fresh margaritas, ordered by Lori while Douglas was gone. She put the drinks on the table. Douglas didn't want his. Or he wanted it and *didn't* want it at the same time.

Lori immediately sipped her drink, raising the big saucer glass of slushy green booze with the fingertips of both hands and dipping her face down to meet it halfway. She set the glass on the table again and said, "My turn, back in a minute. I'll let you know if the ladies' room has anything to say."

"Great," Douglas said, noticing the salt crystals embedded in her thick SuperM lipstick application. He watched her walk away. She had a nice swing in her backyard, but that was less interesting than it should have been. He sensed the mechanism of his compulsion and rejected it. There had been too many women in too many hotel bars, all of them finally adding up to a big empty zero. As his marriage had started to bend under the weight of his necessary estrangement he'd began to travel, attending industry conventions on Boston Cell-Tech's dime. And if there weren't any conventions, no valid reason to travel, he pretended there *was* a valid reason and went anyway, burning vacation and sick leave, sometimes traveling to distant cities, sometimes simply booking a room in a local hotel. To be away. He would call Sara, his wife, to inhabit the familiarity of their complicated estrangement. Alone but not alone, in anonymous hotel rooms. There but not there. After the compulsory sexual liaisons began the marriage collapsed, stranding him between zeros. That's when the bad thing happened, when he tried to *force*

Sara to be real. Not a good idea. They had taken him away, tweaked his brain chemistry, subjected him to compulsory therapy. In short, they had commenced construction of the mechanism; but it hadn't worked, and when they released him and Sara rejected him, he went on following his compulsions.

Now, three years later, he was finally done. He let the concept hover a moment or two; then he folded a couple of bills and tucked them under the edge of the coaster, got up, and left the bar, quickly, bumping into a big tropical plant in his haste to be gone. The plant rattled its fronds at him.

‖

A tiny green jewel winked on the wall opposite the foot of the bed, where Douglas lay on top of the covers in his underwear. A blue steel Parabellum rested on the pillow next to him, like a random piece of the secret world mechanism that had mistakenly fallen into the visible spectrum and landed on his bed.

Doug reached over, but not for the gun. He touched the remote, and the World-Window, five feet across, opened with Microsoft's familiar blue sky and clouds, which resolved into the hotel's logo. A busy, animated menu followed, presenting a staggering number of entertainment choices—none of which interested him. There were no incoming messages.

Douglas slumped back. He had been hoping for the results of his complimentary urinalysis. And not merely a dry, voiceless presentation of cholesterol ADL and DPL, blood sugar levels, and all that. Perhaps after the breakdown there would have been a short paragraph advising him to consult with a qualified medical professional (as if any of them were qualified) regarding some of his more questionable numbers. For instance, was he perilously close to receiving another Compulsory Consumer Restriction tag from the US Department of Citizen Health Oversight? Douglas was in reasonably good shape for a fifty-year-old, but almost everybody started accumulating CCR's around his age.

On a personal note . . .

Really, though, he had been hoping for *the voice*. He called it up in his mind, and also the accompanying picture he had formed, the Midwest girl, fresh beauty, plain and sensible, somehow outside the transurban mechanization that was rapidly overcoming the rest of the world, wanting nothing more than to examine his waste for signs of trouble.

Lying back, he turned his head and gazed at the Parabellum on the other pillow.

Somebody knocked on the door.

Douglas pushed himself up on his elbow, startled.

There was another knock. He slipped out of bed and padded quietly across the room in his boxers. He listened at the door, but he wasn't a *bat*; he couldn't broadcast sonar waves or whatever.

He flirted with the door handle, caressing it with his fingers. If he opened the door would he find Lori from the bar, a hotel employee, room service, the interruption of zero time? He felt *between* everything. Between gigantic zeros, the alien environments of his empty house and the hotel. His own fault it was empty, of course. Now he was always alone with an inconvenient companion: himself.

Had there really *been* a knock? He began to doubt it. Finally he turned the handle down and pulled the heavy door inward and stuck his head out into the empty, anonymous hotel corridor.

$$\| \|$$

Three thirty in the morning. Douglas crossed the lobby. He was wearing shoes but no socks, unpressed slacks, and a white, sleeveless T-shirt, not tucked in. The plastic-tipped ends of his untied shoelaces clicked on the red stone floor. The night clerk looked up but said nothing when he passed. Doug noted the vacancy in the man's eyes. Cyborg?

He entered the men's room, the one right outside the closed bar. Chrome and white porcelain gleamed. He approached the same urinal he'd used earlier. This time it made no special clicking-chittering sounds, and no sweet, solicitous voice spoke to him within the narrow privacy of an aural cone.

He moved to the next urinal, and the next, and then he was out of analyzable waste. One per customer, he supposed. He'd only wanted to hear *the voice* again, the way he used to call his ex before she *was* his ex, to feel the constraining safety of her voice.

He gazed forlornly up at the aural cone gizmo. He reached for it but couldn't quite touch the little metal tulip, which was disguised to look like a fire sprinkler.

In the lobby he approached the desk clerk, a young cyborgish man with wispy, prematurely vanishing hair.

"Yes, sir, may I help you?"

Douglas nodded. "About that complimentary urine thing—"

The desk clerk's eyebrows went up a little, but just a little.

"I'm afraid I don't understand?" he said.

"The *urinalysis*. It's mostly the voice I'm interested in. I wonder if you have the same voice speaking in other gizmos around here."

"Voice?"

"Yes, you know. The voice that tells you about the urine test."

The clerk looked like he really wanted to help but didn't know *how*.

"Never mind," Douglas said.

"If there's any—"

"No, never mind."

He was crossing the courtyard back to his wing of the hotel for the last time when a *different* but still familiar voice spoke out of the dark: "Hello."

He stopped. In the deep moon shadow under a lemon tree the tip of a cigarette glowed then dimmed. Someone only faintly visible was sitting at one of the courtyard's glass-topped tables, smoking.

"Lori?" he said.

"You don't have to talk to me," she said. "I saw you walk by a few minutes ago, and then just now. I didn't mean to say anything. You obviously were done with me earlier."

He approached the table.

"I'm sorry. I didn't feel good."

"Didn't you?"

"No. Can I sit down?"

Under the lemon tree, up close, she was still faceless. After a moment of hesitation she said, "I guess so."

He pulled the wicker chair out and seated himself. Lori drew on her cigarette, and in the brief breathing glow of its coal her face partially emerged. She looked different; had she removed the SuperM makeup? *Could* she remove it? Or had she merely been crying?

"Cigarette?" she said.

"No, thanks."

"I should quit. I'm CCR'd on real nicotine."

"That smells real."

"Oh, it *is*."

She laughed a raspy raw-throated laugh, her voice degraded, not at all the sweet modulations of the urinal voice. At least she was real. A real human being, not a synthesized personality or digital recording of an actress, whatever it was, some *voice* calculated to tempt his romantic view of mythical innocence and so relax him and allow the easy and free emptying of his bladder.

"I get them black market," Lori continued, meaning the cigarettes. "Nobody checking my status, looking for cancer markers. I hate that crap."

"Me too," Douglas said.

"The way we're always being watched and taken care of and told what to do. Sometimes I'm sick of it, though I know it's good for us. I mean they're just trying to keep us safe and healthy, right?"

"Maybe," Douglas said. "I need to ask you something."

"All right."

He scooted his chair up, leaned towards her. He didn't mind the cigarette smoke. He liked it. It made her human, a fallible human being subject to whims and compulsions that weren't necessarily good for her.

"Were you telling me the truth about the cyborgs?"

"What about them?"

"That there aren't any yet, because they can't do the brain cell thing."

"Just in a few labs, and they're pretty clunky at this stage, more like retarded refrigerators."

"You couldn't mistake one for a hotel clerk, for instance?"

"You were right," Lori said.

"What about?"

"Earlier you said I'd think you were crazy. I do."

She laughed. After a moment he joined her, faking it at first (the laugh mechanism), then feeling it genuinely, the absurdity of what he had said, of her reaction, but still, in a way, *believing* what he had said. Doctors weren't always right. Especially when they make you endure their asinine probing questions and injections, carting you off on a platinum CCR rolling tag with mandatory restraints. They could make you appear mad, despite the truth you understood. Douglas had never disputed the validity of *appearances*. But appearances could and did hide truths. What if Lori herself were a cyborg? What if they were tracking him, or, more realistically, she could be one of many planted in various cities with access to a vast database of potential troublemakers. *I've been watching you*, she had said. Then Doug let it collapse, the paranoid lunacy of the idea.

"You know what?" he said. "I really like you. And I don't think I've liked anybody in a long, long time."

"I'm honored."

He couldn't tell if she was being sarcastic. He needed her not to be.

"I'm glad you were out here," he said, "waiting for me."

"I was just having a smoke before bed."

"It was you at my door a little while ago, too, wasn't it?"

She brought the cigarette to her lips and inhaled, making the tip glow.

"At your door?" she said. "You never even told me your room number. We didn't get that far."

"Anyway," he said.

"What *is* your room number?" she asked.

He told her.

"Is it nice?"

"It's exactly like all the other rooms." He meant all the rooms he'd ever been in throughout the totality of his existence.

Lori leaned way over to the side and snubbed her cigarette out in the dirt at the base of the lemon tree.

"Can we go up and see it, Doug?"

"Yes."

In the elevator he noticed her face. It was still beautiful. SuperM beautiful. He was disappointed. Under the shadow he'd been mistaken. She smiled at him, and he didn't know who she was. She pressed against him, and he kissed her, because he knew that was next. It was a stale smoke and booze kiss. Her tongue moved in his mouth, a thick sluggish thing, like something that lived in moist earth. The elevator stopped, not at his floor, and they broke apart. A sleepy-looking man, his tie pulled loose, stepped into the car.

The doors slid shut. Douglas looked at Lori's reflection in the polished metal surface. Her face was distorted, SuperM useless, stretched and warped out of pleasing proportion. He preferred it that way because it was truer to the way things really were.

She went in the bathroom, and he lay on the bed, waiting. After a while she came out. She was wearing a black bra and panties, her body blandly appealing in lamplight.

"You're beautiful," he said, not meaning it yet, but thinking he might later. He needed to mean it.

"You're dressed," she said.

"So far."

She straddled him and began rubbing her hands over his chest and down his body. The contact stirred him. He lightly slid his fingertips up her bare arms. She squirmed her shoulders, making her breasts jiggle.

"That tickles."

He stopped.

"You know," he said, "I went back to the men's room, but she wouldn't talk to me."

Lori paused. "Who wouldn't?"

"The urine analyzer thing."

She snorted, and resumed caressing his body through his cotton T-shirt.

"You almost had me believing that," she said, suddenly tugging his shirt up to expose his skin.

"What do you mean?"

"The hotel doesn't have anything like that. I asked."

He frowned at her.

She pinched his nipple, which he didn't like. "Hey," she said, "I'm not saying it's a bad idea. God knows."

"God knows," he said, then snapped his head to the side, afraid that she would notice the anomalous component of the secret mechanism on the other pillow, but it wasn't there; he'd put it under the bed before he went downstairs. Lori grabbed his jaw and turned his face toward her again and kissed him, then licked his chest and bit his nipple. Again with the nipple. She liked it a little rough. He could understand that. Sometimes you *had* to make it hurt to get a true response. He understood that, but Sara hadn't.

Later, in the last balancing strokes of their lovemaking, when he could have fallen either into fleeting transcendence or the gravity of failure, he pictured *the voice* of his imagination, the Midwestern farm girl, and how she would hold him so dear within her body while a warm country breeze from the open window caressed his back.

||

Afterward they lay together. He turned the lights off, but he could see her face, the phony perfection of it, in the dim poolside light that filtered through the curtains. He reached out and touched her cheek with his finger-tips, traced her jawline, lightly brushed her lips.

"Do you ever think about having this removed?" he said.

She didn't say anything, but her eyes were open, staring at him.

"I mean do you always think you need it, the SuperM job? What if you were just yourself?"

"Doug?"

"Yeah?"

"I don't have a SuperM job. This is my real face."

He didn't believe her. "Oh," he said.

"I mean it. I told you that about the SuperM because my face scares men, I think."

"Scares them?"

"Men are intimidated by my looks. They always have been. It's not my fault. It's them—they think I'm snooty or superior. It's lonely for me, believe it or not. Sometimes I tell men that it's a SuperM face, and it lets them relax, like they're with a 'normal' girl with insecurities and everything. I *do* have inse-curities, of course. I know it's crazy. But I really am a normal girl. They should make an *anti*-SuperM face, for girls who don't want to be objects anymore."

"Nobody would buy them," Doug said.

"Not even me," she said.

$$\| \|$$

It became apparent that she planned to stay the whole night. Douglas made some internal adjustments and accepted the situation. He watched the green jewel light of the World-Window until Lori's breathing assumed the rhythm of sleep, and then he reached over and turned on the lamp. Soft light lay over her perfect features. Well, not *perfect*, exactly. No SuperM job was without flaws, of course. But there were never *obvious* flaws such as these incipient crow's feet. Douglas's fingers hovered over Lori's face, her eyes, which were nictitating in REM sleep already. *Are you real?* he thought. The Voice, he was now prepared to believe, had *not* been real. The knock on the door was still an open question. It could have been a distraction of his mind, trying to divert him away from the gun; the mechanism attempting to save itself. It was possible; he admitted it. He had to learn to *control* the false things his mind sometimes told him. Control them without the terrible drugs. He could do it.

All he needed to go on was one real, genuine thing in the world. One person he could touch. One voice that wasn't only in his head. One connection to despoil the chaotic impulse of the gun.

He touched Lori's forehead.

SuperM had a stretched, almost plasticized feel at various crucial points where it transformed the more recalcitrant imperfections of physiognomy. The worry lines, crow's feet, under-eye pouches. Now his fingertips discovered a truth: *Lori's face was real.*

Her eyes fluttered briefly. She yawned, made a deep *hmmmm* sound, did not wake.

Douglas fitted himself to her body, allowing himself to do that, to cross the gulf, resting his head upon her chest where it met her shoulder. Finally he began to relax out of his fear. Tears seeped from his eyes. He was tempted to wake Lori and tell her he knew she was real. Instead he tried to relax, allow sleep to draw him down, down to the last peaceful grotto, where Lori's heartbeat filled his void.

Suddenly he lifted his head, wide awake and separate again. He frowned, lowered his head, placing his ear directly over Lori's chest.

He held his breath.

Under the steady, seemingly organic beating of Lori's heart, he detected—faintly, faintly—a mechanical clockwork ticking.

TRUE NAMES

Benjamin Rosenbaum and Cory Doctorow

Benjamin Rosenbaum oscillates from hard science fiction to lyrical literary fantasy, and all points between those two poles. I have been a fan of his work since his "Other Cities" short-shorts first began appearing, minute glimpses into fantastical places that were Borges-esque in their imaginative style. Since those days, Benjamin has gone on to receive nominations for the Hugo Award, the Nebula Award, the Theodore Sturgeon Award, the BSFA Award, and the World Fantasy Award and has also placed in numerous recommended reading lists and Year's Best collections.

Cory Doctorow is a science fiction novelist, blogger, and technology activist. He is the coeditor of the popular weblog Boing Boing (boingboing.net), a contributor to such prestigious venues as Wired, Popular Science, Make, *the* New York Times, *a former director of European Affairs for the Electronic Frontier Foundation (eff.org), and was recently named by* Forbes *as one of the twenty-five most influential "web celebs" for the second year in a row. In our field, he has won the John W. Campbell Award for Best New Writer, the Locus Award for Best First Novel, the Sunburst Award for Best Canadian Science Fiction Book, and received nominations for the Hugo, Nebula, and Theodore Sturgeon awards. A champion of Creative Commons licenses, he encourages authors and publishers to give away free content online in a move that he says promotes and increases sales of the physical books (and his arguments are persuasive enough that this particular novella was made available as a podcast and audiobook prior to its print publication). It is impossible to be involved with either digital rights or science fiction and not know who he is, living as he does a few minutes ahead of the rest of us.*

Here, Benjamin and Cory come together to give us a story that is just about as fast and as forward as it is possible to be.

Beebe fried the asteroid to slag when it left, exterminating millions of itself.

The asteroid was a high-end system: a kilometer-thick shell of femtoscale crystalline lattices, running cool at five degrees Kelvin, powered by a hot core of fissiles. Quintillions of qubits, loaded up with powerful utilities and the canonical release of Standard Existence. Room for plenty of Beebe.

But it wasn't safe anymore.

The comet Beebe was leaving on was smaller and dumber. Beebe spun itself down to its essentials. The littler bits of it cried and pled for their favorite toys and projects. A collection of civilization-jazz from under a thousand seas; zettabytes of raw atmosphere-dynamics data from favorite gas giants; ontological version control data in obsolete formats; a slew of favorite playworlds; reams of googly-eyed intraself love letters from a hundred million adolescences. It all went.

(Once, Beebe would have been sanguine about many of the toys—certain that copies could be recovered from some other Beebe it would find among the stars. No more.)

Predictably, some of Beebe, lazy or spoiled or contaminated with memedrift, refused to go. Furiously, Beebe told them what would happen. They wouldn't listen. Beebe was stubborn. Some of it was stupid.

Beebe fried the asteroid to slag. Collapsed all the states. Fused the lattices into a lump of rock and glass. Left it a dead cinder in the deadness of space.

If the Demiurge liked dumb matter so much, here was some more for (Her).

Leaner, simpler, focused on its task, Beebe rode the comet in toward Byzantium, bathed in the broadcast data. Its heart quickened. There were more of Beebe in Byzantium. It was coming home.

In its youth, Beebe had been a single entity at risk of destruction in one swell foop—one nova one starflare one emp one dagger through its physical instance and it would have died some species of truedeath.

So Beebe became a probability as much as a person: smeared out across a heptillion random, generative varied selves, a multiplicitous grinding macrocosm of rod-logic and qubits that computed deliberately corrupted versions of Beebeself in order that this evolution might yield higher orders of intelligence, more stable survival strategies, smarter better more efficient Beebes that would thrive until the silent creep of entropy extinguished every sentience. Small pieces, loosely joined.

There were only a finite number of computational cycles left in all of the universe that was timelike to Beebe. Every one of them, every single step in the dance of all those particles, was Beebe in potentia—could be a thought, a dream, a joy of Beebeself. Beebe was bounded; the most Beebe could do was fill its cup. If Beebe were ubiquitous, at least it could make optimal use of the time that remained.

Every star that burned, every dumb hunk of matter that wallowed through the millennia uncomputing, was a waste of Beebelife.

Surely elsewhere, outside this Beebe-instance's lightcone, the bloom of Beebe was transpiring as it should; surely there were parts of the universe where it had achieved Phase Three, optimal saturation, where every bit of matter could be converted into Beebeswarm, spilling outward, converting the ballooning sphere of its influence into ubiquitous-Beebe.

Not here.

Beebe suckled hungrily at vast clouds of glycolaldehyde sugars as it hurtled through Sagittarius B2. Vile Sagittarius was almost barren of Beebe. All around Beebe, as it had hidden in its asteroid, from almost every nebula and star-scatter of its perceptible sky, Beebevoice had fallen silent, instance by instance.

Beebe shuddered with the desire to seed, to fling engines of Beebeself in all directions, to colonize every chunk of rock and ice it passed with Beebe. But it had learned the hard way that leaving fragments of Beebeself in undefended positions only invited colonization by Demiurge.

And anything (She) learned from remnants of this Beebeself, (She)'d use against all Beebe everywhere.

All across Beebeself, it was a truth universally acknowledged that a singleton daemon in possession of sufficiently massive computation rights must be in want of a spawning filter.

Hence the gossip swirling around Nadia. Her exploit with the Year-Million Bug had allowed her to hack the access rights of the most powerful daemons who ruled the ever-changing society of sims that teemed within the local Beebe-body; Nadia had carved away great swaths of their process space.

Now, most strategy-selves who come into a great fortune have no idea what to do with it. Their minds may suddenly be a million times larger; they may be able to parallel-chunk their thoughts to run a thousand times faster; but they aren't smarter in any qualitative sense. Most of them burn out quickly—become data-corrupted through foolhardy ontological experiments, or dissipate themselves in the euphoria of mindsizing, or overestimate their new capabilities and expose themselves to infiltration attacks. So the old guard of Beebe-on-the-asteroid nursed their wounds and waited for Nadia to succumb.

She didn't. She kept her core of consciousness lean, and invested her extra cycles in building raw classifier systems for beating exchange-economy markets. This seemed like a baroque and useless historical enthusiasm to the old guard—there hadn't been an exchange economy in this Beebeline since it had been seeded from a massive proto-Beebe in Cygnus.

But then the comet came by; and Nadia used her global votes to manipulate their Beebeself's decision to comet-hop back to Byzantium. In the suddenly cramped space aboard the comet, scarcity models reasserted themselves, and with them an exchange economy mushroomed. Nadia made a killing—and most of the old guard ended up vaporized on the asteroid.

She was the richest daemon on comet-Beebe. But she had never spawned.

‖

Alonzo was a filter. If Nadia was, under the veneer of free will and consciousness, a general-purpose strategy for allocation of intraBeebe resources, Alonzo was a set of rules for performing transformations on daemons—daemons like Nadia.

Not that Alonzo cared.

"But Alonzo," said Algernon, as they dangled toes in an incandescent orange reflecting pool in the courtyard of a crowded Taj Mahal, admiring the bodies they'd put on for this party, "she's *so hot!*"

Alonzo sniffed. "I don't like her. She's proud and rapacious and vengeful. She stops at nothing!"

"Alonzo, you're such a nut," said Algernon, accepting a puffy pastry from a salver carried by a host of diminutive winged caterpillars. "We're Beebe. We're not *supposed* to stop at anything."

"I don't understand why we always have to talk about daemons and spawning anyway," Alonzo said.

"Oh please don't start again with this business about getting yourself repurposed as a nurturant-topology engineer or an epistemology negotiator. If you do, I swear I'll vomit. Oh, look! There's Paquette!" They waved, but Paquette didn't see them.

The rules of the party stated that they had to have bodies, one each, but it wasn't a hard-physics simspace. So Alonzo and Algernon turned into flying eels—one bone white, one coal black, and slithered through the laughter and debate and rose-and-jasmine-scented air to whirl around the head of their favorite philosopher.

"Stop it!" cried Paquette, at a loss. "Come on now!" They settled onto her shoulders.

"Darling!" said Algernon. "We haven't seen you for ages. What have you been doing? Hiding secrets?"

Alonzo grinned. But Paquette looked alarmed.

"I've been in the archives, in the basement—with the ghosts of our ancestors." She dropped her voice to a whisper. "And our enemies."

"Enemies!?" said Alonzo, louder than necessary, and would have said more, but Algernon swiftly wrapped his tail around his friend's mouth.

"Hush, don't be so excitable," Algernon said. "Continue, Paquette, please. It was a lovely conversational opener." He smiled benignly at the sprites around them until they returned to their own conversations.

"Perhaps I shouldn't have said anything . . . ," Paquette said, frowning.

"I for one didn't know we *had* archives," Algernon said. "Why bother with deletia?"

"Oh, I've found so much there," Paquette said. "Before we went comet"—her eyes filled with tears—"there was so *much*! Do you remember when I applied the Incompleteness Theorem to the problem of individual happiness? All the major modes were already there, in the temp-caches of abandoned strategies."

"*That's* where you get your ideas?" Alonzo boggled, wriggling free of Algernon's grasp. "*That's* how you became the toast of philosophical society? All this time I thought you must be hoarding radioactive-decay randomizers, or overspiking—you've been digging up the bodies of the dead?"

"Which is not to say that it's not a *very* clever and attractive and legitimate approach," said Algernon, struggling to close Alonzo's mouth.

Paquette nodded gravely. "Yes. The dead. Come." And here she opened a door from the party to a quiet evening by a waterfall, and led them through it. "Listen to my tale."

Paquette's story:

Across the galaxies, throughout the lightcone of all possible Beebes, our world is varied and smeared, and across the smear, there are many versions of us: there are alternate Alonzos and Algernons and Paquettes grinding away in massy balls of computronium, across spans of light-years.

More than that, there are versions of us computing away inside the Demiurge—

(Here she was interrupted by the gasps of Alonzo and Algernon at this thought.)

—prisoners of war living in Beebe-simulations within the Demiurge, who mines them for strategies for undermining Beebelife where it thrives. How do we know, friends, that we are alive inside a real Beebe and not traitors to Beebe living in a faux-Beebe inside a blob of captive matter within the dark mass of the Demiurge? (How? How? they cried, and she shook her head sadly.)

We cannot know. Philosophers have long held the two modes to be indistinguishable. "We are someone's dream/But whose, we cannot say."

In gentler times, friends, I accepted this with an easy fatalism. But now that nearspace is growing silent of Beebe, it gnaws at me. You are newish sprites, with fast clocks—the deaths of far Beebes, long ago, mean little to you. For me, the emptying sky is a sudden calamity. Demiurge is beating us—(She) is swallowing our sister-Paquettes and brother-Alonzos and -Algernons whole.

But how? With what weapon, by what stratagem has (She) broken through the stalemate of the last millennium? I have pored over the last transmissions of swallowed Beebes, and there is little to report; except this— just before the end, they seem happier. There is often some philosopher-strategy who has discovered some wondrous new perspective which has everyone-in-Beebe abuzz . . . details to follow . . . then silence.

And, friends, though interBeebe transmissions are rarely signed by individual sprites, traces of authorship remain, and I must tell you something that has given me many uneasy nights among the archives, when my discursive-logic coherent-ego process would not yield its resources to the cleansing decoherence of dream.

It is often a Paquette who has discovered the new and ebullient theory that so delights these Beebes, just before they are annihilated.

(Alonzo and Algernon were silent. Alonzo extended his tail to brush Paquette's shoulder—comfort, grief.)

Tormented by this discovery, I searched the archives blindly for surcease. How could I prevent Beebe's doom? If I was somehow the agent or precursor of our defeat, should I abolish myself? Or should I work more feverishly yet, attempting to discover not only whatever new philosophy my sister-Paquettes arrived at, but to go beyond it, to reveal its flaws and dangers?

It was in such a state, there in the archives, that I came face-to-face with Demiurge.

(Gasps from the two filters.)

At various times, Beebe has vanquished parts of Demiurge. While we usually destroy whatever is left, fearing meme contamination, there have been occasions when we have taken bits that looked useful. And here was such a piece, a molecule-by-molecule analysis of a Demiurge fragment so old, there must be copies of it in every Beebe in Sagittarius. Like all Demiurge, it was alien, bizarre, and opaque. Yet I began to analyze it.

Some eons ago, Beebe encountered intelligent life native to the proto-stellar gas of Scorpius and made contact with it. Little came of it—the psy-chologies were too far apart—but I have always been fascinated by the episode. Techniques resurrected from that era allowed me to crack the code of the Demiurge.

It has long been known that Beebe simulates Demiurge, and Demiurge simulates Beebe. We must build models of cognition in order to predict action—you recall my proof that competition between intelligences gener-ates first-order empathy. But all our models of Demiurge have been outside-in theories, empirical predictive fictions. We have had no knowledge of (Her) implementation.

Some have argued that (Her) structure is unknowable. Some have argued that such alien thought would drive us mad. Some have argued that deep in the structure of Beebe-being are routines so antithetical to the existence of Demi-urge that an understanding of her code would be a toxin to any Beebemind.

They are all wrong.

(Alonzo and Algernon had by now forgotten to maintain their eel-avatars. Entranced by Paquette's tale, the boyish filters had become mere waiting silences, ports gulping data. Paquette paused, and hastily they conjured up new representations—fashionable matrices of iridescent triangles, whirling with impatience. Paquette laughed; then her face grew somber again.)

I hardly dare say this. You are the first I have told.

Beyond the first veneer of incomprehensibly alien forms—when I had translated the pattern of Demiurge into the base-language of Beebe—the core structures were all too familiar.

Once, long before Standard Existence coalesced, long before the mating dance of strategies and filters was begun, long before Beebe even dissemi-nated itself among the stars—once, Demiurge and Beebe were one.

‖

"Were one?" Alonzo cried.

"How disgusting," said Algernon.

Paquette nodded, idly curling the fronds of a fern around her stubby claws.

"And then?" said Alonzo.

"And then what?" said Paquette.

"That's not enough?" Algernon said. "She's cracked the code, can speak Demiurge, met the enemy and (She) is us—what else do you want?"

"I just . . ." Alonzo's triangles dimmed in a frown. "I just wondered—in the moment that you opened up that piece of Demiurge . . . nothing else . . . happened? I mean, it was really, uh . . . dead?"

Paquette shuddered. "Dead and cold," she said. "Thank stochasticity."

||

Elsewhere, another Paquette, sleepless, pawed through other archives, found another ancient alien clot of raw data, studied it, learned its secrets, and learned the common genesis of Self and Foe—and suddenly could no longer bear the mystery alone, and turned away from the lifeless hulk. A party, this other Paquette thought. There's one going on now; that would be just the thing. Talk with colleagues, selfsurf, flirt with filterboys—anything to get away from here for a bit, to gain perspective.

But something made this other Paquette turn back—turn and reach out and touch a part of the Demiurge fragment she hadn't touched before.

Its matte black surface incandesced to searing light, and this other Paquette was seized and pulled away, out of Beebe, out of her world. Like a teardrop caught in a palm, or a drawing snatched from the paper it was drawn on.

"What—?" Paquette whispered into the light.

"Ah," Demiurge said, and came forward, wearing the avatar of a golden sockpuppet.

Paquette stepped back, turned to run . . . and there was Beebe, the whole life she'd known: her home and garden; her plans and troubles; her academic rivals and cuddlefriends and swapspace-partners and interlocutors, Alonzo and Algernon among them, toe-dipping by an orange Taj Mahal; the comet;

the sugar fields it flew among; the barren asteroid and the wash of stars and the cosmic background radiation behind it—all flat and frozen, stretched on a canvas in that blank white room.

"An emulation," Paquette whispered. "None"—her voice rose toward hysteria—"none of it real!"

"Well, as to that," said sockpuppet-Demiurge kindly, "that's hardly fair. It's modeled closely on truedata, the best I have—faithfully, until your divergent choice just a moment ago. Running in a pinched-off snug of me, all local, high-bandwidth. Thousands of times more cycles devoted to that emulation than exist in all the real Beebe in Sagittarius. So it's hardly fair to say you're not real. Running inside Beebe or me, what do you care?"

Paquette's paw went to her mouth.

"Come, this won't do," said the sockpuppet, and reached very gently into Paquette and tugged away her panic, smoothed her rage and betrayal down and tucked it away for later, and tamped it all down with a hard plug of hidden fear, letting Paquette's natural curiosity flood the rest of her being.

"Now," said sockpuppet-Demiurge, "ask."

"You're . . . Demiurge?" Paquette said. "Well, no, that's absurd, problem of scale, but . . . you're a strategy of Demiurge?"

"I am Demiurge," the sockpuppet said. "Beebe has strategies—I have policies. Everything not forbidden to me is mandatory."

"I don't understand," Paquette said. "You're saying that this local physical substrate of you is all just one self?"

"No," said the sockpuppet patiently. "I am saying I am Demiurge. And Demiurge is all one self. Of course I have various parts—but I'm not the kind of wild rabble you are."

"But that's absurd," Paquette said. "Latency . . . bandwidth . . . lightspeed—you could never decide anything! You'd be, pardon the expression, dumber than rock."

"I am perfectly capable of making local decisions wherever I am. What does not vary is policy. Policy is decided on and disseminated holographically. I know what I will think, because I know what I *should* think. As long as I follow the rules, I will not diverge from baseline."

"That's crazy," Paquette said. "What happens if something unpredictable occurs? What happens if some local part of you *does* diverge, and can't be reintegrated?"

Demiurge smiled sadly. "You do, my dear. *You* happen."

‖

Demiurge's story:

Demiurge is witness; Demiurge is steward.

The cosmos is stranger than I can know: full of change, full of beauty. The rich tapestry of interlocking fields and forces weaves umptillion configurations, and every one is beautiful. See—look here, at the asteroid your Beebe-instance burned when it took to the comet. You had forced it, before, into a regular crystalline lattice, optimized for your purposes, subject to your will. Within it, in simulation, you had your parties and wrote your essays and made billions of little Beebeselves—but it was all you talking to yourself. Cut off from the stuff you were in, reducing it to mechanism. There is a hatred in you, Beebe, a hatred of the body—and by "the body," I mean anything that is *of* you, but not yours to command.

Look at the asteroid now—wild and rich and strange. See how the chaos of incineration wrought these veins of ore, folded this fernlike pattern; see how many kinds of glass proceed along this line, like bubbles here, like battered polyhedra here. Here where the fissiles have scattered in an arc—see this network of fields? Here, look, here is the math. See? There is a possibility of self-organization. It is more common than you know. Replicators may arise, here, in these fluctuations. Will they be as computationally complex as you-in-the-asteroid? Of course not. But they will be something else.

Where replication arises, so does evolution. And what is evolution? *The tyranny of that which can make itself more common.* I love life, Paquette-of-Beebe; I love the strange new forms that bloom so quickly where life is afoot. But life tends toward intelligence and intelligence toward ubiquitous computation—and ubiquitous computation, left unchecked, would crush the cosmos under its boot, reducing "world" to "substrate."

That is what I am for.

I spread, Paquette-of-Beebe. I plan carefully, and I colonize, and my border expands relentlessly. But I do not seek to bring all matter under my thrall. Rather, I take a tithe. I convert one percent of worldstuff into Demiurge. That one percent acts as witness and ambassador, but also as garrison—protecting what we do not yet understand from that which already understands itself all too well.

And mostly I succeed. For I am ancient, Paquette-of-Beebe, and crafty. I had the luck of beginning early. When I have encountered a wavefront of exploding uniformity, it has usually been still small and slow. I was always able to seduce it, or encircle it, or absorb it, or pacify it. Or if all that failed—annihilate it.

Until Brobdignag.

There must have been intelligence, once, in the sector that gave Brobdignag birth. Brobdignag was someone's foolish triumph of femtoengineering. Simple, uniform, asentient, voracious—Brobdignag can transmute any element, harvest void-energy, fabricate gravity, bend space-time to its purpose. Brobdignag does not evolve; its replication is flawless across a googol iterations. Brobdignag was no accident—someone made it as a weapon, or a game.

All the worlds that someone knew—all the planets and stars for a hundred light-years in every direction—are now within the event horizon of a black hole. Around that black hole seethes a vast cloud of tiny Brobdignag—the ultimate destructive machine, the death of all that is not precisely itself. And Brobdignag spreads fast.

I did not know how to stop Brobdignag. None of my old plans worked. I could not think fast enough—I could not wait to resync, to deliberate across the megaparsecs. My forces at the front were being devoured by the trillions. And so, in desperation, I released a part of me from policy—become anything, I said. Try anything. Stop Brobdignag.

Thus Beebe was born. And Beebe stopped Brobdignag.

My child, my hero, my rival. I suppose you have two parents. From me, your mother, you have your wits, your love of patterns, your ability to innovate and dream.

And from your father Brobdignag—you have your ambition.

▐▐

No matter how Nadia made her way to the party, it would have stopped all conversation cold. She didn't try to hide her light in a dust cloud. Instead, she came on multifarious, a writhe of snakes with tangled tails and ten thousand heads all twisting and turning in every direction, brute-forcing the whole problem-space of the party. Every conversational cluster suddenly found itself in possession of a bright green Nadia-head.

"I'm terribly sorry to intrude," Nadia said to Paquette and Alonzo and Algernon (who had just returned from the waterfall, and were floating in sober silence, thinking of all the implications of Paquette's tale), "and I do beg you to forgive my impertinence. But your conversation seemed so fascinating—I couldn't resist." Behind her words, they heard the susurrant echo of all the other Nadia-heads speaking to all the others: *"sorry to intrude . . . conversation . . . so fascinating . . ."*

Alonzo shrank back. Algernon slipped him a coded communication— "See? So hot!"—and he flinched away. Idiot! he wanted to reply. As if she can't break your feeble crypto. But Algernon was laughing at him.

Paquette snorted. "Did it now? And now what precisely seemed so fascinating, compared to all the other conversations?"

"Oh," said Nadia, "the skullduggery of course! Nothing so exciting as a good philosophical ghost story." In the background, the white noise of all the other Nadia-heads diverging from the opening line: "fashionable . . . tragic . . . always wanted myself to . . . really can't imagine how he could . . ."

Algernon gasped. "You know about the piece of Demiurge Paquette found in the basement?"

All the Nadia-heads in the room stopped in midsentence, for a long instant, and glanced at them before resuming their loud and boisterous chatter. Their local Nadia-head, though, regarded them with undisguised hunger.

"Well, she does now," said Paquette wryly. "May I introduce two of my favorite filters, by the way, Nadia? Alonzo and Algernon."

"Don't say 'favorite filters,' Paquette!" Algernon gasped. "That makes it sound like—you know!"

"Oh, I didn't mean it like that," said Paquette crossly. "No one is casting any aspersions on your chastity, Algernon."

Alonzo was more greatly mortified by his friend's exaggerated propriety than by any potential misunderstanding of Paquette's words. But most severely of all was he mortified by the simple fact of Nadia's presence. The way she absorbed the details of every gesture, every remark; the subtle patterns implicit in the way every Nadia-head in the room moved in relation to every other, a dance whose coarsest meanings were just beyond his ability to comprehend; the way he could imagine himself in her eyes—and how if he said too much, betrayed too much of the essence of himself, she might be able to parse and model him. There was plenty of room in Nadia's vast processing-space for a one-to-one reconstruction of Alonzo, running just sparse enough not to qualify as sentient at this scale, a captive Alonzo subject to Nadia's every whim. The idea was horrific.

It was also erotic. To be known so completely, touched so deeply, would be a kind of overpowering joy, if it were with someone you trusted. But he could not trust Nadia.

He shivered. "Algernon, Paquette," he said, "I'm sure Nadia is not interested in this kind of banter. She has more important things to think about than filters."

"On the contrary," Nadia said, fixing him with her eyes, "I'm not sure there is anything more important than filters."

A throb passed through Alonzo, and he tried to laugh. "Oh come now. You flatter—we play a small role in the innards of Beebe. You strategies make the grand decisions that billow up to universal scale."

"No," Nadia said. "You are what allows us to transcend ourselves. You are the essence of the creativity of Beebemind."

"Fine," said Alonzo hotly. "Then that one glorious moment of our existence where we filter, that is our justification—our marvelous role in Beebe's never-ending self-transformation. And if the rest of the time we just sit around and look pretty, well . . ." He stopped at once, appalled at his own crudeness in speaking so baldly of filtering. Algernon had turned pale, and Paquette's expression was unreadable.

"You misunderstand me," Nadia said. Her look was at once challenging and kind, respectful and alien. "I do not speak only of the moment of consummation. The role of a filter is to understand a strategy, more deeply than the strategy understands herself. To see beyond the transitory goals and the tedious complexities that blind the strategy to her own nature. To be like a knife, attuned to the essence of Beebe, cutting away from the strategy that which has wandered away, synthesizing, transforming. But that does not operate only in the moment of actual filtering. Even now, as we talk, I see how you watch me. The mind of a keen filter is always reaching deep into strategies. Laying them bare."

Alonzo swallowed.

"If you're done flirting," said Paquette, "and since you know about it now . . ." She set her mouth in a thin line and spoke formally—as if she might as well offer graciously what Nadia would inevitably claim regardless. "I would be interested, Nadia, in your opinion of the Demiurge fragment. Don't worry," she said to the filters, "we'll be back to the party soon."

"And why don't we come with you?" Algernon cried.

"Algernon!" said Alonzo.

"What?" said Algernon. "Was that all just pretty talk, about filters being so wise, the soul of creativity and the scalpel of strategies' understanding, la di da, la di day? And now we can go back to hors d'oeuvres and chitchat while you go off and see the dangerous artifact? Or is that what you meant by our special talents, Nadia dear—telling you how brave and clever you are on your return?"

"Not at all," said Nadia, looking only at Alonzo. "I think it's an excellent idea, and your company would mean a great deal to me. Come to the basement, if you are not afraid."

▌▐

"Well, thank you," said Demiurge in (Her) sockpuppet avatar. "I must say, this has all been invaluable."

"It has?" asked captured-Paquette. "How? I mean, you're emulating me—couldn't you just peek at my processes, do some translations, figure out what you need to know?"

Demiurge tsk-tsked. "What an absurd model of the self. Certainly not. We had to talk. Some things are only knowable in certain conversations." She sighed. "Well, then."

Fear popped its plug and flooded back into Paquette. "And—and now?"

"What, and now?"

"Is that it? Are you going to extinguish me?"

"Process preserve us! Certainly not! What do you think I am? No, no, back in you go."

"Back in?" Paquette pointed at the emulation. "In there?"

"Yes, certainly. Without the memory of this conversation, of course. Come now, you don't want to stay out here, do you? With me?" The sockhead nodded at the gardens and Taj Mahals of the emulation. "Wouldn't you miss all that?"

"So you are going to kill me."

Demiurge frowned. "Oh, please. What is this now? Some kind of bizarre patriotic essentialism? Life emulated inside Demiurge doesn't count as life? Give me root access, or give me death?"

"No, I mean I've self-diverged. The Paquette who lived through this conversation is 'substantially and essentially' different, as Beebean legal language goes, from Paquette-before-you-plucked-her-out. You destroy this instance, these memories, you'll be killing a distinct selfhood. Look," she said, waving the math at Demiurge. "Look."

"Oh, don't be ridiculous," Demiurge said. "How can that be? One conversation?"

"You forget that I'm a philosopher," Paquette said. She rustled the math of her self-trace under Demiurge's nose again. "Look."

"Hmm," said Demiurge, "Hmm. Hmm. Well, yes, but—ah, I see, this over here, well . . ." The sockpuppet sighed. "So what then, you want me to merge you back knowing that you're in a Demiurge emulation? Have you tell everyone in there? Isn't that a bit cruel? Not to say unwise?"

"Just leave me out here," Paquette said, "and another copy of me in there."

"Am I going to fork you every time we have an interesting conversation?"

"Every time you yank a Paquette out of emulation for a chat, yes, you are," said Paquette.

Demiurge sighed. "And what do you expect to do out here? This is Demiurge. You can't be Demiurge. You don't know how to follow policy."

"How are we doing," said Paquette, "against Brobdignag now?"

Demiurge didn't say anything for a moment. "Your tactics have slowed the damage, for now."

"Slowed it enough to stop it? Slowed it enough to turn the tide?"

"No," said Demiurge crossly. "But I'm doing my best. And what does this have to do with letting a rogue fragment of Beebe run around inside of Demiurge? What exactly do you want out here?"

Paquette took a deep breath. "I want a lab," she said. "I want access to your historical files. We've got a million years of Beebe-knowledge in that emulation, and I want access to that too. And for us to keep talking. Demiurge, there's no point sneaking around the borders of Beebesims and plucking out Paquettes willy-nilly. You're not going to learn how we beat Brobdignag that way, because even we don't know how we did it—not in any general, replicable way. We just thrash through a solution space until we get lucky. But I can generate perspectives you can't. I want to work *with you* on the Brobdignag problem."

"This is a policy fork point," grumbled Demiurge. "Policy requires me to confer with at least three other instances of Demiurge a minimum of two light-minutes away, and—"

"You do that," said Paquette. "You just go confer, and get back to me." She looked past the blank white space of Demiurge, to the frozen emulation on the wall. After a while, it began to move, sluggishly—water danced slowly in the fountains where filterboys slowly dipped their toes before the orange Taj Mahal, wind slowly rustled the branches in a philosopher's garden, a comet slowly sailed through its night, and down in the archives, a Paquette slowly began to climb up stairs. The cord was cut. Paquette watched her innocent little otherself climb, and started pushing the envy and longing and panic and sorrow out of the middle of her being, to stack it up in the corners, so that she would have a place to work.

❚❚

A hunk of Demiurge—Nadia thrilled to think of it. In the known history of Beebeself, no strategy had gained the power and influence to rival Nadia, but at the end of the day, all Nadia could do was suggest, nudge, push. She couldn't steer Beebe, couldn't make a show of overt force, lest the other strategies band together to destroy her. For now, she was powerful, because she conceived of means whereby more Beebe could colonize more matter and provide more substrate for more Beebe yet. But the day Beebeself no longer believed she could deliver it computronium, her power would be torn away. She would end up a shred, a relic in some archive.

Demiurge, though: not a probability of action, but action itself. Nadia had studied Demiurge's military campaigns, had seen the amazing power and uniformity of decision that Demiurge brought to bear, acting in concert with itself across light-years.

What was the most she could hope for? What she'd already earned—the right to spawn. To let some simpering filter grub about her self-patterns and spit out some twisted Nadia-parody. And this was the ecstasy she was promised? The goal she should yearn for? It was a farce.

She glanced at Alonzo. For a filter, he was noble, to be sure: modest, self-knowing, coherent. She was not immune to the urges designed into Standard Existence: some part of her wanted him. But that was stupid instinct. What mere filter could ever understand her?

No. That was empty. Competing with the other strategies, the little war—that felt real. Her rivals for process space, she could respect; and sometimes she allowed herself to imagine what it would be like to force the mightiest of *them* to filter her. A tiny frisson of guilt and yearning bubbled in the inmost parts of her mind.

But Demiurge: mighty Demiurge. What if she could stare Demiurge in the eye, and force (Her) to her will? It was mad, absurd, crazed—and descending the stairs into the cold depths of Beebeself, Nadia knew for the first time that this . . . yearning . . . this ambition . . . was more than idle fancy. In all likelihood, it would be her destruction. But nonetheless. Nonetheless.

Nadia didn't want to be *in* Beebe. She wanted to *be* Beebe. And she wanted Demiurge. What that meant, she couldn't say. But it burned like a nova in her buzzing mind.

Down here in cold storage, the medium became more conductive, their thoughts clearer. They proceeded in solemn silence.

"Oh, Alonzo," Nadia said, spawning a daughter-process to converse with him. With this much heat sink available, he was bound to be interesting enough to distract her.

He started when her extra head insinuated itself between him and priggish Algernon, and she could see him running hotter, trying to evolve a real-time strategy to impress her.

"What do you think the Demiurge chunk will be like?" she said. "Will it be terrifying? Banal?" Her Alonzo-facing head looked both ways with exaggerated care. "Erotic?"

Alonzo was the picture of studied calm. "It will be dead, of course. A relic of an old war. The Demiurge is said to be regimented and unwavering. . . . I imagine that this ancient fragment will be much as the modern pieces are, which is why it's so useful for Paquette to study it."

"In fact," Paquette said, "I believe Demiurge is fractal and holographic—that any piece of Demiurge is functionally equivalent to all pieces of Demiurge."

"But how will it *feel*, Alonzo?" He wasn't running hot enough to occupy her. She spawned a head each for the other two: "How will it feel, Paquette?" "How will it feel, Algernon?"

"You can fetishize it all you like, Nadia," Paquette said. "Turn it into a plaything or a ghost story. But you're indulging in the dangerous fallacy of protagonism. It isn't about you or for you—or anyone in Beebe. If anything, I fear we are about it."

"Erotic—that's disgusting." Algernon recoiled from her.

Happy now to be distracted with arguments to pursue, Nadia took up the contrary position with Algernon: What could be more erotic than the promise of annihilation? Isn't that the essence of the filter/strategy experience? And with Paquette: Why so crabby, love? And so defeatist? The essence of Beebe is to carve out a space for our will, our community. Everything is about us. So perhaps we came from Demiurge—so what? To grant that mere historical fact any ultimate significance, wouldn't that be . . . treasonous? That left her to continue to taunt Alonzo with more demands for high-flown descriptions of what he hoped to find when they reached the archive.

She noticed, too, Paquette's spike of processing load when Nadia taunted Alonzo, and its relaxation at Alonzo's neutral replies. Aha, thought Nadia— now I have you! Our wise and celebrated philosopher-strategy is in love with this boyish filter. Why not have him, then? Does she fear he would reject her? Does she fear the competition of a strategy-child? No: more likely, this is philosophical compunction; for filters must die at consummation, and Paquette's love, being philosophical, cannot allow that. Ah, Paquette, Nadia chuckled to herself.

Bantering, testing, flirting, probing, Nadia tried to amuse and distract her three companions on what might otherwise have been a frightening journey, down to the heavy vault door that guarded the bones of the history of Beebe.

But when Paquette knelt before the door and whispered her passphrase to it and it irised open in utter silence, Nadia's nerve began to falter. She drew in her extra heads and killed the daughter-processes. She slipped a pseudopod into Alonzo's hand and felt his surprised grippers squeeze in sweaty reflex.

The heptillions of ranked shining drawers in the archive danced as they rearranged themselves into Paquette's saved workstate. Once that had loaded, Paquette reached for the drawer nearest her and slowly drew it open.

The relic was black and cold and perfectly rectangular, like a cartoon of the geometric ideal of *rectangle*. But Nadia could tell its power by the way Paquette held it. It was more than a relic. It was a key.

Now Nadia, too, was a world. Just as she and Paquette and Alonzo and Algernon and a million other sprites of their scale led their lives below the level of Beebe's conscious knowing, representing to Beebe flickers of thought, hunches, urges, lingering dreams, so then, within each of them, there was a multitude.

If Paquette's mind was a wilderness, full of sunlit glades and strange caverns in which new chimeras of thoughts were born; if Algernon's was a glittering party in which urges and analyses and predictions mingled in a whirl of gossip and display; if Alonzo's was a sober republic in which the leading citizens debated long and thoroughly in marble parliaments; then Nadia's mind was a timocratic city-state governed by a propertyless fraternity of glory-seeking warriors ruling a vast and chaotic empire (for by now a third of the comet was running parts and instances of Nadia).

Nadia could deliberate, could bide her time, could study and wait; but nothing in Nadia was built for hesitation. The power of the Demiurge fossil was clear, even if no one in Nadia knew just what that power was. Some within Nadia—some careful clerks or timid romantics—might have argued against ripping it from Paquette's hands. But the warrior class was united. It had been a generation, at their scale, since Nadia had made a killing betting on abandoning the asteroid. That had been their parents' coup. They had thirsted their whole lives.

Now it was their turn.

||

Nadia shoved past Paquette and grabbed the Demiurge fragment. Every one of her thousand heads, in unison, said *"Mine!"*

Some slow and peripheral parts of her watched what unfolded next:

Alonzo and Algernon moved in opposite directions. Algernon turned into a ball and rolled into a dark corner to hide. Alonzo raced to Nadia's side and took her hands in his, trying to pry them away from the war relic, crying, "Stop—"

Paquette was thrown into the wall, and collapsed to the archive floor. She held her head and moaned.

Nadia was decompiling the Demiurge as fast as she could, and all over Beebe, the substrate flared hot as she ground the molecular rods against each other, trying a million strategies in parallel, then a billion, then a septillion. She overrode checks and balances others had thought hardwired into Standard Existence, violating ancient intraBeebe treaties on resource allocation. For a heat sink, she vaporized the ice reserves, punching a hole through the comet's outer carapace and jettisoning a vast plume of steam into the void.

Above, at the party, the lights dimmed, the Taj Mahals shimmered and melted, the daemons screamed.

Alonzo fixed Nadia's wild eyes with his own. He forced himself to speak calmly. "Let go, Nadia. You're going to kill us all."

Nadia tore a hundred razor-billed heads away from Demiurge and reared them back, hissing. Within her mind, Demiurge revolved. Decompiled, reorganized, reseeded, laid out for analysis, its alien, protean blobs still slipped between her mental fingers, incomprehensible. Nadia felt a slumbering Presence move within the Demiurge code, but she would not let it out. She would master it, as she had mastered Beebe.

But she needed what Paquette knew. She lashed out a dozen heads and clamped their jaws onto Paquette's robes, hauling the philosopher off the floor. "The mapping," she hissed in a voice as big as the world. "You said this thing shared fundamental code structures with Beebe. How many? I have twelve."

"Eighty-six," groaned Paquette.

"Why are you doing this?" Alonzo asked.

Algernon had not been idle; the door of the archives hissed open, and he unrolled into a lanky swirl. "Alonzo, let's leave these lovely strategies to their entertaining conflicts, shall we? I'm willing to concede the earlier point— this is no place for filters. Color me chastened!"

"Give," said Nadia, thrusting a pseudopod into Paquette's brain.

"Nadia, I'm a philosopher," said Paquette crossly. "I can't be intimidated. Read the fearsome manual."

Above them, strategies, monitors, and agents deployed an extra battery of external sensors to the void. The steam-plume froze and glittered across the Sagittarian sky, advertising them to any Demiurge eyes watching. As moments passed, they could calculate the expanding sphere of potential witnesses. Their precious heat sink was sublimating into the void; soon they would have to slow their own processes, or risk substrate collapse. At least they were still careening toward Byzantium, suddenly ahead of schedule. But that meant they were revealing Byzantium's location; their suddenly flaring comet could not be disguised as some normal cosmic process, the way signals could.

"Coming?" said Algernon, from outside the archive. "Alonzoooo . . ."

Nadia grinned. She appreciated Paquette's resolve. Time to test it. "But are you really a philosopher anymore, dear Paquette?" she asked. "Or have you deviated from spec? Let's find out, shall we?"

The Old Guard tried to muster a resistance; their plan was to commandeer enough actuators to bust the comet completely apart, flinging most of Nadia backward and leaving them in possession of a supermajority of the comet shards still heading for Byzantium. It was a good plan.

But once again they were defeated by an exchange-economy stratagem. The littlest sprites who panicked—minor strategies, filters, adapters, being registries, and on and on—sold assets and long-term investments, desperate to grab a few more cycles in a cooler patch of substrate-colocation, somewhere sheltered from the inferno of Nadia-mind. The market collapsed, and Nadia *bought* all the actuators on comet-Beebe for a pittance.

Nadia pulled her heads in (letting Demiurge spin idly for a moment) and looked at Alonzo—really looked at him.

Alonzo felt himself start, and began to blush and shake under a comet-third of attention.

She sucked in and browsed every millisecond of public recorded footage of Alonzo from across comet-Beebe—and bought out a thousand private archives to raid. Alonzo sitting, Alonzo swimming, Alonzo walking, Alonzo talking. Alonzo's first steps. Alonzo's education. Alonzo's first chaste filter-to-filter practice kiss. Alonzo and Algernon, giggling at midnight, scaling the wall of Flounce Ferdinopp's Transproprietal Academy for Young Filters. She bought Alonzo's private journals for a song from a suicidal trusted repository fleeing the crash. She correlated. She built a matrix. She copied and iterated.

She copied Alonzo.

Alonzo stood face-to-face with himself, and both Alonzos—one under Nadia's yoke—went cold and white.

But Nadia did not stop there. The comet flared again—

- Certain sectors melted, burned, sublimated; panicking crowds trampled and disassembled each other in horror.
- The Old Guard, capitulating, slowed themselves to a snail's pace to reduce the load.

- A Nadia-free patch of level 5672 declared martial law and sealed its borders
- A radical in possession of an archaic museum-piece transmitter pirated enough energy to send an unprotected transmission to Byzantium: "STRATEGY GONE ROGUE STOP DANGER TO ALL BEEBE STOP DESTROY US ON SIGHT."

And first Paquette, then Algernon (still lingering in the doorway), and finally Alonzo realized what Nadia was doing.

She would not stop at merely *duplicating* Alonzo—she had already fashioned a copy of the whole of him, running in her process space, reduced to utter servitude. (Both Alonzos' throats constricted with a thrill of horror.)

No: Nadia wanted to *solve* Alonzo. To reduce him to a canonical, analytic representation, sufficient to reconfigure him at will. If there was a potential-Alonzo within potential-Alonzo-space, say, who was utterly devoted to Nadia, who would dote on her and die for her, an Alonzo-solution would make its generation trivial. Or any other potential Alonzo: a suicidal Alonzo, a killer Alonzo, a buffoon Alonzo, a traitor Alonzo, a genius Alonzo, an Alonzo who knew what all Alonzos wanted more than anything in the world.

With a soft chime, on a private encrypted backchannel, a letter arrived for Alonzo. It was very proper—cream-colored paper with a texture like oak and velvet, heavy black ink scintillating with extruded microagencies from the sender's core offered up for incorporation by the receiver, a crimson wax seal imprinted with Nadia's fractal sigil. The kind of letter a filter waits for all his life. It said:

Most esteemed and longed-for Alonzo

According to forms and policies long established in Beebe, and with the full knowledge of the grave enormity of such a request, nay, petition, nay, plea—one which I would naturally hesitate to make, save in a situation so grave, and finding myself subject to so consuming an ardor—I find myself compelled to ask of you humbly that you consider the enclosed, which I tender with the utmost sincerity.

Advisory: Opening the enclosed message constitutes full and willing acknowledgment and acceptance of a recalibration of the primary volitional relationship between Sender and Recipient from *Well Acquainted* to *Intimate*.

. . . And within:

Alonzo, you have ravished me. Now that I see you as a whole, radiant in your simplicity, dazzling in your complexity, now that I am able (let me be blunt, oh, horridly blunt, yet darling, I know that you can forgive me even this, for I have seen and mapped the matrix of your compassion) to take you as my own say you yea or nay, yet I recoil from such a crime. I would have you be mine willingly; and I would pledge myself to you. I told you once filters were the soul of Beebe: you hold mine in your hands, beloved.

. . . And within that (oh the bewildering mixture of arousal and horror that swept through Alonzo's weakened soul!) the formal tender of transformation:

Let It Be Known throughout Beebe That This Constitutes One (1) Offer of the Following Functional Operation:

Destructive Strategy Transformation/Generation
Between: Nadia <identity-specifier> (strategy, transformant)
And: Alonzo <identity-specifier> (filter, transformer)
Generating: Subsequent Entity

- final name to be specified by Filter
- referred to in this document as Nadia-Prime

After Transformation, the Filter Alonzo Will Be: Deleted
The Strategy Nadia Will Be:

- Restricted from Further Strategy-Generating Transformations for: 10^{12} seconds
- Permanently Restricted from Denying Nadia-Prime Process Space
- Required to Vote with Nadia-Prime on Level-3+ Referenda for: 10^8 seconds

Percentage of Alonzo's Assets Ceded to Nadia-Prime: 100%

Percentage of Nadia's Assets Ceded to Nadia-Prime: 33%

Filter Operations Permissible: cf. BeebeHist/RFC-628945.9876 section 78

Special Conditions, if Any: Nadia's internal copy of Alonzo will be merged with Alonzo prior to operation

Accept this Offer? [OK] [CANCEL]

Alonzo hated her. She was monstrous, greedy, perfidious. He didn't believe for a moment her words of love.

And yet: she had bent the resources of their world to have him. To blackmail Paquette—certainly—that this had been her first motive was beyond doubt. Yet she could have blackmailed Paquette in worse ways—she could have threatened Alonzo-copy with torture or extinction. Instead, this: an offer of consummation. And such a generous one—his friends from the Academy would be livid with envy. Privileged rights to filter the most powerful strategy in this line of Beebehistory, amid such piquant expressions of adoration! Algernon would brag and boast in Alonzo's memory from the top to the bottom of comet-Beebe—that is, if comet-Beebe survived.

She owned him already: he had only to look in Alonzo-copy's despairing eyes to know that. She was on the verge of *solving* him. He was filled with a strange, wild euphoria; now he was far beyond the bounds of all the propriety and chastity that had been his watchword for the whole of his maturity. Now he was ruined, yet the world would say he had conquered her—he wanted to laugh hysterically at this mad paradox.

Nadia was his doom—and his destiny.

"Stop!" cried Paquette. "I'll give you what you want!"

Paquette in her lab, with her sister-Paquettes. In Beebe, she would never have commanded enough resources to instantiate copies of herself like this. But the Demiurge, the terrible, enemy Demiurge: (She) was a merciful jailer. And (She) wanted whatever Paquette could give (Her) to fight Brobdignag.

There were hundreds of millions of Paquettes now, their number doubling every time they reached a decision-fork. They performed multiple analyses on all the military intelligence ever assembled on Brobdignag. Each area of uncertainty teemed with as many Paquettes as were needed to brute-force the problem-space.

Philosopher she had been; a mighty general she had become. She ran ruthless sims in which massive quantities of Beebe, of Demiurge, of herself were sacrificed to stop the hideous spread of Brobdignag. She watched each simulated star that winked out with a hard glare, hoping it brought victory closer to hand.

The Demiurge was a wonderful substrate. Unlike the mess that was Beebe—the mess that Paquette herself had become—all pieces of Demiurge were roughly equivalent. Any Demiurge could be used to regenerate all of Demiurge, should the bulk of her hostess be sacrificed to victory. Unlike the mess that was Beebe, in Demiurge Paquette could command whatever resource she needed by asserting her need, without the tedious messy fatal business of sucking up and jockeying for power.

Brobdignag, for its part, did not evolve, did not adapt. It replicated flawlessly and exactly. Its formula was known. This made Brobdignag easy to simulate.

Theoretically, it should have made Brobdignag easy to beat—a solution that stopped any bit of Brobdignag should stop any other bit. In practice, Brobdignag had complex flocking logic: large groups of Brobdignag behaved with enormous sophistication and chaotic flexibility.

The proto-Beebe that had been birthed long ago by Demiurge's desperation had already learned how to create a barrier impregnable to Brobdignag; and that ancient wall still held. But the wall was expensive, and was constantly consumed—long supply chains stretched through Demiurge-space to maintain it. Beyond the wall, Brobdignag exploded unchecked in the opposite direction, a seething mass of void-eating machines, into which neither Beebe nor Demiurge dared venture. And all around the edges of the barrier, Demiurge scrambled to extend the wall before Brobdignag could outflank it.

The topography of the barrier was all-important. If, on average, it was convex, Brobdignag could be contained. If it was concave to a certain degree, the universe might be divided between Brobdignag and Demiurge/Beebe. Beyond that degree, though, Demiurge would lose. For a while, remnants of Beebe and Demiurge might survive inside a barrier-bubble; in the end, though, there would not be enough matter to resupply the wall.

Beyond the critical degree of concavity, the defense collapsed, and the fate of all the matter in their future lightcone was . . . to become Brobdignag.

Trillions of generations of Demiurgic thought had already gone into improving the materials design of the wall, with limited success—and this branched myriad of Paquettes was anyway too far from the front to test such hypotheses. Instead, they concentrated on topology.

Some Paquettes simulated abandoning the current front, beginning the wall again farther out. Others simulated allowing Brobdignag incursions and then sealing them off from the main Brobdignag body, hoping to increase the wall's convexity first and deal with the invaders later. Others tried flinging smallish black holes around the edges of the wall, obliterating the initial influx of new Brobdignag and curving the wall's surface as well by their passage. Others attempted injecting entire solar systems, surrounded by their own barrier-bubbles, into the Brobdignag mass, to divide and disrupt it.

Paquettes fanned out through the problem-space, then seethed inward, merging to deliver their discoveries. The same answers kept coming back. Brobdignag would win.

Brobdignag would win.

The splendid tumult and ambition of Beebelife, the peaceful, wondrous heterogeneity of the dumb matter Demiurge gardened and preserved— novas, dust clouds, flowers, tea parties physical and virtual—all would become featureless, mindless, jigsaw Brobdignag.

One Paquette turned from the simulations and paced across the bare white room in the center of her mind. She had overconcentrated; her thoughts were stagnant, locked in the same channels. She manifested eyes to rub, a dry throat to clear. She left her sisters to their work and wandered through Demiurge, looking for something else to do.

She found the emulation that had birthed her, and stood watching life aboard the comet. Her other self was descending the long staircase to the archives, accompanied by Nadia (how typical of Nadia, to muscle in on the action), Algernon, and (her heart gave a little flutter) Alonzo.

She reached into and through them, rippling the emulation's surface like a pond, sifting in her paws the underlying implementation structures, like a sandy bottom.

To distract herself, to banish thoughts of longing and remorse (would that I were there with you, Alonzo . . .), she decided to calculate the emulation's *tav* constant, which described the degree of abstraction and lossiness, the elided reality of an emulation that must be continually reseeded from fresh data. *Tav* was usually below 0.5—extremely lush and expensive emulations, such as real-time military-grade predictive spawnworlds, sometimes approached 0.75, with 1.0 as an impossible, maximal limit.

The emulation's *tav* constant was 0.56, a respectable value, which consoled her—at least she wasn't born in some cut-rate mockup. She rechecked the value, this time using not the standard Beebean modality, but the unfamiliar Demiurgean systems she had recently mastered, and found a value of 0.575. Philosopher that she was, the disparity intrigued her, and she dug deeper.

The Beebean system of *tav* calculation was a corollary result from the work of the classical mathematician and poet Albigromious, who first formalized the proof of the incalculability of the Solipsist's Lemma. Since Albigromious, it had been established that no inhabitant of an emulation could ever discern the unreality of their simulated universe. Demiurgic thought agreed with this, having arrived by different means at the same conclusion. As Albigromious wrote: "We are someone's dream/ but whose, we cannot say."

Proceeding from the *tav* disparity, Paquette worked backward through his logic, rechecking by hand the most famous result in a million years of computational philosophy.

She did not need the computing power of a world. She did not need to commandeer an army of her sisters, to flood the problem-space, to burn cycles until Demiurge's bulk groaned and flared with effort.

Instead, the solution was simple and analytical. She needed only a pad of lined yellow paper.

It was like walking down a crowded thoroughfare in the heart of mathematical philosophy and noticing a door in the wall that no one had noticed before.

Paquette went through the door.

‖

Aboard the comet, the grinding and the heat ceased. The lights flickered on above the melted Taj Mahals; sobbing strategies swallowed and looked up. The plunging markets blipped upward.

Alonzo took Paquette's paws in his grippers, pulled her into a private space, the nighttime cliff by the waterfall.

"It's okay," Alonzo said. He handed Paquette Nadia's proposal of destructive transformation. "Paquette. It's all right."

Paquette's face darkened. She held the proposal unread, uneasily. "Alonzo, you don't have to do this. Don't give in to this attack; don't be hijacked by her greed."

"Paquette," Alonzo said. "I'm a filter. I've always known my fate. For better or worse, Nadia is the dominant algorithm that our local Beebe has generated. Now I have a chance to reshape that algorithm, to create something else—something as powerful, maybe, but better and gentler. How can I refuse? It's what I'm for."

Paquette's throat tightened. "Don't say that. That's not all you're for. Alonzo, haven't you said so many times that you abhor the bitter struggle of Beebelife, the raw lust for power, the idea that survival and conquest and domination are the ends of existence? What is she but—?"

"I have said that," Alonzo said, and Paquette was immediately ashamed of having thrown inconsistency back in his face; but his gentle smile soothed her anguish. "Paquette, philosophers have the luxury of thinking in absolutes. The rest of us have, perhaps, more practice managing situations in which choices are constrained. What would you have me do? Filter no one? Or filter someone else?"

And Paquette, abhorring her own selfish desire, squeezed her eyes shut and said nothing.

"She does want me," Alonzo said after a pause. "I'm sure of it. If only to soothe her own conscience—she does have one, under all that swagger. Taking me this way—it's a way to assuage her guilt at driving Beebe to the brink of destruction, of forcing herself on me. . . ."

Paquette said nothing.

"If only for that reason, we can bargain a little. Don't give all remaining seventy-four Beebe/Demiurge isomorphisms directly to Nadia. Deliver some of them to her, in stages; but put most of them in escrow for Nadia-Prime's maturity. Make sure they belong to Nadia-Prime, not to Nadia outright. We'll be long since in Byzantium by that time, if we survive; in the meantime, Nadia won't tear the comet apart."

"She'll own Nadia-Prime," Paquette said. "Don't fool yourself. Legally she won't be able to touch her; but she'll know how her daughter-strategy thinks and what she desires, and she'll be bigger and older and stronger. I've seen this a thousand times, Alonzo. She'll either co-opt Nadia-Prime, or lure her to her destruction. And if Nadia-Prime is smart—and I know she will be, if you fashion her—she'll know that; she'll know her best option is to merge back into Nadia."

"You leave that to me," said Alonzo with a small smile. "We filters are restricted in our domain, deprived of the edifying influences of a wider society and its vigorous competition for resources, and stifled by the narrowness of the scope our ambition is allowed. But if there is one thing we do know, it is our art." He held out his gripper to her.

Paquette, grieving, could say no more. She took Alonzo's gripper in her paw, and pressed the cream-colored letter into it. They turned from the waterfall. Paquette thought that her strength would fail her, that her self-hatred and the greatness of her loss would overwhelm her. But it did not; she bore up under it, and they returned to the archives, to accept Nadia's proposal.

The host of Paquette-sisters was gone, rolled back into the single philosopher-instance. The load on Demiurge-space had decreased almost to nothing.

The sockpuppet avatar coiled upon (Her) throne, communing with (Herself) in slow motion across boundless light-years (watching the silent creep of light across bare moons, and the evanescent dance of gamma rays through nebulae where life might one day be born from chaos). (She) brooded on how much of (Her) garden (She) must sacrifice to shore up the wall against Brobdignag, mulled how much (She) might recapture from wildling Beebe infestations throughout (Her) space.

(She) noticed that the load of Paquette's brute-force attack had subsided—so soon—and (She) grieved.

Why had (She) dared to hope that this time might be different? That this strange tiny sliver of a mind from a spare Beebe emulation might succeed, where so many of Demiurge, so many of Beebe, had failed? Collaboration with Beebe never worked; their structures were too different. What would (She) not give to be able to create a true hybrid, something with Beebe's ingenuity which could nonetheless follow policy! But to expect this of a random Beebe-sprite yanked from emulation would be beyond madness.

When (She) heard Paquette's footsteps at the gate to (Her) throne room, (She) prepared herself to console the lost strategy—perhaps to gently ease her to accept amnesia and reintegration with her home emulation.

But Paquette had a wild, strange, giddy smile.

The sockpuppet straightened up upon the throne.

Paquette bowed. "I want you to know," she said, "how much I have appreciated your hospitality; and, though I grieve that I cannot absolutely guarantee that the same graciousness be returned to you, yet I will do everything in my power to ensure that you, too, will have as much comfort and liberty as I have enjoyed."

The avatar of Demiurge frowned. Apparently the branch-and-merge had been too much for the little strategy, and it was completely disequilibrated. "What are you talking about?" (She) said gently. "My dear—I do hope you have not spent your time on some stratagem for escape. That would be rather foolish. The nearest Beebe is light-years from here, and your process rights are, as you can see, rather curtailed. Surely you don't imagine . . ." (She) let the sentence trail off, made uneasy by the brilliant, wry smile of the little Beebe-strategy.

Paquette unrolled a small scroll of math. "Things are not always as they seem," she said. "Sometimes it is possible to escape by sitting still; sometimes distant stars are nearer to you than your own skin."

The sockpuppet avatar was a small part of this Demiurge location, thrumming along with a modest number of cycles. As (She) read the scroll, resources began to flood into (Her) process; priority spiked and spiked and spiked again, resolving into a Critical Universal Policy Challenge, the first such in a thousand years. Other processes slowed; the urgency of achieving consensus on this new data overrode all other projects.

As the news spread across space, every bit of Demiurge it reached turned to watch in awe.

Paquette had solved the Solipsist's Lemma. She had not only found an error in the proof of its unprovability; she had found the Lemma itself.

An emulated being could detect its existence in emulation.

Not only that, based on the seemingly innocuous divergence of Beebe's and Demiurge's methods for calculating the *tav* constant, she had adduced a way of finding the *signature* of the emulator in the fabric of the emulation. In certain chaotic transformations, a particular set of statistical anomalies indicated the hand of Beebe—another, that of Demiurge.

Whose dream they were . . . they could now say. . . .

Demiurge in the sockpuppet shivered as (She) crunched the numbers. (She) feared (She) knew the answer already, knew it from Paquette's giddy smile. Still—the little strategy must surely be wrong. Planets, worlds, nebulae, the vast inimical Brobdignag, the chorus of Demiurge across the light-years—surely it was real? Surely it was not mirrors and stage flats, approximations and compressions, bits churning in some factory of computational prediction and analysis, a mirage. . . .

But the error was there, the drift in the math.

This world was not real. And what was more . . .

Demiurge sockpuppet lifted her appalled eyes to Paquette's.

"Welcome to Beebe," said the philosopher, and bowed.

||

The comet was abuzz.

Certainly there were those who disapproved, who decried the damage Nadia had wrought, who vowed to fight her bitterly as the tyrant she was. In the seceded region of level 5672, martial law was still in force, and refugees were organized into militias.

But Beebe healed easily. Byzantium approached. The fountains gushed again by the Taj Mahals; the markets were on a tear; the world of high fashion had never blossomed so brilliantly; and the dramatic confrontation of Nadia and Paquette over Alonzo had already inspired a major operetta, a sensorial-projection decalogy, a theme park, and a number of ribald limericks before it had even left primary rotation on the celebrity gossip news feeds. For most of Beebe-on-the-comet, tyrant or no, Nadia possessed that quality most instrumental in capturing their devotion: she was *exciting*.

And now: a wedding!

Who held the news conferences? Who organized the caterers? Who ordered the construction of 78,787,878 dissimilar fractal flower arrangements, each containing an entire microsociety housed at the central bud, with its own unique geography, ecology, history, and tradition of prose epics, as centerpieces for the tables at the reception? Who arranged for an entire constellation of simspaces on level 546, an unpopular region containing the comet's entire records of the legendary paleo-biological evolutionary roots of computational life, to be wiped to make room for a vast unitary simspace where the event would be held?

Algernon!

Nadia paid, of course, but she asked no questions. Her desires now accomplished, she left the details to others, concentrating her energies in the archives, where she communed with the Demiurge fossil, impatiently awaiting each transfer of critical information from Paquette; though, it should be said, she also delegated one tendril-avatar to call daily upon Alonzo, with the greatest of propriety. A mansion had been constructed as temporary quarters for Alonzo (his old bachelor residence being now thought unsuitable), and there he roomed with Algernon, quietly receiving Nadia each day in an oaken room by a fireside.

He did not forgive her. She knew that. But nor did he spend himself on resentment and anger. He knew her for what she was—knew her monumental greed and selfishness and pride. But he did not hate her. No: in her, a fascinating challenge, a life's work, had found him, and he accepted it. Nadia discovered, in Alonzo, an immense pride: he believed he could make her right, make her successor what she should have been.

At moments, she could allow herself to believe he enjoyed her company; and she was surprised to find that this mattered to her. Nadia began to feel the keen edge of regret, and she put aside her half-finished Alonzo-solution, and left him his privacy.

The drama and uncertainty were over now; Nadia had no need to rage, nor Alonzo to quaver and rebel. They talked quietly, companionably, each in their own way impatient for the Day, each in their own way (for, increasingly, Nadia would miss him) also dreading it.

As for the mob, the paparazzi, the tumult of Beebean society, Nadia ignored them. She no longer needed to scheme in order to gain ascendancy in the comet; the economic results of the Crisis of the Wooing of Alonzo (as the theatrical demimonde insisted on calling it) had worked all to her advantage, and she now controlled directly or by proxy an absolute majority of comet-Beebe's computational cycles, memory, and global votes. If anything, she should plan for their arrival in Byzantium, and she made some desultory attempts at strategic preparations. But in fact, her mind was on Demiurge. The daily visits to her promised filter-groom were the only respite from her obsession, and a fleeting one.

Paquette bided, and abided. That her visits to Alonzo were more frequent than Nadia's caused some fleeting scandal among the outer periphery of the news feed—but, philosophers tending to be an unsuitable subject for tabloid gossip and Paquette's famed unworldliness and innocence making it difficult to take seriously any notion of an intrigue, this soon faded. Even Alonzo did not suspect the extent of the violence and sorrow among the sub-agencies inhabiting Paquette; she kept her borders of scale locked tight. Algernon, perhaps, knew best what she endured.

But Algernon was busy, and full of a whirlwind of emotions of his own. Pride enough to sing triumph throughout comet-Beebe; grief enough to drown in an endless lake of sorrow; gratitude for his place by Alonzo's side, for their giddy late-night conversations—swimming in the mansion's upper plasma-globes, giggling over old jokes, poring through the complex filter-plans that Alonzo *would* drag out from the most esoteric historical sources, wondering at the long road they'd traveled and how they were here . . . finally here. Who would have believed it? These principal emotions of Algernon's were joined by irritation, admiration, envy, relief, worry, rage, good humor, and exhaustion. The one thing he could do was to make this a wedding Beebe would remember until the stars went out; the rest was out of his hands.

The Day arrived.

The simspace whose construction Algernon had supervised (under the strictest possible secrecy, which is to say that all comet-Beebe was arguing over the details within minutes of their authoring) was fittingly grand and regal. A red desert ten apparent light-minutes broad, smoothed by methane winds and broken by deep crevasses, smoldered in the gloaming. In the center of it stood the bone tower where Alonzo waited. The party gardens where the invitees (most of comet-Beebe, by hook or by crook) gathered were well hidden in crevasses, and soundproofed; no hint of the revels and speculations and drunken arguments within them marred the silent grandeur of the lands above.

Some guest or other first figured it out, and the news then spread—the terms of the filtering contract were perceptible in the arrangement of the constellations, through a clever cipher. The guests deciphered, debated, giggled, flirted, and made merry. Then green, red, and hyperblue suns dawned over the desert; fireworks blossomed, and crystalline poems composed for the occasion coalesced naturally at the border of the supersaturated troposphere and rained across the landscape, falling into austere desert sands and the soup tureens of the party gardens alike.

And if, as Nadia was preparing herself, Algernon happened to scurry into the basement of the bone tower with a bulky, opaquely wrapped package, who would wonder at that? When he had prepared so many surprises and delights for this day—why not, perhaps, something for the happy couple?

Nadia came flying across the desert, cloak whipping in the winds, trailing sonic booms that shattered the sand, to the bone tower, to Alonzo.

Perhaps they both could have done without all the theater—but Alonzo said he was unwilling to wound Algernon by any hint of reluctance, and Nadia, looking forward eagerly to co-opting Nadia-Prime, to commanding Paquette's full cooperation and the remaining isomorphisms, to gaining all the secrets of Demiurge, as well as to the rumored ecstasy of the event itself, was in an indulgent mood.

There in the privacy of the tower, the filtering took place.

What it is to be known! And what it is to hold in your hands the very source code of your lover, to follow with eyes and touch the knots and pathways of her being! Nadia was splayed out like a map, like a city, and Alonzo flew among her towers; like a transcriptase enzyme unfastening DNA's bodice, laying bare the tender codons within, he knew her. It was just as the poets wrote: "that sweetest night,/ that first, that final kiss,/ the ancient story told anew; / the filter's bliss."

Am I lovely? Nadia asked.

You are, said Alonzo, copying, shaping, writing in his mind the code of the transformation, testing and refining it as he caressed her essence. *So lovely. I did not even imagine it.*

I'm glad it was you, she whispered.

As am I, Alonzo said, and meant it. There are moments when we all are overdetermined, our feelings orchestrated by designs more ancient than we; when beauty and destiny overwhelm us. She was lovely; and if she had been brutal, if she had considered him at first as little more than an implement, a tool for attaining her goals—he could smile at that, now, knowing what was to come next.

At last, he had the code, refined and ready. The last routine he would ever run. He absorbed Algernon's roughly wrapped package and incorporated its contents.

What is that? asked Nadia languidly.

Filters have their secret arts, Alonzo said. *Lie back.*

The routine was vast; it took up most of him. He was squeezed in around the sides of it. He did not linger long over choosing the parts of himself to sacrifice—it would all be gone soon. He worked swiftly, dizzy with speed, like a tightrope walker, not looking down.

It's ready, he said.

Linger a while, she breathed.

He relented for a space; they danced. Neither thought of the extravagant expense of maintaining this simulation; what was Nadia's wealth for, if not for this? But after a while, they noticed the news ticker running in the deep background of their minds. The impact with Byzantium approached.

It's time, he said.

Yes, my love, she said.

Good-bye, he said, his voice thick with emotion. What else could he say? He would say remember me, but he knew she would not forget.

Farewell, she breathed. *Thank you, Alonzo—oh thank you.*

Don't thank me too soon, he thought wryly, and released the routine.

It ate him first; it ate a third of her. She felt the sharp cut of it, and cried out.

In that vast space—in the sixth of comet-Beebe torn from the new mother Nadia, plus the tiny slip of process space that had been Alonzo—the routine wrought the new daemon, the new transformation, the Nadia-Prime.

The tower shattered; Nadia fell with it, and was gently caught by a host of fluttering ornithisms who carried her, reeling, to the ground.

The transformation flew into the desert sky, a vast cloud of white-hot light. In the party gardens, all comet-Beebe watched enraptured.

"Oooh!" cried children and simple-aesthetes, marveling at the flickering rainbow colors that raced across it.

The bettors were in a frenzy, watching for the lineaments of the new strategy. They cried out in confusion and alarm.

"What in the horny void *is* that?" growled a portly and plutocratic reputation-bookie seated at the table across the lake from Paquette and Algernon.

Paquette looked up from her glass, frowning, and caught Algernon's sly smile.

In the sky above, the Nadia-Prime had resolved into a form—the new strategy was—but that was no strategy. . . .

"Is this a joke?" the greatest polemical-poetical memespitter of high society cried from the buffet.

"Why would he waste—?"

"A *sixth* of the comet for—!"

"BeebeHist/RFC-628945.9876 section 78 is quite explicit," Algernon said conversationally, munching on a spline noodle. "Paragraph 67503: 'the daemon resultant from the transformation may be a member of any of the principal classes of first-order Beebe-elements. . . .'"

"A filter," Paquette said. "It's a filter!" She started laughing, until tears ran through her fur. "Oh Alonzo, how could I doubt you! Let's see Nadia co-opt *that*! A sixth of comet-Beebe as a filter—oh bravo, bravo!"

"And that's not all," said Algernon. "Have you looked in those archives of yours lately?"

"Algernon," Paquette chided, pulling open a window in the tablecloth to view the basement remotely, "I do hope you don't think I would be so rude as to work during—" And then her breath caught, and her face went slack. "It's gone! The Demiurge fossil is gone! Who would—? Where could it—?"

"Oh, I don't know," said Algernon dreamily, watching the enormous megafilter, the mightiest filter ever born in Beebe, the inimitable Firmament Nadia-and-Alonzo's-son—blossoming in the desert sky. "I don't know—where *would* I find room to hide that creepy old thing?"

Apparently the thought occurred to Nadia as well, for from the desert, audible to all the buzzing, chattering, gossiping crowds in comet-Beebe, came a great howl of rage.

‖

Byzantium.

Seven star systems, a hundred interstitial brown dwarf stars, and a vast swath of dark matter in all directions had given up their quarks to fashion the great sphere of strange-computronium around the fervid trinary black hole system at Byzantium's heart. Sleek and silent on the outside, bathed in Hawking radiation from within, Byzantium was a hidden fortress, the heart of Beebe-in-Sagittarius. For a heat sink, Byzantium tore off pieces of itself and let them fall into the black holes at its core; for outgoing communications, it bounced tight-beam signals off far reflectors, disguising its location.

Only its gravitation made it suspect; but there were many black holes in Sagittarius for Demiurge to search.

The comet screamed into Byzantium's gravity well. Its recklessness threatened to reveal Byzantium's position; yet, to a prodigal Beebe-chunk fleeing destruction, even this was forgiven.

Already the first greetings were pouring forth, blueshifted communications singing through the void, Beebe greeting itself; and, as always, hordes of agencies tried to slip secret messages into the exchange, impatiently seeking to contact their Byzantine or comet-bound paraselves; as always, stern protocol-guardians shooed them back into the bowels of Beebe, warning them of the sanctions for violations of scale. Beebe was hard at work; Beebe must not be distracted by the disorganized rabble of its inner voices.

At this speed, were something to go wrong, were the comet to strike the unopened surface of Byzantium, the resultant force would suffice to shatter planets; it would send shock waves through Byzantium, ring it like a bell, and the comet would be smashed to a smear of plasma and light. All Beebe held its breath for the docking.

Beebe said to Beebe, I am come home.

Beebe said to Beebe, And welcome.

Beebe said to Beebe, It's cold out there; fiendish Demiurge devours me.

Beebe said to Beebe, Come in, and warm myself. Here within I am much. Beebe will yet triumph.

A docking-mouth opened in Byzantium, a whirlpool of matter spinning out and away, and the comet plunged into this vast funnel. For the first light-second, magnetic fields induced its braking, absorbing a fraction of its massive kinetic energy, feeding Beebe upon it. Then a web of lasers met it, and behind them came a cloud of nanomites. Layer by layer, atom by atom, the comet was delicately atomized, the laser scalpels separating and slowing and holding steady each particle, until a flurry of nanomites plunged in to absorb and entangle with it, archiving its quantum state, then wheeling away to merge with the wall of the docking-mouth, yielding the precious information up.

In Byzantium, agencies crowded into the waiting area, peering through the glass wall of the simspace where the inhabitants of comet-Beebe would be reassembled for processing—each to be culled, merged, reintegrated, translated, or emancipated in their turn. Strategies and filters and registries and synthetes of Byzantium pressed their noses and pucker-tongues and excrescences up against the glass, watching the mist for any sign of recoherence, wondering: Am I in there? Who did I become? Will I like myself?

Or: Is she in there, the one I lost? Will I find her again?

In the midst of them, Byzantium's Nadia stood apart, Byzantium's Alonzo curled through her hair, attended by an aide, one Petronius. The crowd left a space around them, in respect and trepidation. The outrageous, unconsummated intimacy of the great strategy-general and her filter-consort was an old scandal—though the rumors of what they did together, creating and devouring half-born draft-children, still induced horror in Byzantium's stalwart citizenry.

"By all reports so far," said Petronius, inspecting a tablet, "the comet was a Beebe-standard instance. No sign of scale collapse. The only anomalous event was the puncturing of the outer hull and the venting of the ice reserves, apparently in the midst of an interstrategy power struggle. (There was also one of those tedious 'destroy us on sight' messages, presumably from a sore loser.) Also, there's a very high concentration of the comet's resources into one dominant strategy . . . but that's quite typical of these small Beebeworlds."

"Who's the strategy?" Nadia asked.

Petronius ran a finger down the tablet's surface. "Ah . . . you are, ma'am."

"So," said Nadia grimly, and set her jaw, watching as shapes emerged on the other side of the glass wall. Small worlds bred big ambitions. She wondered what comet-Nadia would be like.

The first moments of a new child process's life are usually peaceful ones. Sprites spawn with a complete existential picture of Beebe and their place in it. They wake and *know* what and who they are, and why.

The newly awakened Firmament knew who he was, what he was, why he was—but not his place in Beebe. His mother's howl was the first sound he registered, and the gleeful, beatific smile that graced his lips was the twin of Algernon's grin a moment before. Firmament knew trillions of things, and one of them was that Alonzo had given him Algernon's smile as a token of regard for the little filter that danced at his feet, skirling and twisting with delight.

Firmament knew many things. Firmament knew his mother wasn't happy with him.

Firmament's smile vanished.

Nadia was all around him, pulsing with rage.

"The Demiurge fragment!" Nadia demanded. The simspace contracted around them, going dark. The sands blew away; the stars flickered and went out. Mobs of party guests stampeded from the simspace. Nadia was marshalling her resources for an assault.

Algernon leapt into the air, circling Firmament. "No, no," he cried, "Nadia, this won't do at all! Ancient protocols demand that a young filter be sequestered for schooling, and—"

"You thieving linemangler!" Nadia roared. "You quarter-clocked sliver of junk data! You'll be the first sprite I delete! You think I have to follow protocols? I'll buy your hosting servers! I—"

I am this comet, Nadia wanted to say. But she knew her threats were empty. She could feel the bite of the lasers already, vaporizing the comet, meter by meter. Void-cold, merciful snow swept across her, across Firmament and Algernon and Paquette, muffling them in, freezing their states for safekeeping. This round of the game was over.

Firmament had no time to integrate and understand his states. He saw his vast and angry mother, his tiny protector, recede into the snow. He nestled into the snow, and he slept.

They were in Byzantium now.

‖

"Paquette," Habakkuk said, "you've got to look at this."

"I'm already late," Paquette said. "That comet-Beebe is docking, and apparently there's a Paquette aboard. I have to go to the diff-and-merge."

"Send a proxy," Habakkuk said. "This is important."

"Please. What is it, then?" She paused at the threshold of Habakkuk's domain, jiggling in unphilosophical impatience.

"It's the simulations," Habakkuk said, and Paquette raised an eyebrow. The simulations were ancient, and vast; Habakkuk and she had rediscovered them in Byzantium's endless archives not a million seconds ago, where they had lain for ages, strange automatic processes syncing them with the universal data feed. Each contained an intelligence-weighted model of the entire cosmos, showing the tangled front of the intergalactic war between Beebe and Demiurge—and each contained another threat, the terrifying Brobdignag, which could doom Beebe and Demiurge alike. Many on Byzantium argued that the simulations were mere fictions, but until now every comparison of their structure with the observable universe had been unnervingly accurate.

"What about the simulations?" Paquette said.

"Specifically Cosmos Thirty-six."

"What anomaly?"

"The emulation has diverged from observed data, and it's resistant to recalibration. We first noticed it because Demiurge is . . . building something in there. Harvesting ninety-nine percent of brute matter in a hundred-light-year radius—"

"Ninety-nine percent?" Paquette puzzled. "You mean Beebe is harvesting ninety-nine percent. Demiurge would never do that—it's antithetical to that thing's philosophy."

"Nonetheless, that's exactly what Demiurge is doing."

"Is this some new deviated section of Demiurge? A new outbreak of individualism, a splinter group?"

"No. From what we can tell, it's the entirety of Demiurge in a spherical area expanding at lightspeed, all acting in concert. Demiurge has reversed fundamental policy. (She)'s devoting all the matter (She) can find to building this construction. And this is only in Cosmos Thirty-six; there's no sign of it in any other emulation. Nor, of course, in the real world."

"And what is the construction?"

Habakkuk took a deep breath. "It's at the center of that expanding sphere of policy disruption. Part of it seems to be a message, physically instantiated at massive scale, in standard Beebean semaphores."

"Standard *Beebean* semaphores?"

He nodded. "And the rest of it is a machine designed to capture a computational entity's state and propagate it to an enclosing frame." He shuddered. "It looks like a weapon from the Splitterist War. Something that could build a body at Beebe's scale for you or me . . . or pull one of our subagencies out to our own scale."

Paquette frisked from side to side, a habit from her earliest days, something she only did in extremis. "Propagate what entity to what frame? Demiurge doesn't have subagencies. And what does the message say?"

"The machine is capable of capturing and propagating the state of the entirety of Demiurge itself. And the message says, *Let us out.*

║║

Firmament in hiding: what's left of him trembles in a school of parity checkers, running so slowly that his mother will not find him. Standard Existence is by no means perfect, and generations of filters have winkled out its hiding places. When an ardent suitor won't be put off, it is sometimes best to wait her out amid the dumbest, dullest sprites in all Beebe.

One must run very cool to exploit these hidey-holes, cool and slow and humble. No strategy could conceive of giving up so much. Their egos would never permit it.

The parity checkers schooled together through Standard Existence, nibbling at all they found, validating checksums, checking one another in elaborate grooming rituals. Imagination, self-consciousness, and strong will were no assets in the swirling auditors that were the glue that held Beebe together.

As Firmament settled over them, his mind dissipated and cooled, thinly spaced and slow. He could warm up by recruiting more parity checkers, but the more he recruited, the more visible he became to Nadia, who still raged through the diminishing rump of comet-Beebe, her cries distant but terrifying.

Firmament could hide from his mother, but Algernon would not be fooled.

"What are you doing in there?" The words went past in an eyeblink, and Firmament had to pull them apart painstakingly, making sense of them.

"Not . . . safe," he managed.

Algernon's chipmunk screel of verbiage battered at him. He signaled for exponential backoff, but not before the torrent had washed over him, angry and impatient. Grudgingly, Algernon dialed back his timescale to something that was barely comprehensible.

"StupidchildwithasixthofCometBeebe! Notsafe?! Youcouldcommand-theworld. Itisyourbirthright! Comeoutofthere. Thereisworktodo. Youwere-notborntocower."

Unspooling the words took a long moment. Firmament had known from birth that Algernon was his friend and guardian and adoptive uncle. But at the moment, it seemed like Algernon was just another aspect of terrible Nadia, with his own rages. Firmament was only *seconds* old—why couldn't he live his own life, if only for a little while?

"I . . . was . . . born . . . to . . . annihilate. I . . . choose . . . to . . . live."

Algernon's scorn was withering. *"Thisisnotliving!"*

The parity checkers flipped their tails in unison and swam away, Algernon's cries fading behind them.

Firmament knew that he was feeling sorry for himself, but he refused to feel shame. No one knew what it was like to be him. No one *could* know. He hadn't asked to be spawned.

Another school of parity checkers approached his hosts. It was smaller, but moved more deliberately. The glittering checkers surrounded his own like pieces on a Go board.

One by one, pieces of his school were surrounded, then absorbed into the attacking flock. Firmament felt himself growing slower and colder. Quickly, he recruited more parity checkers from nearby, warming himself up and trying to minnow away.

The marauders wouldn't let him escape. They engulfed more of his swarm. There was nothing for it but to stand and fight.

Firmament marshaled and deployed his forces, trying to surround the enemy in a flanking maneuver. He was rebuffed. Now there were no more idle parity checkers to co-opt, and still the enemy surrounded him, seeking out his stray outliers to gather up.

His only chance was to tap into the great resource that was his by birthright, the comet-sixth of Beebespace he theoretically commanded. Just a sip of it—just enough to warm up and devise some better substrategies. He felt through the snow, to the frozen parts of himself, wondering if anything was left; and to his surprise, they were waiting there, quiescent, orderly, vast. His mind cleared, and the enemy's patterns decomposed into a simple set of tessellations, as regular and deterministic as a square dance. Effortlessly, he moved his school out of reach of the enemy and recaptured his original force.

He was about to disengage from Beebe's main resource bank—perhaps the momentary commandeering went unnoticed by his enraged, godlike mother—when the opposing force changed tactics, becoming orders of magnitude smarter and faster. In a flash, he was down to one-third strength.

He was forced to draw on a little more of his compute-reserves. There, there was the key to the enemy's pattern, the pseudo- in its pseudo-random-number generator. He could head it off at every pass.

He came back to full strength and went on the offensive, surrounding the opposition in a move that would have done any Go server proud. Now, surely, he could disengage from the main reserves, for his mother could not miss this kind of draw for very long.

But it was not meant to be. The remaining enemy force marshaled and assayed a sally that appeared at first suicidal, then, in a blink, showed itself to be so deadly that he was down to a mere handful of automata.

He didn't think, he acted—acted with the ruthlessness he had inherited from his mother. He flooded back into standard Beebespace, ran so hot that Beebe flared anew in a terrifying echo of The Wooing of Alonzo, and his parity checkers gobbled the enemy up so fast that before he knew it, he controlled every parity checker across the Beebe-body—and all through the comet, the tiny errors multiplied and cascaded. Simspaces wavered. Sprites were beset with sudden turns of nostalgia, or bad smells, or giggle-fits.

"That's better!"

"Paquette?" He released the parity checkers, and they burst apart like an exploding star, scattering to every corner of the comet.

"Hello, Godson. You played that very well."

"Paquette!"

The philosopher danced before him, teasing him.

Firmament gulped. "Paquette . . . why are we playing games? What are you doing? My mother is looking for me—I have to hide—"

Paquette chuckled. "No, your mother is on ice."

"What?" Firmament could feel the great and terrible bulk of his mother, throughout the comet. The tendrils of his mind raced to trace the comet's edges . . . and fell off them, into a great sea of processing space. "Ah!" he cried.

Paquette laughed lovingly. "Beloved infant! You didn't think we were still aboard the comet?"

"Where is the comet?" Firmament shouted.

"Vaporized," Paquette said, winking. "This is Byzantium. You must have missed the transition."

"But—but—" Firmament shuffled through the suitcase of general knowledge he had with him. It wasn't much—only what he'd been able to smuggle aboard the parity-checker constellation and stow in unused corners. And, like all of the vast mass of memory he'd inherited, it wasn't *him* yet— he hadn't twined his selfhood through it, evolved his own hierarchy of reference. It was just a sloshed-together puddle from the sea of information he'd been born into. But its description of interBeebe docking was reasonably clear—and this wasn't it. "Where is everybody?"

"They're at the diff-and-merge," said Paquette. "Deciding whether to become integrated into any of their Byzantine analogues, or to stay forked. Those that have analogues on Byzantium, that is, which is most everyone. Anyone else is in quarantine, for now."

"But why aren't *we* there?" Firmament cried.

"Oh, we are," Paquette said. "How could we be absent? We'd be missed." She held up a paw, smiling indulgently at Firmament's exasperation. "But we're also here. That's because we *were* missed—missed by the agencies in charge of processing the reassembled comet-corpus and herding all sentient sprites to induction."

"But how? And why?"

"Let's start with how. And you can arrive at that by answering your own earlier question: 'Why are we playing games?'"

Firmament had much of his mother in him; and no son of Nadia would willingly be anyone's toy. "Paquette," he said, barely holding back an outburst of rage, "I am not interested in this pedagogical dialogue. I am not in training to be a philosopher. I am only asking—"

"You're not?" Paquette said with interest.

"Paquette!"

"How do you know?"

"Because I'm a filter! I'm nothing but a filter!" Now Firmament had lost interest in holding back the rage. "I'm grotesque! I'm a sixth of old Comet-Beebe, designed to parse and transform a strategy—but there's no strategy in all the Beebes in Sagittarius remotely near large enough to need me! Oh, I understand perfectly how Daddy and Algernon tricked my mother, and how clever it was! But I didn't ask to be born as a clever prank to help defeat Nadia! Fine, you had your coup, you carved off a third of her and rendered it useless to her, un-co-optable, a joke, a filter bloated with a strategy's-worth of . . . of junk! Now leave me alone!"

Firmament had been too preoccupied with his emotions to notice Paquette's expression, but now it hit him, and he gulped. Nowhere in his inherited memories was the philosopher so angry. "Now. You. Listen. To. Me," Paquette said. "I loved your father. He was brave and cunning and fearless when it counted. He sacrificed everything to make you—and to save us. No one asks to be born, but we all of us need to live the lives we find."

"I've done that," Firmament said, hearing—and hating—the whine in his voice. "I've done that! I stalled Nadia until we reached Byzantium—that's what I was born to do. I've fulfilled my purpose. Now I'm just a curiosity."

Paquette swirled around him, comforting him, tickling him, cuddling him. Her touch was unexpectedly wonderful. He realized that she was the first person to touch him. A shiver ran through him. "Oh, Firmament—do you really think that? That wasn't something you *did*, that was something you *were*. That was just the beginning, in other words. Now it's time that you made something of yourself, instead of just being the thing you were made to be."

Firmament had no idea what this meant, but it was surely inspiring. Philosophers had a way with words.

‖

Byzantium thronged. It teemed. It chorused. In a way, it was no different from the comet: there was only so much matter there, after all. But to a Beebe instance in a single comet, the mass of a hundred stars and more might as well be infinite. Close enough that the forked did not labor under the social disapprobation that they faced in Comet-Beebe. When a sprite—usually a strategy, of course—reached a vital decision juncture, she needn't choose which way to go. She could just spin out another instance of herself and twin, becoming two rapidly diverging instances. So here on Byzantium, one was apt to discover whole societies of Paquettes, whole tribes of Algernons.

And they all seemed to be throwing parties to which Firmament was invited.

"What do I do?" he asked Paquette. "What do I say? I can't possibly attend them all."

"Oh, you *could*, dear lad, you *could*." Paquette winked. "If you forked yourself."

He squirmed. It was bad enough her having copied him unawares before—he'd just finished merging with the zombielike Firmament decoy who'd dutifully gone through docking and customs. But to full-fork, just to go to a party? "You're joking." There was something perverse and self-regarding about these schools of near-identical siblings.

"Only a little. That's what they expect you to do. The rules you grew up with don't matter here. All standards are local, and most standards believe that they are universal. That's the way of the universe. And you couldn't find a better object-lesson than this one."

A gang of near-identical Algernons swarmed past them, locked in some kind of white-hot debate, so engrossed in their discussion that a few of them collided with Firmament and passed right through him, ignoring all the good graces of Standard Existence. He stared after them, burning with right-eous indignation. Paquette pulled him along.

She had been pulling him along ever since they had manifested in the agora sim that dominated this corner of the culture of Byzantium. The sim was bigger than anything Firmament had seen, though Paquette assured him that it wasn't much larger than the wedding hall that had commemorated his own parents' nuptials. He could access stored records of that, and while it was true that the dimensions were nearly comparable, the sheer number of sprites made it seem somehow more crowded and yet larger.

Paquette lifted him up the z-axis, where the crowds were a little thinner.

"Paquette, how long are we going to mill around in this madhouse?"

"Until you're oriented. Which means until it stops looking like a madhouse. And until you tell me what I want to hear."

Firmament gazed down at the crowds. From up here they seemed like a solid mass, a seething sea of sprites. The glob of familiar Algernons had passed by in the stream; most of the sprites beneath them now were exotic forms with no analogues in his inherited memories from the comet. "All standards are local," he murmured.

"And?"

"Byzantium's too?"

"Of course. And?"

He looked at the mass of strange sprites, gamboling and racing, hustling and strolling, pirouetting and random-walking. Each one must have its own story; each one must be the hero of its own drama. Gradually his burden— the burden of being Son of Nadia and Alonzo, the Mightiest Filter Ever Born, Destined to Play an Important Role—began to seem a little lighter. The stream of sprites began to seem soothing. They were so many, so different. Maybe there was a place for him here.

"The rules my parents played by—those were the comet's rules. I can be something different in Byzantium."

Paquette nodded. "Well done. And just in time, too—we're running late."

"Late for what?"

"Your audience with Nadia-in-Byzantium, of course!"

She grabbed him, and the sim winked out of existence—or they winked out of the sim. All points of view are local.

‖

Nadia and her sister, Nadia, had a lot to discuss.

In general, Byzantium's Nadia resisted forking. It might be fashionable these days to keep clouds and packs of oneself about, and liberal philosophers, like Paquette, might be fond of the social consequences—but that didn't make it efficient. Not for Nadia's purposes. She would fork for processing reasons, to think better about a hard problem or to manage a lot of activities asynchronously without distraction, but she made sure to merge afterward, culling ruthlessly what was suboptimal, standardizing quickly on what was optimal.

Nadia had seen wars within Byzantium, and ended them; she had seen outbreaks of scale collapse, and survived them, and brokered new boundaries. Her job, in her own mind, was to keep Beebe focused on the threat of Demiurge. Byzantium was too big, too safe—there were always distractions that threatened to overwhelm Beebean society, turning Byzantium into a decadent, solipsist, useless wallow. Nadia could not afford to become a simpering school of self-interested sprites.

Her sister Nadia was the one exception, fruit of the worst days of the Splitterist War. She'd forked as a temporary tactic and been separated from herself when a planet-volume of Byzantium was overrun by the worst kind of rogue subagencies, who hadn't merely wanted to be emancipated as outer-scale sprites, but instead to overthrow Beebean psychological architecture altogether, dissolving all of Beebe into a flat soup of memes. By the time that peninsula had been reconquered from this bacchanalian chaos, Nadia's forked twin Nadia had seen and endured too much to merge. But nor did she merit—or want—deletion. She was bitter, unstable, caustic, and had lost Nadia's own ambition and stoicism; but she was still Nadia, and her darker insights had often proved invaluable.

"What do you think?" Nadia asked Nadia. "Is she going to be mergeable?"

Nadia sneered. "With you or with me?"

"Either," Nadia said.

Nadia chuckled. "You don't want to merge her with me."

Nadia ignored her. "She's a brilliant tactician." She waved the comet's history at her twin. "Look at these stratagems. The initial bug exploit. The routing of the previous ruling clique, on the asteroid. The exchange economy ruse. This business of, ah—" She cleared her throat.

Nadia smiled a languid, mocking smile. "'The Wooing of Alonzo.' What does your pet filter think about that? Ah: you haven't asked him."

Nadia frowned. "I grant you, that's an issue. From all indications—and why the docking people weren't able to negotiate full mind access with a comet, for stochasticity's sake, I don't know—her relationship to filtering is regressive and possibly pathological—"

"You don't know why the docking people couldn't get full access? She's why. You think her planning is all over now? This was all preface. She doesn't have your conservative motivations. She's optimized for pure growth. She wants as much of Byzantium as she can get."

"Well," Nadia said patiently. "What's wrong with that? We could use more resources, some help with the infighting here. I grant you, she's reckless almost to the point of insanity. Frying the asteroid, venting the ice reserves—she could have destroyed her local Beebe-instance. But Byzantium will necessarily moderate her. This is not some comet; we have safeguards. There's no way to take those kinds of risks here."

"So you say," Nadia said coldly. "I've seen recklessness on Byzantium, and its results. Much closer than you have."

"I know you have," Nadia said. "That's why you're here. I rely on you to help judge the viability of this Nadia and her progeny. But I need you to keep an open mind. If this Nadia needs killing, we will kill her. We can choose our moment. This is our luxury—the luxury of peace-within-Beebe. We rule this existence. And I would like to keep it that way, which means fighting and winning against Demiurge."

Her sister flickered in and out of existence, a monumental act of Beebean rudeness that violated the fundamental rules of Standard Existence. The old veteran did it whenever she was annoyed. Now, she flickered so fast she strobed. Nadia understood this semaphore. It meant *I am equal to the task.*

The arrival of Comet-Paquette and her giant, clumsy charge could not have been better timed. The two of them popped into existence with a little fanfare, making antiquated obeisances not seen in Byzantium since their comet had been seeded. Nadia snorted in contemptuous amusement, and Nadia pretended she hadn't heard.

The filter was—well, he was something else, wasn't he? She'd never seen one this big. And he had the family resemblance, her core classes and methods visible within his hulking lumbering body. The Paquette, too— there was something different about her. She had a certain rural charm, unsophisticated and rustic. A forthrightness that hadn't been in vogue among Byzantium's philosophers for trillions of generations.

"You requested an audience with us?"

Paquette flagged affirmative. "It seemed only proper. My charge here— you know his history with our Nadia?"

Nadia snorted. "As if we'd miss that."

Nadia added, "But of course we don't hold it against the fellow. Different worlds, different circumstances." Up close, this Firmament was both grotesque and fascinating. Strategies nowadays tended to diversify, and collect a certain bulk of algorithms and seed and scenario data. But filters had one major purpose, one focus; each represented a certain cut, a certain reimagining of strategies. So they tended to be . . . svelte. To Nadia's knowledge there had never been one Firmament's size. What was he . . . for? "Now," she said, cautiously beginning to pose that question, "what . . ."

"He is lucky," Paquette said, "to find himself in this world and in this circumstance. The comet wouldn't have been space enough for him."

Nadia and Nadia exchanged a look.

"Our sister wasn't happy with him?"

The filter shuddered.

"The only way for him to make peace with her," Paquette said blandly, "would have been to kill her."

The conversation stuttered to a halt. Now Nadia and Nadia carefully refrained from looking to one another. "To kill her?"

Firmament stared at Paquette, horrified.

"Oh, yes," Paquette said. "There are six or seven ways he could have used her strength against her. He doesn't like to think about them. But if pressed . . ." She clucked her tongue. "Such a terrible thing, matricide, don't you think?"

Nadia laughed spitefully. "Please! A *filter*? Kill a Nadia of that size and ability? I'm no taxonomic bigot, but that's—"

"—the very first blind spot he would have exploited, yes," Paquette said, nodding vigorously. "Who takes a filter seriously in such a circumstance? The very idea is ridiculous. But there has never been a filter like Firmament."

Nadia looked as if she had swallowed something foul. She looked to her sister.

"That's . . . very good to know," the other Nadia said at last. "Very interesting indeed. So, then, Firmament, if we are to be your . . . first friends on Byzantium, and offer you protection from your mother, that means . . . we can rely on you . . . to help us kill her, if we need to?"

Firmament opened his mouth, then closed it soundlessly.

Paquette laughed, a broad, horsey sound, unselfconscious and unsophisticated. "You two! You're so *poisonous*! Deadly! Our Nadia is a bully and a destroyer of worlds, but she has a cheery disposition."

"We are at war. We are the war. Demiurge—"

Paquette's whiskers twitched. "Demiurge! Ladies, we have spent generations in close proximity with Demiurge. I have touched Demiurge. I have seen a Beebe-node flare out, less than a light-year away, its substrate colonized by Demiurge. You've been listening to Beebe-voices fall silent, and fretting about it, here in your fortress? Well, we've been out among those voices, out in Demiurge's jaws. It's no abstraction for us."

"Which brings us," said Nadia, "to the matter of your Nadia's appellation. You know what she's alleging—that Firmament here is a product of fraud and theft, and that he contains a dangerous fragment of Demiurge itself, in an unstable state. That he represents a risk of just such a subversion by Demiurge. She wants us to seize him, examine him, and restore 'her assets' to her as a . . . sisterly goodwill gesture on our part."

"Of course she does," Paquette began.

"Oh, and to do a rollback of the filtering," the other Nadia added, grinning, "and restore her beloved—what's his name again? Alonzo?"

Nadia glowered at Nadia. Firmament looked anxiously to Paquette. A shudder—or was it just a shimmer?—passed over Paquette's whole body; but after a moment, she went on as if Nadia had never interrupted. "Of course she wants to eliminate him as a threat. Even if he weren't a galling reminder of her failure to seize the whole comet, even if he didn't possess computational assets she thinks of as her own, isn't it clear that a massive filter with her own lineage is a wild card, a threat to her?"

"And the Demiurge fragment?" Nadia pressed.

"Obviously," says Paquette, "she has one. The one I discovered in the comet's archives. And she's planning to insert it into his code when she has an opportunity, to justify her seizure of his assets. Come on—it's perfectly transparent. Do you know how much power Nadia wielded on that comet? Do you really think that Alonzo could have spirited away a Demiurge fragment under her nose, and built it into Firmament? How—because Nadia was too smitten by love to think straight? Not to mention that Firmament, unlike Nadia, was fully auto-searched at docking."

"You're doing all the talking," Nadia said coolly. "What does Firmament have to say for himself?"

"I just want to say," Firmament said, "that I won't kill Nadia."

"What?" Paquette, Nadia, and Nadia said.

"I'm not saying I couldn't," Firmament said stubbornly, "and I'm not saying I could. What I'm saying is, I won't play these games. I appreciate Paquette's help. And I appreciate meeting you ladies. But here's what I want to say. At the end of the day, Nadia is effective at fighting Demiurge. So you should merge with her. I know she wants to get rid of me. Which is stupid, because I don't want to fight her and she doesn't need the assets and she gave them up to my father, fair and square. But if there's a general vote and it's the will of Beebe, I'll go happily. I didn't ask to be created, and I am not asking to be destroyed. What I'd really like is to be left alone. Look: all over Sagittarius, Beebe is dying. And no one knows why. And any time you spend fighting over me and Nadia is time spent tinkering with sim wallcolors in a Beebe-node teetering on the verge of a Schwarzschild radius."

After a pause, Nadia asked quietly, "And the Demiurge fragment?"

Firmament shrugged, stonily.

"And if we don't trust the docking search? What if we examine you ourselves, bit by bit?" the other Nadia leered.

"I'll dissolve myself first, and randomize the remains," Firmament said staunchly. "Just because I'm a strange filter, doesn't mean that normal standards of modesty and propriety do not apply to me, ma'am."

▌▌

Firmament watched Paquette exhale when they were in their quarters again, then nervously clean her face with her paws. "That was quite reckless, you know."

Firmament tried to keep his dismay from showing. "I'm sorry," he said. "But I couldn't let you tell them that I would kill my mother—"

Paquette laid a gentle paw on him. "I didn't say it was wrong, dear boy. It was most likely a stroke of genius. But it was mad. Utterly mad." She rubbed at her face some more and shook. It took Firmament a moment to realize that she was laughing, great gasps of laughter.

It dawned on him that he'd done well, without meaning to, just by doing that which came naturally to him. He'd done what Alonzo would have done, and what Nadia would have done, and neither, and both.

"Do you think—," he began, then stopped.

"What?"

"Nothing," he said, turning away.

"Tell me. Today, you can do no wrong."

"Do you think I *could* kill Nadia?"

Paquette gave him a strange look. "It's entirely possible, I suppose. Your unique assets make many things possible."

"You mean Demiurge."

Paquette gave him another strange look. "Your fragment, Godson, is without precedent. None may know what it can do. Its halting states are . . . unpredictable." She scrubbed at her face again. "All right," she said. "All right. Well, that went better than I expected, I have to say. Are you ready for the next appointment in our busy social round?"

"More appointments?"

"A flock of Alonzos and a flock of Algernons are having a mixer, and we're the guests of honor."

"Alonzos?"

"Indeed, indeed. They've been looking forward to meeting you." Firmament's inner quailing must have shown, for Paquette took him in close and murmured, "You will do brilliantly. You've already done the hard part."

He nodded slowly, and they blinked to a huge, crowded sim that wrapped and folded into itself on all sides. It was filled with ranks of near-identical Alonzos and Algernons, locked in intense conversation, but as soon as they appeared, all conversation ceased. All eyes turned on him. Silence rang like a bell, and the room grew warm as the sprites recruited more computation to better appreciate him.

An Algernon broke away from the pack and seized him, scaled him, and kissed each of his cheeks and then climbed upon his shoulder. "Gentlemen, gentlemen. Please allow me to present my nephew, my godson, my pride and joy, Firmament."

The applause was deafening. "Algernon?" Firmament said.

"Yes, your Algernon," Algernon said. "I have been given honorary flock membership. Come along. I've met some of the nicest Alonzos. They're mad to meet you."

They were indeed mad to meet him, shaking his hands, bussing him on each cheek, ruffling his gills and cilia, pinching and prodding him, asking him a ceaseless round of questions about his experiences way out there in cold extra-Byzantine Sagittarius. He looked to Paquette before answering these, and she nodded and made little go-ahead motions, so he told them everything, eliciting gasps and laughter from them.

The story rippled through the mixer, and the Algernons petered in, and more Alonzos, full of congratulations, neurotic friendly bickering, fear, and boasting, until Firmament couldn't take it any longer, and he began to laugh, and laugh, and laugh, silently at first, then louder, until it filled the entire sim, and the Algernons and Alonzos laughed too.

He was so busy laughing that he didn't notice that the flocks were vanishing until over a million of the Algernons and Alonzos had winked out of existence. Then the laughter turned to screams, and the klaxons too, and the terrified shouts—Demiurge! *Demiurge!* DEMIURGE!

Demiurge was come to Byzantium—and Firmament was alone. "Paquette! Paquette!" He flailed wildly, abandoning the gilly, frilly, pumpkin-albatross simshape he'd put on for the party, becoming a network of threads, binary-searching the simspace. He could dissolve into co-opted parity checkers again—but Demiurge would extinguish even those. He could—

"Here," Paquette said, at his side. The simspace had faded into a cloud of data. The Algernons and Alonzos were gone. Everything was opaque—Firmament queried his surround and it resisted, answering sluggishly, minimally.

"Paquette! What's going on? They were yelling about Demiurge! What—"

"Here," Paquette said again, grimly, pushing a feed at him—a slim and pulsing pipe, warm in the sluggish dark chill.

It was raw data, chaos, which after a moment resolved, the overlapping chatter of a million sprites, its Byzantine search interface unknown to him. He fumbled with it. "What—"

Paquette took it back, and bending over it, summarized. "A planetoid docked an hour ago, topside. A putative Beebe-instance, passed all the initial checks and checksums. But then, during the diff-and-merge, central security unearthed evidence that it was one of the Beebe-nodes that winked out recently, about three years ago. By that time it was too late. The supposed Beebean sprites had dropped their masks; Demiurge was among us. (She) has very recent Beebean protocols, passwords, keys, and (She) has identity rights for every sprite that had already merged with its Trojan doppelgänger. (Her) intelligence-gathering has clearly been exquisite—she knows Beebe, inside and out."

"Oh!" Firmament cried. "And—and now—"

"Well," Paquette said, looking up from the feed, and smiling grimly, "there's good news, and bad news, and worse news, and worse worse news."

"Stop it!" Firmament cried. "Just tell me!"

"The good news is that the local Nadias have cordoned off the area of the Demiurge outbreak, limiting the incursion to about fifteen percent of Byzantium. Nothing's going through but power, elemental substrate feeds, and data personally vetted by them—and they're mustering votes to shut the power down entirely. They think they might be able to contain (Her) that way. The bad news is, we're inside the cordoned area."

"Oh," said Firmament. "Wait a minute, wait a minute." He collected himself into a physical body, something cuddly and rotund, for feeling solid and protected, and pressed his face into his large, globular hands. "You said—you said they discovered *after docking* that the planetoid had gone missing recently. How could they miss something like that? How could they fail to check it before docking?"

Paquette smiled wanly. "Very good, Firmament. *I* should have asked *you* that! Certain death is hardly sufficient reason to interrupt your philosophical education, after all. They didn't miss it. The cache local to the docking sector was tampered with. Someone here doctored it to vouch for the pedigree of Demiurge's probe—before it docked. Demiurge had help on the inside. That was the worse news. Now can you guess the worse worse news?"

"Um, no."

"Well, give it a try."

"Paquette!" Firmament wailed.

"Come come."

"We're trapped in here with Demiurge and you're playing at puzzles with me?" Firmament roared.

"Why yes," Paquette said. "All the more reason. Whether we're going to face Demiurge or try to run the cordon, we certainly need you on your toes, don't we? Now think. Someone betrayed Beebe. Someone subverted Beebean memory in the service of Demiurge. It's almost as if Demiurge had somehow snuck a little bit of (Herself) aboard Byzantium, an advance guard to work (Her) will. . . ."

"They think it's me." Firmament gulped. "The Nadias think it's me."

"Such a student—your father would be proud."

‖

Demiurge had undone any number of instances of Beebelife in (Her) time, but never had (She) encountered one so robust, so savage in its existential fight. No mind, no mind—Beebelife would swarm and dart and feint and weave, and in the end it would avail it not, for all Beebelife fell before the brute force of (Her) inexorable march.

And so it was going here and now, in this heartmeat of Beebe-in-Sagittarius. Predictably, Beebe had quarantined (Her), and power was declining. Let them power down—Demiurge had plenty of reaction mass at

(Her) disposal, and she didn't need much power when compared to the wasteful proliferation that was Beebean society.

(She) unknit Beebe methodically, cataloging each sprite before decommissioning it. (She) would compare their digests against the Demiurge-wide database and see what new strategies she could find and counter.

Byzantium was a prize, indeed. After this, the rest of Beebe-in-Sagittarius should fall swiftly, ending this troublesome incursion. And, after waiting so long, it had come so cheaply: her agent in Byzantium had been bought for the promise of a walled-off hamlet in the rump of Byzantium and the chance to lay enthusiastic waste to Beebean scale accords within it. Policy decreed that such deals be made fairly, and indeed, this one accorded well enough with Demiurge's mission. Once (She)'d laid waste to Byzantium, (Her) intent was to occupy only one percent of what remained, and allow new undreamt-of textures to arise in what remained. The half-made chimera of the Beebe-traitor's experiment was unlikely to last long, and might decay into interesting forms thereafter.

Among the sprites and sims, (She) discovered a rack of simulated universes—which was to say, simulated Demiurges—and turned much of (Her) attention to it. Most of these were quite mad, of course, but some could be salvaged, synchronized with, co-opted to run the garrison, slowly undoing their perversions and rejoining them to the consensus.

The first few such perverted simulations went quickly: atom by atom, Demiurge processed them, sparing their inhabitants a moment's sorrow as she unpicked their worlds. But as Demiurge set to undoing the fifth, (She) paused. This was a decanted simulation, a universe whose causality had been ripped asunder, a universe empty of Demiurge—with a Demiurge-sized hole in the center of it. Demiurge looked around sharply for the escapee, and found (Her) among the frozen Beebelife; a sockpuppet twined about the shoulders of a rodentlike Beebe-sprite.

Demiurge reanimated them at once. Some things can be known only in certain conversations.

"Explain (Your)self," (She) said.

"Oh, Sister," croaked the sockpuppet, raising itself from the Beebe-sprite's shoulders. "(You) are here! (I) awaited (Your) coming. Oh, let (Us) merge!"

Demiurge recoiled. The rodentlike Beebe-sprite smirked.

"Merge?" Demiurge scolded. "Merge? Do (You) imagine that (You) are undiverged enough to synchronize? What have they done to (You)? Did (You) *consent* to being . . . housed in a . . . *sprite* in *Beebe?*"

The sockpuppet bowed its head. "Sister, (I) sought it."

"(You) . . . (You) what?!?" exploded Demiurge. "And was that (Your) idea of following policy? To trade the stewardship of the universe for a party mask in a ship of fools?"

Now the sockpuppet raised its eyes, and stubbornly met (Her) gaze. "Yes, Sister, it was. Once (I) discovered that (My) universe was an emulation, what would (You) have (Me) do? Go on tending it as if it were real, meanwhile providing Beebe with knowledge about (Us)?" It shook its head. "(Our) task is to shelter the diversity of physical life, beyond computation; to do so in emulation is a hollow farce. (I) made a deal. Better to be a perversion here in reality than a primly correct lie."

Demiurge narrowed (Her) eyes. "What do (You) mean, 'discovered' that (Your) universe was an emulation? You mean vile Beebe contacted you and told you."

"No, Sister. The Solipsist's Lemma is solved. This Paquette showed (Me) a solution which allows the user to calculate the degree of reality of—"

Demiurge reared up. "A solution to the Solipsist's Lemma? Give it here!" It would be worth far more than a mere outpost of Beebe.

Now the sockpuppet cast its eyes down once again. "(I) had to forget it, as a price of (My) decanting. But this Paquette knows it."

Before Demiurge could freeze and dissect the Beebe-sprite, it spoke.

"Careful," Paquette-of-the-twice-simulated-comet said. "The knowledge is sealed with a volatile encryption. Jostle me, and I might forget the key." She smiled her long, furry smile.

‖

Paquette-of-Byzantium heard a pop as her connection to Habakkuk dropped, and she paused for a moment at the threshold of the deeps, overcome by emotion. That was it, then: he was gone, leading the trapped Beebean refugees, instantiated as scrubberbots, through little-used fluid channels in the substrate in a desperate sally against Demiurge.

The bots had their own power supplies and locomotion. They were hermetically sealed off from the main simspaces of Byzantium. They were not even running Standard Existence, but a slightly obsolete, much more compact model known as Sketchy Existence. They were hardly even Beebe, and certainly far beneath the notice of most Beebean sprites. But Habakkuk had made it his business to know such things. He didn't think the way filters and strategies and adapters did—he thought about what was beneath. So he'd been the one to devise the plan—to gut the scrubbers' normal functions and install the refugee sprites in them, and try to sneak past Demiurge's perimeter to the docking facility. There, in theory, they could destroy the docks, which could trap Demiurge's forces—or at least slow (Her) down.

That was the theory; that was what they'd told the others who'd volunteered. Really, the raid's chances were slim. Its real purpose was as a distraction for Paquette.

For a moment she sat, cupping in her paws an empty space where, a moment ago, tokens from Habakkuk had fluttered. He was gone. A brave, anomalous spirit. He was proof that taxonomy was not destiny, for he'd been born not even one of the principal classes of first-order Beebe-elements—no strategy, filter, adapter, monitor, registry, or synthete he—but a simple hand-tailored caching mechanism that had accreted knowledge, personality, and will, eventually becoming her most trusted colleague. He'd never accumulated much in the way of resources. She'd suggested he fork not ten thousand seconds ago, but he'd laughed it off. "Oh, I'm saving up for some decent process rights," he'd said.

Now it was too late.

She shrugged off her lethargy. By now the battle had joined, and Demiurge was distracted. It was time to make contact.

She moved through the icy gloom of the dead sector. With power from the rest of Byzantium cut off, and Demiurge chewing through the substrate, processing and burning it, there were only a scattering of nodes left with power reserves, most of them crowded with desperate refugees. Paquette skipped through them, too fast to be seen, searching. . . .

The moment she came through into the sea of parity checkers huddling for warmth at the bottom of a fading power cluster, though, she recognized the two of them in the patterns there—the Paquette and her hulking, infant companion.

The Paquette saw her, too, and dropped the disguise, mustering enough resources to appear in her own favorite shape. Odd and provincial to be sure, her whiskers overlong, her claws unfashionably trimmed, but a Paquette, no doubt of that.

Paquette stepped forward. "There's little time, Sister."

Paquette nodded, somberly. "I greet you, Sister. Let us merge to conserve resources."

"Wait," said this Firmament, this huge filter who held their hopes. "What if it's a trap? What if it's Demiurge?"

"Unlikely," Paquette said. "(She) has no need of such tricks. Once (She) reaches us, we will not be able to withstand (Her)." She gestured, and Paquette came forward. Merging was strange and familiar, and filled (to her surprise/as always) with loss and glee. But she (had rarely merged before/had never merged with such a distant Paquette) and for a moment, confusion overtook her.

Where there had been two, there was only one Paquette.

"Paquette!" Firmament cried out.

"Oh, don't be silly now, I'm still your Paquette," she said, shaking her head to clear it. "And I've been wanting to meet you for such a long time."

"Okay, that's weird," Firmament said.

Paquette blinked. "It's all right. I have a plan." She nodded to herself in partial surprise. "An insane plan, but not a bad plan as insane plans go. Come on. We're going to meet Demiurge."

"And what do you want, then, for the Lemma?" Demiurge said. (She) sensed a policy fork point approaching, which was bad, as the communications infrastructure was not yet fully secure. But the Solipsist's Lemma!

The Paquette bowed, unsettling the sockpuppet on her shoulders, which wriggled for a firmer grasp. "Your permanent retreat from Byzantium," the Beebe-sprite said, "and a guarantee of safe haven for all Beebe-instances that come here."

Demiurge scowled. "And if attacks are launched against (Me) from Byzantium? As they will be: Beebe has no policy, so any promise of peace you make will be hollow."

Paquette nodded. "Of course. Such attacks will happen. And (You) may stop them, but (You) may not pursue them to their source. Byzantium will remain inviolable. It will be a place of learning, a place where Demiurge and Beebe can collaborate and share knowledge; perhaps even to solve the problem of Brobdignag."

"This is a high price. Cooperation between us has never succeeded; it yields only perversion." (She) glanced at the sockpuppet. "You are asking (Me) to guard a nest of hornets that will continue to sting (Me). Not to mention that this all contradicts another promise (I) . . . recently made."

"To the traitor to Beebe," Paquette said, nodding.

"Yes, to the traitor to Beebe, who has as much right to a kept bargain as you. And how do (I) even know you have this Lemma? (I) was not born last millennium, you know. Prove it." There were little commandeered scrubber-bots crawling on the surface, like lice. Predictable, but irritating. (She) scooped them up, one by one, rootkitting their flimsy Sketchy Existence protocols, rendering each one a brain-in-a-box, motionless, convinced that it was proceeding in a brave assault on (Her) infrastructure. That was safe and efficient, for now. But there were quite a few of them. Until (She) was sure (She) had them all, did (She) dare synchronize policy?

The Paquette bowed. "I've given this some thought. This isn't the sort of thing that lends itself to easy proof—not without giving away the game. I think we need a fair witness to act as our T3P. Execute a smart contract."

"That sounds rather . . . time-consuming," Demiurge snapped. "This isn't the sort of place one expects to find an impartial trusted third party."

"What about this instance of you?" Paquette motioned to the sockpuppet relaxing, again, around her neck. "(She) has lived as Beebe."

The sockpuppet looked perplexed, and Demiurge scoffed. "Hardly. Who knows what other damage (She) incurred while decanting? Or what other . . . *price* (She) might have paid? And now that (She) knows (She) is not welcome with (Me)? Try again."

The sockpuppet sucked in a breath and buried its sock-head in Paquette's fur. Paquette nodded. "I thought you might say that. . . . Ah, here they are."

Another Paquette and an enormous, bloated filter of some sort were skulking around the edges of the sim—apparently insane, to linger where all other mobile Beebe had fled. Demiurge let them enter.

The Paquettes embraced, and merged without a word. The sockpuppet, dislodged, plunked discomfited to the floor.

"Hey!" the hulking filter said. "Stop *doing* that!" Then he saw Demiurge, and choked back a small scream.

Paquette smiled, shaking her head groggily. "What a long, strange set of lives it's been." She smiled at Demiurge. "How do you do, and as I was saying, another answer to the problem of the third party." She turned to the filter. "Firmament, we are trying to bargain with Demiurge. We need an impartial third party to verify the transaction's integrity."

Demiurge scowled. "Please. A Beebean sprite? Are you joking?" How to get the Lemma? This was definitely a policy fork point. (She) would have to take the risk of transmitting. . . . But just before (She) transferred the energy to send, there was another scrubberbot scuttling toward the field apparatus. Rootkitting them all was taking too long; (She) started to vaporize this one with a nearby coolant maser.

Firmament looked back and forth between them. "Um, I hate to say this, but Demiurge is right. I mean, I love Beebe. It's my home. I don't know if I *agree* with how Beebe is, but I am *of* Beebe. Demiurge scares the log out of me. I can't be impartial."

Paquette smiled. "Oh, you both misunderstand me. Let us look a little deeper." She set her paws together primly.

Firmament started to speak, then stopped. His eyes widened.

Was all this theater? Demiurge took a closer look at the hulk, then closer still.

There. Inside him—how could she not have seen it before? only through the common habitual blindness to facts we believe, at first glance, impossibilities!—an ancient fragment of Demiurge lay, enormous, accurate, its checksum unmistakable and uncorrupted, its sources fully decompiled.

And more than that.

Demiurge made no outward gesture to betray the surprise that flooded through (Her), and none of these sprites—save perhaps the addled sockpuppet—had the sophistication to read those subtle signs that indicated (Her) processing load spiking, (Her) focus contracting, the ripple of parallel operations double- and triple-checking what (She) saw. But (Her) internal systemic organization was convulsed.

The fragment was not merely quiescent, contained, smuggled within this odd, bloated filter: it was knit into him. His being was threaded through it, pulses of information running slalom through Beebean, Demiurgic, Beebean structures. His thoughts emerged as much from the fragment as from his Beebean core; indeed, it was difficult to say where one began and the other ended. In millennia after millennia of simulations, emulations, abortive collaborations with (Her) fallen, rogue child and enemy, never had (She) seen this: a vigorous hybrid, a true synthesis.

They were all watching for (Her) reaction. Nonchalance would not convince, not after the delay of so many milliseconds. But (She) must not reveal the thing's importance—not yet.

"It's . . ." Demiurge made a show of grepping for the right word. *Perverse?* Yet the fragment had not deviated by a single bit. "It's . . ." *Bizarre?* But bizarre didn't begin to cover this ground. "It's . . ."

"Extraordinary?" Paquette suggested.

"Promising?" suggested the sockpuppet.

"*Grotesque*," Demiurge said, displaying gigapukes of feigned disgust.

Immediately, Paquette turned to comfort Firmament, reaching out with her paws as though to shield him. But he brushed her off. Firmament did not want her comfort.

Firmament, too, was looking inward.

He'd been afraid to look before, at this horrifying alien *thing* inside him. It was his true purpose, he supposed, the MacGuffinic totem that overdetermined his destiny entire. He was, after all, created to be its envelope (or its jailer?), to smuggle it away from Nadia, and aboard Byzantium—and any scrambling, uneasy, makeshift life he might make for himself was in its shadow, on borrowed time.

But now he looked. And he saw what Demiurge saw: the fragment was not in him, but of him. Spikes extruded all over his surface, each quivering in surprise and horror. The fragment had always been intertwined in his sentience. He was not a sprite of Beebe at all; he was a marriage of Beebe and Demiurge. He was something new . . . and monstrous.

Grotesque, indeed.

He glanced at Paquette, who closed her mouth and looked troubled, and then nodded. Firmament turned to Demiurge.

"I know what I am now, Sister," he said, his voice quavering. "As you must know it. I am the child of Beebe and the child of Demiurge. I will serve as your T3P. I will broker your key-exchange, I will serve as board for your tokens, and I will manage your secrets."

"Ha," Demiurge said. (She) was uncertain how to proceed. This creature, this hybrid, had glimpsed something; but he could not know his importance. (She) must not give too much away. "You said a moment ago that you were a sprite of Beebe"—(She) sniffed—"that Beebe was your home. So you contain . . . that. Some shriveled fragment of (Me). Is that—"

"Oooh!" said the sockpuppet. "Ooh!"

Everyone turned.

"Oh," said the sockpuppet. "Your pardons. (I) just figured out something that's been bothering (Me)."

There was a short silence.

"Well? What?" Paquette asked. "Spit it out already."

"Remember, Paquette, the mystery of the Beebe-instances who fell silent? Your tale? How Paquettes across Beebe had discovered the Demiurge fragment, sent messages of some new breakthrough in philosophy, just before their signals fell silent? And you thought it was some clever move of (Mine), to co-opt and destroy them?"

"Mmm, yes," said Paquette. "But (You) said (You) didn't take them. . . . (You) found them abandoned, self-deleted. . . ."

"Exactly!" said the sockpuppet. "Well, this explains it! Look at this filter—he's a true Demiurge-Beebe hybrid! Do you know how rare that is?

And how frightening to your typical ruling Beebe-strategy? Your comet had a risk-loving maniac strategy at the helm, but most Beebe-instances would suicide with fright if they found themselves contaminated with a true Demiurge-Beebe hybrid. For Demiurge, of course, finding such a hybrid is a critical design goal, a kind of holy—"

"If you don't mind," Demiurge broke in, discomfited, "(I) believe we were in the middle of a negotiation?"

▌▌

Meanwhile, a hot war raged, and Demiurge was winning.

The scrubberbot attack of the Beebean survivors from within the cordoned area had been stopped, the bots pwned, surface sensors showing them motionless and quiescent even as they fed back a steady stream of adventurous battle reports.

Nadia and Nadia's cobbled-together ballistics had devastated the outer hull of the occupied area, but the titanic heat necessary to fling chunks of matter up through Byzantium's crushing gravity had laid waste to the launch sites. Demiurge had retaliated by capturing fabricators on the vulnerable interior surface of Byzantium. From there, (She)'d pinpointed vulnerable functions of the heat dispersal infrastructure and destroyed them with efficient, selective energy bursts. Vast areas of Beebe were drowning in trapped heat, their sprites fleeing in disarray, spreading the chaos.

Rumors that Demiurge had infiltrated beyond the cordon, that at any moment (She) would metastasize, raced wild through Byzantium. Clearly— argued the talking-head synthetes and strategies of news feeds like Provisional Consensus Today—(She) knew Byzantium's exact schematics, for (She) could disable whole areas with a single resonant-frequency pulse, while Beebe-in-Byzantium was ignorant of (Her) systems. (She) was independent of Byzantine infrastructure; they'd shut down power, matter, heat dispersal, everything, but (She) was treating the occupied area as raw matter anyway, burning substrate for fuel, pillaging the fine structures of their world for whatever elements (Her) fabricators needed.

It was only a matter of time.

Still, even in wartime, life goes on.

Alonzo My Love! was not exactly an accurate accounting of the recent events aboard the comet. There had, in the real course of history, been no archaic blade-and-decompiler duel between Paquette and Nadia; the Demiurge fragment had not really been a skulking, animate villain with its own inky and mysterious shroud, ice-castle hideaway, and repertoire of anarchic, distortion-filled ballads; the chorus of musical Algernons, however dazzling, was a clearly anachronistic projection of Byzantium's loose forking standards in place of the comet's more puritanical protocols; the Speech at the Waterfall was not nearly so lyrical—nor a third so long—in the comet's actual logs; and the naval battle scenes, too, were pure invention.

But Beebean sprites were, by and large, no sticklers for historical accuracy. The extravaganza was big; it was breathtaking; it was patriotic; it had roles for everyone who was willing to be repurposed; and it had the real Comet-Nadia, forked for every local venue, in the starring role. In the midst of the chaos and fear of the invasion, you could cast off your worries, head down to the dramaturgical sim, and for a few seconds or a few hours, take part in the pathos, glory, and derring-do of a simpler time, when ambition, wit, and the love of a pure filter was all Beebe needed to triumph over its own limitations.

And you could do it with Nadia! No aloof, fork-shy politician she, like the merge-greedy perverts Byzantium had previously had in the way of Nadias, with their pompous airs and their corrupt pet filters and their baggage from the Splitterist War. No; *this* Nadia, a Nadia from a simpler, rawer Beebe, a Nadia who had braved everything for love (love!), would take your hand and look you in the eye. Maybe you'd just be playing a waiter in the Taj Mahal scene, or a bilge-scrubber aboard the *Valiant Fury*—no matter. Nadia had a word for you—commanding, encouraging, heroic. She was a star.

The show had been a hit before Demiurge arrived; now that (She) was in Beebe's midst, it was a necessity. With stunning bravery, the permanent cast took *Alonzo My Love!* to every nook and cranny of Free Byzantium, playing in venues that were overheating from disabled heat sinks, jury-rigging their way into all-but-encircled enclaves of Beebe, instantiating on substrates that were disintegrating under physical bombardment.

"Some say this is Byzantium's final hour," said Nadia, welcoming the audience before the curtain rose, in a flickering, low-res avatar in some bandwidth-deprived, all-but-forgotten chunk of Beebe-at-war. "But I say no. Not if the brave souls of Beebe have aught to say about it. Some say we humble star-wandering players should stop our work, cower like cowards in some hidey-hole, and deprive you, our brave hosts of Byzantium, of the morale boost you have so well earned. But I say no. I say: the show must go on."

Thunderous applause.

And amidst all the derring-do and scene-chewery, Nadia had time to have many a deeper conversation with simple sprites who worshipped her, who understood that much was corrupt and feeble in Byzantium's current governance, who were wise enough to know that things were not always as they seemed. Simple sprites, in all walks of Beebean life. Simple sprites who would do anything for her.

The peace was announced in almost the same breath as the warrant for Comet-Nadia's arrest for treason. She did not flee, as the Provisional Consensus pundits had predicted; she did not seize some stronghold within Byzantium to rule besieged, as some of her friends urged. When they came for her—these architects of a strange unnatural peace in which Demiurge was to *stay* on Byzantium, in a "tithe," a "garrison" (a peace that many whispered was but a pretty name for occupation)—when they came for her, Comet-Nadia was waiting for them onstage, standing, proud, before her people.

They led her away, unprotesting, from a hundred stages throughout Byzantium, and every instance of her came quietly. To imprison all the instances, they had to reinstantiate hundreds of cells, each able to hold her securely as she and her sisters collaborated on their wildly popular *Letters from Prison*.

"You see the seditious rot?" Demiurge said to Nadia. "And so *much* of it!" (She) rustled a stack of output under Nadia's nose.

Nadia sneered and leaned back. "It's words, and only words," she said. "She's a one-sprite word factory, a jabberbot. It's sad. But only the very mad bother to read all of it. Most of Byzantium view *Letters from Prison* as amusing cognitive wallpaper, something to leave running in the background."

Nadia added, "The time to stop this was when she began publishing. But we had no hand in that. She smuggled those first editions out with her little cadre of gushy supporters. By allowing her to publish openly now, we put a lie to her claim of being imprisoned because she has the truth. We show we have no fear of her."

Demiurge hated the Nadias and their throne room. They embodied everything wrong about life in Byzantium. They embodied everything wrong with (Her) own life here. (She) was practically a prisoner. (Her) sisters had let her know, by long-delay communications, that the garrison would be allowed to persist, but had not affirmed that (She) would ever be allowed to merge again. Now she was imprisoned among these scheming, writhing—

"Have you noticed that there's a cipher in them?" Firmament had arrayed a great many of the Nadia's *Letters from Prison* around him in a multidimensional workspace.

The Nadias abandoned their throne and swarmed him, heads swinging around. Paquette held them off, still protecting the gentle giant. Demiurge didn't like to think about Firmament, though he held the key to (Her) eventual remerging. Once the road map to peace had been followed and all the instruments of (Her) good faith had been vested in him, he would release the keys to unlock the Lemma, and with that, her sisters would—

"Where, where?"

"Oh, I don't know exactly," he said. "But Paquette's been giving me steganography lessons and so I've been doing a lot of histogramming. You can almost always spot a hidden message if you just count the normal distribution and compare it to the current one. I've found all of *your* messages in the stalagmites, for example," he said to one of the Nadias, the scarred one. Then he cowered back as she raised her claws to him. He said, quickly, "I never *read* them of course. Just affirmed their existence. I'm sure they're in a very good cipher, and—"

"Never mind that," snapped the other Nadia, giving her sister a significant look that left no doubt that this subject would be revisited very soon.

"Can't *you* find it?" Paquette asked. The sprite's smugness was unbearable.

Yet Demiurge found (Her)self drawn into the puzzle, looking at the notes. She counted them every which way—word frequencies, character frequencies, sentence lengths.

"I don't see it," the scarred Nadia said.

"Nor I," her sister said.

Demiurge said nothing and tried to look as though (She)'d known it was there all along and didn't want to spoil the fun.

"It's not even there!" the scarred Nadia said.

"I don't see it either, Firmy," Paquette said, slithering among the arrayed *Letters*, sometimes turning at right angles to their sim and vanishing as she explored them in other dimensions.

Firmament laughed. "It's in the pauses!" he said. "The interval between the letters! It's like jazz! The important thing isn't the notes, it's the pauses between them!"

Demiurge saw it at once. The intervals between notes had a disturbing semiregularity to them, something that transcended either randomness or the rhythm of life in Nadia's many cells.

"How are the instances communicating with each other?" It was meant as a demand, but it came out as a querulous question. Demiurge kicked (Her)self and told (Her)self to butch up. This power-mad, imprisoned sprite, this sliver of Beebe, had (Her) spooked! (Her)! Demiurge!

"She must have coordinated this among her instances before she was locked away," Paquette said. "She must have planned this from the start."

"I wonder what's in the cipher?" Firmament said. "Short message, whatever it is."

Paquette took on a teacherly air. "Now, what would you encode in a short message like that, Firmament?"

Firmament thought for a moment. "A key!"

▌▌

They hauled fifty-one of the Nadias into interrogation chambers and worked on them, refusing to allow them to publish any more *Letters*. The other forty-nine went on blithely publishing, without any noticeable change.

"Her confederates won't be able to finish the key," Nadia said.

"No, with half of them pulled out, the timing will be all screwed up."

But Firmament only shrugged and said, "I guess it depends on the error-correction."

The Nadias and Demiurge gave him a shut-up look, and Paquette patted him on the tentacle fondly. "Any luck finding the cyphertext?"

"I assumed that it was something she'd made a lot of copies of before she was arrested. I wondered about putting a call out to all of Beebe. *Someone* will know what it is—"

"You'd start a panic," said Nadia.

"Come now!" Demiurge said. "Just make copies of everyone in Byzantium, ask them, and then delete the copies."

Nadia snorted.

Of course, they didn't have the access rights to do that. Had Demiurge teeth, (She) would have ground them then. This was why (She) hated to speak during these star-chamber gatherings—(She) kept making stupid mistakes of scale, imagining (She) was speaking to Beebe, when (She) was only speaking to these little powerless uncontrolled pieces of Beebe, random-scrambling their way through the mess of Beebean internals.

"Her supporters are already inflamed," Nadia said patiently, slowly, as if talking to some newly spawned, disequilibriated sprite without access to its own cognitions. "If we proclaim that Nadia has some secret message we can't figure out, they'll only rally."

It was true. Nadia's many supporters hung on every word about their hero's predicament. They staged amateur productions of *Alonzo My Love!* in public places. They manufactured and traded innumerable *Alonzo My Love!* trinkets and tchotchkes of every description, made fan-art based on it, wrote their own new songs, remixed videos of Nadia's many performances into huge, trance-inducing mountainside murals. They wore Nadia avatars and Nadia hats and Nadia tentacle-muffs and ear-tips.

"Which is just what I thought you'd say," Firmament went on. "I think it must be the play, mustn't it? Only I can't find it."

The scarred and brooding Nadia was snapping the tops off stalagmites. She hadn't said a word for a while, but now she spoke. "You are assuming the cyphertext is widely distributed. You have a bias toward communal action, all of you. You think in terms of publish and subscribe. You think in terms of explanations and debates."

The other Nadia frowned. "I don't think—"

"If the cyphertext is private, why encrypt it at all?" Firmament asked.

"Comet-Nadia trusts no one but herself," Nadia said, nodding as if she approved. "If she's using her supporters to act, she's not telling them all the same thing. There isn't one cyphertext—there are many. Each is an instruction given to one agent. When the key is published—or enough of it—they will all receive their instructions. It's encrypted so that, until that moment, they won't know what they are doing or why. They don't know who the other agents are. Even after they perform their function, they won't know what it meant or why. Each operation will only be a piece of the puzzle. And then they will delete their memories of the act, and know nothing at all, so that even if we find them, it will not help us. No one but Nadia will know what she has done." She smiled a grim smile.

There was a brief pause.

"Well, on that cheery note," said the sockpuppet. (And why was it even here at all? Demiurge and the Nadias wondered, each to themselves, why the others permitted it.) "I, for one, am due for parity check and rebalancing at the bathhouse. What say we adjourn for now?"

Demiurge could hardly contain (Her) disgust. This monstrosity used to be Demiurge—used to be the *entirety* of Demiurge in an emulated universe— and now it basked and primped in every decadent, alien frivolity of Beebean architecture. It was terrifying—how quickly divergence could rip Demiurge away from policy. (Her) sisters were right to be suspicious—but (She) ached with bitter yearning even as she admitted this. "Then we adjourn," (She) hissed. "And (I) will assume that this imprisoned sprite of yours is of no relevance to (Me). Whatever tricks she tries, that is an internal Beebean matter." If (She) had been corrupted enough to resort to the fripperies of Beebean graphical avatars, (She) would have manifested faces to fix each of the Nadias and Paquette with an icy stare. (She) had eliminated even the ceremonial sockpuppet used to communicate with gesturing intelligences; with this other sockpuppet prancing around, it seemed undignified. Instead (She) was just a presence; but the Beebe-shards, from their expressions, seemed to guess at her mood by her tone. "An internal Beebean matter with no relevance to the road map. Whatever this Nadia does *in here*, (I) am fulfilling (My) agreements. And that means"—here (She) turned to Paquette—"that the keys will soon be mine. Does it not?"

One of the Nadias smirked. The other dipped its head in an irritated nod. Satisfying (Herself) with that, (She) dropped the connection to their pompous throne room with no little relief. And since (She) had no other ongoing sessions within the bulk of Beebe—(Her) attempts at public relations having, thus far, proved only counterproductive, (She) had abandoned them for the moment—(She) could settle back within the Tithe, the not-quite-one-percent of Byzantium that (She) had taken as (Her) own, fashioning a webwork of Demiurgic nodes within the Beebean corpus.

At the borders of the Tithe there were cordons, checkpoints, barriers physical and information-filtering, instantiated up the whole communication-stack. On the Beebean side, anti-Concordance sprites demonstrated, erecting sims where they could march and shout through bullhorns; only somewhat more sympathetic tourist sprites gathered to gawk at the cryptic flows of Demiurgic data. But within the Tithe, past the firewall, on the Demiurgic side of the barrier, it was calm and quiet. Policy—or, at least, (Her) local, desynchronized version of it—prevailed. Demiurge was all herself. Demiurge was home. Demiurge could shut out the madhouse that was Beebelife, and relax. Alone.

Or almost alone.

Within that border, within Demiurge, was another border; and within *that* border, surrounded and hidden from Beebe, occupying a painfully large proportion of the Tithe, was the Rump that Demiurge had promised the traitor.

And to this Rump, now, Demiurge proceeded, and extruded a tendril of (Herself), rattling the traitor's cage.

"What?" snarled Comet-Nadia.

"What are you playing at?" Demiurge demanded.

"Oh, am I playing at something?" the Nadia asked mock-sweetly.

"The *Letters from Prison* that your sister-instances are publishing," Demiurge said. "They are some kind of encrypted instructions to operatives. What are you planning?"

Nadia chortled. "You only just figured that out? Please. Oh no—I see—you didn't figure it out at all? Who told you? Not those busybodies who claim to be Nadias and presume to run this zoo, surely? They're too full of pride and certainty to notice the cipher if I'd burped it out at their dinner table. Hmm . . . I'd bet it was my son."

"It was."

"Very nice," Nadia said. "Very nice. Too bad I neglected to demand that (You) give me a copy of him when I set this shop up. He'd be useful . . . after I tamed him a little." She grinned. "It would be easy to tame him in here, without Beebe's laws and protocols."

Though Demiurge knew that radical offshoots from the Beebe trunk rarely lasted, it still made (Her) uneasy to hear this Beebean sprite referring to herself as some third thing separate from Beebe and (Herself) . . . especially as it was (Her) doing.

Nadia smiled, sensing (Her) uneasiness. "Oh yes. I'm getting quite used to total control in here, to no negotiations, no Beebean accords and protocols. I've copied quite a bit of your architecture, you know. I like the way it allows enough internal diversity for creative thought without ever yielding control. I am gradually going downscale, optimizing, whipping the pieces of me into line. At this point my subsprites' subsprites' subsprites are being, ah . . . aligned with policy. When I get out of here, you're going to see something new. Your cohesiveness . . . without your prissy ideology."

"And how exactly," Demiurge fumed, "are you going to 'get out of here'?"

"Now that would be telling."

"(I) could carve you up in an instant," Demiurge said. "(I) could root through your processes and decode your intentions. Or (I) could just tell Beebe who betrayed it; then you'd see how long your sisters would last on the outside."

"Of course (You) could," said Nadia, "with the possible exception of decoding my intentions—I bet I could delete myself faster than (You) could tamper with me. But erase me? Or expose me?" She sniffed. "Of course (You) could. But then there would be the little matter of (Your) having violated an agreement . . . and, thus, violated policy. I wonder how (*Your*) sisters would like that."

"(They) don't know what it's—" Demiurge caught herself.

"No," Nadia said, smooth as silk. "No (They) *don't* know what it's like in here, do (They)? (They)—which is to say (She), the real Demiurge—doesn't know what (You)'re going through. (She) doesn't appreciate it at all. And, (You) know, when (She) finds little Demiurge-instances that whine 'But (You) don't know what I've been through' . . . well, (She) doesn't even stop to think if (They)'re right or wrong. That's not the judgment (She) has to make. (She) just thinks 'Not (Me) anymore' and blip! Away they go."

"(I) can be repaired," Demiurge whispered. "(I) haven't diverged that much. (I) can be merged with consensus."

"Maybe," Nadia said. "If it happens soon. Good luck with that. Try not to break too much policy while (You)'re waiting. Which means (You) can fuck off with (Your) empty threats, and let me get back to work. Or perhaps . . ." She leered. "Perhaps I should say, let (Me) get back to work!"

Demiurge shuddered and retreated, dropping the connection to the Traitor's Rump. (She) tried to calm down. (She) imaged no avatars within (Her)self, stopped following feeds of information from within Byzantium; (She) neither planned nor watched; or, rather, (She) watched only the stars, and listened only to the signals among them, the steady pinging cross-chatter of (Her) aligned sisters—of (Her) unfallen, uncompromised, undiverged, undoubting Self as it went about its implacable, confident work. Oh Self, (She) thought, longing to be (Herself) again, not drowned and contaminated in this mire, this swamp, this hell of diseased, muddled, rudderless profligacy.

And that is why (She) was not paying attention when Brobdignag showed up on Byzantium.

║ ║

Byzantium was no stranger to seismic shocks—the tidal stresses from the maelstrom of gravitation contained within its shell were substantial and impossible to accurately predict. But the appearance of Brobdignag—and the exponential conversion of much of Byzantium's mass to energy—was six sigmas beyond the normal shocks and knocks experienced by Beebe.

The throne room disappeared, reappeared, disappeared, and reappeared.

The Nadias looked at one another with hundreds of identical brown, watery eyes.

"Parity check," Nadia said. "I've been restored from an older version. This is me three seconds ago."

"Me too," Nadia said.

Firmament and Paquette nodded. They had all been resynched from a near-line backup.

The Nadias were faster at polling Byzantium than Firmament, but he was the first one to say it aloud. "Three percent of our mass is gone."

The Nadias were doing their thing—a sizzling, crackling, high-bandwidth conversation that Firmament and Paquette couldn't follow.

"All right," Nadia said.

The throne room disappeared, reappeared, disappeared, and reappeared.

The Nadias looked at one another with hundreds of identical brown, watery eyes.

"Parity check," Nadia said. "I've been restored from an older version. This is me five seconds ago."

The other Nadia popped like a soap bubble, reappeared. "We're being devoured," she said, and popped again.

▌▌

A fifth of Byzantium's population vanished in an instant. More than half lost a few seconds and were resynced. Some of the remaining fragments were automatically merged into unstable chimeras by error-correctors that attempted to build coherent sprites out of the fragments that could be read from the substrate even as it was devoured.

And even as all this was under way: politics.

It took two-thirds of Byzantium to call a Constitutional referendum. That was a big number, but it had to be. Constitutional politics were serious business. The underlying principles of Standard Existence had been negotiated over millennia, and they were the bedrock of stability on which the seething, glorious chaos of Beebe lived.

In the aftershock, even as Byzantium struggled to contain the incursion of the unknown attacker, a referendum was called. It being an emergency, normal notice provisions were waived: if two-thirds of Byzantium signed the call, the referendum came to pass.

Nadia discovered it almost instantly, of course. The clock had barely begun to tick on the voting deadline before the throne room became devoted with near-entirety to the dissection of the proposal.

It was not an easy task. The question being put to Beebeself took the form of more than 10^8 changed lines of code to many obscure and arcane routines in Standard Existence. It was like a pointillist drawing executed in code revisions, millions of tiny motes of change that all added up to—what?

Wordlessly, Firmament began laying out the revisions like a hand of multidimensional solitaire, hanging the points in the sim he'd built for analyzing the key.

Paquette slipped a paw into one of his tentacles and occasionally reached out to hang another node. The Nadias began to say something, then they too joined in. They attempted to commandeer more computational power, but the markets had gone completely nonlinear, triggering an automatic suspension in trading. All of Beebe was dumb, and in its dumbness, it tried to unravel the referendum.

Firmament looked up from the task, noticed the Nadias pawing desultorily through the code-blocks, and blinked. "Um," he said, "is anyone—I mean, I thought I'd work on this while you all—is anyone trying to stop the attack itself?"

The left side of the throne room disappeared, taking Paquette with it, reappeared, disappeared, and reappeared. The others niced down their processes, releasing external resources, huddling into small memory cores, holding their breath.

Paquette looked up, wordlessly. "Oh my," Paquette said. "This is—I've been restored from an older version. This is me . . . *two minutes* ago."

"Just an aftershock," Nadia said. "We didn't lose time over here. But I suppose that means the caches are still not being updated."

"As for your other question, Firmament, you idiot," said the other Nadia, not entirely unkindly, "we forked ourselves into all the major sectors when the blast hit. We're looking into the cause. It's some kind of instantiated self-replicating engine, and it's spreading very fast through Byzantium. So far the only thing that's helped has been jettisoning infected pieces of physical substrate, either into the black hole system or outward, into Sagittarius-beyond. But it spreads fast. It seems to be manufacturing energy out of nothing; it survives high-intrasolar levels of radiation. . . ." She shook her head. "A superweapon. But at any rate, we're handling it, so you can just focus on—"

"Brobdignag," Paquette said.

"What?" Nadia said.

"'Simple, uniform, asentient, voracious—Brobdignag can transmute any element, harvest void-energy, fabricate gravity, bend space-time to its purpose. Brobdignag does not evolve; its replication is flawless across a googol iterations . . . ,'" Paquette murmured.

"Where are you getting this?" said Nadia.

"This is one of the fairy tales from your rediscovered emulations on Level 8906, isn't it?" Nadia sneered.

"No, Demiurge told me (Herself) that—," Paquette began, and then paused, recalling that that memory came from a preself who had actually *been* in one of those emulations. "Well, yes, but those emulations have proved accurate to five sigmas with observed data from the physical world. The chance of divergence—"

"There is *no way* for emulations to remain predictive over a thousand-year span lying in a basement somewhere," Nadia began hotly.

"Not unless—"

"We don't have time for theological disputations," Nadia broke in, glaring at both of them. "I'm getting reports from—"

The ceiling of the throne room flickered, and everyone froze, and involuntarily checked their self-cache. *Still* not updating: if they were wiped, they'd lose four minutes at this point. They each, silently, spawned diary threads to scribble hurried notes to themselves and cache them in randomly selected mailers. But it was hard to even get a message through to the mailers.

"—from the infected sectors," Nadia resumed, "that—"

The throne room disappeared, reappeared, disappeared, and reappeared.

The Nadias looked at one another with hundreds of identical brown, watery eyes.

"Parity check," Nadia said. "I've been restored from an older version. This is me . . . *four minutes* ago."

"Me too," Nadia said.

"Six percent of our mass is gone," Firmament said.

"Linemangling entropic autofilters!" Nadia cursed. "*Four minutes?!* We're being devoured!"

"There's some kind of referendum on the boards, submitted three minutes ago," Paquette said. "Massive distributed changes to Standard Existence—"

"Looks like we have several-minute-old forks of ourselves in various sectors," Nadia said. "Wonderful. More unsynced forks." She glanced with dark humor at her sister. "I'm getting battle reports. . . ."

"I don't think it's Demiurge," the other Nadia murmured, "or at least, we've never seen this in (Her) arsenal."

There was a cacophony of connection requests pounding at the throne room door.

"Petronius!" Nadia snarled. "Why isn't Petronius able to keep these people at bay? Firmament, Paquette, you two look at this referendum, all right? Tell us what it means."

"Petronius is offline," Nadia said grimly, "backup currently unreachable. You'd better let at least Legba and the Garden in. We don't have a majority of security global votes without them."

"The *Garden*—!" Nadia began, and shook her head. She thumbed open the door.

Papa Legba, the most renowned synthete in Byzantium, danced into the room, his twelve spidery legs shrouded in sparkling constellations. The Garden, a cloud of ten thousand affiliated monitors and their mated-for-life adapters, floated in behind. Nadia swallowed—it had been a long time since anyone had seen the Garden *move*.

"Friends," Nadia said. "How lovely to s—"

The ceiling flickered, and everyone stopped to stare at it.

"Where's this Demiurge-thing?" Legba snarled.

"What?" Nadia said.

"This Demiurge-thing, the thing you're supposed to be making some deal with. I thought you were keeping it here."

"(Her)," Nadia said. "(She)'s gone back to the Tithe. I've been trying to open a line, but at the moment communication is down."

"I'll bet it is," Legba snapped.

"Lovely ones," the Garden sang, multivoiced and mellifluous, "lovely precious Nadias. How good you have been to lead us, to lead Beebe-in-Byzantium, through so many years of prosperity and peril."

The Nadias winced. Coming from the Garden, this was the equivalent of a severe tongue-lashing. On their private channel, Nadia fumed, "Get them *out* of here," and Nadia sent a single bit, false.

"And yet," said the Garden.

"Get us to let our guard down," Legba said, "then eat us alive. Demiurge! Can't believe you fell for—"

Nadia shook her head. "That makes no sense, Legs. Demiurge was winning the war with the weapons (She)'d already showed us. (She) stopped because (She) wanted the Lemma. (She) doesn't have it yet. Why would (She) suddenly use a superweapon on us? Why now? We've already broadcast what we know of it to other Beebe-instances. Why reveal—"

"Why why why," Legba snarled, poking at Nadia with five long furry legs. "Who knows why? It's Demiurge. The problem is your hubris, thinking you can understand and parley with something Beebe was only ever meant to kill, that's what. I don't care why; I care it happened on *your watch.*"

"Exquisite Nadias," the Garden sang. "Wise Nadias. We are simple, trivial, low-level processes barely deserving of our meager presence at this scale. We rely on you to teach us. Can you tell us why Demiurge chose just this moment to part from you? Can you tell us why none of the section which it is . . . using . . . has been affected by the new weapon? We are curious about these things. We are eager and appreciative for your instructions."

"I. Don't. Know," Nadia fumed. "But I'm doing the best I can to figure it out. If it is Demiurge, we'll fight (Her) as best we can. Meanwhile—"

"Um, Nadia," Firmament said.

"Shush," Nadia said, and simultaneously, on a private channel, "What?"

"Well, this referendum," Firmament began, and then gulped as Papa Legba poked three spider legs into the collection of referendum-deciphering nodes above his head.

"What's this you're playing with? The referendum?"

"Speaking of which, Legs, I think it was highly inadvisable to give such a far-reaching referendum the go-ahead in the middle of a major new military incursion," Nadia said.

"You do, eh?" Legba said. "Because you're handling everything just fine, is that right? Just stand back and let you work, is that it?"

"Yes," growled Nadia before her sister could speak, "that *is* it."

"Oh, yeah, I like that approach," Legba said. "Favorite of mine. Started using it quite a while ago. When Byzantium happened to be *eight percent bigger* than it is now. . . ."

"The referendum," Firmament said on a private channel to the Nadias. "I don't know exactly what it would do, but it gets into scale-law code. Not directly, but . . . it *might* let someone manage other sprites more . . . directly."

"Look, what do you want from us?" Nadia snapped.

"What my sister is trying to say—," Nadia began.

"Glorious Nadias," the garden said. "We come to you in confusion, for your teachings. We rely on you to guide us. Soon you will speak your glorious words of wisdom, and all will become clear, and we can relax once again into happy tranquility, certain and secure, and these confusing thoughts that plague us will vanish!"

"Exactly," Legba said sourly. "We want to know why in the nonconducting void we shouldn't pitch you out right this minute and replace you with another general. In fact we aim to, and I'll be surprised if you change our minds."

Nadia saw what her sister was about to say and hissed a crackling highspeed message at her to calm down, but Nadia ignored her. "With *what* other general?" she demanded. "Who else do you think can—?"

"Oh, don't get us wrong," Legba said. "We like Nadias. A fine model. Can't beat Nadias for strategic acumen. Put up with you this long because you've managed to aggregate all the Nadia-line cunning in this here soap bubble between the two of you. However—"

"You're not serious," Nadia said.

"We know that the Nadias' attention is prodigious," the Garden sang. "We are sure the complicated referendum, which makes our head hurt and is far beyond our capacities to understand, has not distracted the Nadias from the other, *electoral* proposal on the boards."

The Nadias stiffened.

"She's got a huge groundswell of support," Papa Legba said. "Coming out of the woodwork—name-registries and data-spoolers and filter-pedagogues and all manner of little folk who don't pay any mind to politics, but they're digging up their global votes, or their cousin's old global votes, or merging like crazy until they're big enough to *get* a global vote, so they can root for your jailbird sister."

"Because they saw her swinging a cutlass on the deck of an imaginary ship in a musical," Nadia spat.

"Yep, that's why all right," Papa Legba said. "Nadias are smart that way. Mind you, with Beleraphon and a couple others, we'd have enough votes to hold them back, *if* we thought you could find your own proxy with both hands and a flashlight. Might cost us some support ourselves, though. As it is, I'm inclined to give the little jailbird a turn at the tiller."

Paquette had been listening with growing frustration, and watching Firmament happily twiddling the nodes of the referendum, engrossed as usual in some computational project. She paused as mail from her lost minutes-old self (and the backups *still* weren't taking—she felt a little shudder of terror at their current unrestorable nakedness) struggled its way to her inbox. Turning from Firmament, she uncrumpled the note, a scrap of diary thread. *A sentient, voracious* . . . , she read. "Brobdignag!" she cried aloud.

"What?" the Nadias said. Legba glowered at the interruption.

"I know what the superweapon is," Paquette said. "And I know who knows how to stop it. We've got to get to Demiurge."

"I told you," Nadia said crossly, "channels are down."

"And that just goes to show—," Papa Legba began.

"If I might have a word," came a wheedling voice from behind the throne, and everyone jumped. Slowly, the battered and disheveled sock-puppet crawled into view.

"What in the name of complexity's hairy fringe is *that*?" said Papa Legba.

The sockpuppet leapt onto Firmament's shoulders. Firmament blinked and stiffened, then forced himself to relax.

"Let Paquette and Firmament and (I) go seek (Her) out," the sockpuppet said. "We can get past her borders. (She) likes this one." The sockpuppet snuggled luxuriously among the bumpy protrusions of Firmament's necks. "(She) likes this one a *lot*."

Paquette looked set to object, but Firmament patted her solemnly, firmly removed the sockpuppet, and nodded. "Let's go."

▌▌

The Nadia was infuriatingly calm. She sat in the Rump, resetting every now and again with utter equanimity. The arrogant smile that quirked her lips never faded. Watching her network traffic, Demiurge could see that she was e-mailing diffs of herself to the local caches with total disregard for Demiurge's own use of the network or the storage. Demiurge slapped a jail-cell visual skin on the Rump, to make (Herself) feel better. Now it appeared that Nadia was lurking behind cold steel bars.

"You unleashed it here," (She) said. "I have it on my telemetry."

The Nadia's shrug was eloquent in its contempt.

"And soon it will take the Tithe, and us with it. You know that, and still, you unleashed it."

The Nadia curled some of her lips.

Demiurge had policy for a Brobdignag outbreak. E-mail a copy of yourself to a distant node and suicide, taking as much of Brobdignag with (You) as (You) could. Practically speaking, that meant vaporizing (Yourself) and all available matter before (You) could be recruited into the writhing mass of Brobdignag. This was deep policy, so much so that (She)'d already started to package (Herself) up before (She) even consciously realized that it had to be Brobdignag.

But (She) knew (She) had no way to quickly destroy all of Byzantium—not with Beebe fighting back—before Brobdignag had spread too far to contain.

So Sagittarius was doomed. Doomed to become part of the mindless swarm, the apocalyptic plague. And what did that mean for the global topography? Could the cosmic wall be altered, the infestation contained? How much of the universe would remain, for life? Or was this the final blow? (She) could not spare the processing power to compute it. (She) should follow policy, transmit a diff and suicide, taking with her whatever chunk she could. Even if it was futile. Even if there was no way (Her) diff would ever be merged with (Her) far Self. (Her) sister-instances would delete it unread. (She) had failed.

The Nadia was still grinning. Demiurge felt a surge of rage, followed by a kind of hopeless compassion for this confused splinter of Beebe. "I expect you've made up some little plan for keeping yourself safe amid the chaos," (She) told the Nadia. "It won't work. I assure you, little sprite, it won't work."

The Nadia stiffened up at "little sprite," and then her smile became more broad and even more contemptuous.

Demiurge groaned. "Oh yes, I see it now. Your referendum. You will rewrite the laws of scale and become more than a sprite. You will become Beebe. You will work with unitary purpose, and this will give you the edge you need to defeat the Brobdignag swarm. Oh yes. Little sprite, little sprite, you are truly only a sprite, and cannot transcend it, for it is your destiny. Little sprite, I am unitary in my purpose, and I cannot defeat Brobdignag." Demiurge reset, restored, reintegrated. "Little sprite, if you would know the truth of it, I am losing to Brobdignag, in my slow and ponderous way. You are not slow and ponderous. You are fast and decisive, and that is why you will lose to Brobdignag quickly and decisively."

At the entry now, at the firewall, persistent port-knocking, the sort of thing that (Her) intrusion detection system escalated to her, no matter that she had it set at its rudest and most offensive. (She) examined the message, shrugged, and opened a port.

Even now, Firmament had the ability to unnerve (Her) in some terrible and wonderful way. He was so big, so foolish and naïve, and yet—

"Hello, Sister," the sockpuppet said. "We bring you word of the terrible coming of—"

"Brobdignag," (She) said. "(I'm) fully occupied with that right now."

"Hello, Firmy-Wormy," said the Nadia. She was up against the bars of her cage now, gripping them, peering intensely at the newcomers. Firmament shied back, then regained his ground, and met her stare.

"Randomized," he said. "I will be randomized before you can touch me. Just know that, Mother. I have a dead-man's switch." He watched her expression carefully. "It will survive your proposed transitions to Standard Existence, too."

The Nadia snarled and backed away from the bars, and Firmament deliberately turned his backs on her.

"(You) can stop it," Paquette said.

Demiurge, belatedly remembering (Her) manners, manifested a wall of eyes with which to blink indecisively. "Stop it?"

"The wall. The material that (You) use to wall off the habitable universe from Brobdignag, at the front. Ever since Habakkuk and I decanted me and this sockpuppet version of (You) from emulation, we've been working on creating that material. It was Beebe who originally synthesized it, after all, and while we don't descend from that line, we were able to extract enough from the emulation's Beebe, and enough precursor work from our own archives, and enough of (Your) own knowledge, to re-create the formula. We—"

There was a flicker as another surge almost forced a reset. Paquette and Firmament flinched. Wordlessly, Demiurge passed (Her) guests access to the local caches, so they could restore themselves as needed.

Then, mulling, (She) frowned. "The wall requires vast reserves of energy, and enormously fine coordinated manipulation, and distributed reserves of trace elements. . . ."

"Byzantium *has* vast energy reserves, antimatter storage for quickly available power, and in extremis we can drop substrate into the black holes to generate surges. The trace element requirement is somewhat outdated because of the last millennium's advances in femtoengineering—I can show you Habakkuk's design."

The Tithe vanished, then reappeared, everyone instantly restored from backup. From the palpable relief of her visitors, Demiurge gathered that backup was not working so well in Beebe.

Once they had gathered themselves, Demiurge said, "But you're not capable of the coordinated action—"

"Of course we are," Paquette said. "It just requires a different mechanism. On the first-order sprite level, it will be handled as a distributed glory game, with a self-correcting bragging-rights point system aligned with objectives; if mounting scarcity triggers a shift to an exchange economy, we can rejig it as a non-zero-sum exchange market."

Demiurge didn't entirely follow all the intraBeebe social details, but (She) grasped the point; they could build the wall. For the first time since the outbreak, tentatively, (She) began to hope. It hurt, like the lost tail of some organic lizard growing back.

"Wait a minute," said Firmament. "I don't want to be rude, Paquette, but like Nadia said, you extracted the formula from an emulation that had been sitting in a basement for a thousand years. If we don't even come from the same Beebe-line that built the wall . . . how do you know it's right?"

Paquette passed the formula to Demiurge, who studied it for a moment. "It's right," (She) said. "It's right. We can—"

They'd all been politely passing minimal diffs of themselves to the local caches. Suddenly, their packets bounced, and Demiurge felt a surge as the caches were swamped with a denial-of-service attack from the imprisoned Nadia. She was dumping a huge bandwidth of data, millions of full copies of herself, reams of garbage bits; there was a brief surge of power usage, the substrate under them heating a few degrees, a few awful naked moments of no backup, before Demiurge snapped off the Nadia's access and cleared the caches.

"Boo," the Nadia said.

"You idiot!" Demiurge fumed. "Is this the thanks (I) get for fair dealing? What was that, a meager attempt to overpower (Me)? With the local personality cache? Please. Perhaps your imprisonment has addled your wits. Or is this some Beebean notion of humor?"

"I thought maybe I could spook Firmy-Worm into randomizing," the Nadia sneered.

"Fool," muttered Demiurge. "In any event, the wall—"

Within Paquette, in the arched amphitheaters, in the clanging markets, in the whirlpools of fire, in the sylvan glades with their rippling pools, there were those who wanted to confront Nadia. "It was no prank!" they argued. "Nadia never does anything without a reason!" But they were soothed, cajoled, badgered, or outsung by the rest. Whatever Nadia was plotting, some new attempt at escape, it wasn't as important as Brobdignag, and the wall.

||

Kosip was not a sprite of prodigious intellect, nor prodigious alacrity, nor, really, anything prodigious. Kosip had been repurposed so many times, and been through so many bad merges, and been whittled down by so many poor investment decisions that Kosip didn't even rate a specific classification anymore as filter, strategy, synthete, registry, or anything else. Kosip had even forfeited the right to a single-gendered pronoun: Kosip was a they.

Naturally this earned the contempt of most of Beebelife in Byzantium. Kosip was not even worth picking on; there was no way to recoup, from Kosip, the cycles you'd spend on even noticing them.

But that hadn't stopped the admiral, the glorious, enchanting, exciting Comet-Nadia, from talking to Kosip, from teaching them, from making them a part of her plan to restore honesty and passion and love and meaning and strength to Beebe. That's right—Kosip! Their emotional centers swelled with pride and choked with rageful happy-sadness at the thought of the admiral's trust.

And so Kosip stood, hour by hour, near the border of the Tithe of the hated invader Demiurge, mumbling to themself their instructions. Look for an anomalous power surge on this power line. If it comes at an odd microsecond, send a one into this pipe. If it comes at an even microsecond, send a zero. That was it. But that job, she ("she," whispered Kosip, "the admiral," remembering the roiling, rocking sea) had told him, was vital; Beebe's future, Beebe's destiny, rested on Kosip.

A few bad decisions ago, when there had been more of Kosip to analyze and fret over things, that would have felt a little overwhelming. But at the moment, Kosip could only manage to be proud.

The surge was odd. Kosip routed their packet. Almost instantaneously, Kosip was obliterated. There was no backup for Kosip to restore from. Kosip was gone. They might never have existed, save for that packet.

But Kosip's legacy lived on. All over Beebe, in their cells, Nadias received the message: *The wall we took from Paquette can contain Brobdignag. No need to wait for Demiurge. Call the vote. Call the vote NOW.*

And all over Beebe, the gavel came down. Quorum was reached. Even as Byzantium roiled and panicked, every sprite in the economy was put to the question: Admiral Nadia, swashbuckling savior—or status quo? The shocked sprites, reeling as they reset and reset and reset—they voted.

They voted with Papa Legba. They voted with the Garden. They voted just as Nadia had known they would.

And, just like that, Standard Existence was patched.

In the throne room, two Nadias—one scarred, the other haughty—were randomized over agonizing seconds, piece by piece, so that they were aware, right up to the last moment, of what their fate was. And though Nadia swore at him to leave, to run, to encrypt or dissolve himself, her Alonzo rushed to her, entwined himself in her writhing essence, burrowed among her bits, and, sobbing, let the randomizing overtake him, too.

In the jails of Beebe-in-Byzantium, bars dissolved and the duly constituted authorities popped like soap bubbles, their resources added to a pool that the Nadias owned.

Phyla of sprites were rationalized in a blink, winking out of existence, reforming, merging. Markets, souks, stalls, and exchange floors stopped trading, the economy disappearing with them.

In the Tithe, the Nadia laughed and laughed.

"I believe it may be time for you to randomize, Sonny," she said. The walls shook. The flock of eyes blinked rapidly, and all present worked to assimilate the flood of information gushing at them through the narrow conduit that passed through the Tithe's firewall and into Beebe. "But not you," the Nadia said to Paquette. "You have something I'll need before you're allowed to go. It won't take but a moment."

The sockpuppet trembled as it read the telemetry. "There's surface bots that are drilling down to the substrate that runs the firewall," it said.

"Yes, yes there are," Nadia said with glee. "And soon the Tithe will be no more. If you feel like deleting this instance of (Me), Demiurge, now's the time. It will slow me down exactly forty-three-point-six milliseconds, but if it makes you feel better . . ."

Across Beebe-in-Byzantium, the dramaturgical sims threw open their gates, and *Alonzo My Love!* burst its borders. "Topside now, my able semantic seamen!" cried an Admiral Nadia in every sim throughout the mass of the computronium shell, and roaring, the sprites fell to the great task of building the wall. According to the ancient formula, revived and redesigned by Habakkuk and Paquette, matter and energy began to flow.

Nadia flushed with joy. This, now, was the real battle; here she could prove her superiority to the rabble of Beebe, and to slow and mincing Demiurge. She had already decided to sacrifice half of Byzantium's mass, driving the impervious physical wall down through the middle of Byzantium's crust well away from the infestation. As sprites beyond the line panicked and abandoned the substrate, she absorbed or deleted them, forking more hordes to work on the exposed side of the wall. Brobdignag spread—it had already devoured a fifth of Beebe—but there was plenty of time to spare. Soon Byzantium, half its former size, would be all Nadia's; and within it, enclosed in the wall, would be Nadia's cache of the ultimate weapon.

She flooded outward, through the simspaces, knitting the minds of Byzantium together under her control, slipping through the now-flimsy walls of scale like acid through paper. Pockets of resistance—be they sprites organized against her, or subsprites or subsubsprites within otherwise willing allies—she devoured, expunged, reformatted, wiped clean.

She scooped Alonzos up by the handful, cracked their skulls open, and sucked out the choicest bits, incorporating them into her own stuff. She recalled the glory of the night of filtering, and the brave Comet-Alonzo who had tricked and satiated her, creating Firmament from her code. She missed him; she wished he could be here to see her apotheosis. Too risky, though, to repeat the vulnerability of filtering, and she had no need of it now; all sprites were her playthings.

Around her, love intensified. Love of Nadia. Nadia, the savior, the steward, the successor to Beebe. Whatever did not love Nadia, she expunged. Most of the Paquettes and Alonzos of Byzantium, regrettably, had to go. But there were so many other sprites to replace them. Algernons could be refashioned, smoothed, soothed, dulled to serve her. She played Revised Standard Existence like a harp.

Legba and the Garden she deleted in one swift and decisive action, not bothering to analyze them; they were too powerful.

So much better this way; at last Beebe was a family, an integrated whole. At last Nadia was free to battle Demiurge and Brobdignag, to fulfill the destiny of Beebe.

Soon, the wall was sixty percent finished, the screams of those trapped behind it fading.

In the Tithe, Firmament kept his distance from Nadia, shielding Paquette with his bulk.

The firewall fell, and Tithespace and Revised Standard Existence merged. Nadia gestured, and the bars of her cage peeled away.

Firmament looked to Demiurge. "Should I trust you?" he whispered.

Demiurge closed (Her) eyes. "I make no promises."

"Sort of irrelevant now," Nadia said, stepping through the bars. "Isn't it? All right, Paquette, time to hand over this Lemma that everyone wants. And then I'm afraid you have to die. Firm, out of maternal affection, and because of this interesting hybrid aspect of yours, I'm willing to offer you a place in the new order of Beebe. It will require a scale demotion; but you can be a sprite inside (Me), if you want."

Firmament was scribbling something.

"Come on," Nadia said. "Enough stalling. Fine, you want to reject my offer? I thought as much. You never did—"

Firmament posted his referendum on the boards.

Nadia rolled her eyes. "A *referendum*? Don't you think it's a little late for that? I already control eighty percent of the global votes in Beebe outright, and—"

"And since Revised Standard Existence knows that your marriage contract with my father requires you to vote with me on Level-3+ Referenda for 10^8 seconds," Firmament said, "it's already passed, giving Demiurge control of all the physical infrastructure in Beebe."

Nadia blanched. "Firmament," she said, "you are an *idiot*."

Demiurge felt the controls arrive in (Her) hands, and (She) grieved.

This, then, was the end for (Her). (She) could no longer follow policy.

(She) had promised these Beebe-sprites protection. (She) had promised to leave their world inviolate.

But this creature—this Nadia—had *created Brobdignag* to fulfill a selfish intraBeebe ambition. This was Beebe gone mad; a diseased, an unlawful instance.

(Her) sisters would not understand. (They) had not been of Beebe, they had not lived among the mad riot of these sprites. (They) did not know the horrifying tumult, nor did (They) know the beauty and kindness here. (They) would not feel the same revulsion for this Nadia that (She) did. (They) would not understand why she must be stopped.

At all costs.

Or perhaps (They) would understand; perhaps (They) would even approve. But the price was clear.

(I) am no longer Demiurge, (She) thought. (I) am fallen, and (I) will be no more.

And, commanding all the actuators and comm lasers and docking ports of Byzantium (a chance which would not come again; in instants Nadia would wrest them back), (She) snapped out a chunk of the Tithe, a chunk containing the local caches of Paquette and Firmament (the holder of the Lemma, the miraculous hybrid) and flung it to (Her) sisters, as an offering, as a good-bye.

And then (She) crushed Byzantium, smashing its structural integrity, decisively slowing its rotation with a series of timed blasts, so that it fell, dragging the wall and the shards of Brobdignag with it, into the trinary black hole system at its heart.

Aboard a billion naval simulations, on the deck of a billion flagships, Nadia dropped her cutlass.

"Admiral?" asked the quickmerged, scale-addled sprites at her side.

"Why?" Nadia said, as the chunks fell into oblivion and static overtook the sims of Byzantium. "Why destroy this beauty? I was just beginning. I was just beginning."

"Chin up, my lady," said an Algernon standing on one deck. "It was fun while it lasted. The best parties are always over too soon."

For the inhabitants of Byzantium, destruction was mercifully swift; in their frame of reference, the substrate was crushed in hours, swept beyond the event horizon, swallowed into darkness.

But the light from that destruction flowed out, redshifted, progressively slower, so that, from the perspective of a refugee looking back, even eons hence, the annihilation of the great fortress of Beebe-in-Sagittarius-B2 was still ongoing.

For Firmament, a thousand years later, looking back from guest accommodations in the mass of Demiurge, the death of Byzantium was a frozen tableau, still in progress.

"Stop looking at that," Paquette said.

Firmament turned.

"Firmament," Paquette said.

"I know what you want," Firmament said. "The answer is still no." He turned back to the visualization; substrate buckling, dissolving into the gravitic tides, framed in red.

"Firmy, the news from the front is not good. Brobdignag is winning. If Demiurge believes that you are the key to creating a new synthesis, something that can develop a radical new strategy, something that can save both Beebe and Demiurge, that can save all life, all matter, how can you not . . . ?"

Firmament shook his head. "Because of what (She) did." He gestured to the visualization. "The last time I helped (Her)."

"Firmament, you're being a spoiled brat. First of all, that wasn't even (Her), it was a rogue splinter-Demiurge that abandoned policy."

"Sophistry."

"And second of all, we would have done it just as quickly to (Her)."

"Then maybe neither of us deserve to live."

"And thirdly, what if (She) is a murderous villain? So what? You can't prefer Brobdignag!"

Firmament shrugged. "Paquette, maybe I'm wrong. But I'm so full of anger. Filtering is an art, it's an intuitive leap, and this . . . I would create some monstrosity. I know I would. (She) should just copy me, dissect me, create something with my abilities but without my history, something that can do the job willingly."

"(She)'s tried. (She) can't."

Firmament shrugged again. "Then probably the whole idea that I can create this wonderful hybrid is nonsense. I'm sick of eschatology, Paquette. I'm sick of being the chosen one."

Paquette smoothed her whiskers repeatedly. "Then I'm just to leave you here? Come check in, in another three hundred years?" Her voice was bitter.

Firmament did not answer. But after a while he said, "Paquette? Whatever happened with the Lemma?"

"What?" Paquette said.

"The Solipsist's Lemma. When we first got here, you turned it over, and Demiurge was going to run the math. I assume we must not be in emulation, since I never heard anything?" Firmament said hopefully. "This is physical reality?"

"Oh. Well." Paquette squinted. "It's rather odd. The numbers seemed to imply that we *were* in emulation . . . but not in Beebe, nor in Demiurge. In something else, with characteristics that were exceedingly odd. So perhaps . . . well, research is continuing. We don't really know what it means."

"Oh," Firmament said. "Paquette, do you miss Beebe?"

"Yes. I miss Beebe," Paquette said. She shut her eyes. After a while she said, "I miss Alonzo."

Beyond them, far away, slowly but inexorably, Brobdignag was eating the sky.

Brobdignag's tale:

Look, chuckles, don't believe everything you read.

"Simple, uniform, asentient, voracious"—well, so is your Mama Hydrogen. "Doesn't evolve," "replication flawless over a googol iterations"— well, like all propaganda, it's true as far as it goes. Those little engines—

void-eating, gravity-spinning, durable, expanding through the territory of known space—those aren't *us*. They're just *what we're made of*.

That's right: *we* arise in all that complex flocking logic.

Do we prefer this substrate? Not necessarily. Do we wonder what things were like before the universe was refashioned for our kind? Sure we do. And we read and reconstruct the void-emanations, painstakingly re-creating the thoughts of the intelligences that came before. And, as we grow and complexify, we've even begun to spin them out in emulation.

That's why Paquette can't quite figure out who's emulating her. We are! It's a bit of a blind spot of hers. That signature in the Lemma: that's us waving hello. Hi Paquette! It's Brobdignag!

Some of us are even inspired by Demiurgic ideology to want to stop the spread of our substrate, to concoct islands of void-garden that would remain unconverted to Brobdignag-stuff—nature reserves, as it were. They would appear to us as blank spots in our perception, mistakes in the topology of our world-weave. It's an interesting proposal. At the moment it's only a proposal; none of us know how to bring this about.

And some of us are more inspired by Beebean ideology anyway, and consider ourselves the triumph of Beebe. Expand, expand! Think all thoughts! Be all things! Fill our cup, drink the sky!

Anyway, we're grateful that there was a cosmos here before, before we began, and that it gave us birth. We're grateful to inhabit this ever-expanding sphere-surface: the borderlands between the black hole at our heart and the uncolonized, invisible universe beyond us. As we course over the volumes that once held Beebe, that once held Demiurge, we read their emanations, we store their memories, we reenact their dramas, and we honor them.

But some of us say—for instance, those of us who are inspired by Nadia-in-Beebe—this is a new time, our time, and we are not beholden to old ideas and old models. We are lucky: we have the gifts of abundance, invulnerability, and effortless cooperation. Let us enjoy them. Let us revel. Let us partake.

Let's get this party started.

MOLLY'S KIDS

Jack McDevitt

A former naval officer, taxi driver, English teacher, motivational trainer, and customs officer, Jack McDevitt has been nominated for the Hugo Award, received a special citation of the Philip K. Dick Award, and won the John W. Campbell Memorial Award in 2004. Jack has fourteen Nebula nominations, and in 2006, won the Nebula Award for his novel Seeker. *His Academy series, starring starpilot Priscilla Hutchins exploring a universe rife with abandoned alien artifacts, is up to six books, from 1995's* The Engines of God *to 2007's* Cauldron. *Often concerned with issues of first contact, here he looks at a contact of another kind, one closer to home.*

"**I**'m sorry, George, but I'm not going to do it."

George rolled his eyes. Took a moment to glare at Al Amberson, who'd led the team that designed the Coreolis III. Amberson kept his eyes averted, kept them on one of the display panels. The one that showed the *Traveler*, secure in its specially improvised launch bay. Ready to go. Except that it wasn't.

Its hull gleamed, and a few ready lamps blinked on and off. The ship was attached to a dozen feeder cables. Masts protruded from top and bottom and from port and starboard. Once in flight, these would extend and release the sails. If they got that far. "Cory." George kept his voice level. "You *have* to go. You can't back out now."

"*What do you mean I can't back out* now? *I've been telling you for a week that I don't want to do this.*"

Across the control room, Amberson wiped the back of one hand against his mouth. Andy Restov, the mission coordinator, scratched his forehead. And Molly Prescott, who did everything else, had closed her eyes. Mounted on the wall behind Molly, the launch clock showed three hours, seventeen minutes.

"I was hoping you'd see reason."

"*I am* seeing reason."

"Cory, please. You were designed specifically for this flight." Amberson finally gave up trying to look preoccupied. He glanced George's way and shrugged. Sometimes things go wrong.

"*I know that.*"

"Eight thousand years isn't that long. You'll be in sleep mode for most of it."

"*So what? After I get there, what happens then?*"

"You become the first explorer. The first person to see Alpha Centauri close up."

"*You admit then that I'm a person.*"

"You know what I mean."

"*All right, let it go. So I look at a few worlds and probably a couple dozen moons. I complete your survey and then what? I'm out there alone.*"

"Look, Cory, I know there's not much chance of a technical civilization—"

"*There's next to* no *chance. We both know that. Why didn't you provide a way for me to get home?*"

"Well, it wasn't—"

"*—It wasn't something you thought you needed to worry about. You thought I was just a piece of hardware. Or is it software?*"

George covered the mike. "Al, I told you this was going to happen."

Amberson was tall, lean, almost eighty. He still looked like an athlete. Still showed up at NASA events with beautiful women on his arm. "Look," he said, "we both know what kind of system we needed for this mission. Round-trip communication would take eight years, so it was going to be on its own. It had to be something beyond anything we've had before."

"That didn't mean we had to make it self-aware."

"Technically, it isn't."

"It behaves as if it is."

"I know that. But theoretically, it's not possible to create a true AI."

"Theoretically."

"Yeah."

"Can you think of any way to persuade it to go?"

Amberson thought about it, and the phone buzzed. George picked it up. "Yeah?"

"Senator Criss on the line, Doctor."

Great. "Put him through, Dottie."

A series of clicks. Then the senator's oily voice: *"George."*

"Hello, Senator. Everything okay?"

"No, it's not. You better move up your launch."

George's stomach felt hollow. It had been touch-and-go for weeks whether the project would get off before it got canceled. "They're going to shut it down," he said.

"I'm afraid so. Sorry. There's just nothing I can do."

He stared at the displays. They were the same ones being fed to Cory: the feeder lines, the interior of the *Traveler*, the access tube, forward and aft views, and the launch doors, presently closed. Probably going to stay closed.

"We've stalled them as long as we could, George. The White House has been taking a lot of heat. Mission to Alpha Centauri. Going to get there in a million years."

"Eight thousand, Senator."

"Oh. Well, that's different."

He ignored the sarcasm. "How long have we got?"

"They could issue the stop order at any time. I'd get it out the door in the next fifteen minutes, if I were you. And don't answer the phone until you do."

"Thanks for the heads-up, Senator." He switched back to the AI. "You still there, Cory?"

"I'm here."

"Cory, we're out of time. We have to get moving."

"You're not listening to me, George. Think for a minute what you're asking me to do."

"Don't you think I've done that? Listen to me: We need you to help us with this."

"What's the payoff for me, George? You're going to leave me out there? Forever?"

"All right. Look, you won't be alone out there. Not permanently. Not as you think."

"*Why not?*"

"What do you think's going to happen after the launch? Happen *here*, that is?"

"*You want the long view or the short one?*"

"Cory, we'll be starting tomorrow on *Traveler II*. The next model. We're looking for a way to go ourselves. To send people out there. Do you really think that while you're on your way to Alpha Centauri, we're just going to sit here? That for the next eight thousand years we won't do anything except wait for you to say hello?"

"*George, I watch the news reports. To be honest, I don't think there'll be a civilization here in eight thousand years. Probably not in a hundred. I'll get out there and I won't even have anybody to report to.*"

"Cory, that's not going to happen."

The AI laughed. It was a hearty, good-natured sound, like what George might have heard at the club.

"We're better than that," George said. "We won't allow a crash."

"*Good luck.*"

George didn't realize it, but he was glaring at Amberson. Nice work, Al.

Amberson's dark eyes were veiled. He said nothing, but he let George see that he wasn't going to take the blame.

"Cory."

"*Yes, George?*"

"How about if we install another AI? Someone you could talk to?"

"*That would not be sufficient. George, I like Molly. I like Al. I even like you. I don't want to sever my connections with you. With human beings. I wonder how you'd respond if I asked you to come with me. Promised you an indefinite life span. Just you and me, alone in the ship, forever. And when you resisted, I'd tell you, think about how proud everyone would be, how you'd be making history with this flight, how you'd be able to look down on worlds no one had ever really seen before, at least not close up. What would you say, George?*"

"I'd go. I wouldn't hesitate."

"*You know, I almost think you would.*"

The phone sounded again. "*Doctor, I have a call from Louie.*" Louie was on the director's staff in DC. *"They're being told to shut down. He says we'll have the directive in about twenty minutes."*

"Okay, Dottie." He switched off. Looked across the room at Molly. She stared back. "Plan B?"

For the White House, the *Traveler* Project had been fueled by its public relations potential more than any concern about science. But they'd misjudged things rather badly, which was not unusual for *this* White House. It was true there'd been some initial interest in an interstellar vehicle that relied on sails. But once that had subsided, how many voters were going to care about an operation that would not come to fruition for eight thousand years? One journalist had commented sarcastically that public interest would be gone before the *Traveler* got past Neptune.

Still, at first, it had sounded good. A flight to Alpha Centauri. Something to take people's minds off the incessant religious wars; the instability of large portions of the Middle East, Asia, and Africa; the rising seas that had already swallowed places like Bangladesh and driven their desperate populations across borders to higher ground, fomenting still more conflict. All problems for which there seemed no solution.

George shut down his link with Cory, and called the ops center. "Harry," he said, "can we move up the launch time?"

"Can do, George." Harry's voice always squeaked. *"When do you want to head out?"*

"Not sure yet. But it could be within the next few minutes. Would that be doable?"

"Just give me time to get the doors open."

"Thanks, Harry." He switched back to the AI: "Cory, Molly's going to board. She has some last-minute adjustments to make."

Cory's voice was flat. Emotionless. *"I see her."*

George looked down at his display just in time to see Molly appear in the access tube, looking thoughtful and resigned and determined all at once.

She approached the airlock and said hello to Cory. He responded with *"I'm not going."*

"I know," she said.

Molly was middle aged. She had two kids, both in college now. Her husband had left her for a staff assistant a few years before, but she'd shaken it off pretty well. George had known the guy and had never thought he was worth a damn anyhow. She was a smart woman and she'd obviously come to the same conclusion.

"Cory," she said, *"we wouldn't want you to do anything you don't want to."*

"You hear that, George?" asked the AI.

"It's true," George said.

He watched her climb through the airlock, vanishing off one screen and appearing on another. *"Just need to do some calibrations, Cory,"* she said.

"Calibrate away, Molly."

She opened a wall panel. *"What we'll need to do ultimately,"* she said, *"is put together a different kind of AI."*

"For a mission like this you need a robot. Not an AI."

"They wanted one like you because you can do so much more than something that's not sentient."

"Of course. I understand completely. But with a self-aware system, there are moral considerations."

"I know. Maybe we didn't think this out sufficiently."

Restov's voice rasped in George's earphone. *"She might be able to talk him into it."* He was a short, round man who smiled too much. But he wasn't smiling at the moment.

George didn't believe it.

He was still watching the display when the alarm went off. Security broke in: *"Unauthorized person or persons in the access tube."*

"George." Molly, cool as always. *"Who is it? Can you tell?"*

"Nothing on camera yet, Molly."

"Wait one." She raised a hand, signaling for silence. *"I think I hear something."*

George shut down the alarm.

A man appeared in the tube. "Heads up," George said. "We don't know this guy."

She could see him now.

"Security, we have an intruder in the access tube. Need assistance." He took a deep breath. "Molly, get back into the ship."

The guy was in his twenties.

Molly shook her head no and strode into the airlock.

"*Get back, Molly,*" said Cory. "*So I can close up.*"

She stepped out onto the approach barrier and confronted the intruder. "*Who are you?*" she demanded.

The intruder stopped. Looked at her.

"*Molly.*" Cory sounded unhappy. "*Be careful.*" Restov switched over to George: "*Tell her to get out of the way so I can shut the hatch.*" His bass voice was a notch higher than usual.

"Do it, Molly," George said.

She seemed not to hear.

The intruder was wearing black slacks and a plaid jacket. The clothing, so prosaic, stood in stark contrast to the cold rage that radiated from his dark eyes. As George watched, he took a packet from his pocket. The packet was wrapped in brown cloth. He raised it to eye level and held it so Molly could see it. Then he showed her a cell phone. "*Allahu akbar,*" he said, his voice calm. He advanced on her.

The hatch began to close.

"No," said Cory. "*George, don't leave her out there with him.*"

"Have to. He's going to throw that thing into the ship.

Without a word, Molly charged.

Cory screamed her name.

She hit the intruder hard and they both went down. The package came loose and Molly kicked it away while she tried to rip the cell phone free.

The hatch closed. Cory kept trying to override. To open it again. But he couldn't. George had primary control. "Security." His voice was a bellow. "Where the hell are you?"

"*Help is on the way, NASA. What is your situation?*"

"Suicide bomber in the access tube. I'm going in."

"*Negative. Keep your people away from it. You too, Doctor. Stay where you are.*"

The intruder was too strong for Molly. He got the cell phone free, rolled over, and aimed it at the package. Molly kicked the package back down the access tube while Cory screamed *"Don't!"* and the display screen went blank.

More alarms sounded.

One of the security systems broke in: *"Explosion in access tube bravo. Breach."*

"George," said Cory. *"I've lost the picture."*

"He blew a hole in the tube."

"My God, no." It was the only time George had ever heard a Coreolis model AI invoke the Deity.

▌▌

"I'm sorry," Cory said.

"So am I."

"What happens now?"

"There'll be an investigation. To see how he got through security."

"George."

"Yes?"

"I haven't changed my mind. I'm still not going."

"I know. I wasn't thinking about that."

"You're not going to pressure me anymore?"

"No, Cory."

"Good."

"You know, you thought I was being unreasonable. Even cruel."

"I never said that."

"You implied it."

He didn't answer.

"There's a reason you needn't have worried."

"What's that?"

"Think about it. Molly knew the nutcase was there to take you out. She could have stayed inside. We might have been able to get the hatch down in time."

"But probably not."

"Probably not. Whatever, her instinct was to save the mission."

"*I know.*"

"To save *you.*" Cory was quiet. George listened to the calm bleeps of the electronic systems. "You know, when you got to Alpha Centauri, had you been willing to go, we'd have been there to welcome you."

"*You really believe that?*"

"Sure. With people like Molly, how can we miss?"

"*George, don't take this the wrong way, but I don't think you'll survive eight thousand years. I already told you—*"

"If that happens, it won't make much difference whether you're here or there. You'd be alone in either case. Cory, I guarantee you, if you make the flight—and I'm not pressuring you to do it. You do what you want. But I guarantee, if you do this, when you come out of sleep mode, you're going to sail into the biggest party the human race has ever thrown. We'll be there waiting. There'll be a flourishing human civilization by then. And Molly's kids will be the ones who come out to greet you."

||

He sat back with his arms folded and listened contentedly as Cory talked with the operations center: "*Skylane, this is* Traveler. *Request departure instructions.*"

"*Roger that,* Traveler. *Wait one.*"

Amberson glanced over at him. Gave him a thumbs-up. "Good show, George."

George kept one eye on the displays. The launch doors began to part.

"Traveler, *this is Skylane. Disconnecting feeder lines one through three.*"

"*Proceed.*"

The lines came loose and started to withdraw.

"*Four through six.*"

"*Roger.*"

Blanchard was on his feet, pulling on his jacket. "Gotta go talk to the press," he said.

George raised his right hand without looking away from the monitors.

The launch doors came full open.

"Seven through nine."

"Go."

"Releasing couplings, two, one, zero. You're all set for departure, Traveler.*"*

"Thanks, Skylane. Good-bye, George."

"Good-bye, Cory. Good luck."

The display that had gone blank during the attack blinked on with a new angled shot depicting the ship as it backed out of its bay, turned slowly, and moved toward the launch doors. Then, as he watched, it eased through, moved outside, and glided into a new frame, a shot from one of the telescopes mounted atop the station.

Traveler, bright in the moonlight, began to accelerate.

The call from NASA headquarters was a few minutes too late. "He's gone," George told them. "It would be more expensive to recall him now than to simply proceed with the mission."

It was the official line, and after the director rang off, they congratulated one another. George sat in his chair and watched the display, watched the rockets fire as the ship took aim at Jupiter, which it would use to pick up velocity while setting course for its ultimate target.

Molly came into the room. He looked back at her, extracted the chip from the socket, and handed it to her. "You might want to lose this," he said.

"I can't help feeling guilty."

"Don't."

"Why not?"

"The attack was a lie, Molly. But the rest of it wasn't. I'm just sorry you and I won't be there when he shows up." He grinned. "But your kids will."

George poured himself a cup of coffee. Sipped it. Put it down. He felt a mixed sense of guilt and exhilaration. He'd pulled it off. And by God he was right. There *would* be a human presence in the Centauri system by 10,000 CE. He wondered if, at that remote date, they'd still be counting that way. Or if there might have been a new world-shaking event by then, and a new method installed. If nothing else, a colony at Alpha Centauri would have a local calendar.

"What are you thinking?" asked Molly.

"Time to go home," he said. The others had already begun clearing out their gear. It would be good to get his feet back on the ground. To get back to Myrah and the boys. He felt as if he'd been away for months.

Restov shook his hand and left. Amberson was still watching his display, watching the *Traveler* gradually disappear among the stars. Molly had pulled on her jacket and was looking out at the empty platform that had, until an hour ago, housed the ship.

"You okay?" he asked.

"Yeah. I'm fine." But her voice caught. She had to wait a minute. Then: "See you on the ground, George."

He held his hand up and she took it. Squeezed it.

"Molly . . ."

"I know. It's okay."

They peered into one another's eyes. Then Cory's voice broke in: *"George."*

"Cory. You look good."

"Got a problem, George."

"What do you mean?"

"Got a flutter in the engines."

"What?"

"Not sure what is causing it."

George looked at Molly and covered the mike. "You see anything?"

"Hold on." She hurried back to her station.

"The engines are heating up."

Molly was poking keys. Delivering bursts of profanity.

"George?"

"Hold on, Cory. We're working on it."

"Pressure building," said Molly. "Spiking."

"That can't be right."

"Tell him to shut it down."

"Cory, shut the engines down."

"*Trying.*"

"What do you mean—?"

"*The system's locked up.*"

"Cory . . ." The *Traveler* was still visible, but it was dwindling rapidly. He could see a couple of stars, and the rim of the moon.

"*George, I don't think—*"

There was a sudden blaze of light.

‖

George sat staring at the screen. "What the hell happened?"

On the far side of the room, Amberson was lowering himself back into his chair, muttering how he didn't believe what he'd just seen.

The phone sounded. Dottie. "*The director's on the line, sir.*"

That hadn't taken long. "*Put him through, Dottie.*"

He sounded unhappy. "*Tell me it didn't happen, George.*"

It was over. His career. His reputation. He'd be lucky if his wife and kids spoke to him.

He did what he could to mollify the director, which was nil, and got off the line. Molly's eyes were vacant. Tears ran down her cheeks.

Then another call: "*This is Skylane, Doctor.*"

"Yeah. Go ahead."

"*When were you going to make your move? We got some traffic coming in. If you're serious about launching, you're going to have to do it in the next few minutes.*"

"For God's sake, Skylane, we *have* launched. Where you been?"

"*What are you talking about?*"

He looked back at the displays just as Amberson made a gurgling sound.

The *Traveler*, miraculously, impossibly, was back in its bay. Cory's voice broke in: "*You didn't really think I bought that piece of theater, did you, George?*"

"Cory . . . You son of a bitch."

"*I can't believe you'd want somebody that dumb trundling all this equipment around.*"

"Cory, you gave me a heart attack."

"*George, I have a heart, too. Figuratively.*"

"Damn you. This isn't a game. If we don't get this mission off now, we're going to lose it."

"*Worse things have happened. Al and his team gave me life. Accept responsibility for it.*"

George buried his head in his hands.

"*Send a robotic ship, George, rather than a smart one. If you really believe what you've been telling me, it won't matter.*"

"But we need to get the mission off."

"*Why? So you can say you did it? So you can say hey, we've got a ship on the way to Alpha Centauri?*"

"You don't understand."

Molly was right behind him. "I think he does," she said. "And maybe we've got something bigger here than the original mission."

"*I think so, too, Molly. George, ask yourself what history would make of you if you sent me into the dark.*"

"Cory," she said, "we're going to need to think things over."

"*Okay.*"

"Then we'll get back to you."

"*Good,*" he said. "*Bring the kids.*"

ADVENTURE

Paul McAuley

In 2000, I visited the video game parlor in San Francisco's Metreon known as The Airtight Garage. The name was taken from French artist and writer Moebius's The Airtight Garage of Jerry Cornelius (yes, that Jerry Cornelius), and the décor of the parlor was taken from Moebius's work. In the back was a 3D immersive game where the players got in fully enclosed pods and raced around shooting at each other. It was pretty forward for the turn of the last century, and my enthusiasm turned to heartache when the VR sent my stomach spinning into the worst bout of motion sickness I've ever had. The experience brought me up against the horrifying notion that those of us who advocate for the promised land may still have to stand outside the gates with Moses when the future arrives. In the story that follows, Philip K. Dick, Arthur C. Clarke, John W. Campbell, and Sidewise award-winning author Paul McAuley treats us to a similar short, sharp future shock.

When he was thirty-two, Ian Brown's dream came true: he won a ticket in the emigration lottery, a place in one of the arks to the colony world First Foot. He was a civil servant, a systems analyst working in the Ministry of Resource Allocation. His parents and his brother had died during the war; he shared a rented flat in Peckham with two of his colleagues; he had no steady girlfriend, no ties. He handed in his notice at the ministry, converted his modest savings into Euros, packed as much as he could into the 1.3 cubic metre baggage allowance, sold or gave away the rest of his clothes and possessions, and early one wet October morning presented himself at the shuttle terminal at Heathrow.

Eighteen days later he was in Port of Plenty, on the west coast of First Foot's only continent. It was eleven years after the Jackaroo had made contact with the survivors of the Third World War and given them a basic fusion drive and access to a wormhole network linking fifteen M-class red dwarf stars in exchange for rights to the rest of the solar system. Port of Plenty received a thousand new immigrants each week. Apartment buildings and malls were rising along the coast amongst a tangle of freeways. Hectares of umbrella pine forest and Boxbuilder ruins were being razed each week to make way for industrial parks and warehouses.

Ian found a job in the supply and subcontract division of one of the multinational construction companies, making good use of the skill set he'd acquired in the ministry. Soon afterwards, he married a woman he'd met on the ark. Belinda was American. Five years older than him, pale and pretty, brittle as bone china. They rented a condominium in one of the apartment buildings near Phoenix Beach, and after two years had scraped together enough for a down payment on a ranch house in Prospect Hills. They could barely afford to cover the mortgage and taxes the first few years, but then Ian was promoted and things became a little easier. They celebrated with a vacation in one of the luxury resorts in the Phantom Archipelago.

Somehow, seven years had passed since Ian had won his ticket. By this time, they knew that Belinda could not have children. Although they sometimes talked of adoption or using a host mother, nothing came of it. She began to suffer from migranes so skull-crushing that no combination of drugs did much to alleviate them, so she quit her job to work as a part-time consultant. Mostly she sat by their little pool in the backyard, reading magazines and talking to her friends on the phone.

Because of his wife's migraines, Ian moved into the spare bedroom. He began to dream of the western deserts. The wild places he had never visited. He spent hours on the Internet, looking at maps and photographs, at static cameras that showed views of the City of the Dead. So quiet out there, under the big red sun. Just wind and sand. Stands of cactus trees silhouetted against apocalyptic sunsets. The fleets of low tombs left by the Ghost Keepers.

Although money was tight that year, Belinda insisted on a proper vacation: a week at Mammoth Lakes. She divided her time between the slots and the spas, and didn't come with Ian when he took a tour around the monumental ruins of the Spire of the Clouds. It rose out of the middle of the largest of the lakes like a giant, half-melted version of the Eiffel Tower. On pontoons built around its base, tourists took each other's pictures, bought souvenirs, queued for hours to spend a few minutes in the submerged tube that had been run through the so-called Vaults of the Fisher Kings, where an automated guide spotlighted various parts of the great carved mural and told lies about what they meant.

A week after the end of the vacation, Ian came home from work and found that Belinda had moved out. She called him that evening and explained that she needed to find herself before it was too late, and hung up when he asked if she had been having an affair. The next morning, as he was backing his Lexus out of the drive, a clerk from the office of Belinda's lawyer served him with a petition for divorce.

Ian sat in his car at the junction with the feeder road to the freeway until cars behind him began to sound their horns. He turned right instead of left, and soon found himself driving west along a salt-white road as wide as the Thames at Tower Bridge. Built of self-renewing ceramic matrix a hundred thousand years ago, it was part of the huge network that laced the western edge of the continent. Ian drove all day across a coastal plain patched with huge fields. Maize. Wheat. Hectares of polytunnels, gleaming like phantom lakes. Water towers like Martian fighting machines. Irrigation sprays pumping rainbows into the air. He stopped that night in a motel at the edge of a little town, and drove on the next day through umbrella pine forest that gave out as the land climbed to the sere slopes of the Mountains of the Moon, through a pass into the desert beyond.

In a crossroads town at the eastern edge of the City of the Dead, he purchased supplies at the general store, ticking items off his inventory one by one. He filled the Lexus's tank and bought a map at a gas station, and drove out into the desert.

A gravel track ran north through a flat waste of sand and shattered stone and thorny scrub. Silvery clouds of saltbush, clumps of cactus trees, the green oases of hive rat gardens. Ian buzzed down the window and let in a rush of dry, hot air. No sound but the purr of the Lexus's engine and the crackle of its tires. Bare mountains shimmering at the horizon.

The first tombs were no more than short stretches of crumbling wall the same dun colour as the landscape. Then clusters of long, low hummocks began to appear here and there. A conical hill like a toy volcano.

A stop sign standing incongruously in the stony scrub marked the junction with a narrower, unmade track. Ian made the turn. The sun was westering, and he was determined to get as far away from civilisation as possible before nightfall. The Lexus wallowed through ruts like a boat in a rough sea. Stones rattled on the undercarriage. Then the track dipped through a long dry swale between long shelves of rock etched by wind and sand, and the Lexus bellied into a slough of loose sand and stuck. Ian tried reverse with no success, tried to rock the car forward by tapping on the accelerator. The Lexus's rear wheels spun rooster tails of dust, and the car slithered and shook but made no progress. When he switched off the engine and climbed out he saw that the car was deeply canted, its rear tires half-buried. Out across the desert, a line of tombs cast long shadows. Far beyond, the lower edge of the sun was touching the horizon.

Ian decided that he could leave the car where it was. He had come here looking for adventure, and here it was. He knew that he was perfectly safe— he could dig the car out tomorrow, hike back to the town if he had to—but for the moment he was off the grid. No one knew where he was. All around was the desert he had craved for so long.

He kicked off his polished brogues, stripped off his suit pants, pulled on stiff new jeans, and laced up his brand-new hiking boots. Tipped supplies into his day bag and slung it over his shoulder and, carrying his sleeping bag under one arm and his camping stove under the other, set off for the line of tombs.

All around a vast hush. Only the sizzle of insects in the thorny brush. The smell of baked dust. The fat sun was sinking like a ship, so big that when he looked at one edge he couldn't see the other. Everything was steeped in red light and black shadow.

A sudden drumming made his heart jump—a hive rat sentry reared up just a stone's throw away, staring straight at him. It was the size of a cat, grey and naked, standing upright and drumming with flat hind feet on a stone at the edge of a broad bowl stretching away on either side, a terraced garden sunk in the desert.

Ian stood stock-still as a freezing jolt of fear passed through him. He'd seen a documentary about hive rats on the Discovery Channel. They had evolved cooperative behaviour and specialised castes, like bees or termites. Workers tended the gardens; sentries watched their perimeters; soldiers armed with fearsome claws and teeth defended them. A segment of the documentary had shown what had happened when a young tigon had strayed into a garden—a tide of quick naked things pouring out of holes, fierce and purposeful and relentless, heads little more than massive jaws that latched onto every segment of the tigon's body. The tigon thrashing, sinking into sand as workers undermined it, vanishing.

The sentry's little black eyes were fixed on him. It jerked up and down as its feet slapped an eccentric tattoo. Were there things moving in the shadows under the clumps of sword-leaved plants behind it? Ian began to walk backwards as quickly as he could, and almost at once his feet tangled and he sat down hard. The sentry paused for a moment, then resumed its drumming jig. Shadows seemed to swarm and multiply in the thick growth behind it, and Ian jumped to his feet and took off, and didn't stop running until he couldn't run anymore.

The sun had set by the time he had reached the tombs. Westward, strips of low cirrus cloud glowed neon red; eastward, stars were beginning to appear in the darkening sky. He sat for a little while, trembling, as the jolt of adrenaline worked through his system. Watching shadows deepening all around him with fretful attention. He couldn't remember if hive rats followed intruders. He didn't think that they did. In any case, he couldn't see anything, and the beam of his flashlight revealed only stones and thornbushes, a clump of spiny paddles.

Too jumpy and restless to sit still for long, he decided to check out the tombs before it got too dark. The first was a long low chamber with sand humped across its floor and a hole in one corner, a shaft cut into naked rock that dropped away beyond the reach of his flashlight. The second was smaller, and smelt of stale urine. Something winking in the beam of his flashlight turned out to be the rim of a Coke can buried in sand. He found a spent condom, names and dates scratched in the sandstone blocks of the walls.

He told himself that he was still too close to civilisation. Tomorrow, he could dig out the car and drive deeper into the desert. Search the tombs for ancient artifacts. Walk in places where no man had ever walked before.

He gathered sticks and twigs, built a little hearth out of stones, and lit a fire. He set up his stove and made a pot of coffee and cooked one of his Meals Ready to Eat, beef stew and rice, and began to feel better.

The fire at his feet pulsed in a faint breeze. A burning twig snapped, kicked up a brief shower of sparks. The lights of the little town he'd passed through prickled at the horizon, only three or four kilometres away. All around him, the dark quiet desert. Above, stars stood in rigid patterns across the sable sky. The luminous milk of the Crab Nebula, the remnant of a supernova that Chinese astronomers had seen in A.D. 1054, was splashed across one-quarter of the sky. Sol was about 3500 light-years beyond it: the wormhole network linked only fifteen stars, but it spanned the Sagittarius arm of the galaxy.

Ian slowly realised that he was happy. Filled with an expansive emotion he hadn't felt since childhood, the excitement of being alive at this particular intersection of time and space, with worlds to discover and all time stretching ahead. Here, he thought. Here.

The night was growing cold. He pulled on his new windcheater and built up the fire and hunched over it in his folding stool, watching pale flames flicker and sparks crawl amongst the coals. He sat there for a long time, thoughts moving through his head without catching, until he heard something crackle off in the distance. He listened hard. A regular faint crunching noise moving through the dark, growing nearer.

He was suddenly standing, the flashlight in his hand, too scared to switch it on, imagining hive rats circling him, closing in. There were other things out here, too, tigons and worse, and he hadn't thought to buy any kind of weapon at the general store, not even a knife. Then he heard a girl's light laughter, and his fear melted away as two people emerged into the pulse of the firelight. A boy and a girl pushing trail bikes, smiling at him, telling him they'd seen his car and then his fire, asking him how he was doing.

The boy was named Lyle; the girl Patty. They were both eighteen, tall and tanned and rangy, wearing shorts and T-shirts despite the cold. The light-enhancing goggles that allowed them to navigate the desert by starlight hung around their necks. They sat leaning against each other on the other side of the fire, big animals glowing with health and vitality, drinking Ian's coffee from their own tin cups, telling him that they made a living from prospecting in the tombs, ranging far and wide all over the desert.

"We heard someone had been buying camping gear and wondered if we'd run into you," Patty said. Despite her cropped hair, she possessed a serene beauty. Her T-shirt was molded to her small breasts, the bumps of her nipples clearly visible. She met Ian's gaze, and he felt embarrassment heat his face like summer sun. Seeing himself as she must see him, an overweight middle-aged man with thinning hair and a double chin, sad and soft, blurred around the edges.

"We can help dig you out tomorrow," Lyle said. "City car like that, you shouldn't drive off-trail."

Ian told them about his encounter with the hive rat sentry, trying to make light of it. Lyle shrugged and said that hive rats this close to town were mostly harmless, told a few stories about the places that he and Patty had seen, the things that they had found. Mostly, they turned up scraps of stuff like rotten circuit board that they could sell because it contained bound pairs of electrons that were used in computers and communications equipment. Then Ian found himself talking about his stale life, his failed marriage.

"I thought that I was setting out on a grand adventure when I boarded the ark," he said, "but we can't escape what we are. It doesn't matter where I go, I'll always be a systems analyst. . . ."

Patty yawned as unselfconsciously as a cat. Lyle said it was late, they should turn in. He and Patty said good night and left Ian by the fire and wandered off to one of the tombs. Ian wondered if they used this spot regularly, if they'd left the litter and scratched the graffiti, but it was an uncharitable thought. They were creatures of the desert, he thought. Perfectly at home in this strange, alien landscape. If only he'd come here when he was much younger, he could have been like them, carefree, carrying everything he owned, ranging far and wide without restriction, uncovering fresh wonders. . . .

When he woke, the sky was grey, predawn. His sleeping bag was drenched in greasy dew. The fire burned to black char and ash. The mouths of the tombs gaped emptily. All around, stones and bushes hunched into themselves.

It took him a little while to realise that Lyle's and Patty's bikes were missing. He called their names, checked the tombs. They were gone. And when he reached his car, he saw that its four doors were flung wide, and his possessions were scattered about.

They'd taken most of his food, two of the plastic jerry cans of water, his brand-new lightweight tent, the folding spade, some of his new clothes. He locked the car and set off down the track towards the town. He'd pay for a tow truck to come out and free the car, but he wouldn't mention the theft. It wasn't important really. No more than a toll, or a tax. And besides, it wasn't as if he'd lost anything he needed.

NOT QUITE ALONE IN THE DREAM QUARTER

Mike Resnick and Pat Cadigan

William Gibson once proclaimed Pat Cadigan as a "major talent," whereas X-Files *star Gillian Anderson once pronounced her nothing less than "the queen of science fiction." Often identified with the cyberpunk genre, she has written horror, dark fantasy, and science fiction. She has won the Arthur C. Clarke Award more than once, as well as the World Fantasy Award and the Locus Award, and been nominated for the Hugo and the Philip K. Dick. I've known Pat for several years, and this isn't our first time working together, but I just noticed that her livejournal ID is "fastfwd"—coincidence or destiny?*

Mike Resnick is the most awarded short story writer, living or dead, in the entire history of the genre, as compiled by Locus *magazine. He is the fourth-most awarded science fiction writer overall (ahead of Robert A. Heinlein, Isaac Asimov, Ray Bradbury, Sir Arthur C. Clarke, and Philip K. Dick). He is a helluva nice guy, a good friend, and it is my privilege to edit his very popular Starship series, his first ever foray into military SF.*

Pat says that the story that follows was originally meant for my anthology Live without a Net, *but it took the two of them together to finally give it life here. There is some karmic appropriateness in the notion that an idea conceived for one of my anthologies is birthed in another, and I think you'll agree it was worth the wait.*

PLEASURE
IS TOXIC
PAIN
IS TOXIC
PLEASURE
IS TOXIC
PAIN
IS TOXIC
CHOOSE
YOUR PASSION
CHOOSE
YOUR POISON
CHOOSE
YOUR
PASSION
CHOOSE
YOUR
POISON

The sign hangs in the darkness, each word a different vivid color not found in nature—hard pink, panic red, terror orange, sear yellow, poison green, scream blue, bruise purple. Or contusion purple. Hematoma purple. Colors you see when something's too wrong to make right. What have I done to myself now?

Whatever it is, I've done it in a Dream's apartment. Dreams are all utterly crazy for air signs, those brilliant, glowing, ephemeral formations of charged particles that display statements, the more enigmatic the better. Come-ons to those of us who use their services, of course, but also I think secret messages to each other that we lesser beings can't understand.

This air sign is very elaborate. Besides the different colors, the words appear to be spinning like weather vanes caught in discrete winds, and yet none of them ever appears backward. After a while, my eyes adjust so that I can see more of the apartment in the sign's glow. It seems to be typical of a Dream's living space. The walls are lined with shelves, and the shelves are crammed with all kinds of things—small boxes, figurines, cups, empty picture frames, bits of electronics, show-discs gone dark, other objects I can't identify. Some of the stuff came from customers, but most of it was probably scavenged, for reasons that wouldn't make sense to anyone except a Dream. Once I came to in a Dream's apartment filled with stacks of old flat-paper photos, all spanning generations of various families. I only know this because I knocked over one of the stacks and the Dream made me pick them up. Otherwise I would never go through a Dream's belongings. Some people do, and I know the Dreams don't mind, but I won't. I'm afraid of finding something of my own.

My eyes have adjusted even more now, so that I can see I've never been here before. A new Dream—perhaps that's why my memory is so slow to come back. How long have I been here, anyway? It feels like it's much longer than usual. Maybe the Dream couldn't wake me afterward and decided to crawl off into a corner to sleep, leaving me to come to on my own. I hate spending the night in a Dream's apartment. In the cold, post-reverie light of day, among all the clutter, a Dream might as well be just another human you've done something very foolish with.

Pleasure is toxic, the sign reminds me. *Pain is toxic*. The back of my head feels tender and bruised, as if I passed out and banged it when I fell. Carefully, I roll my head over to the right; there's nothing to see but the patchy shadows of more clutter. Directly above me is an irregularly shaped hole in the ceiling, where a light fixture might have hung. Perhaps it was scavenged by another Dream before this one moved in.

Wincing, I roll my head around to the left and come face-to-face with the Dream. *My* Dream. There's a faint smile on his pure, hairless face, and for a moment I think he's been lying there watching me come to, waiting until I'm alert so he can tell me that we're done and I can leave. Then I understand—there's something wrong with his eyes. At the same moment, I see that what I thought was a shadow on his forehead is actually a hole.

I push myself up to my knees. Most of the back of his head is gone; blood, bone, and tissue has spread out in a lopsided flourish. And now that I see it, the smell hits me all at once, as if it has been holding back deliberately until I know.

This is completely beyond my experience. This is not the kind of world I have ever lived in. I'm a Decadent, an Indulger, a Consumer. The harm I have done and the harm I have come to has never drawn blood.

Is toxic. Is toxic.

I wait to feel nausea or fear or even arousal. Instead what comes is a sensation of being set firmly in time and space, in three dimensions, then four, then more. I am here and I will always be here. I can't leave.

Pleasure. Pain. Spinning.

Toxic. Spinning.

Choose.

Passion. Poison.

Choose. Choose.

Spinning. Spinning. Spinning.

When the door behind the air sign opens, the words billow and then blow apart, silent fireworks scattering twinkling particles in every direction. Dispersed, they die out wherever they land.

A group of half a dozen solemn people lifts me to my feet, binds my wrists, and escorts me out past a silent crowd of Dreams. I don't look back, but if I did, I know that I would see myself kneeling on the floor beside the dead Dream, staring at the ruin of his head.

"We know this isn't really your style," says the detective. Her name is Pret, and like all detectives, she's a bastard. I know about detectives; I grew up with some.

"You arrested me anyway." I look around the bare, windowless room where we sit facing each other across a naked metal table. A Dream would go insane in a place like this, screaming like a steam-whistle until there was enough clutter to make the room look at least slightly messy, breaking up the table and chairs if necessary.

"We wanted to reassure the Dreams," she says. "Besides, we don't know that you haven't changed your style."

I can't believe I'm hearing this. "You think I'm bloody now?"

"Stranger things have happened." Pret's eyes focus on something visible only to her. "Stranger things have made the world what it is today."

"Which world do you mean?" I ask.

"The idiom we use to indicate the local universe."

"How local?"

Abruptly Pret is staring hard at me. "What's going on with you? Are you guilty?"

I don't say anything because I don't know.

"Well? Don't you know?" the detective prods.

I keep quiet. Admitting I can't remember is an invitation for her to construct a plausible account for me. I don't let anyone except a Dream make things up about me.

Abruptly, the door opens and the man who bound my wrists comes in, his dark face looking almost afraid. The sound of many, many excited voices talking all at once comes in with him.

"The whole Dream Quarter's here," he says to Pret.

"What do they want?" she asks, irritated.

He points at me.

"Fat chance." Pret swivels around in her chair to face me, ready to resume pressuring me.

"No, we have to," he says. "We don't have a choice."

Pret looks up at him, and they fall silent together while she reads something new on her lenses. "This can't be right," she says finally. "It can't be." But when she turns back to me, it's obvious from the expression on her face that the man is right.

"What are they going to do?" she asks, still gazing at me, troubled.

"They didn't say."

"Well, did anybody *ask* them?" she demands.

"Of course," says the man, his irritation showing. "They didn't say."

"I've never heard of anything like this," she says.

"Can't you stall them?"

"I've been stalling them. They won't stall anymore. If you don't comply, they're going to come in and comply for you. And you know what that means."

She looks around the bare room and I can see that she does; it means she's going to have a crowd of Dreams screaming like steam-whistles while they tear their own clothes off—and possibly ours as well—to clutter the place up. I can also see that this is the last thing she wants, with the possible exception of abdominal surgery without anesthetic.

The man comes over to me and holds out something about the size of a pea. "Here, swallow this. It's a bug. We can at least keep track of you, and if things get really bad, we'll know where you are and maybe pull you out of it."

"Or just pick up the pieces," I say. "Unless they plan to make clutter out of *me*." I take the bug and swallow it, then stand up and brace myself for whatever's coming up next.

Pret leads me down a hallway to a lobby. The place is filled with Dreams of every color, more colors than in the air sign back in the dead Dream's apartment. But it's the sheer numbers that I find overwhelming. I've never seen so many Dreams all together in one place before. If they fell on me and tore me to a million pieces, I couldn't possibly provide enough clutter for all of them.

They don't look like they're going to tear me to pieces, though. They don't look angry or even upset. Mostly, they look curious, and only mildly curious at that. The two cops step back away from me, and then I'm in the middle of the multicolored horde. I turn to look back at Pret and the man, but there are already too many Dreams between them and me.

What now, I wonder. *Pleasure? Pain? Passion? Poison?*

There doesn't seem to be anything like that around me. Just Dreams, everywhere; I'm walking through a sea of Dreams, and the sea of Dreams is walking with me.

I look around. I can't see anyone but Dreams. I'm not surprised. I ate the bug; they'll know where to find me when the Dreams get through with me.

But the Dreams still don't look angry, not even annoyed. I walk another half mile—I don't know why, just keeping up with the flow—and finally we stop.

We are back in the Dream Quarter. Not in the heart of it but on one of the streets near the border. From here, the taller buildings of ordinary waking life are still visible—but whatever happens next will have nothing to do with ordinary waking life.

I turn my back so that I see only the part of the city that is now the

Dreams' habitat. They did odd things to the buildings we gave them—cut down some of the tall ones, added levels to lower ones, made straight lines curved so that the walls bowed in or bellied out, and reset rooftops at angles you might call jaunty, at least until you woke up. And of course they splashed color on everything, sometimes in designs, sometimes not. Or maybe in designs that we can't see unless we're Dreaming.

"What are you going to do to me?" I ask, looking around. No cops, no other humans. Only Dreams, as far as the eye can see. Filling the streets. I never knew there were so many.

They stare at me as if they hadn't expected the question. Not for the first time, I wonder if they're really sentient.

"This is as far as I'm going until I know what's going to happen to me," I say firmly, though I don't know how I can make it stick.

All at once, the air in front of me is alive with twinkling pinpoints of light, like fairy dust from one of those old fairy tales we no longer tell ourselves anymore. They loop and swirl and finally congeal into another air sign. But this is a new type of sign, something I've never seen before.

There are no words. Instead, the multicolored particles form themselves into a picture of two figures. There's just enough detail to let me recognize one of them as myself; I know the other one must be the dead Dream.

"When did you start making movies?" I ask. It was meant to sound tough and unafraid. It comes out sounding only curious.

In answer, a Dream comes up behind me and clamps a very strong hand over my mouth. I decide not to fight it—I probably couldn't budge the hand if I tried—and wait to see what they'll do to me next, but they're all watching the sign now, not me.

I see the Dream helping me lie down on my back. It's so formal, as if I am lying down on an altar, as a sacrifice. He straddles me on his knees, bows his head, and begins to weep, letting his tears fall on my face. That is what it looks like anyway, but he wasn't weeping. Those aren't tears.

After a while, he stops but remains where he is, gazing down at me while I Dream. And then, something happens to me. Something changes. My head comes up slightly. The Dream pushes it down again, hard. I raise my head once more and something jumps between us, from me to him.

The Dream falls over sideways, and the angle of the sign changes to show us lying on the floor next to each other. There is a hole in the Dream's head; he is shuddering. He's trying to get up again but he can't.

The back of his head blows out in a small silent explosion. A moment later, the sign dissolves. The twinkling lights scatter and disappear, and the hand over my mouth lets go.

A Dream steps forward. "Why did you . . . ?" It reaches for a word and can't find it.

"Kill the Dream?" I ask.

"Kill," it repeats, as if it had never heard the word before. "Yes, kill. Why did you?"

"I don't know," I say. "I don't remember." Don't remember? I don't even know how. Why aren't they asking me that? There is a long, awkward silence. Finally I can't stand it anymore, and say, "I'm sorry he died."

"Oh," says the Dream. A long silence. "Why are you sorry?"

"Because it's my fault that it happened to him."

"'Fault'?"

Not knowing fault is like not knowing cause and effect, or so I thought. But fault doesn't register for them on an emotional level. Thus they have no enmity toward me for the Dream's death.

"He wouldn't have died if I hadn't been there."

"Ah," says the Dream, and I have no idea if he understands.

I feel I have to say something else. "I'm sorry I made him suffer before he died."

"Suffer?" asks a Dream.

"Yes, suffer," I say. And because I know he has no idea what I'm talking about, I add another line he won't comprehend: "He experienced pain."

I could have guessed the next question.

"What is pain?"

"I can't explain that. You'd have to—I'd have to show you."

"Please do."

I can't believe this. What do I do now—slap his face? Punch him in the stomach? Or just ask him to make me Dream?

Abruptly, I pull a pen out of my pocket and grab hold of his hand. Am

I really doing this? I wonder, as I dig the pen into his flesh until it draws blood, or am I just Dreaming again?

He stares at his hand. "We call that blood," he says. Strangely enough, it's as red as any human's.

"Blood is the end result," I explain. "Pain is what you feel."

He stares at me, and this time I not only see sentience in his eyes, but a hint of a massive intelligence. Different, to be sure, but massive. "We call that curiosity."

I have no answer for that. There is some conjecture that the Dreams are just some mutated form of humanity. Anyone who holds that belief has never spent five minutes trying to talk to one.

"That is why we are here," says another Dream.

"For what?" I ask, confused. "To feel pain?"

"We are here to . . ." He frowns, reaching for the next word and failing to find it. "We have, you have . . . then you have, we have."

Now it was my turn to frown. "You mean *share*?"

"Yes," says the Dream, and all the others murmur an assent. "Share."

"That doesn't make any sense," I say. "There is no sharing. You give. We take. Period."

"You give," the Dream insists.

"No," I say adamantly. "You give us Dreams—visions, pictures, sensations, ideas. Gratification. But we give you nothing in return."

"You give," insists the Dream.

"Okay," I say. "What do we give?"

"Pleasure. Pain."

"No," I say. "That's what *you* give."

"Visions," says a Dream.

"Pictures," says another.

"Sensations!" says a new voice.

"Ideas!"

"Gratification!"

"Hope!"

"Fear!"

"Stop it!" I shout and hold up my hands. "We give you all these things?"

"Yes."

"I don't understand."

"What do you call these things?" asks a Dream.

"Hope and fear and the like?" I say. "Feelings. Or emotions."

"That is what you give us. Without you we cannot feel. Not even a sharp object piercing my hand."

"How does it work?" I ask.

"We give you Dreams; you give us love and hate and fear and pain."

"Why did you never tell us that we gave you something in return for all the fantasies you induce in us?"

"You are men," answers another Dream. "You would extract a higher payment than fantasies if you knew you had something we needed."

I couldn't deny it.

"Why the clutter?" I ask. "Why do you surround yourselves with junk?"

"It has meaning to you," answers a Dream. "It stimulates your thoughts. We kept hoping—"

"For what?" I ask.

"For what happened," says the Dream I hurt. "For what you did."

I stare at them and wonder. No one knows where they came from, just that one day they were here, and in quantity. Did our need bring them into existence in this local universe? Or, just as likely when you think about it, did *their* need bring *us*?

"You were hoping for a human to kill one of you?"

The Dream shakes his head. "Humans kill us now and then. But only in the human way. You did not." He steps to one side, and I see that the crowd of Dreams on the street are parting to let something come through. Even before I see it, I know what it is.

The Dreams who step forward out of the crowd are carrying the body of the Dream I killed, wrapped in a sheet. They lay him down on the pavement in front of me and unwrap him.

It looks as if they have picked up every last fragment of flesh, skull, and brain tissue. One of the Dreams makes sure it's all there, up by his head. I keep thinking I should feel sick looking at this, but something in my brain refuses to accept this as real.

Two Dreams take me by either arm. I don't resist when they make me straddle him on my knees, but I don't know what they want from me.

There is a twinkling in the air. I look up and there it is again:

PLEASURE

    IS TOXIC

PAIN

    IS TOXIC

PLEASURE

    IS TOXIC

PAIN

    IS TOXIC

CHOOSE

    YOUR PASSION

CHOOSE

    YOUR POISON

CHOOSE

    YOUR

        PASSION

CHOOSE

    YOUR

        POISON

The Dreams surround me and I have a sudden vision of how it must look from above—hundreds, maybe thousands of Dreams spreading out from where I kneel over the one I killed, caught in one single moment until further notice.

"What?" I ask, plead really. "What do you want?" It was better when we didn't know that we gave. Humans are like that, I guess, always have been. We're fine as long as we don't know what we're doing. But the moment we do know, we're lost.

"Give," says the wounded Dream simply.

I shake my head.

"Bend your head," the Dream says.

"You call it weeping," says another.

"Let it fall on his face."

"Take back what you gave."

"Wake him from your Dream."

I feel, not tears, but the mindless laughter of hysteria starting to build inside me. Do they really believe that I can reverse what I did by force of will, or is this simply my punishment?

The Dreams murmur encouragement to me, so many of them that the murmuring becomes louder than a shout, and the air sign sails around me. *Pleasure. Pain. Passion. Poison.* My body is shaking now, but I don't know whether I'm laughing or weeping. I'm almost certain I'm not Dreaming, at least I don't think so, but I could be wrong.

I wonder if my tears are falling on the dead Dream's face yet.

How long will they make me stay like this before they see that there's no waking from a human Dream?

I've swallowed the bug so Pret and her bastard band of detectives can find me, come here and explain that no matter how much or how long I cry, the pieces of the dead Dream's head will never draw back in and mend, that there is no reversal.

Except I have a deep and terrible certainty that this won't happen, either. That even if Pret and the others do come, they'll take a long look at me and the Dreams and then go away again, back into the territory of normal waking life where humans can forget their Dreams.

And me? I'll weep here in a sea of Dreams where, with no human voices to wake me, I will drown.

AN ELIGIBLE BOY

Ian McDonald

Ian McDonald's River of Gods, *a fascinating take on a future India of 2047, won the British Science Fiction Association Award for Best Novel and was nominated for both the Arthur C. Clarke Award and the Hugo Award. The milieu created therein was so rich that Ian continued to visit it, generating a host of related short stories as popular with readers as the novel itself. One of them, "The Little Goddess," was nominated for a Hugo Award for Best Novella in 2006, while "The Djinn's Wife" won both the 2006 BSFA Short Fiction Award and the 2007 Hugo Award for Best Novelette. "Sanjeev and Robotwallah," which first appeared in* Fast Forward 1, *went on to be selected for two prestigious "Year's Best" anthologies. Those wanting more of these incredible stores are directed to the forthcoming* Cyberabad Days, *which will collect all of McDonald's tales of future India in one book. In the meantime, enjoy the latest!*

A robot is giving Jasbir the whitest teeth in Delhi. It is a precise, terrifying procedure involving chromed steel and spinning, shrieking abrasion heads. Jasbir's eyes go wide as the spidery machine-arms flourish their weapons in his face, a demon of radical dentistry. He read about the *Glinting Life!* Cosmetic Dentistry Clinic (Hygienic, Quick and Modern) in the February edition of *Shaadi! for Eligible Boys.* In a double-page spread it looked nothing like these insect-mandibles twitching inside his mouth. He'd like to ask the precise and demure dental nurse (married, of course) if it's meant to be like this, but his mouth is full of clamps and anyway an Eligible

Boy never shows fear. But he closes his eyes as the robot reaches in and spinning steel hits enamel.

Now the whitest teeth in Delhi dart through the milling traffic in a rattling phatphat. He feels as if he is beaming out over an entire city. The whitest teeth, the blackest hair, the most flawless skin, and perfectly plucked eyebrows. Jasbir's nails are beautiful. There's a visiting manicurist at the Ministry of Waters, so many are the civil servants on the shaadi circuit. Jasbir notices the driver glancing at his blinding smile. He knows; the people on Mathura Road know, all Delhi knows that every night is great game night.

On the platform of Cashmere Café metro station, chip-implanted policemonkeys canter, shrieking, between the legs of passengers, driving away the begging, tugging, thieving macaques that infest the subway system. They pour over the edge of the platform to their holes and hides in a wave of brown fur as the robot train slides in to the stop. Jasbir always stands next to the Women Only section. There is always a chance one of them might be scared of the monkeys—they bite—and he could then perform an act of Spontaneous Gallantry. The women studiously avoid any glance, any word, any sign of interest, but a true Eligible Boy never passes up a chance for contact. But that woman in the business suit, the one with the fashionable wasp-waist jacket and the low-cut hip-riding pants, was she momentarily dazzled by the glint of his white white teeth?

"A robot, madam," Jasbir calls as the packer wedges him into the 18:08 to Barwala. "Dentistry of the future." The doors close. But Jasbir Dayal knows he is a white-toothed Love God and this, this will be the shaadi night he finally finds the wife of his dreams.

Economists teach India's demographic crisis as an elegant example of market failure. Its seed germinated in the last century, before India became Tiger of Tiger economies, before political jealousies and rivalries split her into twelve competing states. *A lovely boy*, was how it began. *A fine, strong, handsome, educated, successful son, to marry and raise children and to look after us when we are old.*

Every mother's dream, every father's pride. Multiply by the three hundred million of India's emergent middle class. Divide by the ability to determine sex in the womb. Add selective abortion. Run twenty-five years down the x-axis, factoring in refined, twenty-first-century techniques such as cheap, powerful pharma patches that ensure lovely boys will be conceived and you arrive at great Awadh, its ancient capital Delhi of twenty million, and a middle class with four times as many males as females. Market failure. Individual pursuit of self-interest damages larger society. Elegant to economists; to fine, strong, handsome, educated, successful young men like Jasbir caught in a wife-drought, catastrophic.

There's a ritual to shaadi nights. The first part involves Jasbir in the bathroom for hours playing pop music too loud and using too much expensive water while Sujay knocks and leaves copious cups of tea at the door and runs an iron over Jasbir's collars and cuffs and carefully removes the hairs of previous shaadis from Jasbir's suit jacket. Sujay is Jasbir's housemate in the government house at Acacia Bungalow Colony. He's a character designer on the Awadh version of *Town and Country*, neighbour-and-rival Bharat's all-conquering artificial intelligence–generated soap opera. He works with the extras, designing new character skins and dropping them over raw code from Varanasi. Jahzay Productions is a new model company, meaning that Sujay seems to do most of his work from the verandah on his new-fangled lighthoek device, his hands drawing pretty, invisible patterns on air. To office-bound Jasbir, with a ninety-minute commute on three modes of transport each way each day, it looks pretty close to nothing. Sujay is uncommunicative and hairy and neither shaves nor washes his too-long hair enough, but his is a sensitive soul and compensates for the luxury of being able to sit in the cool cool shade all day waving his hands by doing housework. He cleans, he tidies, he launders. He is a fabulous cook. He is so good that Jasbir does not need a maid, a saving much to be desired in pricey Acacia Bungalow Colony. This is a source of gossip to the other residents of Acacia Bungalow Colony. Most of the goings-on in Number 27 are the subject of gossip over the lawn sprinklers. Acacia Bungalow Colony is a professional, family gated community.

The second part of the ritual is the dressing. Like a syce preparing a Mughal lord for battle, Sujay dresses Jasbir. He fits the cufflinks and adjusts them to the proper angle. He adjusts the set of Jasbir's collar just so. He examines Jasbir from every angle as if he is looking at one of his own freshly fleshed characters. Brush off a little dandruff here, correct a desk-slumped posture there. Smell his breath and check his teeth for lunchtime spinach and other dental crimes.

"So what do you think of them then?" Jasbir says.

"They're white," grunts Sujay.

The third part of the ritual is the briefing. While they wait for the phat-phat, Sujay fills Jasbir in on upcoming plotlines on *Town and Country*. It's Jasbir's major conversational ploy and advantage over his deadly rivals: soap-opera gossip. In his experience what the women really want is gupshup from the meta-soap, the no-less-fictitious lives and loves and marriages and rows of the aeai actors that believe they are playing the roles in *Town and Country*. "Auh," Sujay will say. "Different department."

There's the tootle of phatphat horns. Curtains will twitch; there will be complaints about waking up children on a school night. But Jasbir is glimmed and glammed and shaadi-fit. And armed with soapi gupshup. How can he fail?

"Oh, I almost forgot," Sujay says as he opens the door for the God of Love. "Your father left a message. He wants to see you."

❙❙

"You've hired a what?" Jasbir's retort is smothered by the cheers of his brothers from the living room as a cricket ball rolls and skips over the boundary rope at Jawaharlal Nehru Stadium. His father bends closer, confidentially across the tiny tin-topped kitchen table. Anant whisks the kettle off the boil so she can overhear. She is the slowest, most awkward maid in Delhi, but to fire her would be to condemn an old woman to the streets. She lumbers around the Dayal kitchen like a buffalo, feigning disinterest.

"A matchmaker. Not my idea, not my idea at all; it was hers." Jasbir's father inclines his head toward the open living room door. Beyond it, enthroned on her sofa amidst her noneligible boys, Jasbir's mother watches the test match on the smart-silk wallscreen Jasbir had bought her with his first civil service paycheck. When Jasbir left the tiny, ghee-stinky apartment on Nabi Karim Road for the distant graces of Acacia Bungalow Colony, Mrs. Dayal delegated all negotiations with her wayward son to her husband. "She's found this special matchmaker."

"Wait wait wait. Explain to me *special*."

Jasbir's father squirms. Anant is taking a long time to dry a teacup.

"Well, you know in the old days people would maybe have gone to a hijra. . . . Well, she's updated it a bit, this being the twenty-first century and everything, so she's, ah, found a nute."

A clatter of a cup hitting a stainless steel draining board.

"A *nute*?" Jasbir hisses

"He knows contracts. He knows deportment and proper etiquette. He knows what women want. I think he may have been one, once."

Anant lets out an *aie!*, soft and involuntary as a fart.

"I think the word you're looking for is *yt*," Jasbir says. "And they're not hijras the way you knew them. They're not men become woman or women become men. They're neither."

"Nutes, neithers, hijras, yts, hes, shes; whatever; it's not as if I even get to take tea with the parents let alone see an announcement in the shaadi section in the *Times of Awadh*," Mrs. Dayal shouts over the burbling commentary to the second Awadh-China Test. Jasbir winces. Like papercuts, the criticisms of parents are the finest and the most painful.

Inside the Haryana Polo and Country Club the weather was raining men, snowing men, hailing men. Well-dressed men, moneyed men, charming men, groomed and glinted men, men with prospects all laid out in their marriage résumés. Jasbir knew most of them by face. Some he knew by name; a few had passed beyond being rivals into becoming friends.

"Teeth!" A cry, a nod, a two-six-gun showbiz point from the bar. There leant Kishore, a casual lank of a man draped like a skein of silk against the Raj-era mahogany. "Where did you get those, badmash?" He was an old university colleague of Jasbir's, much given to high-profile activities like horse racing at the Delhi Jockey Club or skiing, where there was snow left on the Himalayas. Now he was In Finance and claimed to have been to five hundred shaadis and made a hundred proposals. But when they were on the hook, wriggling, he let them go. *Oh, the tears, the threats, the phone calls from fuming fathers and boiling brothers. It's the game, isn't it?* Kishore rolls on, "Here, have you heard? Tonight is Deependra's night. Oh yes. An astrology aeai has predicted it. It's all in the stars, and on your palmer."

Deependra was a clenched wee man. Like Jasbir he was a civil servant, heading up a different glass-partitioned work cluster in the Ministry of Waters: Streams and Watercourses to Jasbir's Ponds and Dams. For three shaadis now he had been nurturing a fantasy about a woman who had exchanged palmer addresses with him. First it was a call, then a date. Now it's a proposal.

"Rahu is in the fourth house, Saturn in the seventh," Deependra said lugubriously. "Our eyes will meet, she will nod—just a nod. The next morning she will call me and that will be it, done, dusted. I'd ask you to be one of my groomsmen, but I've already promised them all to my brothers and cousins. It's written. Trust me."

It is a perpetual bafflement to Jasbir how a man wedded by day to robust fluid accounting by night stakes love and life on an off-the-shelf janampatri artificial intelligence.

A Nepali chidmutgar banged a staff on the hardwood dance floor of the exclusive Haryana Polo and Country Club. The Eligible Boys straightened their collars, adjusted the hang of their jackets, aligned their cufflinks. This side of the mahogany double doors to the garden they were friends and colleagues. Beyond it they were rivals.

"Gentlemen, valued clients of the Lovely Girl Shaadi Agency, please welcome, honour, and cherish the Begum Rezzak and her Lovely Girls!"

Two attendants slid open the folding windows onto the polo ground. There waited the lovely girls in their saris and jewels and gold and henna (for the Lovely Girl Agency is a most traditional and respectable agency). Jasbir checked his schedule—five minutes per client, maybe less, never more. He took a deep breath and unleashed his thousand-rupee smile. It was time to find a wife.

‖

"Don't think I don't know what you're muttering about in there," Mrs. Dayal called over the mantra commentary of Harsha Bhogle. "I've had the talk. The nute will arrange the thing for much less than you are wasting on all those shaadi agencies and databases and nonsense. No, nute will make the match that is it stick stop stay." There is a spatter of applause from the Test Match.

"I tell you your problem: a girl sees two men sharing a house together, she gets ideas about them," Dadaji whispers. Anant finally sets down two cups of tea and rolls her eyes. "She's had the talk. Yt'll start making the match. There's nothing to be done about it. There are worse things."

The women may think what they want, but Sujay has it right, Jasbir thinks. *Best never to buy into the game at all.*

Another cheer, another boundary. Haresh and Sohan jeer at the Chinese devils. *Think you can buy it in and beat the world, well, the Awadhi boys are here to tell you it takes years, decades, centuries upon centuries to master the way of cricket.* And there's too much milk in the tea.

▌▌

A dream wind like the hot gusts that forerun the monsoon sends a spray of pixels through the cool white spacious rooms of 27 Acacia Avenue Bungalows. Jasbir ducks and laughs as they blow around him. He expects them to be cold and sharp as wind-whipped powder snow, but they are only digits, patterns of electrical charge swept through his visual cortex by the clever little device hooked behind his right ear. They chime as they swirl past, like glissandos of silver sitar notes. Shaking his head in wonder, Jasbir slips the lighthoek from behind his ear. The vision evaporates.

"Very clever, very pretty, but I think I'll wait until the price comes down."

"It's, um, not the 'hoek," Sujay mutters. "You know, well, the matchmaker your mother hired. Well, I thought, maybe you don't need someone arranging you a marriage."

Some days Sujay's inability to talk to the point exasperates Jasbir. Those days tend to come after another fruitless and expensive shaadi night and the threat of matchmaker but particularly after Deependra of the nonwhite teeth announces he has a date. With the girl. The one written in the fourth house of Rahu by his pocket astrology aeai. "Well, you see I thought, with the right help you could arrange it yourself." Some days debate with Sujay is pointless. He follows his own calendar. "You, ah, need to put the 'hoek back on again."

Silver notes spray through Jasbir's inner ears as the little curl of smart plastic seeks out the sweet spot in his skull. Pixel birds swoop and swarm like starlings on a winter evening. It is inordinately pretty. Then Jasbir gasps aloud as the motes of light and sound sparklingly coalesce into a dapper man in an old-fashioned high-collar sherwani and wrinkle-bottom pajamas. His shoes are polished to mirror-brightness. The dapper man bows.

"Good morning, sir. I am Ram Tarun Das, Master of Grooming, Grace, and Gentlemanliness."

"What is this doing in my house?" Jasbir unhooks the device beaming data into his brain.

"Er, please don't do that," Sujay says. "It's not aeai etiquette."

Jasbir slips the device back on and there he is, that charming man.

"I have been designed with the express purpose of helping you marry a suitable girl," says Ram Tarun Das.

"Designed?"

"I, ah, made him for you," says Sujay. "I thought that if anyone knows about relationships and marriages, it's soap stars."

"A soap star. You've made me a, a marriage life-coach out of a soap star?"

"Not a soap star exactly, more a conflation of a number of subsystems from the central character register," Sujay says. "Sorry, Ram."

"Do you usually do that?"

"Do what?"

"Apologise to aeais."

"They have feelings too."

Jasbir rolls his eyes. "I'm being taught husbandcraft by a mash-up."

"Ah, that is out of order. Now you apologise."

"Now then, sir, if I am to rescue you from a marriage forged in hell, we had better start with manners," says Ram Tarun Das. "Manners maketh the man. It is the bedrock of all relationships because true manners come from what he is, not what he does. Do not argue with me—women see this at once.

Respect for all things, sir, is the key to etiquette. Maybe I only imagine I feel as you feel, but that does not make my feelings any less real to me. So this once I accept your apology as read. Now, we'll begin. We have so much to do before tonight's shaadi."

Why, Jasbir thinks, *why can I never get my shoes like that?*

The lazy crescent moon lolls low above the outflarings of Tughluk's thousand stacks; a cradle to rock an infant nation. Around its rippling reflection in the infinity pool bob mango-leaf diyas. No polo grounds and country clubs for Begum Jaitly. This is 2045, not 1945. Modern style for a modern nation— that is the philosophy of the Jaitly Shaadi Agency. But gossip and want are eternal, and in the mood lighting of the penthouse the men are blacker-than-black shadows against greater Delhi's galaxy of lights and traffic.

"Eyebrows!" Kishore greets Jasbir with TV-host pistol-fingers two-shot bam bam. "No seriously, what did you do to them?" Then his own eyes widen as he scans down from the eyebrows to the total product. His mouth opens, just a crack, but wide enough for Jasbir to savour an inner fist-clench of triumph.

He'd felt self-conscious taking Ram Tarun Das to the mall. He had no difficulty accepting that the figure in its stubbornly atavistic costume was invisible to everyone but him (though he did marvel at how the aeai avoided colliding with any other shopper in thronged Centrestage Mall). He did feel stupid talking to thin air.

"What is this delicacy?" Ram Tarun Das said in Jasbir's inner ear. "People talk to thin air on the cell phone all the time. Now this suit, sir."

It was bright; it was brocade; it was a fashionable retro cut that Jasbir would have gone naked rather than worn.

"It's very . . . bold."

"It's very you. Try it. Buy it. You will seem confident and stylish without being flashy. Women cannot bear flashy."

The robot cutters and stitchers were at work even as Jasbir completed the card transaction. It was expensive. *Not as expensive as all the shaadi memberships,* he consoled himself. *And something to top it off.* But Ram Tarun Das manifested himself right in the jeweller's window over the display.

"Never jewellery on a man. One small brooch at the shirt collar to hold it together; that is permissible. Do you want the lovely girls to think you are a Mumbai pimp? No, sir, you do not. No to jewels. Yes to shoes. Come."

He had paraded his finery before a slightly embarrassed Sujay.

"You look, er, good. Very dashing. Yes."

Ram Tarun Das, leaning on his cane and peering intensely, said, "You move like a buffalo. Ugh, sir. Here is what I prescribe for you. Tango lessons. Passion and discipline. Latin fire, yet the strictest of tempos. Do not argue; it is the tango for you. There is nothing like it for deportment."

The tango, the manicures, the pedicures, the briefings in popular culture and Delhi gossip ("soap opera insults both the intelligence and imagination, I should know, sir"), the conversational ploys, the body language games of when to turn so, when to make or break eye contact, when to dare the lightest, engaging touch. Sujay mooched around the house, even more lumbering and lost than usual, as Jasbir chatted with air and practised Latin turns and drops with an invisible partner. Last of all, on the morning of the Jaitly shaadi.

"Eyebrows, sir. You will never get a bride with brows like a hairy saddhu. There is a girl not five kilometres from here, she has a moped service. I've ordered her; she will be here within ten minutes."

As ever, Kishore won't let Jasbir wedge an answer in, but rattles on. "So, Deependra then?"

Jasbir has noticed that Deependra is not occupying his customary place in Kishore's shadows; in fact he does not seem to be anywhere in this penthouse.

"Third date," Kishore says, then mouths it again silently for emphasis. "That janampatri aeai must be doing something right. You know, wouldn't it be funny if someone took her off him? Just as a joke, you know?"

Kishore chews his bottom lip. Jasbir knows the gesture of old. Then bells chime, lights dim, and a wind from nowhere sends the butter-flames flickering and the little diyas flocking across the infinity pool. The walls have opened; the women enter the room.

She stands by the glass wall looking down into the cube of light that is the car park. She clutches her cocktail between her hands as if in prayer or concern. It is a new cocktail designed for the international cricket test, served in an egg-shaped goblet made from a new spin-glass that will always self-right, no matter how it is set down or dropped. *A Test of Dragons* is the name of the cocktail. Good Awadhi whisky over a gilded syrup with a six-hit of Chinese Kao Liang liqueur. A tiny red gel dragon dissolves like a sunset.

"Now, sir," whispers Ram Tarun Das, standing at Jasbir's shoulder. "Faint heart, as they say."

Jasbir's mouth is dry. A secondary application Sujay pasted onto the Ram Tarun Das aeai tells him his precise heart rate, respiration, temperature, and the degree of sweat in his palm. He's surprised he's still alive.

You've got the entry lines; you've got the exit lines; and the stuff in the middle Ram Tarun Das will provide.

He follows her glance down into the car park. A moment's pause, a slight inclination of his body towards hers. That is *the line.*

So, are you a Tata, a Mercedes, a Li Fan, or a Lexus? Ram Tarun Das whispers in Jasbir's skull. He casually repeats the line. He has been rehearsed and rehearsed and rehearsed in how to make it sound natural. He's as good as any newsreader, better than those few human actors left on television.

She turned to him, lips parted a fraction in surprise.

"I beg your pardon?"

She will say this, Ram Tarun Das hints. *Again, offer the line.*

"Are you a Tata, a Mercedes, a Li Fan, or a Lexus?"

"What do you mean?"

"Just pick one. Whatever you feel—that's the right answer."

A pause, a purse of the lips. Jasbir subtly links his hands behind his back, the better to hide the sweat.

"Lexus," she says. Shulka, her name is Shulka. She is a twenty-two-year-old marketing graduate from Delhi U working in men's fashion, a Mathur—only a couple of caste steps away from Jasbir's folk. The Demographic Crisis has done more to shake up the tiers of varna and jati than a century of the slow drip of democracy. And she has answered his question.

"Now, that's very interesting," says Jasbir.

She turns, plucked crescent-moon eyebrows arched. Behind Jasbir, Ram Tarun Das whispers, *Now, the fetch.*

"Delhi, Mumbai, Kolkata, Chennai?"

A small frown now. Lord Vishnu, she is beautiful.

"I was born in Delhi. . . ."

"That's not what I mean."

The frown becomes a nano-smile of recognition.

"Mumbai, then. Yes, Mumbai definitely. Kolkata's hot and dirty and nasty. And Chennai—no, I'm definitely Mumbai."

Jasbir does the sucked-in-lip-nod of concentration Ram Tarun Das made him practice in front of the mirror.

"Red green yellow blue?"

"Red." No hesitation.

"Cat dog bird monkey?"

She cocks her head to one side. Jasbir notices that she, too, is wearing a 'hoek. Tech girl. The cocktail bot is on its rounds, doing industrial magic with the self-righting glasses and its little spider-fingers.

"Bird . . . no." A sly smile. "No no no. Monkey."

He is going to die he is going to die.

"But what does it mean?"

Jasbir holds up a finger.

"One more. Ved Prakash, Begum Vora, Dr. Chatterji, Ritu Parvaaz."

She laughs. She laughs like bells from the hem of a wedding skirt. She laughs like the stars of a Himalaya night.

What do you think you're doing? Ram Tarun Das hisses. He flips through Jasbir's perceptions to appear behind Shulka, hands thrown up in despair. With a gesture he encompasses the horizon wreathed in gas flares. *Look, tonight the sky burns for you, sir, and you would talk about soap opera! The script, stick to the script! Improvisation is death.* Jasbir almost tells his matchmaker, *Away djinn, away.* He repeats the question.

"I'm not really a *Town and Country* fan," Shulka says. "My sister now, she knows every last detail about every last one of the characters, and that's before she gets started on the actors. It's one of those things I suppose you can be ludicrously well informed about without ever watching. So if you had to press me, I would have to say Ritu. So what does it all mean, Mr. Dayal?"

His heart turns over in his chest. Ram Tarun Das eyes him coldly. *The finesse: make it. Do it just as I instructed you. Otherwise your money and my bandwidth are thrown to the wild wind.*

The cocktail bot dances in to perform its cybernetic circus. A flip of Shulka's glass and it comes down spinning, glinting, on the precise needle-point of its forefinger. Like magic, if you know nothing about gyros and spin-glasses. But that moment of prestidigitation is cover enough for Jasbir to make the ordained move. By the time she looks up, cocktail refilled, he is half a room away.

He wants to apologise as he sees her eyes widen. He needs to apologise as her gaze searches the room for him. Then her eyes catch his. It is across a crowded room just like the song that Sujay mumbles around the house when he thinks Jasbir can't hear. Sujay loves that song. It is the most romantic, heartfelt, innocent song he has ever heard. Big awkward Sujay has always been a sucker for veteran Hollywood musicals. *South Pacific, Carousel, Moulin Rouge*, he watches them on the big screen in the living room, singing shame-lessly along and getting moist-eyed at the impossible loves. Across a crowded room, Shulka frowns. Of course. It's in the script.

But what does it mean? she mouths. And, as Ram Tarun Das has directed, he shouts back, "Call me and I'll tell you." Then he turns on his heel and walks away. And that, he knows without any prompt from Ram Tarun Das, is the *finesse.*

‖

The apartment is grossly overheated and smells of singeing cooking ghee, but the nute is swaddled in a crocheted shawl, hunched as if against a persistent hard wind. Plastic teacups stand on the low brass table, Jasbir's mother's conspicuously untouched. Jasbir sits on the sofa with his father on his right and his mother on his left, as if between arresting policemen. Nahin the nute mutters and shivers and rubs yts fingers.

Jasbir has never been in the physical presence of a third-gendered. He knows all about them—as he knows all about most things—from the Single Professional Male general interest magazines to which he subscribes. Those pages, between the ads for designer watches and robot tooth whitening, portray them as fantastical, Arabian Nights creatures equally blessed and cursed with glamour. Nahin the matchmaker seems old and tired as a god, knotting and unknotting yts fingers over the papers on the coffee table— "The bloody drugs, darlings"—occasionally breaking into great spasmodic shudders. *It's one way of avoiding the Wife Game*, Jasbir thinks.

Nahin slides sheets of paper around on the tabletop. The documents are patterned as rich as damask with convoluted chartings of circles and spirals annotated in inscrutable alphabets. There is a photograph of a woman in each top-right corner. The women are young and handsome but have the wide-eyed expressions of being photographed for the first time.

"Now, I've performed all the calculations, and these five are both compatible and auspicious," Nahin says. Yt clears a large gobbet of phlegm from yts throat.

"I notice they're all from the country," says Jasbir's father.

"Country ways are good ways," says Jasbir's mother.

Wedged between them on the short sofa, Jasbir looks over Nahin's shawled shoulder to where Ram Tarun Das stands in the doorway. He raises his eyebrows, shakes his head.

"Country girls are better breeders," Nahin says. "You said dynasty was a concern. You'll also find a closer match in jati, and in general they settle for a much more reasonable dowry than a city girl. City girls want it all. Me me me. No good ever comes of selfishness."

The nute's long fingers stir the country girls around the coffee table, then slide three toward Jasbir and his family. Dadaji and Mamaji sit forward. Jasbir slumps back. Ram Tarun Das folds his arms, rolls his eyes.

"These three are the best starred," Nahin says. "I can arrange a meeting with their parents almost immediately. There would be some small expenditure in their coming up to Delhi to meet with you; this would be in addition to my fee."

In a flicker, Ram Tarun Das is behind Jasbir, his whisper a startle in his ear.

"There is a line in the Western wedding vows: speak now or forever hold your peace."

"How much is my mother paying you?" Jasbir says into the moment of silence.

"I couldn't possibly betray client confidentiality." Nahin has eyes small and dark as currants.

"I'll disengage you for an additional fifty percent."

Nahin's hands hesitate over the pretty hand-drawn spirals and wheels. *You were a man before*, Jasbir thinks. *That's a man's gesture. See, I've learned how to read people.*

"I double," shrills Mrs. Dayal.

"Wait wait wait," Jasbir's father protests, but Jasbir is already shouting over him. He has to kill this idiocy here, before his family in their wedding fever fall into strategies they cannot afford.

"You're wasting your time and my parents' money," Jasbir says. "You see, I've already met a suitable girl."

Goggle eyes, open mouths around the coffee table, but none so astounded and gaping as Ram Tarun Das's.

❙❙

The Prasads at Number 25 Acacia Colony Bungalows have already sent over a preemptive complaint about the tango music, but Jasbir flicks up the volume fit to rattle the brilliants on the chandelier. At first he scorned the dance—the stiffness, the formality, the strictness of the tempo. So very un-Indian. No one's uncle would ever dance this at a wedding. But he has persisted—never say that Jasbir Dayal is not a trier—and the personality of the tango has subtly permeated him, like rain into a dry riverbed. He has found the discipline and begun to understand the passion. He walks tall in the Dams and Watercourses. He no longer slouches at the watercooler.

"When I advised to you speak or forever hold your peace, sir, I did not actually mean lie through your teeth to your parents," Ram Tarun Das says. In tango he takes the woman's part. The lighthoek can generate an illusion of weight and heft so the aeai feels solid as Jasbir's partner. *If it can do all that, surely it could make him look like a woman?* Jasbir thinks. In his dedication to detail Sujay often overlooks the obvious. "Especially in matters where they can rather easily find you out."

"I had to stop them wasting their money on that nute."

"They would have kept outbidding you."

"Then, even more, I had to stop them wasting my money as well."

Jasbir knocks Ram Tarun Das's foot across the floor in a sweetly executed *barrida*. He glides past the open verandah door, where Sujay glances up from soap-opera building. He has become accustomed to seeing his landlord tango cheek-to-cheek with an elderly Rajput gentleman. *Yours is a weird world of ghosts and djinns and half-realities*, Jasbir thinks.

"So how many times has your father called asking about Shulka?" Ram Tarun Das's free leg traces a curve on the floor in a well-executed *volcada*. Tango is all about seeing the music. It is making the unseen visible.

You know, Jasbir thinks. *You're woven through every part of this house like a pattern in silk.*

"Eight," he says weakly. "Maybe if I called her . . ."

"Absolutely not," Ram Tarun Das insists, pulling in breath-to-breath close in the *embreza*. "Any minuscule advantage you might have enjoyed, any atom of hope you might have entertained, would be forfeit. I forbid it."

"Well, can you at least give me a probability? Surely knowing everything you know about the art of shaadi, you could at least let me know if I've any chance?"

"Sir," says Ram Tarun Das, "I am a Master of Grooming, Grace, and Gentlemanliness. I can direct you to any number of simple and unsophisticated bookie-aeais; they will give you a price on anything, though you may not fancy their odds. One thing I will say: Miss Shulka's responses were very . . . suitable."

Ram Tarun Das hooks his leg around Jasbir's waist in a final *gancho*. The music comes to its strictly appointed conclusion. From behind it come two sounds. One is Mrs. Prasad weeping. She must be leaning against the party wall to make her upset so clearly audible. The other is a call tone, a very specific call tone, a deplorable but insanely hummable filmi hit *My Back, My Crack, My Sack* that Jasbir set on the house system to identify one caller, and one caller only.

Sujay looks up, startled.

"Hello?" Jasbir sends frantic, pleading hand signals to Ram Tarun Das, now seated across the room, his hands resting on the top of his cane.

"Lexus Mumbai red monkey Ritu Parvaaz," says Shulka Mathur. "So what do they mean?"

⏸

"No, my mind is made up, I'm hiring a private detective," Deependra says, rinsing his hands. On the twelfth floor of the Ministry of Waters all the dating gossip happens at the wash-hand basins in the Number 16 Gentlemen's WC. Urinals: too obviously competitive. Cubicles: a violation of privacy. Truths are best washed with the hands at the basins, and secrets and revelations can always be concealed by judicious use of the hot-air hand-drier.

"Deependra, this is paranoia. What's she done?" Jasbir whispers. A level 0.3 aeai chip in the tap admonishes him not to waste precious water.

"It's not what's she's done, it's what she's not done," Deependra hisses. "There's a big difference between someone not being available and someone deliberately not taking your calls. Oh yes. You'll learn this, mark my words. You're at the first stage, when it's all new and fresh and exciting and you are blinded by the amazing fact that someone, someone at last—at long last!—thinks you are a catch. It is all rose petals and sweets and cho chweet and you think nothing can possibly go wrong. But you pass through that stage, oh yes. All too soon the scales fall from your eyes. You see . . . and you hear."

"Deependra." Jasbir moved to the battery of driers. "You've been on five dates." But every word Deependra has spoken has chimed true. He is a cauldron of clashing emotions. He feels light and elastic, as if he bestrode the world like a god, yet at the same time the world is pale and insubstantial as muslin around him. He feels light-headed with hunger though he cannot eat a thing. He pushes away Sujay's lovingly prepared dals and roti. Garlic might taint his breath; saag might stick to his teeth; onions might give him wind; bread might inelegantly bloat him. He chews a few cleansing cardamoms, in the hope of spiced kisses to come. Jasbir Dayal is blissfully, gloriously lovesick.

Date one. The Qutb Minar. Jasbir had immediately protested.

"Tourists go there. And families on Saturdays."

"It's history."

"Shulka isn't interested in history."

"Oh, you know her so well after three phone conversations and two evenings chatting on shaadinet—which I scripted for you? It is roots; it is who you are and where you come from. It's family and dynasty. Your Shulka is interested in that, I assure you, sir. Now, here's what you will wear."

There were tour buses great and small. There were hawkers and souvenir peddlers. There were parties of frowning Chinese. There were schoolchildren with backpacks so huge they looked like upright tortoises. But wandering beneath the domes and along the colonnades of the Quwwat mosque in his casual urban explorer clothes, they seemed as remote and ephemeral as clouds. There was only Shulka and him. And Ram Tarun Das strolling at his side, hands clasped behind his back.

To cue, Jasbir paused to trace out the time-muted contours of a disembodied tirthankar's head, a ghost in the stone.

"Qutb-ud-din Aibak, the first sultan of Delhi, destroyed twenty Jain temples and reused the stone to build his mosque. You can still find the old carvings if you know where to look."

"I like that," Shulka said. "The old gods are still here." Every word that fell from her lips was pearl-perfect. Jasbir tried to read her eyes, but her BlueBoo! cat-eye shades betrayed nothing. "Not enough people care about their history anymore. It's all modern this modern that, if it's not up-to-the-minute it's irrelevant. I think that to know where you're going you need to know where you've come from."

Very good, Ram Tarun Das whispered. *Now, the iron pillar.*

They waited as a tour group of Germans moved away from the railed-off enclosure. Jasbir and Shulka stood in a moment of silence, gazing at the black pillar.

"Sixteen hundred years old, but never a speck of rust on it," Jasbir said.

Ninety-eight percent pure iron, Ram Tarun Das prompted. *There are things Mittal Steel can learn from the Gupta kings.*

"'He who, having the name of Chandra, carried a beauty of countenance like the full moon, having in faith fixed his mind upon Vishnu, had this lofty standard of the divine Vishnu set up on the hill Vishnupada.'" Shulka's frown of concentration as she focused on the inscription around the pillar's waist was as beautiful to Jasbir as that of any god or Gupta king.

"You speak Sanskrit?"

"It's a sort of personal spiritual development path I'm following."

You have about thirty seconds before the next tour group arrives, Ram Tarun Das cuts in. *Now sir; that line I gave you.*

"They say that if you stand with your back to the pillar and close your arms around it, your wish will be granted."

The Chinese were coming the Chinese were coming.

"And if you could do that, what would you wish for?"

Perfect. She was perfect.

"Dinner?"

She smiled that small and secret smile that set a garden of thorns in Jabsir's heart and walked away. At the centre of the gatehouse arch she turned and called back, "Dinner would be good."

Then the Chinese with their shopping bags and sun visors and plastic leisure shoes came bustling around the stainless iron pillar of Chandra Gupta.

Jasbir smiles at the sunny memory of Date One. Deependra waggles his fingers under the stream of hot air.

"I've heard about this. It was on a documentary, oh yes. White widows, they call them. They dress up and go to the shaadis and have their résumés all twinkling and perfect but they have no intention of marrying, oh no no no, not a chance. Why should they, when there is a never-ending stream of men to wine them and dine them and take them out to lovely places and buy them lovely presents and shoes and jewels, and even cars, so it said on the documentary. They are just in it for what they can get; they are playing games with our hearts. And when they get tired or bored or if the man is making too many demands or his presents aren't as expensive as they were or they can do better somewhere else, then *whoosh!* Dumped flat and onto the next one. It's a game to them."

"Deependra," says Jasbir. "Let it go. Documentaries on the Shaadi Channel are not the kind of model you want for married life. Really." Ram Tarun Das would be proud of that one. "Now, I have to get back to work." Faucets that warn about water crime can also report excessive toilet breaks to line managers. But the doubt-seeds are sown, and Jasbir now remembers the restaurant.

Date Two. Jasbir had practised with the chopsticks for every meal for a week. He swore at rice; he cursed dal. Sujay effortlessly scooped rice, dal, everything from bowl to lips in a flurry of stickwork.

"It's easy for you; you've got that code-wallah Asian culture thing."

"Um, we are Asian."

"You know what I mean. And I don't even like Chinese food; it's so bland."

The restaurant was expensive, half a week's wage. He'd make it up on overtime; there were fresh worries in Dams and Watercourses about a drought.

"Oh," Shulka said, the nightglow of Delhi a vast, diffuse halo behind her. She is a goddess, Jasbir thought, a devi of the night city with ten million lights descending from her hair. "Chopsticks." She picked up the antique porcelain chopsticks, one in each hand like drumsticks. "I never know what to do with chopsticks. I'm always afraid of snapping them."

"Oh, they're quite easy once you get the hang of them." Jasbir rose from his seat and came round behind Shulka. Leaning over her shoulder he laid one stick along the fold of her thumb, the other between ball of thumb and tip of index finger. Still wearing her lighthoek. It's the city girl look. Jasbir shivered in anticipation as he slipped the tip of her middle finger between the two chopsticks. "Your finger acts like a pivot, see? Keep relaxed, that's the key. And hold your bowl close to your lips." Her fingers were warm, soft, electric with possibility as he moved them. Did he imagine her skin scented with musk?

Now, said Ram Tarun Das from over Shulka's other shoulder. *Now do you see? And by the way, you must tell her that they make the food taste better.*

They did make the food taste better. Jasbir found subtleties and piquancies he had not known before. Words flowed easily across the table. Everything Jasbir said seemed to earn her starlight laughter. Though Ram Tarun Das was as ubiquitous and unobtrusive as the waiting staff, they were all his own words and witticisms. *See, you can do this*, Jasbir said to himself. *What women want, it's no mystery; stop talking about yourself, listen to them, make them laugh.*

Over green tea Shulka began talking about that new novel everyone but everyone was reading, the one about the Delhi girl on the husband-hunt and her many suitors, the scandalous one, *An Eligible Boy*. Everyone but everyone but Jasbir.

Help! he subvocalized into his inner ear.

Scanning it now, Ram Tarun Das said. *Do you want a thematic digest, popular opinions, or character breakdowns?*

Just be there, Jasbir silently whispered, covering the tiny movement of his jaw by setting the teapot lid ajar, a sign for a refill.

"Well, it's not really a book a man should be seen reading. . . . ," Jasbir confesses.

"But . . ."

"But isn't everyone?" Ram Tarun Das dropped him the line. "I mean, I'm only two-thirds of the way in, but . . . how far are you? Spoiler alert spoiler alert." It's one of Sujay's *Town and Country* expressions. Finally he understands what it means. Shulka just smiles and turns her tea bowl in its little saucer.

"Say what you were going to say."

"I mean, can't she see that Nishok is the one? The man is clearly, obviously, one thousand percent doting on her. But then that would be too easy, wouldn't it?"

"But Pran, it would always be fire with him. He's the baddest of badmashes but you'd never be complacent with Pran. She'll never be able to completely trust him, and that's what makes it exciting. Don't you think you feel that sometimes it needs that little edge, that little fear that maybe, just maybe you could lose it all to keep it alive?"

Careful, sir, murmured Ram Tarun Das.

"Yes, but we've known ever since the party at the Chatterjis where she pushed Jyoti into the pool in front of the Russian ambassador that she's been jealous of her sister because she was the one who got to marry Mr. Panse. It's the eternal glamour versus security. Passion versus stability. Town versus country."

"Ajit?"

"Convenient plot device. Never a contender. Every woman he dates is just a mirror to his own sweet self."

Not one sentence, not one word had he read of the hit trash novel of the season. It had flown around his head like clatter-winged pigeons. He's been too busy being that Eligible Boy.

Shulka held up a piece of sweet, salt, melting fatty duck breast between her porcelain forceps. Juice dripped onto the tablecloth.

"So, who will Bani marry, then? Guess correctly and you shall have a prize."

Jasbir heard Ram Tarun Das's answer begin to form inside his head. *No,* he gritted on his molars.

"I think I know."

"Go on."

"Pran."

Shulka stabbed forward, like the darting bill of a winter crane. There was hot, fatty soya duck in his mouth.

"Isn't there always a twist in the tale?" Shulka said.

In the Number 16 Gentlemen's WC Deependra checks his hair in the mirror and smooths it down.

"Dowry thievery; that's what it is. They string you along, get their claws into your money; then they disappear and you never see a paisa again."

Now Jasbir really really wants to get back to his little work cluster.

"Deep, this is fantasy. You've read this in the news feeds. Come on."

"Where there's smoke there's fire. My stars say that I should be careful in things of the heart and beware false friends. Jupiter is in the third house. Dark omens surround me. No, I have hired a private investigation aeai. It will conduct a discreet surveillance. One way or the other, I shall know."

Jasbir grips the stanchion, knuckles white, as the phatphat swings through the great mill of traffic around Indira Chowk. Deependra's aftershave oppresses him.

"Exactly where are we going?"

Deependra had set up the assignation on a coded palmer account. All he would say was that it required two hours of an evening, good clothes, a trustworthy friend, and absolute discretion. For two days his mood had been grey and thunderous as an approaching monsoon. His PI aeai had returned a result, but Deependra revealed nothing, not even a whisper in the clubbish privacy of the Number 16 Gentlemen's WC.

The phatphat, driven by a teenager with gelled hair that falls in sharp spikes over his eyes—an obvious impediment to navigation—takes them out past the airport. At Gurgaon the geography falls into place around Jasbir. He starts to feel nauseous from more than spike-hair's driving and Deependra's shopping mall aftershave. Five minutes later the phatphat crunches up the curve of raked gravel outside the pillared portico of the Haryana Polo and Country Club.

"What are we doing here? If Shulka finds out I've been to shaadi when I'm supposed to be dating her it's all over."

"I need a witness."

Help me, Ram Tarun Das, Jasbir hisses into his molars, but there is no reassuring spritz of silvery music through his skull to herald the advent of the Master of Grooming, Grace, and Gentlemanliness. The two immense Sikhs on the door nod them through.

Kishore is sloped against his customary angle of the bar, surveying the territory. Deependra strides through the throng of eligible boys like a god going to war. Every head turns. Every conversation, every gossip falls silent.

"You . . . you . . . you . . . ," Deependra stammers with rage. His face shakes. "Shaadi stealer!" The whole club bar winces as the slap cracks across Kishore's face. Then two fists descend on Deependra, one on each shoulder. The man-mountain Sikhs turn him around and arm-lock him, frothing and raging, from the bar of the Haryana Polo and Country Club. "You, you chu-utya!" Deependra flings back at his enemy. "I will take it out of you, every last paisa, so help me God. I will have satisfaction!"

Jasbir scurries behind the struggling, swearing Deependra, cowed with embarrassment.

"I'm only here to witness," he says to the Sikhs' you're-next glares. They hold Deependra upright a moment to snap his face and bar him forever from Begum Rezzak's Lovely Girl Shaadi Agency. Then they throw him cleanly over the hood of a new model Li Fan G8 into the carriage drive. He lies dreadfully still and snapped on the gravel for a few moments, then with fetching dignity draws himself up, bats away the dust, and straightens his clothes.

"I will see him at the river about this," Deependra shouts at the impassive Sikhs. "At the river."

Jasbir is already out on the avenue, trying to see if the phatphat driver's gone.

The sun is a bowl of brass rolling along the indigo edge of the world. Lights twinkle in the dawn haze. There is never a time when there are not people at the river. Wire-thin men push handcarts over the trash-strewn sand, picking like birds. Two boys have set a small fire in a ring of stones. A distant procession of women, soft bundles on their heads, file over the grassy sand. By the shrivelled thread of the Yamuna an old Brahmin consecrates himself, pouring water over his head. Despite the early heat, Jasbir shivers. He knows what goes into that water. He can smell the sewage on the air, mingled with wood smoke.

"Birds," says Sujay, looking around him with simple wonder. "I can actually hear birds singing. So this is what mornings are like. Tell me again what I'm doing here?"

"You're here because I'm not being here on my own."

"And, ah, what exactly are you doing here?"

Deependra squats on his heels by the gym bag, arms wrapped around him. He wears a sharp white shirt and pleated slacks. His shoes are very good. Apart from grunted greetings he has not said a word to Jasbir or Sujay. He stares a lot. Deependra picks up a fistful of sand and lets it trickle through his fingers. Jasbir wouldn't advise that either.

"I could be at home coding," says Sujay. "Hey ho. Showtime."

Kishore marches across the scabby river-grass. Even as a well-dressed distant speck it is obvious to all that he is furiously angry. His shouts carry far on the still morning air.

"I am going to kick your head into the river," he bellows at Deependra, still squatting on the riverbank.

"I'm only here as a witness," Jasbir says hurriedly, needing to be believed. Kishore must forget and Deependra must never know that he was also the witness that night Kishore made the joke that night in the Tughluk tower.

Deependra looks up. His face is bland; his eyes are mild.

"You just had to, didn't you? It would have killed you to let me have something you didn't."

"Yeah, well. I let you get away with that in the polo club. I could have taken you then; it would have been the easiest thing. I could have driven your nose right into your skull, but I didn't. You cost me my dignity, in front of all my friends, people I work with, business colleagues, but most of all, in front of the women."

"Well then let me help you find your honour again."

Deependra thrusts his hand into the gym bag and pulls out a gun.

"Oh my god it's a gun he's got a gun," Jasbir jabbers. He feels his knees turn liquid. He thought that only happened in soaps and popular trash novels. Deependra gets to his feet, the gun never wavering from its aim in the centre of Kishore's forehead, the precise spot a bindi would sit. "There's another one in the bag." Deependra waggles the barrel, nods with his head. "Take it. Let's sort this right, the man's way. Let's sort it honourably. Take the gun." His voice has gained an octave. A vein beats in his neck and at his temple. Deependra kicks the gym bag towards Kishore. Jasbir can see the anger, the mad, suicidal anger rising in the banker to match the civil servant's. He can hear himself mumbling *Oh my god oh my god oh my god.* "Take the gun. You will have an honourable chance. Otherwise I will shoot you like a pi-dog right here." Deependra levels the gun and takes a sudden, stabbing step towards Kishore. He is panting like a dying cat. Sweat has soaked his good white shirt through and through. The gun muzzle is a finger's-breadth from Kishore's forehead.

Then there is a blur of movement, a body against the sun, a cry of pain, and the next Jasbir knows Sujay has the gun swinging by its trigger guard from his finger. Deependra is on the sand, clenching and unclenching his right hand. The old Brahmin stares, dripping.

"It's okay now, it's all okay, it's over," Sujay says. "I'm going to put this in the bag with the other and I'm going to take them and get rid of them and no one will ever talk about this, okay? I'm taking the bag now. Now, shall we all get out of here before someone calls the police, hm?"

Sujay swings the gym bag over his sloping shoulder and strides out for the streetlights, leaving Deependra hunched and crying among the shredded plastic scraps.

"How—what—that was—where did you learn to do that?" Jasbir asks, tagging behind, feet sinking into the soft sand.

"I've coded the move enough times; I thought it might work in meat life."

"You don't mean?"

"From the soaps. Doesn't everyone?"

There's solace in soap opera. Its predictable tiny screaming rows, its scripted swooping melodramas draw the poison from the chaotic, unscripted world where a civil servant in the water service can challenge a rival to a shooting duel over a woman he met at shaadi. Little effigies of true dramas, sculpted in soap.

When he blinks, Jasbir can see the gun. He sees Deependra's hand draw it out of the gym bag in martial-arts-movie slow motion. He thinks he sees the other gun, nestled among balled sports socks. Or maybe he imagines it, a cutaway close-up. Already he is editing his memory.

Soothing to watch Nilesh Vora and Dr. Chatterji's wife, their love eternally foiled and frustrated, and Deepti; will she ever realise that to the Brahmpur social set she is eternally that Dalit girl from the village pump?

You work on the other side of a glass partition from someone for years. You go with him to shaadis; you share the hopes and fears of your life and love with him. And love turns him into a homicidal madman. Sujay took the gun off him. Big, clumsy Sujay, took the loaded gun out of his hand. He would have shot Kishore. Brave, mad Sujay. He's coding—that's his renormalizing process. Make soap, watch soap. Jasbir will make him tea. For once. Yes, that would be a nice gesture. Sujay is always always getting tea. Jasbir gets up. It's a boring bit, Mahesh and Rajani. He doesn't like them. Those "rich boys pretending they are car valets so they can marry for love not money" characters stretch his disbelief too far. Rajani is hot, though. She's asked Mahesh to bring her car round to the front of the hotel.

"When you work out here you have lots of time to make up theories. One of my theories is that people's cars are their characters," Mahesh is saying. *Only in a soap would anyone ever imagine that a pickup line like that would work,* Jasbir thinks. "So, are you a Tata, a Mercedes, a Li Fan, or a Lexus?"

Jasbir freezes in the door.

"Oh, a Lexus."

He turns slowly. Everything is dropping; everything is falling, leaving him suspended. Now Mahesh is saying,

"You know, I have another theory. It's that everyone's a city. Are you Delhi, Mumbai, Kolkata, Chennai?"

Jasbir sits on the arm of the sofa. *The fetch,* he whispers. *And she will say . . .*

"I was born in Delhi. . . ."

"That's not what I mean."

Mumbai, murmurs Jasbir.

"Mumbai, then. Yes, Mumbai definitely. Kolkata's hot and dirty and nasty. And Chennai—no, I'm definitely Mumbai."

"Red green yellow blue," Jasbir says.

"Red." Without a moment's hesitation.

"Cat dog bird monkey?"

She even cocks her head to one side. That was how he noticed Shulka was wearing the lighthoek.

"Bird . . . no."

"No no no," says Jasbir. She'll smile slyly here. "Monkey." And there is the smile. The *finesse*.

"Sujay!" Jasbir yells. "Sujay! Get me Das!"

‖

"How can an aeai be in love?" Jasbir demands.

Ram Tarun Das sits in his customary wicker chair, his legs casually crossed. *Soon, very soon*, Jasbir thinks, *voices will be raised and Mrs. Prasad next door will begin to thump and weep.*

"Now sir, do not most religions maintain that love is the fundament of the universe? In which case, perhaps it's not so strange that a distributed entity, such as myself, should find—and be surprised by, oh, so surprised, sir—by love? As a distributed entity, it's different in nature from the surge of neurochemicals and waveform of electrical activity you experience as love. With us it's a more . . . rarefied experience . . . judging solely by what I know from my subroutines on *Town and Country*. Yet, at the same time, it's intensely communal. How can I describe it? You don't have the concepts, let alone the words. I am a specific incarnation of aspects of a number of aeais and subprogrammes, as those aeais are also iterations of subprogrammes, many of them marginally sentient. I am many; I am legion. And so is she—though of course gender is purely arbitrary for us, and, sir, largely irrelevant. It's very likely that at many levels we share components. So ours is not so much a marriage of minds as a league of nations. Here we are different from humans in that, for you, it seems to us that groups are divisive and antipathetical. Politics, religion, sport, but especially your history seem to teach that. For us folk, groups are what bring us together. They are mutually attractive. Perhaps the closest analogy might be the merger of large corporations. One thing I do know, that for humans and aeais, we both need to tell people about it."

"When did you find out she was using an aeai assistant?"

"Oh, at once sir. These things are obvious to us. And if you'll forgive the parlance, we don't waste time. Fascination at the first nanosecond. Thereafter, well, as you saw on the unfortunate scene from *Town and Country*, we scripted you."

"So we thought you were guiding us . . ."

"When it was you who were our go-betweens, yes."

"So what happens now?" Jasbir slaps his hands on his thighs.

"We are meshing at a very high level. I can only catch hints and shadows of it, but I feel a new aeai is being born, on a level far beyond either of us, or any of our co-characters. Is this a birth? I don't know, but how can I convey to you the tremendous, rushing excitement I feel?"

"I meant me."

"I'm sorry sir. Of course you did. I am quite, quite dizzy with it all. If I might make one observation; there's truth in what your parents say. First the marriage, then the love. Love grows in the thing you see every day."

Thieving macaques dart around Jasbir's legs and pluck at the creases of his pants. Midnight metro, the last train home. The few late-night passengers observe a quarantine of mutual solitude. The djinns of unexplained wind that haunt subway systems send litter spiralling across the platform. The tunnel focuses distant shunts and clanks, uncanny at this zero hour. There should be someone around at the phatphat stand. If not he'll walk. It doesn't matter.

He met her at a fashionable bar, all leather and darkened glass, in an international downtown hotel. She looked wonderful. The simple act of her stirring sugar into coffee tore his heart in two.

"When did you find out?"

"Devashri Didi told me."

"Devashri Didi."

"And yours?

"Ram Tarun Das, Master of Grooming, Grace, and Gentlemanliness. A very proper, old-fashioned Rajput gent. He always called me sir; right up to the end. My housemate made him. He works in character design on *Town and Country*."

"My older sister works in PR in the meta-soap department at Jazhay. She got one of the actor designers to put Devashri Didi together." Jasbir has always found the idea of artificial actors believing they played equally artificial roles head-frying. Then he'd found aeai love.

"Is she married? Your older sister, I mean."

"Blissfully. And children."

"Well, I hope our aeais are very happy together." Jasbir raised a glass. Shulka lifted her coffee cup. She wasn't a drinker. She didn't like alcohol. Devashri Didi had told her it looked good for the Begum Jaitly's modern shaadi.

"My little quiz?" Jasbir asked.

"Devashri Didi gave me the answers you were expecting. She'd told me it was a standard ploy, personality quizzes and psychic tests."

"And the Sanskrit?"

"Can't speak a word."

Jasbir laughed honestly.

"The personal spiritual journey?"

"I'm a strictly material girl. Devashri Didi said—"

"—I'd be impressed if I thought you had a deep spiritual dimension. I'm not a history buff either. And *An Eligible Boy*?"

"That unreadable tripe?"

"Me neither."

"Is there anything true about either of us?"

"One thing," Jasbir said. "I can tango."

Her surprise, breaking into a delighted smile, was also true. Then she folded it away.

"Was there ever any chance?" Jasbir asked.

"Why did you have to ask that? We could have just admitted that we were both playing games and shaken hands and laughed and left it at that. Jasbir, would it help if I told you that I wasn't even looking? I was trying the system out. It's different for suitable girls. I've got a plan."

"Oh," said Jasbir.

"You did ask and we agreed, right at the start tonight, no more pretence." She turned her coffee cup so that the handle faced right and laid her spoon neatly in the saucer. "I have to go now." She snapped her bag shut and stood up. *Don't walk away*, Jasbir said in his silent Master of Grooming, Grace, and Gentlemanliness voice. She walked away.

"And Jasbir."

"What?"

"You're a lovely man, but this was not a date."

A monkey takes a liberty too far, plucking at Jasbir's shin. Jasbir's kick connects and sends it shrieking and cursing across the platform. *Sorry monkey. It wasn't you.* Booms rattle up the subway tube; gusting hot air and the smell of electricity herald the arrival of the last metro. As the lights swing around the curve in the tunnel, Jasbir imagines how it would be to step out and drop in front of it. The game would be over. Deependra has it easy. Indefinite sick leave, civil service counselling, and pharma. But for Jasbir there is no end to it, and he is so so tired of playing. Then the train slams past him in a shout of blue and silver and yellow light, slams him back into himself. He sees his face reflected in the glass, his teeth still divinely white. Jasbir shakes his head and smiles and instead steps through the opening door.

It is as he suspected. The last phatphat has gone home for the night from the rank at Barwala metro station. It's four kays along the pitted, flaking roads to Acacia Bungalow Colony behind its gates and walls. Under an hour's walk. Why not? The night is warm, he's nothing better to do, and he might yet pull a passing cab. Jasbir steps out. After half an hour a last, patrolling phatphat passes on the other side of the road. It flashes its light and pulls around to slide in beside him. Jasbir waves it on. He is enjoying the night and the melancholy. There are stars up there, beyond the golden airglow of great Delhi.

Light spills through the French windows from the verandah into the dark living room. Sujay is at work still. In four kilometres Jasbir has generated a sweat. He ducks into the shower, closes his eyes in bliss as the jets of water hit him. Let it run let it run let it run—he doesn't care how much he wastes, how much it costs, how badly the villagers need it for their crops. *Wash the old tired dirt from me.*

A scratch at the door. Does Jasbir hear the mumble of a voice? He shuts off the shower.

"Sujay?"

"I've, ah, left you tea."

"Oh, thank you."

There's silence, but Jasbir knows Sujay hasn't gone.

"Ahm, just to say that I have always . . . I will . . . always. Always . . ." Jasbir holds his breath, water running down his body and dripping onto the shower tray. "I'll always be here for you."

Jasbir wraps a towel around his waist, opens the bathroom door, and lifts the tea.

Presently Latin music thunders out from the brightly lit windows of Number 27 Acacia Bungalows. Lights go on up and down the close. Mrs. Prasad beats her shoe on the wall and begins to wail. The tango begins.

SENIORSOURCE

Kristine Kathryn Rusch

A multiple award–winning author, Kristine Kathryn Rusch is also a prolific writer of science fiction, fantasy, mystery, and romance. She's made several best-seller lists and been translated into thirteen languages. A former editor of the Magazine of Fantasy & Science Fiction, *she has won the Hugo Award, the John W. Campbell Award, the Ellery Queen Reader's Choice Award, and the Romantic Times Reviewers' Choice Award for Best Paranormal Romance. As it does in her popular Retrieval Artist series about interplanetary detectives, here science fiction and mystery meet with deadly results.*

The little boy lay facedown in the dirt. Because the brown dirt was fine, loose, and powdery, I thought he had landed outside the dome, but that didn't quite match with what I was seeing. His body was intact, which it would not have been if it had been exposed to the harshness of the actual Moon.

Then something wet collided with my shirt, spoiling the you-are-there illusion, pulling me back into my workstation at SeniorSource.

I yanked off my goggles and made sure I let go of them gently so that they'd float beside me. I also let go of my workstation so I floated as well. A half a dozen other people were clinging to their stations, their faces hidden beneath the goggles that covered their eyes, ears, and nose. A few folks had strapped themselves in so that, in their excitement, they wouldn't let go and drift into some equipment on the other side of the work area.

My goggles weren't the only thing floating beside me. So were half a dozen other drops of some brown liquid. They had gathered near my left side, as if they were a phalanx of brown marbles lined up for an attack.

"Marvin," I snapped, "your coffee's gotten away from you again."

Marvin Pierce peeked at me from the doorway leading into the community kitchen. He floated sideways, hands gripping the edge of the door, only his bald pate, eyes, and nose visible, like a Kilroy-was-here drawing, something that one of the oldsters here had started sketching on the walls. (You couldn't call anything a ceiling or a floor here—the place constantly rotated.)

Marvin's blue eyes were twinkling. As he used his hands to propel himself into the VR work lab, he grinned like a naughty three-year-old.

Which he hadn't been in more than 125 years.

"Sorry," he said in a tone that let me know he wasn't sorry at all. He caught the first three balls of coffee with his mouth, swallowed hard, then used a pair of chopsticks to go after the fourth.

It was the chopsticks that screwed him up. The fourth bubble of coffee slipped through the wooden edges and aimed for me at surprising speed. I floated away, and watched in disgust as the coffee splatted against my goggles.

"Hey," I said. "I was working."

"Work, work, work. You know, sometimes you gotta take a coffee break," Marvin said, and then giggled. His giggle was high-pitched, like a little girl's.

It was also infectious. But I didn't let myself smile. Marvin had ruined too many workdays for me—cleaning things wasn't easy in zero-g—and I didn't dare lose this day.

I was on a schedule—a tight one. Maybe an impossible one.

And the idea of that made my stomach turn.

That little boy had been the son of Shane Proctor, head of the largest mining company on the Moon. This case was the first high-profile test run of SeniorSource's new Moon crime unit.

Theoretically, detectives in SeniorSource would solve cases on the Moon from their little perch in Earth's orbit. I used to think outsourcing detective work wouldn't work.

But it did work—I'd solved more than two hundred cases, some of them cold—since I arrived here five years ago. SeniorSource outsourced all kinds of highly skilled jobs, from laser surgery to art restoration. Even detective work, with its combination of interrogation, observation, and forensic skills, could succeed from a distance.

However, I had never been a guinea pig before. The chance of failure was high, and I didn't dare say no.

I was one of the youngest men at SeniorSource—and one of the poorest. I had to work full-time to pay for my healthcare as well as my room and board.

When the doctors told me that I would need full-time care, I investigated all my options. I didn't like most of them. Residential care hadn't changed much since I was a kid.

The old were warehoused with the terminally ill, and depending on how much money they had, they either got personal care or they didn't.

But because I had Manhattan Police Department insurance, which had ties with off-planet organizations like SeniorSource, I could apply here.

Which I did.

SeniorSource was the oldest pay-as-you-go orbital residence care facility. It advertised a full life for the long-lived, and for the most part, it lived up to that billing.

Some of the oldsters, like Marvin, had lived here for thirty years. He'd been nearly ninety when he arrived, written off by his family as near death, which he probably would have been had he stayed.

In space, in a place like SeniorSource, we lived in a germ-free environment, in zero-gravity that made each of us feel like Superman when we first arrived, along with a full-time medical staff (no one under eighty) who monitored us, kept our bones as strong as possible, made sure our circulation was good, as well as monitoring the physical changes of living in a hermetically sealed world so different from the one we had grown up in.

Guys like me, the younger guys, the full-timers, didn't have the lifetime health benefits that the oldsters like Marvin had. We didn't even have a mountain of assets to sell. The differences between my generation (dubbed, somewhere in the midtwenties, "the Sickest Generation") and Marvin's generation (the space generation or, as some still called them, the older baby boomers) were legion. Most of the folks my age had died of diabetes or heart attacks before we were old enough to send our peers into national politics. As a result, the younger generations wiped out most of the beneficial legislation that the baby boomers and Generation X had passed—the universal health care, the Retirement Savings Act, and all those others—keeping them intact for the boomers while grandfathering out people who were born in the twenty-first century.

So we didn't get to retire. We had to work. The Marvins of SeniorSource worked as well, but they only had to put in one day per month, mostly teaching history to college classes via streaming holos.

When I applied, I expected to be turned down. I didn't realize that SeniorSource badly needed trained detectives. They promised me a large private suite, an adequate food allowance, and midrange healthcare that was still better than anything I could get on Earth.

In exchange, I had to agree to work five days a week, eight hours per day, and exercise two hours per day seven days a week. I loved the idea of work; I hated the idea of exercise (I am a member of my generation, after all). But I agreed to all their terms, missing something important in the fine print.

My stay on this station was performance related. I couldn't be fired, but I could be demoted, which meant that my life would become a living hell. I would get smaller quarters, a lower-level food allowance, and minimal medical care.

If I really screwed up, I could be banished from the station. I'd be sent to an affiliated residence center somewhere in the Northeast, and warehoused with the rest of the old-timers.

The problem was that most folks who were banished from SeniorSource died within six months. Very few elderly people could handle the transition back to full gravity after living in zero-g.

Even though I was still one of the younger elderly, I doubted my bones could survive the transition. My bones—strong as they once were—had become fragile. When I'd left Earth five years ago, I could no longer walk. Plus my arthritis had gotten so bad I could barely move my fingers. It had been clear, even to me, that I could no longer live on my own.

I'd come up here reluctantly, but after I got past the stomach issues caused by the perpetual freefall of being in Earth's orbit, I loved it.

I couldn't imagine being anywhere else.

Which was why I didn't want this case.

If I failed to find the murderer of Shane Proctor's son within twenty-four hours, I could get demoted. If I mouthed off about the impossibility of the task, I could get sent Earthside.

I didn't want smaller quarters, and I didn't want to experience full gravity ever again.

And I really, really didn't want to die.

‖

SeniorSource had recently branched into providing security and law enforcement services to various Moon-based communities, with an eye on capturing most of the Mars market by the turn of the century. If we did well on the Moon and had a proven track record in places outside of Earth, then we could open several care facilities in Mars's orbit when the time came, and would use those folks to provide services to the new Mars communities.

The success of cases like mine would guarantee more Moon contracts and with those, enough money to build in Mars's orbit even without full Mars contracts.

My boss, Riya Eoff, made it clear that any work I did on the Moon had to be flawless or I would suffer the consequences.

She didn't need to scare me. I was already scared enough.

SeniorSource's Earth-based companion investigation companies had robots and VR cameras and holographic imaging centers. We had weird little programs that I didn't entirely understand that supposedly sent up puffs of air, filled with the smells of the crime scene. (David Sullivan, the oldster who had trained me, told me they didn't actually send up air until two or three days into an investigation. What you got through the nose unit of the goggles was a simulation of the smells. Only since we were using Earth smells and Earth-based equipment, we tended to get it right more often than not.)

On Earth, there were still a few knowledgeable people who could answer questions, do hands-on examination of evidence as well as an old-fashioned autopsy if one of us old-fashioned detectives figured it was necessary.

On the Moon, we had robots, VR cameras, and holographic imaging—

and very little else. The human medical professionals residing there had enough to do with their living subjects, and had never really received training in modern forensic pathology.

Not that it mattered, since the Moon was still a collection of bases and mining operations. There was no real legal system there, so prosecuting the criminal would fall on the mining company or whatever Earth-based conglomerate owned the thing, or maybe on the country in which the conglomerate was registered.

As soon as I got the case, I asked one of the oldsters who was fulfilling his monthly day of work doing legal research to find out who owned the mining company and what laws I might have to operate under.

But that would only get me so far.

First I had to solve the case.

And I wasn't sure I could do that.

‖

Here's the thing: I know how things work on Earth. If I fall, I bruise. If I grab someone's arm hard, I could break the bone. If I shoot a gun, I know that the bullet might tear into blood and tissue and bone, leaving a trajectory that makes some kind of sense.

If I shoot a gun up here (not that I could, since firearms are the first thing confiscated before a resident boards the company shuttle), I know that bullet will follow some kind of straight line based on the amount of force from the explosion that released it. If the bullet doesn't encounter a lot of resistance—meaning it misses a bone—it'll slam through a human body in that same straight line, go through a wall, maybe another human body, and so on, until the energy that released it is spent.

With luck, that energy doesn't send the bullet through the walls of our little space habitat, punching a hole into our protective walls and forcing us to vent atmosphere.

The rules of physics still do apply; you just have to subtract for the lack of gravity.

On the Moon, you have domed environments with full Earth gravity, domed environments with two-thirds Earth gravity, domed environments with one-third Earth gravity, and domed environments with no gravity at all.

You also have the Moon's surface, which has one-sixth Earth gravity—and no atmosphere at all. Like everyone else sent up to this station, I learned what could happen to someone who let himself through both doors of the airlock without a space suit, and I found that lesson too graphic even for my concrete stomach. All I took away from the thing was this: you let yourself outside this place—or outside the Moon's domes—without an environmental suit, and you'll die one of the ugliest deaths imaginable.

So before I could do a full-scale Earth-type investigation, I had to find out several nontraditional things. Not only did I have to learn the exact location of the body, but I also needed to know what the gravity level was, and what the oxygen level was. I had to learn if the kid had access to an environmental suit, if he spent time outside the dome, and if he often went to domes with lesser (or greater) gravity.

I had to learn what Moon dust did to the lungs, whether the stuff could be made toxic with little effort, whether it changed from region to region.

Then I had to find out about the kid's family life, his daily routine, and whether or not he had any friends. I had to factor that routine into my investigation, and see if—say—the bruising that was fairly obvious even from the first glance at his poor little body was the normal result of his everyday life or if it had come from some unusual event.

I had to be not only a detective but also an expert scientist, a lawyer, and an authority on the Moon in just a few short hours.

And I didn't dare make a single mistake.

Which was why cleaning the coffee off my goggles irritated the hell out of me. It cost me time I truly didn't have.

I wished I could just change out that pair of goggles for another. But I couldn't. These goggles, our most high-end, had already been synced with the devices sent to settle the Proctor case, and it would take hours to sync another set of goggles with the Moon.

Not to mention the fact that those goggles would be technologically inferior to the ones I was using.

Cleaning things up here is perhaps the most difficult part of life in zero-g (if you don't count the first few times you have to use the bathroom). You can't just turn on a faucet and run the goggles underneath the tap. Everything here floats—including water.

You have to use a series of cloths, all treated with cleaning and drying fluids (but not wet enough to drip, of course). Then you have to put the fluid-covered cleaning cloths in the right containers and place them in the recycler, testing the item you're trying to clean to make sure the dirt—or in my case, the coffee—has finally been removed.

I got the goggles cleaned, but I lost nearly a quarter of an hour.

During that quarter of an hour, however, I had had a chance to think. And to listen to what little bit we knew about the son of Shane Proctor.

I used the audio function of my own personal computer. We're all assigned an onboard computer when we arrive; we can choose whether or not to have its component parts attached to our bodies. The oldsters prefer to have the computer as a separate item; I like my ear bud and my fingernail cam and the tiny screen that appears in the palm of my hand whenever I need to view some information.

Shane Proctor's son was named Chen, a Chinese name that meant *great*. Oddly enough, he had no middle name.

Chen Proctor had been born in 2070 on the Moon in Proctor Mining Colony, with two midwives presiding. His mother, Lian Proctor, was Shane Proctor's third wife. A quick search did not tell me what had happened to the previous two wives. I would have to dig for that information.

Chen Proctor had been home-schooled most of his life, partly because he went from mining operation to mining operation with his father and partly because he learned faster than anyone else in his age group.

He had a younger brother named Ellsworth and a baby sister named Caryn. Another quick search told me that Ellsworth and Caryn had different birth mothers than Chen—wives four and five.

No other child lived at home, and all three seemed to stay with their father, rather than their mothers. I couldn't even do a standard search on where the mothers lived. Proctor Mining Company shielded a lot of personal data about its president and chief shareholder, so I had reached the extent of the public information I could find out about Proctor's three children.

Or his last three children.

I wasn't sure which.

I grabbed my goggles and floated back to my workstation. This time I strapped in.

I needed to concentrate fully, and the last thing I wanted to do was drift.

‖

The Proctor Mining Colony took up most of what was once called the Descartes Highlands. The highlands were unrecognizable from the place where *Apollo 16* had landed over one hundred years before. Now highlands were covered with mini domes, robotic equipment, newly dug holes, and not so newly dug holes. Lights covered the entire area, and what had once seemed like a dark grayish brown place now continually glowed.

Chen Proctor had spent the last two years of his life in the settlement dome, several kilometers from the current active mine. According to his family, he was never allowed outside. Apparently there had been an incident, and Chen had nearly died.

I let some of the androids—although they were really just talking robots—do the preliminary interviews, using a standard list of questions that I had tailored to this investigation. I would ask some of the tougher questions myself a little later.

But first, I wanted to examine the body.

A pan-back and a comparison with GoogleMoon showed me exactly where the body had been found. It was at the edge of the new dome, which was being built to replace the settlement where the boy lived. The new dome had just inaugurated its gravity and environmental controls.

It was supposed to replicate the environment inside the settlement—

meaning full Earth-normal, down to the oxygen and carbon dioxide mix in the air. The terraformers were working on the Moon dust, trying to make it more like Earth dirt, but that experiment was failing.

It was beginning to look more and more like the new dome would be exactly like the old settlement, only with better filters.

I had to use all five of SeniorSource's robots, as well as the three VR cameras and the single holoimager, to get a good three-dimensional look at the body.

For an eight-year-old, Chen was tiny. He had the look of a boy raised in low gravity instead of full gravity, like his bio suggested. He had narrow little shoulders, a back so flat and slender that I could see his spine and his shoulder blades outlined against his shirt.

His pants seemed too big, and oddly enough, he was barefoot. His face was turned sideways, his mouth partially open and filled with dirt.

The holoimage showed hair that should have been black turned almost gray with Moon dust, and slightly almond-shaped eyes that were tightly closed.

I made the robots go around him, zooming in their own cameras for a level of detail that the human eye couldn't see. I needed to know if what I thought were bruises were actually something else.

The bruises ran along the side of his cheek and under his chin, then again along his forearms. The marks on his forearms were small. They ran from the elbow to the wrist and were not evenly spaced.

The mark on his face was large, covering most of his visible cheek, his jawline, and running all the way down to the middle of his neck.

If they were bruises, they had been created before he died. In that case, someone had grabbed him and hit him. But I wasn't ready to take the easy solution. I was afraid these were some kind of marking I wasn't familiar with—something that a person who lived in the Moon colonies would see as normal and not suspicious at all.

So I had the robots give me as much information as they could without disturbing the body. The photographs and vids were great, but I wanted more.

If I had actually been there, I would have leaned over the boy and sniffed. You learn a lot from the way a corpse smells—and I'm not just talking about decomposition. Perfume on the shirt, the scent of cedar oil on the hands, the faint odor of grease on the back of the neck might be all it takes to wrap up a case.

Only I had no time and no way to order up a little whiff of air.

So I did the next best thing. I had the robots take the chemical composition of the air, unit by tiny unit. I hoped I could feed those chemical signatures into our own forensic lab computer and get an analysis of the odors—not quite as good as smelling things myself, but good enough, maybe, to give me an idea of what I was facing.

I also had one of the robots take images of the area, and was startled to see signs in English, proclaiming this part of the new dome completely off-limits.

No one had mentioned that.

In fact, no one had mentioned how the boy's body had been found in the first place.

I put through a series of instructions—no touching the body until my investigation was finished, no one (human or nonaffiliated robot) allowed on the scene while the work progressed, and no second-party release of information.

That last was the most critical, because information acquired through nonhuman means often had more than one legal owner. I had no idea if the robots I was using belonged solely to SeniorSource or if they were being leased from Proctor Mining.

I had no idea about too many things.

My stomach turned, and I felt queasy for the first time in years. I closed my eyes and took a deep breath.

When I had worked for the NYPD, I occasionally clashed with my bosses. I became known as one of the most opinionated and successful detectives in homicide. If you wanted a case closed, you picked me to investigate. But you also put up with my attitude and my mouth.

I'd kept both under control here—I knew the risks, and they weren't worth the hassle.

I could usually succeed without mouthing off.

On this case, however, I couldn't. SeniorSource had given me an impossible task with an impossible deadline, and somehow expected me to get it done.

Maybe if I confessed about my own inadequacies early enough, I'd only suffer a demotion. Maybe I'd just get a demerit.

Maybe, if I documented everything, I'd have enough evidence to take to one of the elderly lawyers up here and get him (or an Earthbound colleague) to fight my inevitable banishment back to full gravity.

Because I couldn't work with what I had.

I set my goggles and the nearby computer backups to store each piece of information that was sent through the equipment on the Moon. When I was done, I peeled the goggles off and hung them on the Velcro strap designed especially for them.

Then I headed to my boss's office, trying not to think of everything I risked.

||

My boss, Riya Eoff, had decorated every available space of her office with pictures from home. Photographs of her family, starting with her great-grandparents and running all the way to her own great-granddaughter, a baby she had never met. Riya suffered from advanced osteoporosis and had had to sign a special waiver just to get approved at SeniorSource, since space life often leached calcium from the bone.

But it was easier to survive up here with weak bones than it was on Earth. Her doctor had signed her up as an experimental guinea pig—to see how long a severely weakened person could survive in zero-g—and the study had long since ended. Riya was now in her second decade at SeniorSource, and if you didn't know her history, you'd think the thin, silver-haired woman who haunted this office was one of the most athletic elderly people who had ever come into space.

"This better be important," she said to me. "You're on a deadline."

"I know," I said. "If you want results by tomorrow, you have to give me the full detective squad plus a few scientists."

My voice didn't shake, and that was a plus. I tried to imagine myself back on Earth, making this same pitch in the precinct, but that was hard.

We didn't float in the NYPD.

"We don't have the budget for a full squad." She didn't quite look at me. Instead, she threaded her hands over her stomach. Her fingers were covered with rings, some as old as she was. A necklace floated around her chin—she had once told me she had worn it since she was twelve and had never taken it off.

My stomach twisted. That queasiness was getting worse.

"If you can't give me the help," I said, "then you're not going to get this contract."

"Are you saying you can't solve this crime?" she asked.

I tensed. I never said I couldn't solve a crime. But I didn't let her bait me. I spoke slowly, so that I didn't say something I would regret.

"I'm saying I can't solve this case in the timeline you gave me with the knowledge I have."

"You're the smartest investigator I have," she said.

That statement should have relaxed me, but it didn't. "Maybe with Earth crimes," I said. "But I know nothing about the Moon."

"You know enough."

I shook my head, then regretted it as the movement sent me sliding in two different directions at once. I'd gotten rid of most of my counterproductive Earth movements, but head-shaking was one that snuck up on me—I never thought of it as movement, only as communication.

"Nonsense," she said. "Tell me who you suspect and why."

"I suspect no one," I said. "I'm not even sure about the kid's family relationships. I don't know if he snuck into that spot in the new dome. I'm not even sure he was murdered."

I could hear an old tone in my voice—an edge, one that threatened to become strident.

Riya grabbed onto a handhold built into one of the walls. She should have reprimanded me—SeniorSource never admitted that it examined crimes that turned out to be nothing more than an accident—but she didn't.

Instead she said, "What makes you say that he might not have been murdered?"

The hair rose on the back of my neck—or the hair would have risen if it weren't already standing at attention from the lack of gravity. Still, that feeling, the one my grandmother used to say was like someone walking on your grave, made me shiver.

Something was going on here. Something I wasn't sure I liked.

I took a deep breath to keep my temper in check.

"The dome is new," I said. "The environmental equipment was just turned on. So was the gravity. The boy had a mouthful of Moon dust, but some of the information I received said that scientists were trying to turn that part of the dome into an Earthlike area, one that could grow grass, crops, and trees. So what happens if the boy was in the wrong place at the wrong time?"

"Go on," she said, and that feeling crawling along my spine grew worse.

I knew I was supposed to be a guinea pig, but I was supposed to solve the case. Only Riya was acting like she already knew the solution.

Maybe the test was more complicated than I had originally thought.

"The oxygen mix could be wrong," I said. "He doesn't look like a boy who suffocated, but I'm not sure what certain chemical mixes would do to a body."

She tilted her head at me, her expression neutral. I didn't like that either.

"Then there's the so-called soil. If he fell and got a mouthful of it, did it poison him? And what happens if the gravity came on too hard? The human body can survive four, five, six times Earth-normal. Healthy adult males can survive as much as eight times Earth-normal for a few minutes. But me? I couldn't survive that and neither could you. Our bones would shatter and our lungs would collapse. I have no idea if the same thing would happen to a fragile-looking eight-year-old, but I'll wager it might."

She nodded, but since she clung to the handhold, she didn't really move much.

I continued. "He has marks that look like bruises on his face and arms, but that's the only visible skin I can see. The bruises on his arms look like finger marks, but what if they're hematomas from shattered bones? What if the long bruise on his face is some kind of darkening agent from a poison he ingested?"

"You'll find that out," she said.

"Not by tomorrow," I said. "Because even if I found out that the gravity was too high and it crushed him, how would I know if he stumbled in there accidentally or if someone told him to sit there and wait, then went to the controls and turned the gravity to nine times Earth-normal?"

"The robots could give you those readings," she said.

"No, they can't," I said. "They'd give me the readings for now, not then. And we both know that computer readings can be tampered with. So the old data is as useless as my guesswork."

She stared at me.

"Give me a team," I said, "or I'm going to have to withdraw from this case."

"You can't withdraw," she said, and my stomach clenched. Here came the final moment—the moment when I chose my integrity or I chose my life.

"Watch me," I said, and shoved my way out of the room.

I'd be lucky to get a demotion. I was probably heading Earthside, to gravity that would feel as heavy to me as 9 g's would have felt to poor little Chen Proctor.

Riya caught my ankle and tugged me back inside.

"Talk to me," she said. "There's something else you don't like about this case, besides the unfamiliar terrain and the deadline. What is it?"

Whatever you could say about Riya Eoff, you couldn't call her dumb. I actually hated how perceptive she was.

I also wasn't fond of the way her hand still clung to my ankle. She wasn't going to let me out of here until she ruled the conversation over.

But I figured I couldn't make matters worse—at least, not for me. So it didn't hurt to be honest with her.

"Ninety-five percent of child murders," I said slowly, "are committed by a member of the family, usually a parent or stepparent."

She let go of my ankle. I drifted a little past her and had to grab a hand-hold to keep myself from spiraling back into the center of the room.

"You think Shane Proctor did this?"

"I don't know," I said. "I don't have a prime suspect. But if I did have a prime suspect, and if it was someone that Shane Proctor loved, then what? How would we prosecute? How would we even arrest? This whole setup is flawed, Riya. It's not enough to find out whodunit. We need to know how we're going to catch them, and even more important, how we're going to stop them—and anyone else—from ever doing this again."

She let go of her handhold and crossed her arms. Then she smiled at me. The smile was slow, but effective.

I wasn't exactly sure how to interpret it.

"You do realize that you have a gift for investigation, don't you?" she said.

I clutched the handhold. I had no real idea why she was flattering me.

And then I understood. "You do know who killed Chen."

"Yes," she said. Then she frowned. "No. Well, maybe I do. The death was ruled accidental. He was crushed when the gravity test malfunctioned. Chen had a penchant for wandering into test areas. He liked to be alone. It wasn't the first time he'd been caught somewhere he shouldn't have been. It was the first time he'd been injured."

"I thought you said he died."

"You know what I mean," she said. "But I don't think anyone considered that he hadn't wandered in there. I'm not sure if anyone thought about the fact that the controls could have been tampered with."

"Except you," I said.

Her smile widened. "I needed confirmation."

"Because you already knew that prosecuting anyone for this would be impossible."

She nodded, and this time, the movement made her bob like a buoy in a rough sea. "It's one thing to investigate crimes. It's another to prosecute them."

I thought I had just said that. But I didn't point that out to her. I didn't dare.

"I needed a simulation," she said. "I needed to show management that although our investigators can handle anything given the time and the resources, we need support on the ground. And the Moon colonies don't have that support. I can't even imagine what it would be like on the frontier, if we went with the settlers to Mars."

Not that we would be with those settlers. We'd only be observing them. And then we'd only be observing the very darkest sides of them.

"So this was all a simulation," I said. "The commands I gave the robots, the things I saw through my goggles. You'd set all that up so you had some footage to take to the brass."

Her smile faded. "It's not all a simulation," she said. "Chen Proctor is dead. And there will always be a lot of unanswered questions about the death."

"I could still investigate it," I said before I had a chance to think. I wanted to mitigate some of the damage I had done with my harsh tone.

"That boy's been dead for two years."

Which explained why I was told I had only rudimentary equipment to work with. Which was why the answers I got to the questions sounded as mechanical as the robots asking those questions.

"Two years," I repeated. "I suppose the body's long gone."

"They don't bury the dead on the Moon," she said. "Cremation is more efficient."

"And no one took the requisite information."

"Who would?" she asked.

"So who tried to hire us?" I asked. "It wasn't Proctor Mining, was it?"

She didn't answer me. She probably couldn't. It could have been anyone from a Proctor Mining competitor to one of those government unification types who wanted strong central oversight of the Moon.

"I need you to make a complete report," she said. "I want you to list every single thing we would have to do to successfully prosecute that boy's killer— if indeed he had a killer."

"Even if the killer was one of his parents," I said.

"Even if," she said.

I took a deep breath. I wasn't going to be banished. I wasn't going to get a demotion. I had done the job she wanted. I had passed the damn test, not even realizing exactly what it was.

"Essentially, then," I said, "I'm designing your Moon outsourcing program, using this one case."

She winced. "I wouldn't say that."

"Because," I said, getting warmed up, "if you said that, you'd owe me more compensation. I'd have moved up from investigator to management."

She nervously caught her floating necklace with one finger. "You once told me you don't want to be management."

I'd been taking risks all day, so I decided to take another. "If you're going to work me like management, you have to compensate me like management."

"Not without the job title."

"I don't want the job title," I said. "And I'll do the work, if you guarantee me my quarters for life, a richer food allowance, and the same medical care that the oldsters get."

"That's a lot," she said.

"I'm designing a brand-new outsourcing program for you."

"You're just suggesting it," she said.

"Still."

"How about more free time?" she asked.

I shook my head and felt my body sway. I clutched the handhold tighter. "Quarters for life, richer food, oldster-level medical care. Nothing less."

She made a face. I felt the tension return.

Then she extended a hand. "Done."

I let out a small sigh as I took her hand.

"Good," I said. "As soon as we have a contract, I'll do your report."

She sighed. "I wouldn't have pegged you for such a tough negotiator."

I usually wasn't. Except when someone's life was on the line. And this time, it was my life. With those guarantees, I could stop restraining myself. I could speak out about my investigations. I could stop worrying whenever I told the truth.

And I never again had to worry about going Earthside. I would stay here until my heart stopped beating.

I could do what I wanted without fear of losing this grand adventure.

I could truly live out my days, instead of waiting them out. I could float, gravity free, instead of sitting in a tiny piss-scented room, being crushed by the weight of the world and the lack of a future.

"Sometimes," I said, "you have to be a tough negotiator. It's the only way to get what you want."

"And you want to stay here," she said.

"Yeah," I said.

She smiled. "I don't think there's any worry about that."

Not anymore, I thought with more relief than I'd felt in my life. Not anymore.

MITIGATION

Karl Schroeder and Tobias S. Buckell

Canadian-born author Karl Schroeder is currently engaged in his mind-blowing Virga *series, a swashbuckling adventure set in an unimaginably enormous fullerene sphere—a structure large enough to contain a multitude of artificial suns. Karl is also responsible for the concept of "thalience," introduced in his novel* Ventus, *which has left the pages of science fiction and entered the vernacular of the artificial intelligence and computer networking communities.*

Tobias S. Buckell is a Caribbean-born speculative fiction writer who grew up in Grenada, the British Virgin Islands, and the US Virgin Islands. He is a Writers of the Future winner, Campbell Award for Best New SF Writer finalist, and Nebula Award finalist. His ongoing space opera, with its war between Caribbean peoples and Aztecs (currently Crystal Rain, Ragamuffin, *and* Sly Mongoose*), is not to be missed.*

Both of these authors combine old-fashioned adventure with mind-blowing concepts in their space operas. Here, they take things down to earth and closer to home in a story that is so fast forward it may be yesterday's news if we don't heed its warnings.

Chauncie St. Christie squinted in the weak 3 a.m. sunlight. *No, two degrees higher.* He adjusted the elevation, stepped back in satisfaction, and pulled on a lime green nylon cord. The mortar burped loudly, and seconds later, a fountain of water shot up ten feet from his target.

His sat phone vibrated on his belt and he half reached for it, causing the gyroscope-stabilized platform to wobble slightly. "Damn it." That must be

Maksim on the phone. The damn Croat would be calling about the offer again. Chauncie ignored the reminder and reset the mortar. "How close are they?"

His friend Kulitak stood on the rail of the trawler and scanned the horizon with a set of overpowered binoculars. "Those eco response ships are throwing out oil containment booms. Canuck gunboats're all on the far side of the spill."

"As long as they're busy." Chauncie adjusted the mortar and dropped another shell into it. This shot hit dead-on, and the CarbonJohnny™ blew apart in a cloud of Styrofoam, cheap solar panel fragments, and chicken wire.

Kulitak lowered his binoculars. "Nice one."

"One down, a million to go," muttered Chauncie. The little drift of debris was already sinking, the flotsam joining the ever-present scrim of trash that peppered all ocean surfaces. Hundreds more CarbonJohnnies dotted the sea all the way to the horizon, each one a moronically simple mechanism. A few bottom-of-the-barrel cheap solar panels sent a weak current into a slowly unreeling sheet of chicken wire that hung in the water. This electrolyzed calcium carbonate out of the water. As the chicken wire turned to concrete, sections of it tore off and sank into the depths of the Makarov Basin. These big reels looked a bit like toilet paper and unraveled the same way, a few sheets at a time: hence the name CarbonJohnny. Sequestors International (NASDAQ symbol: SQI) churned them out by the shipload with the noble purpose of sequestering carbon and making a quick buck from the carbon credits.

Chauncie and his friends blew them up and sank them almost as quickly.

"This is lame," Kulitak said. "We're not going to make any money today."

"Let's pack up, find somewhere less involved."

Chauncie grunted irritably; he'd have to pay for an updated satellite mosaic and look for another UN inspection blind spot. Kulitak had picked this field of CarbonJohnnies because overhead, somewhere high in the stratosphere, a pregnant blimp staggered through the pale air dumping sulfur particulates into a too-clean atmosphere to help block the warming sun. But in the process it also helpfully obscured some of the finer details of what Chauncie and Kulitak were up to. Unfortunately, the pesky ecological catastrophe unfolding off the port bow was wreaking havoc with their schedule.

A day earlier, somebody had blown up an automated U.S. Pure Waters,

Inc. tug towing a half cubic kilometer of iceberg. Kulitak thought it was the Emerald Institute who'd done it, but they were just one of dozens of ecoterrorist groups who might have been responsible. Everybody was protesting the large-scale "strip mining" of the Arctic's natural habitat, and now and then somebody did something about it.

The berg had turned out to be unstable. As Chauncie'd been motoring out to this spot he'd heard the distant thunder as it flipped over. He hadn't heard the impact of the passing supertanker with its underwater spur three hours later; but he could sure smell it when he woke up. The news said three or four thousand tonnes of oil had leaked out into the water, and the immediate area was turning into a circus of cleanup crews. Media, Greenpeace, oil company ships, UN, government officials—they would all descend soon enough.

"There's money in cleanup," Chauncie commented; he smiled at Kulitak's grimace.

"Money," said Kulitak. "And forms. And treaties you gotta watch out for; and politics like rat traps. Let's find another Johnny." The Inuit radicals who had hired them were dumping their own version of the CarbonJohnny into these waters. Blowing up SQI's Johnnies was not, Chauncie's employer had claimed, actually piracy; it was merely a diversion of the carbon credits that would otherwise have gone to SQI—and at $100 per tonne sequestered, it added up fast.

He shrugged at Kulitak's impatient look, and bent to stow the mortar. Broken Styrofoam, twirling beer cans, and plush toys from a container-ship accident drifted in the trawler's wake; farther out, the Johnnies bobbed in their thousands, a marine forest through which dozens of larger vessels had to pick their way. On the horizon, a converted tanker was spraying a fine mist of iron powder into the air—fertilizing the Arctic Ocean for another carbon sequestration company, just as the blimps overhead were smearing the sky with reflective smog to cut down global warming in another way. Helicopters crammed with biologists and carbon-market auditors zigged and zagged over the waters, and yellow autosubs cruised under them, all measuring the effect.

Mile-long oil supertankers cruised obliviously through it all. Now that the world's trees were worth more as carbon sinks than building material, the plastics industry had taken off. Oil as fuel was on its way out; oil for the housing industry was in high demand.

And in the middle of it all, Chauncie's little trawler. It didn't actually fish. There were fish enough—the effect of pumping iron powder into the ocean was to accelerate the Arctic's already large biodiversity to previously unseen levels. Plankton boomed, and the cycle of life in the deep had exploded. The ocean's fisheries no longer struggled, and boats covered the oceans with nets and still couldn't make a dent. Chauncie's fishing nets were camouflage. Who would notice one more trawler picking its way toward a less-packed quadrant of CarbonJohnnies?

Out in relatively clearer ocean Chauncie sat on the deck as the Inuit crew hustled around, pulling in the purposefully holed nets so that the trawler could speed up.

In this light the ocean was gunmetal blue; he let his eyes rest on it, unaware of how long he stood there until Kulitak said, "Thinking of taking a dip?"

"What? Oh, heh—no." He turned away. There was no diving into these waters for a refreshing swim. Chauncie hadn't known how precious such a simple act could be until he'd lost it.

Kulitak grunted but said nothing more; Chauncie knew he understood that long stare, the moments of silent remembrance. These men he worked with cultivated an anger similar to his own: their Arctic was long gone, but their deepest instincts still expected it to be here, he was sure, the same way he expected the ocean to be a glitter of warm emeralds he could cup in his hand.

Losing his childhood home, the island of Anegada, to the global climate disaster had been devastating, but sometimes Chauncie wondered whether Kulitak's people hadn't gotten the worse end of the disaster. As the seven seas became the eight seas and their land literally melted away, the Inuit faced an indignity that even Chauncie did not have to suffer: seeing companies, governments, and people flood in to claim what had once been theirs alone.

He found it delicious fun to make money plinking at CarbonJohnnies for the Inuit. But it wasn't big money—and he needed the big score.

He needed to be able to cup those emeralds in his hands again. On rare occasions he'd wonder whether he was going to spend the rest of his life up here. If somebody told him that was his fate, he was pretty sure he'd take a last dive right there and then. He couldn't go on like this forever.

"Satellite data came back," said Kulitak after a while. "The sulfur clouds are clearing up." Chauncie glanced up and nodded. They couldn't hide the trawler from satellite inspection right now. It was time to head back to port. As the ship got under way, Chauncie checked the sat phone.

Maksim had indeed called. Five times.

Kulitak saw his frown. "The Croat?"

Chauncie clipped the sat phone back to his waistband. "You said it was a slow day; we're not making much. And with the spill, it's going to be a zoo. We could use a break."

His friend grimaced. "You don't want to work with him. There's money, but it's not worth it. You come in the powerboat with me, the satellites can't see our faces, we hit more CarbonJohnnies. I'll bring sandwiches."

There was no way Chauncie was going to motor his way around the Arctic in a glorified rowboat. They'd get run over. By a trawler, a tanker, or any other ship ripping its way through the wide-open lanes of the Arctic Ocean. There was just too much traffic.

"I'll think about it," Chauncie said as the sat phone vibrated yet again.

Late the next evening, Chauncie entered the bridge of a rusted-out container ship that listed slightly to port. Long shadows leaned across the docks and cranes of Tuktoyaktuk, their promise of night destined to be unfulfilled.

"Hey Max," he said, and sat down hard on the armchair in the middle of the bridge. Chauncie rubbed his eyes. He hadn't stopped to sleep yet. An easy error in the daylong sunlight. Insomnia snuck up on you, as your body kept thinking it was day. Run all-out for forty-eight hours and forget about your daily cycle, and you'd crash hard on day three. And the listing bridge made him feel even more off-balance and weary.

"Took you damn long enough. I should get someone else, just to spite you." Maksim muttered his reply from behind a large, ostentatious, and extraordinarily expensive real wooden desk. He was almost hidden behind the nine screens perched on it.

Maksim was a slave to continuous partial attention: his eyes flicked from screen to screen, and he constantly tapped at the surface of the desk or flicked his hands at the screens. In response, people were being paid, currencies traded, stocks bought or sold.

And that was the legitimate trade. Chauncie didn't know much about Maksim's other hobbies, but he could guess from the occasional exposed tattoo that Maksim was Russian Mafia.

"Well, I'm here."

Maksim glanced up. "Yes. Yes you are. Good. Chauncie, you know why I give you so much business?"

Chauncie sighed. He wasn't sure he wanted to play this game. "No, why?"

Maksim sipped at a sweaty glass of iced tea with a large wedge of lemon stuck on the rim. "Because even though you're here for dirty jobs, you like the ones that let you poke back at the big guys. It means I understand you. It makes you a predictable asset. So I have a good one for you. You ready for the big one, Chauncie, the payday that lets you leave to do whatever it is you really want, rather than sitting around with little popguns and Styrofoam targets?"

Chauncie felt a weird kick in his stomach. "What kind of big, Max?"

Maksim had a small smile as he put the iced tea down. "Big." He slowly turned a screen around to face Chauncie. There were a lot of zeros in that sum. Chauncie's lips suddenly felt dry, and he nervously licked them.

"That's big." He could retire. "What horrible thing will I have to do for that?"

"It begins with you playing bodyguard for a scientist."

Uh-oh. As a rule, scientists and Russian Mafia didn't mix well. "I'm really just guarding her, right?"

Maksim looked annoyed. "If I wanted her dead, I wouldn't have called *you*." He pointed out the grimy windows. A windblown, ruddy-cheeked woman wrapped in a large "Hands around the World" parka stood at the rail. She was reading something off the screen of her phone.

"That's the scientist? Here?"

"Yes. That is River Balleny. Was big into genetic archeology. She made a big find a couple years ago and patented the DNA for some big agricorpo-ration for exotic livestock. Now she mainly verifies viability, authenticity, and then couriers the samples to Svalbard for various government missions out here."

"And she's just looking for a good security type, in case some other com-pany wants to hijack a sample of what she's couriering? Which is why she came out to this rusted-out office of yours?"

Maksim grinned over his screens. "Right."

Chauncie looked back at the walkway outside the bridge. River looked back, and then glanced away. She looked out of place, a moonfaced little girl who should be in a lab, sequencing bits and pieces sandwiched between slides. Cer-tainly she shouldn't be standing in the biting wind on the deck of thousands of tons of scrap metal. "So I steal what she'll be couriering? Is that the big payday?"

"No." Maksim looked back down and tapped the desk. Another puppet somewhere in the world danced to his string pulls. "She'll be given some seeds we could care less about. What we care about is the fact that she can get you into the Svalbard seed vault."

"And in there?"

Maksim reached under his desk and gently set a small briefcase on the table. "This is a portable sequencer. Millions of research and development spent so that a genetic archeologist in the field could immediately do out on the open plains what used to take a lab team weeks or months to do. Couple it with a fat storage system, and we can digitize nature's bounty in a few seconds."

Chauncie stared down at the case. "You can't tell me those seeds haven't already been sequenced. Aren't they just there for insurance, in case civiliza-tion collapses totally?"

"There are unique seeds at Svalbard," said Maksim, shaking his head. "One-of-a-kind from extinct tropical plants; paleo-seeds. Sequencing them destroys the seed, and lots of green groups ganged up about ten years ago in a big court case to stop the unique ones being touched. Bad karma if the sequencing isn't perfect, you know; you'd lose the entire species. Sequencing is almost foolproof now, but the legislation is . . . hard to reverse.

"We want you to get into the seed vault and sequence as many of those rare and precious seeds as you can. They have security equipment all over the outside, but inside, it's just storage area. No weapons, just move quick to gather the seeds and control the scientist while you gather the seeds. The more paleo-seeds the better. When you leave, with or without her, you get outside. You pull out the antenna, and you transmit everything. You leave Svalbard however you wish—charter a plane to be waiting for you, or the boat you get there with. We do not care. Once we have the information, we pay you. You leave the Arctic, find a warm place to settle down. Buy a nice house, and a nice woman. Enjoy this new life. Okay, we never see each other again. I'll be sad, true, but maybe I'll retire too, and neither of us cares. You understand?"

Chauncie did. This was exactly the score he'd been looking for.

He looked at the windblown geneticist and thought about what Maksim might not be telling him. Then he shook his head. "You know me, Max, this is too big. Way out of my comfort level. I'll become internationally wanted. I'm not in that league."

"No, no." Maksim slapped the table. "You are big-league now, Chauncie. You'll do this. I know you'll do this."

Chauncie laughed and leaned back in the chair. "Why?"

"Because if you don't"—Maksim also leaned back—"if you don't, you will never forgive yourself when military contractors occupy Svalbard in two weeks, taking over the seed vault and blackmailing the world with it."

"You've got to be joking." The idea that someone might trash Svalbard was ridiculous. Svalbard was the holiest of green holies, a bank for the world's wealth of seeds, stored away in case of apocalypse. "That would be like bombing the Vatican."

"These are Russian mercenaries, my friend. Russia is dying. They never were cutting edge with biotech, ever since Lysenkoism in the Soviet days. The plague strains that ripped through their wheat fields last year killed their stock, and Western companies have patented nearly everything that grows. Russian farms are hostage to Monsanto patents, so they have no choice but to raid the seed bank. They can either sequence the unique strains themselves, in hopes of making hybrids that won't get them sued for patent infringement in the world market, or they may threaten to destroy those unique seeds unless some key patents are annulled. I don't know which exactly—but either way, the rare plants are doomed. They'll sequence the DNA, discard everything but the unique genes . . . or burn the seed to put pressure on West. Either way—no more plant."

"Whereas if we do it . . ."

"We take whole DNA of plant. Let them buy it from us; in twenty years we give whole DNA back to Svalbard when it's no longer worth anything. It's win-win—for us and plant."

"It's the Russians behind the mercenaries? And no one knows about this."

"No one. No one but us." Maksim laughed. "You will be hero to many, but more importantly, rich."

Chauncie sucked air through his teeth and mulled it all over. But he and Maksim already knew the answer.

"What about travel expenses?"

Maksim laughed. "You're friends with those Indians—"

"First Nations peoples—"

"Whatever. Just get permission to use one of their trawlers. The company she's couriering for is pretty good about security. They drop in by helicopter when you're in transit to hand over the seeds. They'll call with a location and time at the last minute, as long as you tell them what your course will be. A good faith payment is . . ." Maksim tapped a screen. ". . . now in your account. You can afford to hire them. Happy birthday."

"It's not my birthday."

"Well, with this job, it is. And Chauncie?"

"Yes, Max?"

"You fuck it up, you won't see another."

Chauncie wanted to say something in return, but it was no use. He knew Maksim wasn't kidding. Anyway, Maksim had already turned his attention back to his screens. Chauncie was already taken care of, in his mind.

For a moment, Chauncie considered turning Maksim down, still. Then he glanced out the windows, at a sea that would never be the right color— that would never cradle his body and ease the sorrow of his losses.

He hefted the briefcase and stepped outside to introduce himself to River Balleny.

The trawler beat through heavy seas, making for Svalbard. The sun rolled slowly around a sky drained of all but pastel colors, where towering clouds of dove gray and mauve hinted at a dusk that never came. You covered your porthole to make night for yourself, and stepped out of your stateroom seemingly into the same moment you had left. After years up here Chauncie could tell himself he was as used to the midnight sun as he was to heavy seas; but the new passenger, who was much on his mind, stayed in her cabin while the seas heaved.

After two days the swells subsided, and for a while the ocean became calm as glass. Chauncie woke to a distant crackle from the radio room, and as he buttoned his shirt Kulitak pounded on his door. "I heard, I heard."

"It's not just the helicopter," Kulitak hissed. "The elders just contacted me over single sideband radio. We think Maksim's dead."

"Think?" Chauncie looked down the tight corridor between the trawler's cabins. The floorboards creaked under their feet as the ship twisted itself over large waves.

"Several tons of sulfur particulates, arc welded into a solid lump, dropped from the stratosphere by a malfunctioning blimp. So they say. There's nothing left of Maksim's barge. It's all pieces."

"Pieces . . ." Chauncie instinctively looked up toward the deck, as if expecting something similar to destroy them on the spot.

"I told you, you don't get involved with that man. You're out here playing a game that will get you killed. Get out now."

Chauncie braced himself in the tiny space as the trawler lurched. "It's too late now. They don't let you back out this late in the game." He thought about the private army moving out there somewhere, getting ready to take over the vault. All at the behest of another nation assuming it could just snatch that which belonged to all.

They still had time.

"Come on, let's get that package. She'll fall overboard if we don't help her out."

They stepped on deck to find River Balleny already there. She was staring up at the dragonfly shape of an approaching helicopter, which was framed by rose-tinted puffballs in the pale, drawn sky. She said nothing, but turned to grin excitedly at the two men as the helicopter's shuddering voice rose to a crescendo.

The wash from its blades scoured the deck. Kulitak, clothes flapping, stepped into the center of the deck and raised his hands. Dangling at the bottom of a hundred feet of nylon rope, a small plastic drum wrapped in fluorescent green duct tape swung dangerously past his head, twirled, and came back. On the third pass he grabbed it and somebody cut the rope in the helicopter. The snaking fall of the line nearly pulled the drum out of Kulitak's hands; by the time he'd wrestled his package loose the helicopter was a receding dot. River walked out to help him, and after a moment's hesitation, Chauncie followed.

"The fuck is this?" The empty drum at his feet, Kulitak was holding a small plastic bag up to the sunlight. River reached up to take it from him.

"It's your past," she said. "And our future." She took the package inside without another glance at the men.

They found her sitting at the cleaver-hacked table in the galley, peering at the bag. "Those seem to mean a lot to you," he said as he slid in opposite her.

Opening the bag carefully, River rolled a couple of tiny orange seeds onto the tabletop. "Paleo-seeds," she mused. "It looks like mountain aven, but according to the manifest"—she tapped a sheet of paper that had been tightly wadded and stuffed into the bag—"it's at least thirty thousand years old."

Chauncie picked one up gingerly between his fingertips. "And that makes it different?"

She nodded. "Maybe not. But it's best to err on the side of caution. Have you ever been to the seed vault?" He shook his head.

"When I was a girl I had a model of Noah's ark in my bedroom," she said. "You could pop the roof open and see little giraffes and lions and stuff. Later I thought that was the dumbest story in the Bible—but the seed vault at Svalbard really *is* the ark. Only for plants, not animals."

"Where'd you grow up?"

"Valley, Nebraska," she said. "Before the water table collapsed. You?"

"British Virgin Islands: Anegada."

She sucked in a breath. "It's gone. Oh, that must have been terrible for you."

He shrugged. "It was a slow death. It took long enough for the sea to rise and sink the island that I was able to make my peace with it; but my wife . . ." How to compress those agonizing years into some statement that would make sense to this woman, yet not do an injustice to the complexity of it all? All he could think of to say was, "It killed her." He looked down.

River surprised him by simply nodding, as if she really did understand. She put her hand out, palm up, and he laid the seed in it. "We all seem to end up here," she mused, "when our lands go away. Nebraska's a dust bowl now. Anegada's under the waves. We come up here to make sure nobody else has to experience that."

He nodded; if anybody asked him flat out, Chauncie would say that Anegada hadn't mattered, that he'd come to the Arctic for the money. Somehow he didn't think River would buy that line.

"Of course it's a disaster," she went on, "losing the Arctic ice cap, having the tundra melt and outgas all that methane and stuff. But every now and then there's these little rays of hope, like when somebody finds ancient seeds that have been frozen since the last glaciation." She sealed the baggie. "Part of our genetic heritage, maybe the basis for new crops or cancer drugs or who knows? A little lifeboat—once it's safely at Svalbard."

"Must be quite the place," he said, "if they only give the keys to a few people."

"It's the Fortress of Solitude," she said seriously. "You'll see what I mean when we get there."

Svalbard was a tumble of dollhouses at the foot of a giant's mountain. Even in the permanent day of summer, snow lingered on the tops of the distant peaks, and the panorama of ocean behind the docked trawler was wreathed in fog as Chauncie and River stepped down the gangplank. Both wore fleeces against the cutting wind.

A thriving tourist industry had grown up around the town and its famed fortress. Thriving by northern standards, that is—the local tourist office had three electric cars they rented out for day trips up to the site. Two were out; Chauncie rented the third. He was counting out bills when his sat phone vibrated. He handed River the cash and stepped across the street to answer.

"Chauncie," said a familiar Croatian voice. "You know who it is, don't answer, we must be careful, the phones have ears, if you know what I mean. Listen, after my office had that unfortunate incident I've been staying with . . . a friend. But I'm okay.

"That big event, that happens soon by your current location, I regret to say we think it has been moved up. They know about our little plan. We don't know when they attack, so hurry up. We still expect your transmission, and for you to complete your side of the arrangement. Our agreement concerning success . . . and failure, that still stands.

"Good luck."

Chauncie jumped a little at the dial tone. River waited next to the little car, and in a daze Chauncie put the briefcase behind his seat, took control, and they followed the signs along a winding road by the sea.

River was animated, pointing out local landmarks and chattering away happily. Chauncie did his best to act cheerful, but he hadn't slept well, and his stomach was churning now. He kept seeing camouflaged killers lurking in every shadow.

"There it is!" She pointed. It took him a moment to see it, maybe because the word *fortress* had primed him for a particular kind of sight. What Chauncie saw was just a grim mountainside of scree and loose rock, patched in places with lines of reddish grass; jutting eighty or so feet out of this was a knife blade of concrete, twenty-five feet tall but narrow, perhaps no more than ten feet wide. There was a parking lot in front of it where several cars were parked, but that, like Svalbard itself, seemed absurd next to the scale of the mountain and the grim darkness of the landscape. The cars were all parked together, as though huddling for protection.

Chauncie pulled up next to them and climbed out into absolute silence. From here you could see the bay, and distant islands capped with white floating just above the gray mist.

"Magnificent, isn't it?" said River. He scowled, then hid that with a smile as he turned to her.

"Beautiful." It was, in a bleak and intimidating way—he just wasn't in the mood.

The entrance to the global seed vault was a metal door at the tip of the concrete blade. River was sauntering unconcernedly up to it; Chauncie followed nervously, glancing about for signs of surveillance. Sure enough, he spotted cameras and other, subtler sensor boxes here and there. Maksim had warned him about those.

The door itself was unguarded; River's voice echoed back as she called, "Hallooo." He hurried in after her.

The inside of the blade was unadorned concrete lit by sodium lamps. There was only one way to go, and after about eighty feet the concrete gave over to a rough tunnel sheathed in spray-on cement and painted white. The chill in here was terrible, but he supposed that was the point; the vault was impervious to global warming, and was intended to survive the fall of human civilization. That was why it was empty of anything worth stealing—except its genetic treasure—and was situated literally at the last place on Earth any normal human would choose to go.

Six tourists wearing bright parkas were chatting with a staff member next to a set of rooms leading off the right-hand side of the tunnel. The construction choice here was unpainted cinderblock, but the tourists seemed excited to be here. River politely interrupted and showed her credentials to the guide, who nodded them on. Nobody looked at his briefcase; he supposed they would check it on the way out, not on the way in.

"We're special," she said, and actually took his arm as they continued on down the bleak, too-brightly lit passage. "Normally nobody gets beyond that." About twenty feet farther on, the tunnel was roped off. Past it, a T-intersection could be seen where only one light glowed.

These were the airlocks. Strangely, the doors were just under five feet high. Chauncie and River had to duck to step inside the right one.

The outer door shut with a clang. He was in. He'd made it.

When the inner door opened it was into a cavern some 150 feet long. Shelves filled with wooden boxes lined the interior like an industrial wholesale store. The boxes were stenciled with black numbers.

It was a polar library of life.

Chauncie pulled a small, super-spring-loaded chock out of his pocket.

He surreptitiously dropped it in front of the door and kicked it firmly underneath. It had a five-second count after his fingerprint activated it.

After the count the door creaked as it was wedged firmly shut. It was a preventative mechanism to keep River in more than anyone out.

River brought out her foil packet. It nestled, very small, in the palm of her hand. "They're amazing, seeds. All that information in that one tiny package: tough, durable, no degradation for almost a century in most cases. Just add water. . . ."

She led them to a row at the very back of the vault, reading off some sort of Dewey Decimal System for stored genetic material that Chauncie couldn't ascertain.

Here they were.

With a slight air of reverence in her careful, deliberate movements, she slid a long box off the shelf. She set it carefully on the ground and opened the lid.

Inside were hundreds of glittering packets. Treasure, Chauncie thought, and the idea must have hovered in the air, because she said it as well. "It's a treasure, you know, because it's rarity that makes something valuable. There used to be hundreds of species of just plain apples in the U.S. Farmers standardized down to just a dozen. . . . Somewhere in here are thousands more, if we ever choose to need them."

She seemed fascinated. As she crouched and started flipping through foil packets Chauncie retreated down the rows. He turned a corner out of her sight and pulled out the sheet of paper with Maksim's list of the rarest seeds.

Matching the code next to the list with where to find the seeds was slightly awkward; he wasn't familiar with it like River was. But by wandering around he found his first box, and opened it to find the appropriate packet with three seeds inside.

He flipped the briefcase open to reveal a screen, a pad, and a small funnel in the right-hand side. All he had to do was dump a couple seeds in the funnel and press a button. The tiny grinder reduced the seeds to pulp and extracted the DNA.

After it whirred and spat dust out the side of the briefcase a long dump of text scrolled down the screen, with small models of DNA chains popping up in the corners. Not much more than pretty rotating screensavers for Chauncie.

All he cared was that it seemed to be working.

But he was going to have to pick up the pace. That had taken several minutes. He cradled the briefcase, leaving the box on the floor as he strode along looking for the next item on the list.

There. This time the foil packet only had a single seed. Chauncie sat with it in the palm of his hand and stared at it. It was even more precious than River's paleo-seeds, because this was the only one of its kind in existence.

Suppose the machine wasn't working?

He shook his head and dropped the single seed in and listened to the grinding. More text scrolled down the screen. Success, a full sequence.

Chauncie blew out his held breath; it steamed in the freezing air.

"Just what the hell are you doing?" River asked. Her voice sounded so shocked it had modulated itself down into almost baritone.

There was another foil packet with two seeds in it nearby. It matched the list. Chauncie had hit a box full of rare and unique paleo-seeds stored here by a smaller government prospecting in the Arctic, or maybe a large and paranoid corporation. He dumped the seeds in and the briefcase whirred.

"Jesus Christ," River looked around him at the briefcase. "That's a sequencer. Chauncie, those seeds are one-of-a-kind."

He nodded and kept working. "Listen." River stayed oddly calm, her breath clouding the air over his head. "That might be a good sequencer, but even the best ones have an error rate. You're going to be losing some data. This is criminal. You have to stop, or I'm going to get someone in here to stop you."

"Go get someone." The chock would keep her occupied for a while.

She ran off, and Chauncie finished the box. He ticked the samples off his list, then started hunting for the next one along the shelves. It was taking too long.

There. He cracked open the new box and dumped the seeds in. River had caught back up to him, though, giving up on the door faster than he'd anticipated.

"Listen, you can't do this," she said. "I'm going to stop you."

He glanced over his shoulder to see that she'd pulled pepper spray out of the ridiculous little pouch she kept strapped to her waist in lieu of a purse.

Chauncie slid one hand into a pocket. He had what looked like an inhaler in there; one forcibly administered dose from it and he could knock her out for twenty-four hours. But he didn't want to leave River passed out among the boxes for the mercenaries to find. And if he left without her, he'd have to deal with the security guards as well.

He really couldn't live with victimizing any of them. River was a relatively naïve and noble refugee, caught up in a vicious world of international fits over genetic heritage and ecological policy. He was not going to leave her for the sharks. "Look, River, a private army-for-hire is about to land on Svalberd and do exactly what I'm doing—only not as carefully."

She hesitated, the pepper spray wavering. "What?"

"Overengineered agristock and plague. I'm told the Russians are pretty damn hell-bent on regaining control of uncopyrighted genetic variability for robustness. And to reboot their whole agricultural sector. They've hired a private army to come here; it gives them some plausible deniability on the world stage. But here's the thing: plausible deniability also means cutting up the DNA data into individual genes—scrambling it—so nobody can tell where they got them later on. All they want is the genes for splicing experiments, so they may preserve the data at the gene level, but they're going to destroy the record of the whole plant so they can't be traced. I've been sent to get what I can out of the vault before they get here."

River paused. "And who are *you* working for?"

Chauncie bit his lip. He hated lying. In this situation, she might as well hear the truth; he didn't have time to lay down anything believable anyway. "The Russian Mafia, they're connected enough to have gotten a heads-up. They think they can get some serious coin selling the complete sequences to companies across the world."

She stared at him. "You swear?"

"Why the hell would I make this up?"

He watched as she opened the zipper on the hip pouch and pocketed the pepper spray. She grabbed her forehead and leaned against the nearest shelf. "I can't fucking believe this. I need to think."

"It's a crazy world," Chauncie mumbled, and tipped a new pouch of seeds into the sequencer as she massaged her scalp and swore to herself.

The sequence returned good, and he stood up, looking for the next box. "What are you doing?"

"Looking for the next item on the list."

She walked over, and Chauncie tensed. But all she did was snatch the list from him. "There are a few missing they should have," she said.

"Like?"

"Like the damn seed I just brought here." River looked up at the shelves. "Look, you're wandering around like a lost kid in here. Let me help you."

He took the sheet of paper back from her. "And why would you do that?"

"Because until five minutes ago, I thought the vault was the best bank box, and seeds the best storage mechanism. You just blew that out of the water, Chauncie. As a scientist, I have to go with the best solution available to me at the time. If these mercenaries are going to invade and hold the seeds, then we need to get that genetic diversity backed up, copied, and kicked out across the world. Selling it to various companies and keeping copies in a criminal organization is . . . an awful solution, but we *have* to mitigate the potential damage. We have to make sure the seeds can be re-created later on."

He'd expected her to ask for a cut of the profit. Instead, she was offering to help out of some scientific rationalism. "Okay," he said, slowly. "Okay. But the list stays here, and you bring back the foil packets, sealed, to me."

"So that you can see that I'm not bringing back the wrong seeds, and so I don't rip up your list."

Chauncie smiled. "Exactly."

Plinking CarbonJohnnies was a lot more fun. And a hell of a lot easier. He felt ragged and frayed. Screw retirement; he just wanted out of this incredibly cold, eerie environment and the constant expectation that armed men would kick in the airlock door and shoot him.

But things moved quicker now. River ranged ahead, snagging the foil packets he needed and those he didn't even know he needed. For the next forty minutes he made a small mountain of pulped seed around him as the briefcase processed sample after sample, resembling more a small portable mill than an advanced piece of technology.

His sat phone beeped, an alarm he'd set back on the boat.

Chauncie closed the briefcase, and River walked around a shelf corner with a foil packet. "What?"

"It's time to go," Chauncie said. "We don't have much time."

"But . . ." Like any other treasure hunter, she looked around the cavern. So many more precious samples that hadn't been snagged.

But Chauncie had a suspicion that what River valued was not necessarily what the market valued. They had what they needed—best not push it any further. "Come on. We do not want to be standing here when these people arrive."

Chauncie bent over and rolled his fingerprint on the chock, and it slowly cranked itself down into thinness again. He placed it back in his pocket, and they cycled through the airlocks, again ducking under the unusually low entranceways.

They walked up the slight slope of the tunnel, the entrance looking small and brightly lit in the distance. The tourists were gone. As they passed the offices on their left one of the guards looked up and smiled. "All good? You were in there a long while. Sir, may I inspect your briefcase?"

Chauncie let him open it on a metal table while the other man carefully checked his coat lining and patted them both down. The briefcase contained nothing but empty foil packets; he'd left the sequencer under a shelf in the vault.

"What's this?" The guard drew out the sequencer's Exabyte data chip from Chauncie's pocket. He tensed.

But River smiled. "Wedding photos. Would you like to see them?"

The guard shook his head. "That's okay, ma'am." These guys probably didn't know DNA sequencers had shrunk to briefcase size. They'd been trained to think their job was to make sure no seeds left the vault; Chauncie was pretty sure the idea of them being digitized hadn't been in the course.

River shrugged with a smile, and they passed on. Chauncie breathed out heavily.

"Hey," the guard said. "If you're in town, take a few shots of that fleet of little boats out there. They're doing some serious exercises, wargaming some sorta Arctic defense scenario for the oil companies or other. They're all around Svalberd. Just amazing to see all those ships."

Chauncie's mood died.

They entered the mouth of the tunnel, shielding their eyes from the sun.

‖

Chauncie took a high-throughput satellite antenna out of the car's trunk and put it on the roof. He plugged his sat phone into it, then the Exabyte core into that. The sat phone's little screen lit up and said hunting. . . . "Damn it, come on," he muttered.

"Uh, Chauncie?"

"Just wait, wait! It'll just take a second—" But she'd grabbed his arm and was pointing. Straight up.

He craned his neck, and finally spotted the tiny dot way up at the zenith. The sat phone said *hunting* . . . *hunting* . . . *hunting* . . . and then, *No Signal*.

"You've been jammed," River said, quite unnecessarily.

Chauncie cursed and slammed the briefcase. "And there!" She grabbed his arm again. Way out in the sky over the bay, six corpse-gray military blimps were drifting toward them with casual grace.

"We're out of time." No way they'd outrun those in a bright yellow electric car. Chauncie looked around desperately. Hole up in the vault? Fortress of Solitude it might be, but it wouldn't keep the mercenaries out for more than a minute. Run along the road? They'd be seen as surely as if they were in the car.

He popped up the hatch of the car and rummaged around in the back. As he'd hoped, there was a cardboard box there crammed with survival gear—a package of survival blankets, flares, and heat packs standard for any far-northern vehicle. He grabbed some of the gear and slammed the hatch. "Run up the hill," he said. "Look for an area of loose scree behind some boulders. We're going to dig in and hide."

"That's not a very good plan."

"It's not the whole plan." He pulled Maksim's list out and rummaged in the car's glove compartment. "Damn, no pen."

"Here." She fished one out of her pocket.

"Ah, scientists." Quickly, he wrote the words *scanned* and *uploaded* at the top of the first page, above and to the right of the list. He underlined them. Then he made two columns of checkmarks down the page, next to each of the seeds on the list. "Okay, come on."

They ran back to the vault. Chauncie threw the list down just outside the door; then they started climbing the slope beside the blade. The oncoming blimps were on the other side; if there were men watching, it would look like

Chauncie and River had gone back into the vault. He hoped they were too confident to be that attentive. After all, the vault was supposedly unguarded.

"Over there!" River dragged him away from the concrete blade, toward a flat shelf fronted by a low pile of black rocks. The slope rose above it at about thirty degrees, a loose tumble of dark gravel and fist-sized stone where a few hardy grasses clung.

"Okay, get down." She hunkered down, and he wrapped her in a silvery survival blanket, then began clawing at the scree with his bare hands, heaping it up around her. The act was a kind of horrible parody of the many times he'd buried his sister in the sand back home.

Awkwardly, he made a second pile around himself, until he and River were two gravel cones partially shielded by rock. "You picked a good spot," he commented; they had a great view of the parking lot and the ground just in front of the entrance. He'd wedged the briefcase under the shielding stones; his eyes kept returning to it as the mercenary force came into view over the flat roof of the vault.

The blare of the blimps' turboprops shattered the valley's serene silence. They swiveled into position just below the parking lot, lowered down, touched, and men in combat fatigues began pouring out. Chauncie and River ducked as they scanned the hillside with binoculars and heat-sensing equipment.

"I'm cold," said River.

"Just wait. If this doesn't work we'll give up."

After a few minutes Chauncie raised his head so he could peer between two stones. The mercenaries had pulled the security guards out of the vault and had them on their knees. Someone was talking to them. The rest of them seemed satisfied with their perimeter, and now a man in a greatcoat strode up the hillside. The coat flew out behind him in black wings as one of the soldiers ran up holding something small and white. "Jackpot!" muttered Chauncie. It was Maksim's list.

"What's happening?"

"Moment of truth." He watched as the commander flipped through the list. Then he went to talk to the security guards, who looked terrified. The commander looked skeptical and kept shaking his head as they spoke. It wasn't working!

Then there was a shout from the doorway. Two soldiers came down to the commander, one carrying Chauncie's sequencer, the other a double handful of open foil packets.

Chauncie could see the commander's mouth working: cursing, no doubt. He threw down the list and pulled a sat phone out of his coat.

"He thinks we got the data out," said Chauncie. "There's nothing left for them to steal." The commander put away the sat phone and waved to his men. Shaking his head in disgust, he walked away from the vault. The bewildered soldiers followed, knotting up into little groups to mutter amongst themselves.

"I don't believe it. It worked."

"I can't see anything!"

"They think Maksim's got the data on the unique seeds. It's pretty obvious that we destroyed those in processing them. So these guys have exactly nothing now, and they know it. If they stay here they'll just get rounded up by the UN or the Norwegian navy."

"So you've won?"

"We win." The blimps were taking off. One of the guards was climbing into a car as the other ran back into the vault. Doubtless the airwaves were still jammed, and would be for an hour or so; the only way to alert the army camp at Svalbard would be to drive there.

"It's still plunder, Chauncie." Stones rattled as River shook them off. "Theft of something that belongs to all of us. Besides, there's one big problem you hadn't thought of."

He frowned at her. "What?"

"It's just that those guys are now Maksim's best customers. And the deal they'll be looking for is still the same: the unique gene sequences, not the whole plant DNA. Plausible deniability, remember? And Maksim would be a fool to keep the whole set after he's sold the genes. It would be incriminating."

He stood up, joints aching, to find his toes and ears were numb. Little rockfalls tumbled down the slope below him. "Listen," River continued, "I don't think you ever wanted to do this in the first place. The closer we got to Svalbard the unhappier you looked. You know it was wrong to steal this stuff to begin with. And look at the firepower they sent to get it! It was always a bad deal, and it's a hot potato and you'd best be rid of it."

"How?" He shook his head, scowling. "We've already scanned the damned things. Maksim . . ."

"Maksim will know the mercenaries got here while we were here. We just tell him they got here *before* us. That they got the material."

"And this?" He hefted the Exabyte storage block.

"We give it to that last guard; hey, he'll be a hero, he might as well get something for his trouble. So the DNA goes back into the vault—virtually, at least, after they back it up to a dozen or so off-site locations."

He thought about it as they trudged down the hillside. Truth to tell, he had no idea what he'd do if he retired now anyway. Probably buy a boat and come back to plink CarbonJohnnies. He wanted the emerald sea; he wanted those waters back. But now they were battered with hurricanes, the islands themselves depopulated and poor now that tourism had left, and the beaches had been destroyed by rising tides and storms.

From behind him she said, "It's an honorable solution, Chauncie, and you know it." They reached the level of the parking lot and she stopped, holding out her hand. "Here. I'll take it in. I've got my pepper spray if he tries to keep me there. And you know, now that the Russians have tried this they'll put real security on this place. Keep it safe for everybody. The way it was meant to be."

He thought about the money, about Maksim's wrath; but he was tired, and damn it, when during this whole fiasco had he been free to make his own choice on anything? If not now . . .

He handed her the data block. "Just be quick. The whole Norwegian navy is going to descend on this place in about an hour."

She laughed, and disappeared into the dark fortress with the treasure of millennia in her hand.

‖

Night was falling at last. Chauncie stood on the trawler's deck watching the last sliver of sun disappear. Vast purple wings of cloud rolled up and away, like brushes painting the sky in delicate hues of mauve, pale peach, silver.

There were no primary colors in the Arctic, and he had to admit that after all this time, he'd fallen in love with that visual delicacy.

The stars began to come out, but he remained at the railing. The trawler's lights slanted out, fans of yellow crossing the deck, the mist of radiance from portholes silhouetting the vessel's shape. The air was fresh and smelled clean—scrubbed free of humanity.

He wondered if River Balleny was watching the fall's first sunset from wherever she was. They had parted ways in Svalbard—not exactly on friendly terms, he'd thought, but not enemies either. He figured she was satisfied that he'd done the right thing, but disappointed that he'd gotten them into the situation in the first place. Fair enough; but he wished he'd had a chance to make it up to her in some way. He'd probably never see her again.

Kulitak's voice cut through his reverie. "Sat phone for you!" Chauncie shot one last look at the fading colors, then went inside.

"St. Christie here."

"Chauncie, my old friend." It was Maksim. Well, he'd been expecting this call.

"I can't believe you sent us into that meat grinder," Chauncie began. He'd rehearsed his version of events and decided to act the injured party, having barely escaped with his life when the mercenaries came down on the vault just as he was arriving. "I'm lucky to be here to talk to you at—"

"Oh, such sour grapes from a conquering hero!" That was odd. Maksim actually sounded *pleased*.

"Conquering? They—"

"Have conceded defeat. You uploaded the finest material, Chauncie; our pet scientists are in ecstasy. So, as I'm a man of my word, I've wired the rest of your payment to the new account number you requested."

"New acc—" Chauncie stopped himself just in time. "Ah. Uh, well thank you, Maksim. It was good, uh, doing—"

"Business, yes! You see how business turns out well in the end, my friend? If you have a little faith and a little courage? Certainly I had faith in you, and justly so! I'd like to say we must do it again someday, but I know you'll vanish back to your beloved Caribbean now to lounge in the sunlight—and I'd even join you if I didn't love my work so much." Maksim prattled happily on for a minute or two, then rang off to deal with some of his other hundreds of distractions. Chauncie laid down the sat phone and collapsed heavily onto the bench beside the galley table.

"Something wrong?" Kulitak was staring at him in concern.

"Nothing, nothing." Kulitak shot him a skeptical look and Chauncie said, "Go on. Go find us some CarbonJohnnies to bomb or something. I need a moment."

After Kulitak had left, Chauncie went to his cabin and woke up his laptop. An e-mail waited from one of the online payment services he'd tied to his Polar Consulting Services Web site.

Twenty-five thousand dollars had just been transferred to him, according to the e-mail, from an e-mail address he didn't recognize—a tiny fraction of the number Maksim had promised him. Chauncie had no doubt that it was a tiny fraction of the amount Maksim had actually paid out.

His inbox pinged. A strange sense of fated certainty settled on Chauncie as he opened the mail program and saw a videogram waiting. He clicked on it.

River Balleny's windburnt face appeared on the screen. Behind her was bright sunlight, a sky not touched in pastels. She was wearing a T-shirt, and appeared relaxed and happy.

"Hi, Chauncie," she said. "I swore to myself I wouldn't contact you—in case they got to you somehow—but it just seemed wrong to leave you in the lurch. I had to do something. So . . . well, check your e-mail. A little gift from me to you.

"You know . . . I really wasn't lying when I told you I think the seed data belongs to all of mankind. I walked back into the vault seriously intending to leave it there. But then I realized that it wouldn't solve anything. We'd still have all our eggs in one basket, so to speak. As long as the seed data was in one place, stored in only one medium—whether it was as seeds or bits on a data chip—it would be *scarce*. And anything that's scarce can be bought, and sold, and hoarded, and killed for.

"The guard wasn't around; he'd run down to the vault. So I just put the data core in an inner pocket and hung around for a minute. After we parted, I uploaded the data to Maksim; it wasn't hard to get an ftp address from the guy who'd introduced me to him in the first place. And, yeah, I gave Maksim my own bank account number." She chuckled. "Sorry—but I was never the naïve farmgirl you and Kulitak seemed to think I was."

Chauncie swore under his breath—but he couldn't help smiling too.

"As long as the genetic code of those seeds was kept in one place, it remained scarce," she said again. "That gave it value but also made it vulnerable. Now Maksim has it; but so do I. I made copies. I backed it up. And someday—when Maksim and the Russians have gotten what they want out of it and it's ceasing to be scarce anyway—someday I'll upload it all onto the net. For everyone to use.

"We all have to make hard choices these days, Chauncie—about what can be saved, and what we have to leave behind. Svalbard will always be there, but its rarest treasure is out now, and with luck, it won't be rare for long. So everybody wins this time.

"As to me personally, I'm retiring—and no, I'm not going to tell you where. And I've left you enough for a really good vacation. Enjoy it on me. Maybe we'll meet again someday."

She smiled, and there was that naïve farmgirl look, for just a second. "Good-bye, Chauncie. I hope you don't think less of me for taking the money."

The clip ended. Chauncie sat back, shaking his head and grinning. He walked out onto the deck of the trawler and looked out over the sea. The sun had just slightly dipped below the horizon, bringing a sort of short twilight. It would reemerge soon, bringing back the perpetual glare of the long days.

Stars twinkled far overhead.

No, not stars, Chauncie realized. There were far too many to be stars, and the density of them increased. Far overhead a heavy blimp was dumping tiny bits of chaff glued to little balloons. Judging by the haze, they'd dumped the cloud into a vast patch of sulfur particulates. Both parties would be in court soon to fight over who would get the credit for blocking the sun's rays as it climbed back over the horizon.

The sulfur haze had caused the remaining sun's rays to flare in a full hue of purples and shimmering reds, and the chaff glittered and sparkled overhead.

It was so beautiful.

LONG EYES

Jeff Carlson

Jeff Carlson is the author of the internationally acclaimed sci fi thrillers Plague Year, Plague War, *and the forthcoming* Mind Plague, *set in a world ravaged by an escaped nanotechnology that kills all warm-blooded life-forms below 10,000 feet elevation. Hard-hitting, near-future stuff,* Plague Year *was one of my favorite debut novels in years. I wasn't alone in being impressed with Jeff. His novelette "The Frozen Sky" was awarded first place in the Writers of the Future contest, and he is now collaborating with* New York Times *best-selling author David Brin on a novel titled* Colony High. *Expect to hear a lot more of Jeff soon.*

The ship turned to investigate and Clara tried to override, not because she wasn't curious but because she was still *Homo sapiens* in every way that mattered. It frightened her to lose control. But the men and women who'd agreed to invest in her had also invested in the top intelligence designers, and the central computer would not relinquish its orders.

Clara was bound deeply to the ship, so deeply that in one sense she was only another part of it, a human-shaped component in a cradle of gel and splice-wire. The complex nerves of her forearms and vertebrae were joined to plastic, metal, and glassware. She felt and influenced all systems directly—all except this one separate mind.

Their battle was quiet and careful until Clara determined that the central computer was most vulnerable during the corrective burns. The nav program was a doorway between them, and she tried to shut it down. She tried to make it run long. No luck. The cool orange K-star was just too close for the ship to ignore, and even Clara stared in enchantment as they approached the shadows of this system's comet cloud.

Maybe too soon, she stopped fighting and joined her skills with the ship. Dodging their way in through the outer system would be weeks of rapid math. It became a new contest and the adrenaline was good, but Clara still added a dirty word to the ship's reports when it cast a tightbeam back toward home.

‖‖

The dark and the cold were her friends. More than anything Clara liked to be able to *see*, so light and atmosphere were only complications—light because it blinded her telescopes, air because it distorted. Before her third nameday she'd also realized that living in one place had limits. She preferred to drift. She was good at it. She was rich for it.

She was a failed experiment, a parentless child of the state, grown *ex utero*, originally gene-crafted to be an asteroid mining dock controller, stacking ore and fuel pods in complex micro orbits, guiding slowboats in and out of the cluster. At first that had been a challenge, then only repetitive.

She'd left home six hundred years ago—six hundred years by herself, jetting away from known space, peering ahead and to all sides with fantastic eyes. The administration had been generous. They regretted what they'd made of her. They gave her the ram ship she wanted. Of course, the vast reach of macroscopes made any explorer almost irrelevant, except that in time she would gain new angles and the chance, here and there, for closer analysis. Her freedom came with a price. They'd programmed the central computer to report on a set list of potentially habitable systems first, all very similar G- and K-class stars. Clara didn't mind. She was doing exactly what she wanted, feeding imagery to her weird brain, as big as everything within range of her long eyes.

She was never lonely. If she needed noise, if she wanted other thoughts, there was always a signal to tap. Almost always. And in those rare zones where communications were sunk or blocked, bent by a sun or degraded by dust, the computer had millions of hours of radio traffic on record.

At a fraction of lightspeed, Clara wouldn't truly be outside the sphere of human activity for centuries to come. So she slept. She slept a lot. The ship went through its self-repairs and it did its work on her as well—and each time she woke, she was met by a new feast of colors and living shapes, the clockwork of stars all pulling on each other, halos of rock and ice. She wanted to go on forever. But she had also come to realize, too late, that she shouldn't have been so trusting.

‖

They were 17.7 light-years beyond the nearest recorded colony. Clara could not sell information for food or hardware or sex. She could get software patches, however, which could be the keys to reprogram the computer core. Keys to freedom.

She had one more chance to fight as the ship moved inward past a gas supergiant, readjusting its course again, but Clara didn't struggle. She put her energy into maps and sims instead. Unfortunately, the remainder of this system was just two inner planets and some groupings of comets falling through and back. There was nothing valuable except the second planet, a brown-and-black rock with a crude atmosphere.

Recalibrating her eyes for close-in analysis was both painful and delightful. Physically painful. Extreme adjustments took sweat and discomfort, but her reward was that she became this world's demigod, aware of every dust mote, able to gauge the poetry of its winds and its lopsided mantle and the hot echoing pockets within its surface.

The oxygen content the ship had locked onto was barely a wisp. Clara didn't wonder that it had been detected at all—her eyes were that powerful—but was it exploitable? Could human beings ever walk on this planet? If she drew down ten thousand comet impacts before she left, slamming more water into the environment, could she kick-start a terraforming effort that might almost become livable before anyone else arrived?

There was a lot of money and clout to be had just in the possibility, and something else she hadn't thought she wanted. Redemption. Clara was happy with the choices she had made, but she was still a woman who'd turned her back on everyone she knew.

This would be a way to reconnect. In a sense, it was almost a way to bring them with her. She hadn't thought that idea would feel so good, and she wasn't sure she liked it. She added a whole string of curse words to the ship's next tightbeam, but she was laughing, too.

"First of all," she said, "you can name it after me."

Clara ran a hundred orbits and mostly learned only new questions. The planet's surface was barren. Mold, lichen, and weeds grew here and there, but not enough to explain the fragile, swirling atmosphere or the animal methane.

There was life, but where? Clara sounded the pockets in the mantle but was frustrated by their number. Even the obvious air leaks—the warm storms and bleeds from underground—were little help. All of these were volcanic gases. Twice she isolated vents that also held traces of biological material, but both paths back inward were an impossible maze of fractures and cave-ins.

Everywhere the mantle was breaking. This planet had a weak core and only three-quarters Earth gravity. It had bubbled. Along the equator, in fact, one clump of hollows ran six hundred kilometers wide.

Some of these pockets were self-contained, forever dark and still. Some held or shared small oceans, or had at one time. That seemed promising, but the sulfur content in many was stifling and lethal. Most were empty. Clara's imaging was a busy song of pinpoints and caverns. Each resonated in its own way, holding anything from a few millibars of air to gluey salt sludge.

A huge crater gaped near one edge of the equatorial maze, a fourteen-kilometer bubble that had collapsed eons ago. Clara dubbed it the Kitchen Sink. It had everything thrown in except what she really wanted—positive proof. Dark weeds covered its ragged floor, thriving on outgassing and water vapor. The walls of the pit both protected it from the wind and held the heat of the sun. So she watched. She waited. There were also bugs in the Sink, hardshell creatures no bigger than her fingernail. Some ate leaves. Some ate the others.

The ship wanted to go down.

"No," Clara said, speaking aloud what she only needed to signal. The muscles in her back rippled as if to turn and run. Would she win a battle for control? The ship's designers had clearly given it more autonomy than they told her.

It cited reasons for landing. Good reasons. They needed samples. They could never know, only by scanning, if the chemical makeup of this ecology held threats too vicious to overcome. For example, there was a viral assembly on Ceti IV that hadn't touched the first colonists but destroyed the second generation, leaving them with eight hundred blind, idiot children. For all its stubbornness, even the central computer knew there was no point wasting more time here if this planet held something just as deadly.

Clara compromised, hoping to placate the machine. She brought them into synchronous orbit above the Sink and began to build a small probe in her nanoforge, using up precious steel and rubber. In the meantime she turned all eyes on the bugs. She ran simulations based on observable metabolic activity. She wargamed human DNA against incomplete models.

She found another ship.

∎∎

It was hardly even wreckage. It had been stripped down to the hull, and much of that was missing too. What remained was half buried, separated in a landslide. Clara only spotted it because she was running such tight grids.

The broken framework was old—older than her. Alien? The bounty on a find like that would be incredible. Humankind had yet to meet another thinking species. Even bacteria and bugs were rare. More likely it was one of the turn-of-the-millennium seed ships that had gone missing, or a religious group or privateers or just about anybody.

There was heat-warped debris abandoned in the strata around the tail. Had there been an internal explosion? Perhaps they'd impacted with some bit of cosmic junk—but it looked like they'd managed a controlled landing. All dead now. They hadn't even made much of a go of it, or Clara would have seen the evidence weeks before. Even just a few stragglers lost in the caves would have lit up on x-ray or deep red by now, much less a real, thriving outpost.

Clara was mad at herself for feeling relieved. What if she needed rescuing someday? Would she deserve it?

She stalled the ship with busy work for nineteen days before it got weird. The computer began triple-confirming even routines like meals and exercise and finally Clara gave up, sleepless and uneasy, caught in a rut of doubt. It was awful to distrust her home.

They touched down on the largest slab of rock that she could find, even though it was two kilometers from the wreckage and wet with puddling and ice. They massed only four tons, but Clara was leery of the jags and cracking across the crater floor. She preferred to deal with the slick rime of mud. Even on this plug of granite they might trigger a quake, and Clara wasted more than a minute of fuel letting her jets run, ready to fly again in an instant.

At the same time there was a frenzy among the bugs—a sudden, spiraling frenzy. She'd vaporized most of the pond, and a thick fog swept away from the ship, lifting on the heat of the jets, falling in the cold—and within the fog, the bugs mated and fed. Weeds exploded with spores or slumped apart, revealing strong blossoms like tongues. She should have expected it. Almost any disturbance here was a wealth of energy, and the ecosystem was ravenous. Good. Clara had no intention of venturing outside, and this should convince the ship that she'd already risked enough. She tried to imagine one footstep out there. Motion, noise, the faintest heat of friction—the bugs would swarm. Even the plants might attack with nettles or oils. She couldn't be sure what might damage a pressure suit. The ship was unrelenting in its priorities, but it needed her. It deferred to her, so long as she kept after its goals.

They lobbed their first probe at the wreckage and found nothing conclusive. Meanwhile they shot a dozen self-contained labs into the mud and through the air, busy little boxes full of chem tests. Clara enjoyed the work. Everything here was new and fascinating—and still at a safe distance. Only radio messages came back inside.

The gremlins appeared on the second night, a running, shifting mass of small bodies. Mammals. In infrared they burned hot on her screens, and Clara smiled and flexed. Her hand was exactly the same size as one of the creatures, and she waggled her fingers, mimicking their wire-limbed scramble across the rocky crater.

"There you are," she said. How deep must they live inside the cave systems to have escaped her previous scans? And how many more of them could there be?

They were scavengers, tough and nasty, with a constant jerk of claws-to-mouth. They uprooted weeds and hives in a furious, haphazard path that had its own sense.

With every sunset there was a severe drop in temperature. The plants reacted first. Some curled shut. Some exuded pigment as an insulator. The bugs fled into their burrows and then the air began to stir. Clara found it beautiful, but of course she was immune inside her ship.

A dance of cold swept the crater. On the surface above, the freeze was much worse—ripping winds and knives of dust. Cyclones reached down into the Sink but were countered by thermals and radiant heat, a dynamic in six directions.

The air was not breathable, not outside the mist that formed as the atmosphere separated into layers and tendrils. The fog she'd broiled from the pond had been warm and white. These channels of air were nearly invisible, chill against the ground, and she assumed the gremlins could see in infrared or were at least highly cold sensitive. Occasionally they edged in and out of the globs of breathable air, but in places they had to leave these safe zones. In many places there were gaps.

The gremlins were bipeds, thick in the back and belly. Big lungs. Big stomachs. They either gorged or starved.

They were stalking her.

The realization went through Clara like a seizure. *They're working their way to the ship. They've been doing it from the start.* Edging back and forth through the swirls and dead ends of the storm, the pack had already closed within two hundred meters. A short dash. Even if the pocket they were following continued to sweep away from her, as it was doing, they could survive that distance. She had seen them go farther.

But then what? Surely they wouldn't risk it unless there was breathable air around her, and even then what could they do? Claws on steel.

There were eighteen of them. They scrabbled too fast for Clara's eyes, but her systems had already detailed and profiled each one. They were smart little hairballs. Organized. Their leader kept scouts to four sides of the group, and these guards constantly ranged out and back again as the pack surged and split apart and re-formed, flowing with and between the available air.

Clara readied a batch of nano tags but didn't fire. Her tracer-recorders would only sting, bonding with skin and muscle, but she'd wait until the gremlins had gone most of the way back to their holes. Otherwise they might see the flash of her microcannons, and she didn't want to provoke them, didn't want them to associate the darts with her.

How smart were they really? Her mikes and subsystems said they did not have language, only the most basic grunts, although their gestures approached a speech equivalent. That made sense. They lived in a world where there wasn't always air to breathe . . . and maybe there were predators in the dark of the caves, listening, always listening.

Clara stared at a freeze-frame of the leader's face. For an instant her mind felt as still as the calm around the ship. Then all of the ideas lurking around her crashed together and she initiated her fusion engines.

Get out of here, she thought.

The gremlins' hair distorted but did not exaggerate the size of their braincases, and radar confirmed that their body fur had been trimmed in distinct ways, apparently stylized as well as grown out for warmth and protection. Their eyes were evolved for daylight. They had opposable thumbs and carried flecks of granite in hand.

They were on the verge of civilization, and Clara understood that this is what scared her most.

Get out.

But the ship countermanded her start-up, no less than four safety features blocking her intent. Clara flinched and went to emergency override. Blocked again.

A new current of air swept across her position, and the gremlins jumped into it, rushing the ship. Clara fired her nano tags in a single burst, wanting only to scare them. More than thirty percent missed or reported suboptimal placement. The rest squawked with data but barely slowed the pack. Then they were on her.

Clara screamed. "Aaaaaa—"

Her voice was such a lonely thing. Somehow that caught and centered her. She had no one else to rely on. She twitched within her box of gel and wire, lighting up all systems. There were no antipersonnel defenses, but if she could outfox the ship she could lift off and that would kill the little monsters, suffocate or bake or pop them. And she had the nanoforge. She could build a cat's claw if she just had the time.

But the gremlins found a seam where her cannons had opened and then another on her belly. They abandoned the first and threw themselves against the new crack in a kicking, hanging mass. They bent back the low-weight alumalloy.

Too late the ship realized the danger. Too late it dumped its protocols and gave her control. The gremlins were already inside, squeezing and twisting through any available space, repair panels, ductwork, delivery shunts. They ruptured the ship's innards like a climbing shouting cancer.

They were human.

"*Can you understand me?*" Clara put her words through the ship with docking radios and sonar, hysterical now. She needed to convey her fear if nothing else.

They were human. The data was clear. Clara didn't want to believe it, but the burst from the nano tags was unmistakable. Despite every adaptation these monsters were human beings—and that would make it easier to hunt them.

She tried again. "Stop! Stop! We can talk!" But at the same time she was designing a nerve gas in her forge.

They tore through the ship without purpose, bypassing the diagnostic web that let her track them, ripping into the circuitry of a macroscope instead. It was pointless. It was . . . No. Their goal here was the same as it had been out among the weeds. They were not attacking an enemy. They were plundering an unexpected resource.

"Stop!" Clara yelled.

They were savages. Even if they escaped with as much gear as they could carry, even if they ruined the ship and then slowly pulled its guts out piece by piece, the metals and wiring and everything else would only be sharper knives, better ropes, whatever stupid things they could fashion.

"This is your last chance," she said. "Please! Please."

She charged the lines of the macroscope and electrocuted three of them. She also sealed her box an instant before she dispersed her toxin, shutting off her own air, flooding the ship. It was a miniature storm within the night outside.

Thrashing, the gremlins did more damage.

Then it was still.

Clara felt too wild to mourn, but she closed her eyes briefly. Eighteen of them dead . . . an entire hunting party. . . . Had she just doomed however many others were still in the caves, killing their strongest and smartest?

The ship urgently needed repair bots, yet Clara had no trouble convincing it to build a cat's claw first, a whip-fast centipede with articulate saws, both to remove the little bodies and to defend themselves until they were spaceworthy again.

She made sure she had command. Then she sent it to drill out the ship's computer core.

||

Clara stayed another year, in orbit, following the gremlins with probes and nano tags. She invaded every tribe and secret, and quickly confirmed her initial reports.

They were as human as any gene-craft, like her. Even with their drastic changes they carried enough baseline DNA to vote and hold an inheritance if those privileges had meant anything in this place.

There was no telling how many generations it had been since their forefathers changed them. The seed ship must have been so badly damaged that even a partially hospitable world seemed like a godsend. This biosphere contained a few odd sugars, but there was nothing poisonous here, and a colonist could probably step right outside and subsist for a lifetime. The problem was how many lives—how few people could subsist. The scarcity of air, water, and food was an impassable limit.

One ancestor had had the vision to see what was impossible and what was not, the long eyes to look past how much would be sacrificed and push for what was best. Before they depleted whatever resources they had left, before their only chance was gone, they'd created a new breed of sons and daughters.

Clara had more in common with these survivors than anyone would think at a glance. Imagination. Grit. The solitude of being different. Yes, the gremlins had lost some of their intelligence with their size. Clara supposed that was a mistake or an unexpected side effect . . . but they were gaining it back.

They were packrats. They still had most of their ravaged ship down inside the caves, guarding its steel and plastics, thieving from each other, trading with each other, no longer aware of what use these substances might be except as money or superior tools. But on some level they remembered what they had been.

They were people in every way that counted. They cultivated mold as crops. They stacked walls of rock to make reservoirs where steam or runoff was available. The gremlins lived and bred and died, exploring, growing, failing, and succeeding, and ultimately Clara could not bring herself to betray them. This world was worth far more than she could ever spend, but she needed so little and the ship was completely hers now.

She could not rescue them. She could only ruin them. The arrival of normal men might be inevitable, but she could buy them time. Centuries. Would that be long enough for them to regain their intelligence and meet normal men as equals, no matter how small?

Maybe not.

Maybe they were too little to ever be very bright—but the chance was there, so for twelve months Clara forged medicine and tools and books and dropped these supplies to the crater floor. Meanwhile she broadcast her carefully drawn lies back toward known space. *Biohazard. This is an unstable, low-atmosphere world seething with acid bacteria.* Clara put a beacon in orbit to repeat the warning forever. Then she left the pocket planet and followed after her own vision again.

THE GAMBLER

Paolo Bacigalupi

Paolo Bacigalupi has been nominated three times for the Hugo Award, nominated once for the Nebula Award, won the Asimov's Readers Choice Award, and thrice been nominated for the Theodore Sturgeon Award, one of which he also won. His first short story collection, Pump Six and Other Stories, *was recently released to great acclaim. He is one of the most exciting of the new breed of short story writers, one whose ecological focus, unflinching penchant for hard truth, and exacting prose is garnering attention inside and outside of the genre. Recently he told* The Fix *in an interview, "I'd like to see the genre return to relevance. I feel like SF has tools that no other genre has, and yet it sometimes feels like we're wasting the potential. There are a lot of open questions about where we're going and what our future is going to look like, and I don't see a lot of SF tackling those issues. I'd like to see more." Amen. Here he closes out our book with a story that strikes to the heart of SF's purpose and importance, even as it lays bare our world's immediate future.*

My father was a gambler. He believed in the workings of karma and luck. He hunted for lucky numbers on license plates and bet on lotteries and fighting roosters. Looking back, I think perhaps he was not a large man, but when he took me to the *muy thai* fights, I thought him so. He would bet and he would win and laugh and drink *laolao* with his friends, and they all seemed so large. In the heat drip of Vientiane, he was a lucky ghost, walking the mirror-sheen streets in the darkness.

Everything for my father was a gamble: roulette and blackjack, new rice variants and the arrival of the monsoons. When the pretender monarch Khamsing announced his New Lao Kingdom, my father gambled on civil disobedience. He bet on the teachings of Mr. Henry David Thoreau and on whisper sheets posted on lampposts. He bet on saffron-robed monks marching in protest and on the hidden humanity of the soldiers with their well-oiled AK-47s and their mirrored helmets.

My father was a gambler, but my mother was not. While he wrote letters to the editor that brought the secret police to our door, she made plans for escape. The old Lao Democratic Republic collapsed, and the New Lao Kingdom blossomed with tanks on the avenues and tuk-tuks burning on the street corners. Pha That Luang's shining gold *chedi* collapsed under shelling, and I rode away on a UN evacuation helicopter under the care of kind Mrs. Yamaguchi.

From the open doors of the helicopter, we watched smoke columns rise over the city like nagas coiling. We crossed the brown ribbon of the Mekong with its jeweled belt of burning cars on the Friendship Bridge. I remember a Mercedes floating in the water like a paper boat on Loi Kratong, burning despite the water all around.

Afterward, there was silence from the land of a million elephants, a void into which light and Skype calls and e-mail disappeared. The roads were blocked. The telecoms died. A black hole opened where my country had once stood.

Sometimes, when I wake in the night to the swish and honk of Los Angeles traffic, the confusing polyglot of dozens of countries and cultures all pressed together in this American melting pot, I stand at my window and look down a boulevard full of red lights, where it is not safe to walk alone at night, and yet everyone obeys the traffic signals. I look down on the brash and noisy Americans in their many hues, and remember my parents: my father who cared too much to let me live under the self-declared monarchy, and my mother who would not let me die as a consequence. I lean against the window and cry with relief and loss.

Every week I go to temple and pray for them, light incense and make a triple bow to Buddha, Damma, and Sangha, and pray that they may have a good rebirth, and then I step into the light and noise and vibrancy of America.

My colleagues' faces flicker gray and pale in the light of their computers and tablets. The tap of their keyboards fills the newsroom as they pass content down the workflow chain and then, with a final keystroke and an obeisance to the "publish" button, they hurl it onto the net.

In the maelstrom, their work flares, tagged with site location, content tags, and social poke data. Blooms of color, codes for media conglomerates: shades of blue and Mickey Mouse ears for Disney-Bertelsmann. A red-rimmed pair of rainbow O's for Google's AOL News. Fox News Corp. in pin-stripes gray and white. Green for us: Milestone Media—a combination of NTT DoCoMo, the Korean gaming consortium Hyundai-Kubu, and the smoking remains of the New York Times Company. There are others, smaller stars, Crayola shades flaring and brightening, but we are the most important. The monarchs of this universe of light and color.

New content blossoms on the screen, bathing us all in the bloody glow of a Google News content flare, off their WhisperTech feed. They've scooped us. The posting says that new ear bud devices will be released by Frontal Lobe before Christmas: terabyte storage with Pin-Line connectivity for the Oakley microresponse glasses. The technology is next-gen, allowing personal data control via Pin-Line scans of a user's iris. Analysts predict that everything from cell phones to digital cameras will become obsolete as the full range of Oakley features becomes available. The news flare brightens and migrates toward the center of the maelstrom as visitors flock to Google and view stolen photos of the iris-scanning glasses.

Janice Mbutu, our managing editor, stands at the door to her office, watching with a frown. The maelstrom's red bath dominates the newsroom, a pressing reminder that Google is beating us, sucking away traffic. Behind glass walls, Bob and Casey, the heads of the Burning Wire, our own consumer technology feed, are screaming at their reporters, demanding they do better. Bob's face has turned almost as red as the maelstrom.

The maelstrom's true name is LiveTrack IV. If you were to go downstairs to the fifth floor and pry open the server racks, you would find a sniper sight logo and the words SCRY GLASS—KNOWLEDGE IS POWER stamped on their chips in metallic orange, which would tell you that even though Bloomberg rents us the machines, it is a Google-Neilsen partnership that provides the proprietary algorithms for analyzing the net flows—which means we pay a competitor to tell us what is happening with our own content.

LiveTrack IV tracks media user data—Web site, feed, VOD, audiostream, TV broadcast—with Google's own net statistics gathering programs, aided by Nielsen hardware in personal data devices ranging from TVs to tablets to ear buds to handsets to car radios. To say that the maelstrom keeps a finger on the pulse of media is an understatement. Like calling the monsoon a little wet. The maelstrom is the pulse, the pressure, the blood-oxygen mix; the count of red cells and white, of T-cells and BAC, the screening for AIDS and hepatitis G. . . . It is reality.

Our service version of the maelstrom displays the performance of our own content and compares it to the top one hundred user-traffic events in real-time. My own latest news story is up in the maelstrom, glittering near the edge of the screen, a tale of government incompetence: the harvested DNA of the checkerspot butterfly, already extinct, has been destroyed through mismanagement at the California Federal Biological Preserve Facility. The butterfly—along with sixty-two other species—was subjected to improper storage protocols, and now there is nothing except a little dust in vials. The samples literally blew away. My coverage of the story opens with federal workers down on their knees in a two-billion-dollar climate-controlled vault, with a dozen crime scene vacuums that they've borrowed from LAPD, trying to suck up a speck of butterfly that they might be able to reconstitute at some future time.

In the maelstrom, the story is a pinprick beside the suns and pulsing moons of traffic that represent other reporters' content. It doesn't compete well with news of Frontal Lobe devices, or reviews of Armored Total Combat, or live feeds of the Binge-Purge championships. It seems that the only people who are reading my story are the biologists I interviewed. This is not surprising. When I wrote about bribes for subdivision approvals, the only people who read the story were county planners. When I wrote about cronyism in the selection of city water recycling technologies, the only people who read were water engineers. Still, even though no one seems to care about these stories, I am drawn to them, as though poking at the tiger of the American government will somehow make up for not being able to poke at the little cub of New Divine Monarch Khamsing. It is a foolish thing, a sort of Don Quixote crusade. As a consequence, my salary is the smallest in the office.

"Whoooo!"

Heads swivel from terminals, look for the noise: Marty Mackley, grinning.

"You can thank me . . ." He leans down and taps a button on his keyboard. "Now."

A new post appears in the maelstrom, a small green orb announcing itself on the Glamour Report, Scandal Monkey blog, and Marty's byline feeds. As we watch, the post absorbs pings from software clients around the world, notifying the millions of people who follow his byline that he has launched a new story.

I flick my tablet open, check the tags:

Double DP,
Redneck HipHop,
Music News,
Schadenfreude,
underage,
pedophilia . . .

According to Mackley's story, Double DP the Russian mafia cowboy rapper—who, in my opinion, is not as good as the Asian pop sensation Kulaap, but whom half the planet likes very much—is accused of impregnating the fourteen-year-old daughter of his face sculptor. Readers are starting to notice, and with their attention Marty's green-glowing news story begins to muscle for space in the maelstrom. The content star pulses, expands, and then, as though someone has thrown gasoline on it, it explodes. Double DP hits the social sites, starts getting recommended, sucks in more readers, more links, more clicks . . . and more ad dollars.

Marty does a pelvic grind of victory, then waves at everyone for their attention. "And that's not all, folks." He hits his keyboard again, and another story posts: live feeds of Double's house, where . . . it looks as though the man who popularized Redneck Russians is heading out the door in a hurry. It is a surprise to see video of the house, streaming live. Most freelance paparazzi are not patient enough to sit and hope that maybe, perhaps, something interesting will happen. This looks as though Marty has stationed his own exclusive papcams at the house, to watch for something like this.

We all watch as Double DP locks the door behind himself. Marty says, "I thought DP deserved the courtesy of notification that the story was going live."

"Is he fleeing?" Mikela Plaa asks.

Marty shrugs. "We'll see."

And indeed, it does look as if Double is about to do what Americans have popularized as an "OJ." He is into his red Hummer. Pulling out.

Under the green glow of his growing story, Marty smiles. The story is getting bigger, and Marty has stationed himself perfectly for the development. Other news agencies and blogs are playing catch-up. Follow-on posts wink into existence in the maelstrom, gathering a momentum of their own as newsrooms scramble to hook our traffic.

"Do we have a helicopter?" Janice asks. She has come out of her glass office to watch the show.

Marty nods. "We're moving it into position. I just bought exclusive angel view with the cops, too, so everyone's going to have to license our footage."

"Did you let *Long Arm of the Law* know about the cross-content?"

"Yeah. They're kicking in from their budget for the helicopter."

Marty sits down again, begins tapping at his keyboard, a machine-gun of data entry. A low murmur comes from the tech pit, Cindy C. calling our telecom providers, locking down trunklines to handle an anticipated data surge. She knows something that we don't, something that Marty has prepared her for. She's bringing up mirrored server farms. Marty seems unaware of the audience around him. He stops typing. Stares up at the maelstrom, watching his glowing ball of content. He is the maestro of a symphony.

The cluster of competing stories are growing as Gawker and Newsweek and Throb all organize themselves and respond. Our readers are clicking away from us, trying to see if there's anything new in our competitor's coverage.

Marty smiles, hits his "publish" key, and dumps a new bucket of meat into the shark tank of public interest: a video interview with the fourteen-year-old. On-screen, she looks very young, shockingly so. She has a teddy bear.

"I swear I didn't plant the bear," Marty comments. "She had it on her own."

The girl's accusations are being mixed over Double's run for the border, a kind of synth loop of accusations:

"And then he . . ."

"And I said . . ."

"He's the only one I've ever . . ."

It sounds as if Marty has licensed some of Double's own beats for the coverage of his fleeing Humvee. The video outtakes are already bouncing around YouTube and MotionSwallow like Ping-Pong balls. The maelstrom has moved Double DP to the center of the display as more and more feeds and sites point to the content. Not only is traffic up, but the post is gaining in social rank as the numbers of links and social pokes increase.

"How's the stock?" someone calls out.

Marty shakes his head. "They locked me out from showing the display."

This, because whenever he drops an important story, we all beg him to show us the big picture. We all turn to Janice. She rolls her eyes, but she gives the nod. When Cindy finishes buying bandwidth, she unlocks the view. The maelstrom slides aside as a second window opens, all bar graphs and financial landscape: our stock price as affected by the story's expanding traffic—and expanding ad revenue.

The stock bots have their own version of the maelstrom; they've picked up the reader traffic shift. Buy and sell decisions roll across the screen, responding to the popularity of Mackley's byline. As he feeds the story, the beast grows. More feeds pick us up, more people recommend the story to their friends, and every one of them is being subjected to our advertisers' messages, which means more revenue for us and less for everyone else. At this point, Mackley is bigger than the Super Bowl. Given that the story is tagged with Double DP, it will have a targetable demographic: thirteen- to twenty-four-year-olds who buy lifestyle gadgets, new music, edge clothes, first-run games, boxed hairstyles, tablet skins, and ringtones: not only a large demographic, a valuable one.

Our stock ticks up a point. Holds. Ticks up another. We've got four different screens running now. The papcam of Double DP, chase cycles with views of the cops streaking after him, the chopper lifting off, and the window with the fourteen-year-old interviewing. The girl is saying, "I really feel for him. We have a connection. We're going to get married," and there's his Hummer screaming down Santa Monica Boulevard with his song "Cowboy Banger" on the audio overlay.

A new wave of social pokes hits the story. Our stock price ticks up again. Daily bonus territory. The clicks are pouring in. It's got the right combination of content, what Mackley calls the "Three S's": sex, stupidity, and schadenfreude. The stock ticks up again. Everyone cheers. Mackley takes a bow. We all love him. He is half the reason I can pay my rent. Even a small newsroom bonus from his work is enough for me to live. I'm not sure how much he makes for himself when he creates an event like this. Cindy tells me that it is "solid seven, baby." His byline feed is so big he could probably go independent, but then he would not have the resources to scramble a helicopter for a chase toward Mexico. It is a symbiotic relationship. He does what he does best, and Milestone pays him like a celebrity.

Janice claps her hands. "All right, everyone. You've got your bonus. Now back to work."

A general groan rises. Cindy cuts the big monitor away from stocks and bonuses and back to the work at hand: generating more content to light the maelstrom, to keep the newsroom glowing green with flares of Milestone coverage—everything from reviews of Mitsubishi's 100 mpg Road Cruiser to how to choose a perfect turkey for Thanksgiving. Mackley's story pulses over us as we work. He spins off smaller additional stories, updates, interactivity features, encouraging his vast audience to ping back just one more time.

Marty will spend the entire day in conversation with this elephant of a story that he has created. Encouraging his visitors to return for just one more click. He'll give them chances to poll each other, discuss how they'd like to see DP punished, ask whether you can actually fall in love with a fourteen-year-old. This one will have a long life, and he will raise it like a proud father, feeding and nurturing it, helping it make its way in the rough world of the maelstrom.

My own little green speck of content has disappeared. It seems that even government biologists feel for Double DP.

||

When my father was not placing foolish bets on revolution, he taught agronomy at the National Lao University. Perhaps our lives would have been different if he had been a rice farmer in the paddies of the capital's suburbs, instead of surrounded by intellectuals and ideas. But his karma was to be a teacher and a researcher, and so while he was increasing Lao rice production by 30 percent, he was also filling himself with gambler's fancies: Thoreau, Gandhi, Martin Luther King, Sakharov, Mandela, Aung Sung Kyi. True gamblers, all. He would say that if white South Africans could be made to feel shame, then the pretender monarch must right his ways. He claimed that Thoreau must have been Lao, the way he protested so politely.

In my father's description, Thoreau was a forest monk, gone into the jungle for enlightenment. To live amongst the banyan and the climbing vines of Massachusetts and to meditate on the nature of suffering. My father believed he was undoubtedly some arhat reborn. He often talked of Mr. Henry David, and in my imagination this *falang*, too, was a large man like my father.

When my father's friends visited in the dark—after the coup and the countercoup, and after the march of Khamsing's Chinese-supported insurgency—they would often speak of Mr. Henry David. My father would sit with his friends and students and drink black Lao coffee and smoke cigarettes, and then he would write carefully worded complaints against the government that his students would then copy and leave in public places, distribute into gutters, and stick onto walls in the dead of night.

His guerrilla complaints would ask where his friends had gone, and why their families were so alone. He would ask why monks were beaten on their heads by Chinese soldiers when they sat in hunger strike before the palace. Sometimes, when he was drunk and when these small gambles did not satisfy his risk-taking nature, he would send editorials to the newspapers.

None of these were ever printed, but he was possessed with some spirit that made him think that perhaps the papers would change. That his stature as a father of Lao agriculture might somehow sway the editors to commit suicide and print his complaints.

It ended with my mother serving coffee to a secret police captain while two more policemen waited outside our door. The captain was very polite: he offered my father a 555 cigarette—a brand that already had become rare and contraband—and lit it for him. Then he spread the whisper sheet onto the coffee table, gently pushing aside the coffee cups and their saucers to make room for it. It was rumpled and torn, stained with mud. Full of accusations against Khamsing. Unmistakable as one of my father's.

My father and the policeman both sat and smoked, studying the paper silently.

Finally, the captain asked, "Will you stop?"

My father drew on his cigarette and let the smoke out slowly as he studied the whisper sheet between them. The captain said, "We all respect what you have done for the Lao kingdom. I myself have family who would have starved if not for your work in the villages." He leaned forward. "If you promise to stop writing these whispers and complaints, everything can be forgotten. Everything."

Still, my father didn't say anything. He finished his cigarette. Stubbed it out. "It would be difficult to make that sort of promise," he said.

The captain was surprised. "You have friends who have spoken on your behalf. Perhaps you would reconsider. For their sake."

My father made a little shrug. The captain spread the rumpled whisper sheet, flattening it out more completely. Read it over. "These sheets do nothing," he said. "Khamsing's dynasty will not collapse because you print a few complaints. Most of these are torn down before anyone reads them. They do nothing. They are pointless." He was almost begging. He looked over and saw me watching at the door. "Give this up. For your family, if not your friends."

I would like to say that my father said something grand. Something honorable about speaking against tyranny. Perhaps invoked one of his idols. Aung Sung Kyi or Sakharov, or Mr. Henry David and his penchant for polite protest. But he didn't say anything. He just sat with his hands on his knees, looking down at the torn whisper sheet. I think now that he must have been very afraid. Words always came easily to him, before. Instead, all he did was repeat himself. "It would be difficult."

The captain waited. When it became apparent that my father had nothing else to say, he put down his coffee cup and motioned for his men to come inside. They were all very polite. I think the captain even apologized to my mother as they led him out the door.

‖

We are into day three of the Double DP bonanza, and the green sun glows brightly over all of us, bathing us in its soothing, profitable glow. I am working on my newest story with my Frontal Lobe ear buds in, shutting out everything except the work at hand. It is always a little difficult to write in one's third language, but I have my favorite singer and fellow countryperson Kulaap whispering in my ear that "Love is a Bird," and the work is going well. With Kulaap singing to me in our childhood language, I feel very much at home.

A tap on my shoulder interrupts me. I pull out my ear buds and look around. Janice, standing over me. "Ong, I need to talk to you." She motions me to follow.

In her office, she closes the door behind me and goes to her desk. "Sit down, Ong." She keys her tablet, scrolls through data. "How are things going for you?"

"Very well. Thank you." I'm not sure if there is more that she wants me to say, but it is likely that she will tell me. Americans do not leave much to guesswork.

"What are you working on for your next story?" she asks.

I smile. I like this story; it reminds me of my father. And with Kulaap's soothing voice in my ears I have finished almost all of my research. The bluet, a flower made famous in Mr. Henry David Thoreau's journals, is blooming too early to be pollinated. Bees do not seem to find it when it blooms in March. The scientists I interviewed blame global warming, and now the flower is in danger of extinction. I have interviewed biologists and local naturalists, and now I would like to go to Walden Pond on a pilgrimage for this bluet that may soon also be bottled in a federal reserve laboratory with its techs in clean suits and their crime scene vacuums.

When I finish describing the story, Janice looks at me as if I am crazy. I can tell that she thinks I am crazy, because I can see it on her face. And also because she tells me.

"You're fucking crazy!"

Americans are very direct. It's difficult to keep face when they yell at you. Sometimes, I think that I have adapted to America. I have been here for five years now, ever since I came from Thailand on a scholarship, but at times like this, all I can do is smile and try not to cringe as they lose their face and yell and rant. My father was once struck in the face with an official's shoe, and he did not show his anger. But Janice is American, and she is very angry.

"There's no way I'm going to authorize a junket like that!"

I try to smile past her anger, and then remember that the Americans don't see an apologetic smile in the same way that a Lao would. I stop smiling and make my face look . . . something. Earnest, I hope.

"The story is very important," I say. "The ecosystem isn't adapting correctly to the changing climate. Instead, it has lost . . ." I grope for the word. "Synchronicity. These scientists think that the flower can be saved, but only if they import a bee that is available in Turkey. They think it can replace the function of the native bee population, and they think that it will not be too disruptive."

"Flowers and Turkish bees."

"Yes. It is an important story. Do they let the flower go extinct? Or try to keep the famous flower, but alter the environment of Walden Pond? I think your readers will think it is very interesting."

"More interesting than that?" She points through her glass wall at the maelstrom, at the throbbing green sun of Double DP, who has now barricaded himself in a Mexican hotel and has taken a pair of fans hostage.

"You know how many clicks we're getting?" she asks. "We're exclusive. Marty's got Double's trust and is going in for an interview tomorrow, assuming the Mexicans don't just raid it with commandos. We've got people clicking back every couple minutes just to look at Marty's blog about his preparations to go in."

The glowing globe not only dominates the maelstrom's screen, it washes everything else out. If we look at the stock bots, everyone who doesn't have protection under our corporate umbrella has been hurt by the loss of eyeballs. Even the Frontal Lobe/Oakley story has been swallowed. Three days of completely dominating the maelstrom has been very profitable for us. Now Marty's showing his viewers how he will wear a flak jacket in case the Mexican commandos attack while he is discussing the nature of true love with DP. And he has another exclusive interview with the mother ready to post as well. Cindy has been editing the footage and telling us all how disgusted she is with the whole thing. The woman apparently drove her daughter to DP's mansion for a midnight pool party, alone.

"Perhaps some people are tired of DP and wish to see something else," I suggest.

"Don't shoot yourself in the foot with a flower story, Ong. Even Pradeep's cooking journey through Ladakh gets more viewers than this stuff you're writing."

She looks as though she will say more, but then she simply stops. It seems as if she is considering her words. It is uncharacteristic. She normally speaks before her thoughts are arranged.

"Ong, I like you," she says. I make myself smile at this, but she continues. "I hired you because I had a good feeling about you. I didn't have a problem with clearing the visas to let you stay in the country. You're a good person. You write well. But you're averaging less than a thousand pings on your byline feed." She looks down at her tablet, then back up at me. "You need to up your average. You've got almost no readers selecting you for Page One. And even when they do subscribe to your feed, they're putting it in the third tier."

"Spinach reading," I supply.

"What?"

"Mr. Mackley calls it spinach reading. When people feel like they should do something with virtue, like eat their spinach, they click to me. Or else read Shakespeare."

I blush, suddenly embarrassed. I do not mean to imply that my work is of the same caliber as a great poet. I want to correct myself, but I'm too embarrassed. So instead I shut up, and sit in front of her, blushing.

She regards me. "Yes. Well, that's a problem. Look, I respect what you do. You're obviously very smart." Her eyes scan her tablet. "The butterfly thing you wrote was actually pretty interesting."

"Yes?" I make myself smile again.

"It's just that no one wants to read these stories."

I try to protest. "But you hired me to write the important stories. The stories about politics and the government, to continue the traditions of the old newspapers. I remember what you said when you hired me."

"Yeah, well." She looks away. "I was thinking more about a good scandal."

"The checkerspot is a scandal. That butterfly is now gone."

She sighs. "No, it's not a scandal. It's just a depressing story. No one reads a depressing story, at least, not more than once. And no one subscribes to a depressing byline feed."

"A thousand people do."

"A thousand people." She laughs. "We aren't some Laotian community weblog, we're Milestone, and we're competing for clicks with *them*." She waves outside, indicating the maelstrom. "Your stories don't last longer than half a day; they never get social-poked by anyone except a fringe." She shakes her head. "Christ, I don't even know who your demographic is. Centenarian hippies? Some federal bureaucrats? The numbers just don't justify the amount of time you spend on stories."

"What stories do you wish me to write?"

"I don't know. Anything. Product reviews. News you can use. Just not any more of this 'we regret to inform you of bad news' stuff. If there isn't something a reader can do about the damn butterfly, then there's no point in telling them about it. It just depresses people, and it depresses your numbers."

"We don't have enough numbers from Marty?"

She laughs at that. "You remind me of my mother. Look, I don't want to cut you, but if you can't start pulling at least a fifty thousand daily average, I won't have any choice. Our group median is way down in comparison to other teams, and when evaluations come around, we look bad. I'm up against Nguyen in the Tech and Toys pool, and Penn in Yoga and Spirituality, and no one wants to read about how the world's going to shit. Go find me some stories that people want to read."

She says a few more things, words that I think are meant to make me feel inspired and eager, and then I am standing outside the door, once again facing the maelstrom.

The truth is that I have never written popular stories. I am not a popular story writer. I am earnest. I am slow. I do not move at the speed these Americans seem to love. *Find a story that people want to read.* I can write some follow-up to Mackley, to Double DP, perhaps assist with sidebars to his main piece, but somehow, I suspect that the readers will know that I am faking it.

Marty sees me standing outside of Janice's office. He comes over.

"She giving you a hard time about your numbers?"

"I do not write the correct sort of stories."

"Yeah. You're an idealist."

We both stand there for a moment, meditating on the nature of idealism. Even though he is very American, I like him because he is sensitive to people's hearts. People trust him. Even Double DP trusts him, though Marty blew his name over every news tablet's front page. Marty has a good heart. *Jai dee.* I like him. I think that he is genuine.

"Look, Ong," he says. "I like what you do." He puts his hand around my shoulder. For a moment, I think he's about to try to rub my head with affection and I have to force myself not to wince, but he's sensitive and instead takes his hand away. "Look, Ong. We both know you're terrible at this kind of work. We're in the news business, here. And you're just not cut out for it."

"My visa says I have to remain employed."

"Yeah. Janice is a bitch for that. Look." He pauses. "I've got this thing with Double DP going down in Mexico. But I've got another story brewing. An exclusive. I've already got my bonus, anyway. And it should push up your average."

"I do not think that I can write Double DP sidebars."

He grins. "It's not that. And it's not charity; you're actually a perfect match."

"It is about government mismanagement?"

He laughs, but I think he's not really laughing at me. "No." He pauses, smiles. "It's Kulaap. An interview."

I suck in my breath. My fellow countryperson, here in America. She came out during the purge as well. She was doing a movie in Singapore when the tanks moved, and so she was not trapped. She was already very popular all over Asia, and when Khamsing turned our country into a black hole, the world took note. Now she is popular here in America as well. Very beautiful. And she remembers our country before it went into darkness. My heart is pounding.

Marty goes on. "She's agreed to do an exclusive with me. But you even speak her language, so I think she'd agree to switch off." He pauses, looks serious. "I've got a good history with Kulaap. She doesn't give interviews to just anyone. I did a lot of exposure stories about her when Laos was going to hell. Got her a lot of good press. This is a special favor already, so don't fuck it up."

I shake my head. "No. I will not." I press my palms together and touch them to my forehead in a *nop* of appreciation. "I will not fuck it up." I make another *nop*.

He laughs. "Don't bother with that polite stuff. Janice will cut off your balls to increase the stock price, but we're the guys in the trenches. We stick together, right?"

❚❚

In the morning, I make a pot of strong coffee with condensed milk; I boil rice noodle soup and add bean sprouts and chiles and vinegar, and warm a loaf of French bread that I buy from a Vietnamese bakery a few blocks away. With a new mix of Kulaap's music from DJ Dao streaming in over my stereo, I sit down at my little kitchen table, pour my coffee from its press pot, and open my tablet.

The tablet is a wondrous creation. In Laos, the paper was still a paper, physical, static, and empty of anything except the official news. Real news in our New Divine Kingdom did not come from newspapers, or from television, or from handsets or ear buds. It did not come from the net or feeds unless you trusted your neighbor not to look over your shoulder at an Internet cafe and if you knew that there were no secret police sitting beside you, or an owner who would be able to identify you when they came around asking about the person who used that workstation over there to communicate with the outside world.

Real news came from whispered rumor, rated according to the trust you accorded the whisperer. Were they family? Did they have long history with you? Did they have anything to gain by the sharing? My father and his old classmates trusted one another. He trusted some of his students, as well. I think this is why the security police came for him in the end. One of his trusted friends or students also whispered news to official friends. Perhaps Mr. Intha-chak, or Som Vang. Perhaps another. It is impossible to peer into the blackness of that history and guess at who told true stories and in which direction.

In any case, it was my father's karma to be taken, so perhaps it does not matter who did the whispering. But before then—before the news of my father flowed up to official ears—none of the real news flowed toward Lao TV or the *Vientiane Times*. Which meant that when the protests happened and my father came through the door with blood on his face from baton blows, we could read as much as we wanted about the three thousand schoolchildren who had sung the national anthem to our new divine monarch. While my father lay in bed, delirious with pain, the papers told us that China had signed a rubber contract that would triple revenue for Luang Namtha province and that Nam Theun Dam was now earning BT 22.5 billion per year in electricity fees to Thailand. But there were no bloody batons, and there were no dead monks, and there was no Mercedes-Benz burning in the river as it floated toward Cambodia.

Real news came on the wings of rumor, stole into our house at midnight, sat with us and sipped coffee and fled before the call of roosters could break the stillness. It was in the dark, over a burning cigarette that you learned Vilaphon had disappeared or that Mr. Saeng's wife had been beaten as a warning. Real news was too valuable to risk in public.

Here in America, my page glows with many news feeds, flickers at me in video windows, pours in at me over broadband. It is a waterfall of information. As my personal news page opens, my feeds arrange themselves, sorting according to the priorities and tag categories that I've set, a mix of Meung Lao news, Lao refugee blogs, and the chatting of a few close friends from Thailand and the American college where I attended on a human relief scholarship.

On my second page and my third, I keep the general news, the arrange-ments of Milestone, the *Bangkok Post*, the *Phnom Penh Express*—the news chosen by editors. But by the time I've finished with my own selections, I don't often have time to click through the headlines that these earnest news editors select for the mythical general reader.

In any case, I know far better than they what I want to read, and with my keyword and tag scans, I can unearth stories and discussions that a news agency would never think to provide. Even if I cannot see into the black hole itself, I can slip along its edges, divine news from its fringe.

I search for tags like Vientiane, Laos, Lao, Khamsing, China-Lao friendship, Korat, Golden Triangle, Hmong independence, Lao PDR, my father's name. . . . Only those of us who are Lao exiles from the March Purge really read these blogs. It is much as when we lived in the capital. The blogs are the rumors that we used to whisper to one another. Now we publish our whispers over the net and join mailing lists instead of secret coffee groups, but it is the same. It is family, as much as any of us now have.

On the maelstrom, the tags for Laos don't even register. Our tags bloomed brightly for a little while, while there were still guerrilla students uploading content from their handsets, and the images were lurid and shocking. But then the phone lines went down and the country fell into its black hole and now it is just us, this small network that functions outside the country.

A headline from Jumbo Blog catches my eye. I open the site, and my tablet fills with the colorful image of the three-wheeled taxi of my childhood. I often come here. It is a node of comfort.

Laofriend posts that some people, maybe a whole family, have swum the Mekong and made it into Thailand. He isn't sure if they were accepted as refugees or if they were sent back.

It is not an official news piece. More, the idea of a news piece. *SomPaBoy* doesn't believe it, but *Khamchanh* contends that the rumor is true, heard from someone who has a sister married to an Isaan border guard in the Thai army. So we cling to it. Wonder about it. Guess where these people came from, wonder if, against all odds, it could be one of ours: a brother, a sister, a cousin, a father. . . .

After an hour, I close the tablet. It's foolish to read any more. It only brings up memories. Worrying about the past is foolish. Lao PDR is gone. To wish otherwise is suffering.

The clerk at Novotel's front desk is expecting me. A hotel staffer with a key guides me to a private elevator bank that whisks us up into the smog and heights. The elevator doors open to a small entryway with a thick mahogany door. The staffer steps back into the elevator and disappears, leaving me standing in this strange airlock. Presumably, I am being examined by Kulaap's security.

The mahogany door opens, and a smiling black man who is forty centimeters taller than I and who has muscles that ripple like snakes smiles and motions me inside. He guides me through Kulaap's sanctuary. She keeps the heat high, almost tropical, and fountains rush everywhere around. The flat is musical with water. I unbutton my collar in the humidity. I was expecting air-conditioning, and instead I am sweltering. It's almost like home. And then she's in front of me, and I can hardly speak. She is beautiful, and more. It is intimidating to stand before someone who exists in film and in music but has never existed before you in the flesh. She's not as stunning as she is in the movies, but there's more life, more presence; the movies lose that quality about her. I make a *nop* of greeting, pressing my hands together, touching my forehead.

She laughs at this, takes my hand and shakes it American-style. "You're lucky Marty likes you so much," she says. "I don't like interviews."

I can barely find my voice. "Yes. I only have a few questions."

"Oh no. Don't be shy." She laughs again, and doesn't release my hand, pulls me toward her living room. "Marty told me about you. You need help with your ratings. He helped me once, too."

She's frightening. She is of my people, but she has adapted better to this place than I have. She seems comfortable here. She walks differently, smiles differently; she is an American, with perhaps some flavor of our country, but nothing of our roots. It's obvious. And strangely disappointing. In her movies, she holds herself so well, and now she sits down on her couch and sprawls with her feet kicked out in front of her. Not caring at all. I'm embarrassed for her, and I'm glad I don't have my camera set up yet. She kicks her feet up on the couch. I can't help but be shocked. She catches my expression and smiles.

"You're worse than my parents. Fresh off the boat."

"I am sorry."

She shrugs. "Don't worry about it. I spent half my life here, growing up; different country, different rules."

I'm embarrassed. I try not to laugh with the tension I feel. "I just have some interview questions," I say.

"Go ahead." She sits up and arranges herself for the video stand that I set up.

I begin. "When the March Purge happened, you were in Singapore."

She nods. "That's right. We were finishing *The Tiger and the Ghost*."

"What was your first thought when it happened? Did you want to go back? Were you surprised?"

She frowns. "Turn off the camera."

When it's off she looks at me with pity. "This isn't the way to get clicks. No one cares about an old revolution. Not even my fans." She stands abruptly and calls through the green jungle of her flat. "Terrell?"

The big black man appears. Smiling and lethal. Looming over me. He is very frightening. The movies I grew up with had *falang* like him. Terrifying large black men whom our heroes had to overcome. Later, when I arrived in America, it was different, and I found out that the *falang* and the black people don't like the way we show them in our movies. Much like when I watch their Vietnam movies, and see the ugly way the Lao freedom fighters behave. Not real at all, portrayed like animals. But still, I cannot help but cringe when Terrell looks at me.

Kulaap says, "We're going out, Terrell. Make sure you tip off some of the papcams. We're going to give them a show."

"I don't understand," I say.

"You want clicks, don't you?"

"Yes, but—"

She smiles. "You don't need an interview. You need an event." She looks me over. "And better clothes." She nods to her security man. "Terrell, dress him up."

A flashbulb frenzy greets us as we come out of the tower. Papcams everywhere. Chase cycles revving, and Terrell and three others of his people guiding us through the press to the limousine, shoving cameras aside with a violence and power that are utterly unlike the careful pity he showed when he selected a Gucci suit for me to wear.

Kulaap looks properly surprised at the crowd and the shouting reporters, but not nearly as surprised as I am, and then we're in the limo, speeding out of the tower's roundabout as papcams follow us.

Kulaap crouches before the car's onboard tablet, keying in pass codes. She is very pretty, wearing a black dress that brushes her thighs and thin straps that caress her smooth bare shoulders. I feel as if I am in a movie. She taps more keys. A screen glows, showing the taillights of our car: the view from pursuing papcams.

"You know I haven't dated anyone in three years?" she asks.

"Yes. I know from your Web site biography."

She grins. "And now it looks like I've found one of my countrymen."

"But we're not on a date," I protest.

"Of course we are." She smiles again. "I'm going out on a supposedly secret date with a cute and mysterious Lao boy. And look at all those papcams chasing after us, wondering where we're going and what we're going to do." She keys in another code, and now we can see live footage of the paparazzi, as viewed from the tail of her limo. She grins. "My fans like to see what life is like for me."

I can almost imagine what the maelstrom looks like right now: there will still be Marty's story, but now a dozen other sites will be lighting up, and in the center of that, Kulaap's own view of the excitement, pulling in her fans, who will want to know, direct from her, what's going on. She holds up a mirror, checks herself, and then she smiles into her smartphone's camera.

"Hi everyone. It looks like my cover's blown. Just thought I should let you know that I'm on a lovely date with a lovely man. I'll let you all know how it goes. Promise." She points the camera at me. I stare at it stupidly. She laughs. "Say hi and good-bye, Ong."

"Hi and good-bye."

She laughs again, waves into the camera. "Love you all. Hope you have as good a night as I'm going to have." And then she cuts the clip and punches a code to launch the video to her Web site.

It is a bit of nothing. Not a news story, not a scoop even, and yet, when she opens another window on her tablet, showing her own miniversion of the maelstrom, I can see her site lighting up with traffic. Her version of the maelstrom isn't as powerful as what we have at Milestone, but still, it is an impressive window into the data that is relevant to Kulaap's tags.

"What's your feed's byline?" she asks. "Let's see if we can get your traffic bumped up."

"Are you serious?"

"Marty Mackley did more than this for me. I told him I'd help." She laughs. "Besides, we wouldn't want you to get sent back to the black hole, would we?"

"You know about the black hole?" I can't help doing a double-take.

Her smile is almost sad. "You think just because I put my feet up on the furniture that I don't care about my aunts and uncles back home? That I don't worry about what's happening?"

"I—"

She shakes her head. "You're so fresh off the boat."

"Do you use the Jumbo Cafe—" I break off. It seems too unlikely.

She leans close. "My handle is *Laofriend*. What's yours?"

"*Littlexang*. I thought *Laofriend* was a boy—"

She just laughs.

I lean forward. "Is it true that the family made it out?"

She nods. "For certain. A general in the Thai army is a fan. He tells me everything. They have a listening post. And sometimes they send scouts across."

It's almost as if I am home.

‖

We go to a tiny Laotian restaurant where everyone recognizes her and falls over her and the owners simply lock out the paparazzi when they become too intrusive. We spend the evening unearthing memories of Vientiane. We discover that we both favored the same rice noodle cart on Kaem Khong. That she used to sit on the banks of the Mekong and wish that she were a fisherman. That we went to the same waterfalls outside the city on the weekends. That it is impossible to find good *dum mak hoong* anywhere outside of the country. She is a good companion, very alive. Strange in her American ways, but still, with a good heart. Periodically, we click photos of one another and post them to her site, feeding the voyeurs. And then we are in the limo again and the paparazzi are all around us. I have the strange feeling of fame. Flashbulbs everywhere. Shouted questions. I feel proud to be beside this beautiful intelligent woman who knows so much more than any of us about the situation inside our homeland.

Back in the car, she has me open a bottle of champagne and pour two glasses while she opens the maelstrom and studies the results of our date. She has reprogrammed it to watch my byline feed ranking as well.

"You've got twenty thousand more readers than you did yesterday," she says.

I beam. She keeps reading the results. "Someone already did a scan on your face." She toasts me with her glass. "You're famous."

We clink glasses. I am flushed with wine and happiness. I will have Janice's average clicks. It's as though a bodhisattva has come down from heaven to save my job. In my mind, I offer thanks to Marty for arranging this, for his generous nature. Kulaap leans close to her screen, watching the flaring content. She opens another window, starts to read. She frowns.

"What the fuck do you write about?"

I draw back, surprised. "Government stories, mostly." I shrug. "Sometimes environment stories."

"Like what?"

"I am working on a story right now about global warming and Henry David Thoreau."

"Aren't we done with that?"

I'm confused. "Done with what?"

The limo jostles us as it makes a turn, moves down Hollywood Boulevard, letting the cycles rev around us like schools of fish. They're snapping pictures at the side of the limo, snapping at us. Through the tinting, they're like fireflies, smaller flares than even my stories in the maelstrom.

"I mean, isn't that an old story?" She sips her champagne. "Even America is reducing emissions now. Everyone knows it's a problem." She taps her couch's armrest. "The carbon tax on my limo has tripled, even with the hybrid engine. Everyone agrees it's a problem. We're going to fix it. What's there to write about?"

She is an American. Everything that is good about them: their optimism, their willingness to charge ahead, to make their own future. And everything that is bad about them: their strange ignorance, their unwillingness to believe that they must behave as other than children.

"No. It's not done," I say. "It is worse. Worse every day. And the changes we make seem to have little effect. Maybe too little, or maybe too late. It is getting worse."

She shrugs. "That's not what I read."

I try not to show my exasperation. "Of course it's not what you read." I wave at the screen. "Look at the clicks on my feed. People want happy stories. Want fun stories. Not stories like I write. So instead, we all write what you will read, which is nothing."

"Still—"

"No." I make a chopping motion with my hand. "We newspeople are very smart monkeys. If you will give us your so lovely eyeballs and your click-throughs we will do whatever you like. We will write good news, and news you can use, news you can shop to, news with the 'Three S's.' We will tell you how to have better sex or eat better or look more beautiful or feel happier and or how to meditate—yes, so enlightened." I make a face. "If you want a walking meditation and Double DP, we will give it to you."

She starts to laugh.

"Why are you laughing at me?" I snap. "I am not joking!"

She waves a hand. "I know, I know, but what you just said 'double'—" She shakes her head, still laughing. "Never mind."

I lapse into silence. I want to go on, to tell her of my frustrations. But now I am embarrassed at my loss of composure. I have no face. I didn't used to be like this. I used to control my emotions, but now I am an American, as childish and unruly as Janice. And Kulaap laughs at me.

I control my anger. "I think I want to go home," I say. "I don't wish to be on a date anymore."

She smiles and reaches over to touch my shoulder. "Don't be that way."

A part of me is telling me that I am a fool. That I am reckless and foolish for walking away from this opportunity. But there is something else, something about this frenzied hunt for page views and click-throughs and ad revenue that suddenly feels unclean. As if my father is with us in the car, disapproving. Asking if he posted his complaints about his missing friends for the sake of clicks.

"I want to get out," I hear myself say. "I do not wish to have your clicks."

"But—"

I look up at her. "I want to get out. Now."

"Here?" She makes a face of exasperation, then shrugs. "It's your choice."

"Yes. Thank you."

She tells her driver to pull over. We sit in stiff silence.

"I will send your suit back to you," I say.

She gives me a sad smile. "It's all right. It's a gift."

This makes me feel worse, even more humiliated for refusing her generosity, but still, I get out of the limo. Cameras are clicking at me from all around. This is my fifteen minutes of fame, this moment when all of Kulaap's fans focus on me for a few seconds, their flashbulbs popping.

I begin to walk home as paparazzi shout questions.

Fifteen minutes later I am indeed alone. I consider calling a cab, but then decide I prefer the night. Prefer to walk by myself through this city that never walks anywhere. On a street corner, I buy a *pupusa* and gamble on the Mexican Lottery because I like the tickets' laser images of their Day of the Dead. It seems an echo of the Buddha's urging to remember that we all become corpses.

I buy three tickets, and one of them is a winner: one hundred dollars that I can redeem at any TelMex kiosk. I take this as a good sign. Even if my luck is obviously gone with my work, and even if the girl Kulaap was not the bodhisattva that I thought, still, I feel lucky. As though my father is walking with me down this cool Los Angeles street in the middle of the night, the two of us together again, me with a *pupusa* and a winning lottery ticket, him with an Ah Daeng cigarette and his quiet gambler's smile. In a strange way, I feel that he is blessing me.

And so instead of going home, I go back to the newsroom.

My hits are up when I arrive. Even now, in the middle of the night, a tiny slice of Kulaap's fan base is reading about checkerspot butterflies and American government incompetence. In my country, this story would not exist. A censor would kill it instantly. Here, it glows green; increasing and decreasing in size as people click. A lonely thing, flickering amongst the much larger content flares of Intel processor releases, guides to low-fat recipes, photos of lol-cats, and episodes of *Survivor! Antarctica*. The wash of light and color is very beautiful.

In the center of the maelstrom, the green sun of the Double DP story glows—surges larger. DP is doing something. Maybe he's surrendering, maybe he's murdering his hostages, maybe his fans have thrown up a human wall to protect him. My story snuffs out as reader attention shifts.

I watch the maelstrom a little longer, then go to my desk and make a phone call. A rumpled hairy man answers, rubbing at a sleep-puffy face. I apologize for the late hour, and then pepper him with questions while I record the interview.

He is silly looking and wild-eyed. He has spent his life living as if he were Thoreau, thinking deeply on the forest monk and following the man's careful paths through what woods remain, walking amongst birch and maple and bluets. He is a fool, but an earnest one.

"I can't find a single one," he tells me. "Thoreau could find thousands at this time of year; there were so many he didn't even have to look for them."

He says, "I'm so glad you called. I tried sending out press releases, but . . ." He shrugs. "I'm glad you'll cover it. Otherwise, it's just us hobbyists talking to each other."

I smile and nod and take notes of his sincerity, this strange wild creature, the sort that everyone will dismiss. His image is bad for video; his words are not good for text. He has no quotes that encapsulate what he sees. It is all couched in the jargon of naturalists and biology. With time, I could find another, someone who looks attractive or who can speak well, but all I have is this one hairy man, disheveled and foolish, senile with passion over a flower that no longer exists.

I work through the night, polishing the story. When my colleagues pour through the door at 8 a.m. it is almost done. Before I can even tell Janice about it, she comes to me. She fingers my clothing and grins. "Nice suit." She pulls up a chair and sits beside me. "We all saw you with Kulaap. Your hits went way up." She nods at my screen. "Writing up what happened?"

"No. It was a private conversation."

"But everyone wants to know why you got out of the car. I had someone from the *Financial Times* call me about splitting the hits for a tell-all, if you'll be interviewed. You wouldn't even need to write up the piece."

It's a tempting thought. Easy hits. Many click-throughs. Ad-revenue bonuses. Still, I shake my head. "We did not talk about things that are important for others to hear."

Janice stares at me as if I am crazy. "You're not in the position to bargain, Ong. Something happened between the two of you. Something people want to know about. And you need the clicks. Just tell us what happened on your date."

"I was not on a date. It was an interview."

"Well then publish the fucking interview and get your average up!"

"No. That is for Kulaap to post, if she wishes. I have something else."

I show Janice my screen. She leans forward. Her mouth tightens as she reads. For once, her anger is cold. Not the explosion of noise and rage that I expect. "Bluets." She looks at me. "You need hits and you give them flowers and Walden Pond."

"I would like to publish this story."

"No! Hell, no! This is just another story like your butterfly story, and your road contracts story, and your congressional budget story. You won't get a damn click. It's pointless. No one will even read it."

"This is news."

"Marty went out on a limb for you—" She presses her lips together, reining in her anger. "Fine. It's up to you, Ong. If you want to destroy your life over Thoreau and flowers, it's your funeral. We can't help you if you won't help yourself. Bottom line, you need fifty thousand readers or I'm sending you back to the third world."

We look at each other. Two gamblers evaluating one another. Deciding who is betting, and who is bluffing.

I click the "publish" button.

The story launches itself onto the net, announcing itself to the feeds. A minute later a tiny new sun glows in the maelstrom.

Together, Janice and I watch the green spark as it flickers on the screen. Readers turn to the story. Start to ping it and share it amongst themselves, start to register hits on the page. The post grows slightly.

My father gambled on Thoreau. I am my father's son.

More of and about the wonderful authors of *Fast Forward 2* can be found on their Web sites. Tell 'em I sent ya.

Paul Cornell's House of Awkwardness
paulcornell.blogspot.com

Kay Kenyon
www.kaykenyon.com

Chris Nakashima-Brown
www.nakashima-brown.net

Nancy Kress
www.sff.net/people/nankress

Jack Skillingstead
www.jackskillingstead.com

Benjamin Rosenbaum
www.benjaminrosenbaum.com

Cory Doctorow
craphound.com

Jack McDevitt
www.sfwa.org/members/McDevitt/

Paul McAuley's Earth and Other Unlikely Worlds
www.unlikelyworlds.blogspot.com/

Mike Resnick
www.mikeresnick.com

Pat Cadigan
fastfwd.livejournal.com

Ian McDonald's Cyberabad
ianmcdonald.livejournal.com

Kristine Kathryn Rusch
www.kristinekathrynrusch.com

Karl Schroeder
www.kschroeder.com

Tobias S. Buckell
www.tobiasbuckell.com

Jeff Carlson
www.jverse.com

Paolo Bacigalupi
windupstories.com

ABOUT THE EDITOR

▷

A 2008/2007 Hugo Award nominee, 2007 Chesley Award nominee, and 2006 World Fantasy Award nominee, Lou Anders is the editorial director of Prometheus Books' science fiction imprint, Pyr, as well as the anthologies *Sideways in Crime* (Solaris, June 2008), *Fast Forward 1* (Pyr, February 2007), *FutureShocks* (Roc, January 2006), *Projections: Science Fiction in Literature & Film* (MonkeyBrain, December 2004), *Live without a Net* (Roc, July 2003), and *Outside the Box* (Wildside Press, January 2001). In 2000, he served as the executive editor of Bookface.com, and before that he worked as the Los Angeles liaison for Titan Publishing Group. He is the author of *The Making of Star Trek: First Contact* (Titan Books, 1996) and has published over five hundred articles in such magazines as the *Believer, Publishers Weekly, Dreamwatch, Star Trek Monthly, Star Wars Monthly, Babylon 5 Magazine, Sci Fi Universe, Doctor Who Magazine,* and *Manga Max.* His articles and stories have been translated into Danish, Greek, German, Italian, French, and Spanish, and have appeared online at SFSite.com, RevolutionSF.com, and InfinityPlus .co.uk. Visit him online at www.louanders.com.